D0502251

The Actress

a novel

Amy Sohn

Simon & Schuster

New York   London   Toronto   Sydney   New Delhi

90

Simon & Schuster
1230 Avenue of the Americas
New York, NY 10020

First Simon & Schuster hardcover edition July 2014

SIMON & SCHUSTER and colophon are registered trademarks of Simon & Schuster, Inc.

For information about special discounts for bulk purchases, please contact Simon & Schuster
Special Sales at 1-866-506-1949 or business@simonandschuster.com.

The Simon & Schuster Speakers Bureau can bring authors to your live event. For more
information or to book an event, contact the Simon & Schuster Speakers Bureau at 1-866-
248-3049 or visit our website at www.simonspeakers.com.

Interior design by Akasha Archer
Jacket design by Jackie Seow
Jacket art © Ilona Wellmann/Archangel Images

Manufactured in the United States of America

10 9 8 7 6 5 4 3 2 1

Library of Congress Cataloging-in-Publication Data

Sohn, Amy.
   The actress : a novel / Amy Sohn. — First Simon & Schuster hardcover edition.
      pages cm
   1. Actresses—Fiction. 2. Gay actors—Fiction. 3. Fame—Fiction. 4. Secrets—Fiction. I.
Title.
   PS3569.O435A26 2014
   813'.54—dc23

                                            2014005673

ISBN 978-1-4516-9861-9
ISBN 978-1-4516-9863-3 (ebook)

for my manager

And she had loved him, she had so anxiously and yet so ardently given herself—a good deal for what she found in him, but a good deal also for what she brought him and what might enrich the gift.

—Henry James, *The Portrait of a Lady*

The Actress

Act One

1

The velvet curtains parted, and Maddy watched Steven Weller step into the room, his girlfriend on his arm. Gracefully, he began to move through the crowd, laughing, clapping backs, kissing women. He was trim, though not tall, and blessed with a full and apparently natural hairline envied by millions of middle-aged men.

As she watched him glad-hand, she was surprised to feel her cheeks grow warm. In her job as a restaurant hostess in New York, she was never starstruck by the actors and baseball players who came in to eat, priding herself on being able to keep her cool. But here at the Mile's End Film Festival, not thirty feet from Steven Weller, she felt jumpy and wowed.

"I thought the new one was Venezuelan," said Sharoz, Maddy's producer. "She doesn't look Venezuelan." The girlfriend, who had a few inches on Steven, stood just behind him, nodding faintly. She didn't appear to be participating in the conversations so much as endorsing them.

"That was the last one," Maddy said. "The real estate agent he met on a plane. This one is the Vegas cocktail waitress."

"Cady Pearce," said Maddy's boyfriend, Dan, from her other side.

"You know her name?" Maddy said, planting a hand on his chest. An NYU film school graduate and theory nerd, he never read the trades. "Since when do you follow Hollywood gossip?"

"My barber gets *People*."

"Did you guys notice that he never stays with any woman more than a year?" Sharoz asked. "And usually only from one awards season to the next. The man is so gay."

"Just because a guy is single in his mid-forties doesn't mean he's gay,"

Maddy said. "Maybe he just hasn't met the right person." For years there had been rumors of Weller's homosexuality, but Maddy felt they were a sign of the entertainment industry's increasing puritanism, its tendency to fetishize marriage and domesticity.

Her costar Kira was coming over, unmistakable in her white-blond buzz cut, sleeveless orange jumper, and knee-high moon boots, looking like the catalog model she was. Unlike the others, she had skipped the opening-night selection, Weller's new vehicle *The Widower*, to meet an old friend for drinks. "Is that the new one?" Kira asked, tossing her head in Weller's direction. She spoke in a hoarse voice that resulted from childhood nodules on her vocal cords. "She's even taller than the real estate agent."

"I heard he has a longtime boyfriend," Sharoz said. "They've been together fifteen years."

"You mean Terry McCarthy?" Maddy asked. McCarthy, an actor turned screenwriter, had been Weller's friend since they were both struggling young actors in L.A.

"Not Terry McCarthy," Sharoz said. "A Korean-American flight attendant for United."

"How do you know?"

"This guy I grew up with went to Hobart with the sister of the flight attendant's best friend," Sharoz answered. Sharoz, a striking, long-haired girl from Tehrangeles, had been Dan's classmate at NYU and was one of those detail-oriented people who never seemed harried even in the midst of crises, like the dozens they'd had on *I Used to Know Her*.

Maddy noticed Kira holding one hand in front of her eyes and squinting at Weller. "What are you doing?" Maddy asked.

"You can always tell by the mouth," Kira said. "Yep, yep. Definite gay mouth." She moved her hand in front of Maddy's field of vision so it blocked Weller's forehead and eyes.

Maddy watched his mouth move, unsure what she was looking for. He had a thin lower lip that veered slightly off to the side. "What makes a mouth gay?" she asked.

"The palsy. Gay men have slightly palsied lips."

"I hate to disappoint you, Kira, but I think he's straight," Dan said. "He was married, after all."

"And we all know why Julia Hanson left him," Sharoz said.

A middle-aged actress who was now experiencing a mid-career comeback with a cable procedural, Hanson had been married to Weller for a few years during the 1980s. She had never spoken publicly about the marriage, but in recent months there had been chatter, in the tabloids and on the Internet, that they had divorced because he was gay.

"Even if he is . . . with men," Maddy said, "who cares? It's his business."

"That is so heteronormative," Kira said. "He has an obligation to come out. By staying in the closet, he's doing a disservice to young gay men and women. It's disingenuous." Kira had become a women's studies major at Hampshire College on the heels of a bad breakup from a Northampton Wiccan.

"Everyone in Hollywood is disingenuous," Dan said. "They do drugs, they cheat on their spouses, they have illegitimate children. If I were him, I would never come out. He would lose all the macho roles. The guy wants to work."

"He would work," Kira said. "He's successful enough that it wouldn't hurt. His female fans would still fantasize about him."

"Just—with another guy in bed at the same time," Sharoz said, and the women giggled.

Across the room, Cady Pearce said something, and Steven Weller laughed so loudly that they could hear it. She was either the funniest cocktail waitress in all of Las Vegas or Steven Weller was very easily amused.

A server passed by with a tray. Not caring how it looked to anyone else, Maddy grabbed four pigs in blankets. The others clustered around, too, double-fisting food. After flying into Salt Lake City, they'd barely had time to change clothes at the condos before rushing off to *The Widower*. Mile's End, the festival, was not all that different from a Mile's End film: You were always cold, hungry, and short on time.

The party was in a private room on the third level of the Entertainer, a lodge/club on Mountain Way, and it was hosted by the studio that was distributing *The Widower*. Guest-list-only, it was much more intimate than the official Mile's End–hosted, post-*Widower* party raging two levels below. This crowd was older, with white teeth, tan skin, and cashmere sweaters.

"How did you get us in here, anyway?" Maddy asked Sharoz. "Had to be some kind of mistake."

"It was Ed. He owns Mile's End." Ed Handy was their producer's rep, and Sharoz's words were not hyperbole; the *New York Times* Arts section had recently run a front-page profile entitled "Ed Handy Owns Mile's End."

"Do you think those guys downstairs chasing cheddar with sponsored vodka know what they're missing?" Maddy asked.

"Of course," said Sharoz. "That's what this festival is about, varying levels of access."

Both Sharoz and Dan had been to Mile's End once before, with a short about a gamine subway busker who falls for a conductor. Maddy, who hadn't known Dan then, had never been. She had never even been to Utah. Ever since they got accepted, Dan had been calling her "a virgin to the festival." She understood that his smugness was a cover for his anxiety—*I Used to Know Her* was about to premiere at the biggest independent festival in the country—but she still didn't like it. She wanted to feel that they were all the same, united by what had brought them together in the first place: the desire to make good work.

"So what did you guys think of *The Widower*?" Kira asked.

"Not one true moment in the entire eighty-five minutes," Dan said. "Mile's End has become like Lifetime television." This was a frequent complaint of Dan's: that the festival had become less edgy now that it was entering its twenty-fifth year. But Maddy took it with a grain of salt, because if he really hated the festival, he never would have submitted.

Like all opening-night selections, *The Widower* had been chosen for maximum audience appeal. It wasn't in competition, and its Mile's End screenings were publicity for a spring theatrical release by Apollo Classics, the mini-major division of Apollo Pictures. Weller played an aging dad in Reno trying to remake his life. It was the latest in his independent-film phase, in which he played unglamorous roles that showcased his gravitas and graying sideburns.

"I thought it was moving," Sharoz told Kira. "I got choked up when he took the dad hiking."

"Come on," Dan said. "The guy has no process." In one of Weller's recent "small" films, *Beirut Nights*, which had been nominated for a slew of awards, he had played an over-the-hill CIA operative. The critics had made much of a moment when he found a small boy's body in the middle of the road, pushed a lock of hair from the boy's face, and cried a single tear. Weller had been still and very contained, without the histrionics that most actors used when they cried, but there was a cut just before the tear fell out, and after they saw the film, Dan told Maddy that he must have used glycerin drops.

Steven Weller was best known for having played Stan Gerber, a libidinous divorce attorney, on the hit NBC drama *Briefs* in the mid to late '90s. He did seven seasons, winning women's hearts across America. Maddy was fourteen when *Briefs* came on the air, and she thought he was so sexy, she had a poster of him from *Tiger Beat* on the wall next to her bed. She would kiss it every night before she went to sleep. After *Briefs*, he ventured into big-budget, high-profile action films and romantic comedies, his quote said to have climbed to $8 million per film. There had been a bump or two along the way—his biggest flop, *Bombs Away*, was about hostage negotiators who fall in love—but since then he had gotten choosier about his roles and was now considered one of the top ten actors over forty.

In interviews, he was quick to mock himself and his success, pointing to the element of luck in his career. Maddy didn't know if his disbelief at his fame was real or an act designed to make him more likable. Several years ago he had bought a palazzo in Venice and spent a few months there in the spring and summer, entertaining luminaries. He was an antiscenester, or so it was said.

"I think he has process," Maddy said. "He's just not very showy."

Though she found some of the writing twee, Maddy had enjoyed *The Widower*. Weller wasn't genius—her best friend in grad school, Irina, called him a "hack-tor"—but Maddy found herself responding to his less important scenes. In one, he kissed a woman too eagerly at the end of a date, and the woman recoiled, and Maddy felt that his posture as he walked away showed everything about his character.

"The only reason people think he can act is because he's a handsome guy who makes himself look less handsome in his films," Dan said. "Which is ultimately kind of offensive."

"I don't understand," Sharoz said.

"Weller's attractive but takes these unattractive roles," Kira said, "so it seems like he's transforming himself, except the whole time the audience knows it's really him, so they want to sleep with the character even though he's a sad sack, which makes them feel deep and generous instead of totally shallow and looksist."

Ed Handy was approaching, cell phone in one hand and a tumbler in the other. A paunchy bald man in his early fifties, he carried himself like a male model. "Welcome to Mile's End," Ed said. "It used to be all prostitution and saloons. Now we service a different kind of whore."

"How many times have you used that line?" Dan asked.

"Hundreds. You have to understand, every conversation here has been spoken."

"Does that bother you?" Maddy asked.

"Not at all. Repetition relaxes me."

A middle-aged woman, maybe late fifties, with shiny brown hair, blue eyes, and perfectly aligned teeth, came over and kissed Ed on both cheeks. Maddy had noticed her earlier, circulating gracefully. She wore dark jeans tucked into riding boots and an off-white sweater that hugged her boosted breasts. To her left was an extremely short young man with intense light blue eyes.

"This is Bridget Ostrow," Ed said. Steven's longtime manager-producer, Bridget Ostrow was one of the most powerful women in entertainment. "Bridget produced The Widower."

"Congratulations," Dan said, smiling widely. "Loved it. Loved it."

When Maddy glanced at him, he didn't make eye contact. She hadn't expected him to be rude but was surprised to see him being so phony. "And this is Bridget's son, Zack," Ed said. "Zack's at the Bentley Howard Agency in New York." Bentley Howard, which had offices on both coasts, was one of the top five entertainment agencies. Ed turned to the Know Her crew. "These guys made I Used to Know Her. Dan Ellenberg here's the director. A New York dancer goes home to Vermont to try to prevent her best friend's wedding to this total sleazeball—I identified with him the most—and realizes they've grown in different directions. Maddy helped write it, it's based on her hometown. Bridge, these two girls, Maddy Freed and Kira Birzin, are brilliant. First screening is Saturday at ten."

"A.M.?" Zack asked.

"Yes," Ed said. "If you guys are up, it would be fantastic if you came." Maddy glanced anxiously at Dan. He had been furious when he first got the screening schedule. On Friday night, Bentley Howard was throwing a party for *Rap Sheet*, a film about a car thief turned rapper, at Mountain Way Pub and Grill. This meant that at ten the next morning, most Mile's Enders would be sleeping off hangovers, not seeing films. Dan was convinced the bad timing would harm their chances of distribution.

"I had already made a note to see it," Zack said.

"I'll be there, too," Bridget said, glancing over Dan's shoulder at another face in the crowd.

"Your film has great buzz," Zack said, clapping Dan on the back.

"Everything has buzz here," said Dan. "It's like the old man who told his friend his knee surgeon was the best, and the friend said, 'They're all the best.' " Zack laughed and rubbed his palm against his nose. Maddy didn't know if it was a nervous tic or a sign of drug addiction.

Dan turned to Bridget. "I'm a big admirer of your movies. I loved *Frogs*." *Frogs* was an ensemble retelling of the Exodus story set in the adult entertainment industry. Weller had played a porn director who blows out his brains.

"Interesting that you used the word 'movies,' " Bridget said. Her voice was melodious and pleasing, with the trace of an outer-borough accent. "Steven likes to say we have to make the movies to keep making the films."

Maddy caught Zack rolling his eyes. What was it like to be Bridget Ostrow's son, trying to carve out your own niche as an agent? Clearly, mother and son were not in perfect harmony—but if he didn't admire her on some level, he wouldn't have gone into representation.

"It was so wonderful meeting you all," Bridget said abruptly, glancing at Steven and Cady across the room.

Zack gave out business cards to the foursome. "I'll see you Saturday morning if not before," he said. As they left, Ed beside them, Maddy noticed that mother and son had the same gait, pigeon-like, the heads bobbing, the bodies undulating slightly, as they moved.

"How come you were sucking up to Bridget when you didn't like her movie?" Maddy asked Dan.

"We're here to network," he said testily. "Her client is one of a dozen actors who can get a project made by attaching himself. If she remembers me a couple years down the line, I could wind up directing Steven Weller."

"But you hated his performance."

"I could get better work out of him."

In New York, Maddy was used to being the social one, going out with fellow New School alums to plays and movies, while Dan preferred staying inside or seeing foreign films with Maddy and no one else. She always tried to get him to come with her—he might meet actors for his films, producers—but he said he didn't believe in networking. He'd trot out some line he attributed to Hunter S. Thompson: "An artist must have a strong sense of revulsion for the banalities of everyday socializing." Now all his high-art soliloquies seemed a handy way of casting an unwilling lack of success as a willing one.

Steven Weller was holding court in the center of the room. Bridget's eyes were on him, but her body was turned slightly away. She looked like a Secret Service agent scanning the room for danger.

It occurred to Maddy that Bridget Ostrow probably knew things about Steven Weller that no one else did, even Cady Pearce. Over the years she must have seen his insecurity, fear, anger, everything a celebrity had to hide from the rest of the world. A manager couldn't yell at her star client or act jealous when he got all the attention. She couldn't cross him (or let him find out if she did), and when she disagreed, she had to do so gently, respectfully. Maddy wasn't sure which one had the real power—Weller, with his fame, or Bridget, who had made the fame possible.

Dan said he wanted another drink, and Maddy followed him to the bar. As he tried to get the bartender's attention, she leaned back to face the room. She closed her eyes and tilted her head, the din thrumming in her ears, phrases like "entire ecosystem" and "digging deep."

There was a skylight, and through it she could see the moon. She wanted to call her father on her cell and tell him she was at an elite party, a stone's throw from a movie star, and then she remembered that she couldn't. She sighed and lowered her chin. Her gaze fell on the group huddled around Steven Weller. Everyone was zeroed in on him, but he was staring, unblinkingly, at her.

2

On the bed, Dan was typing furiously into his phone as Maddy unpacked. To save money, they had rented a condo twenty minutes from town; Kira and Sharoz were in the one next door. The apartment looked like it hadn't been altered since the 1970s, complete with old board games, linoleum floors, and a cream-colored fridge.

Maddy removed the jeans and slouchy sweaters she had brought along—Dan and Sharoz had told her that in Mile's End, it was gauche to be anything but casual—and lay down beside him. He was emailing their hired publicist, Reid Rasmussen, about the first screening, trying to make sure they got bodies. She took one of his hands. He had long pale fingers, and she loved to lace them through hers. "I think we're going to win Dramatic," she said.

"Ahh! Don't say that. I don't want to jinx it."

"What's the point of being here if we can't fantasize?" Maddy loved doing theater, but since graduation she had done mostly Off-Off-Broadway, and Actors' Equity showcases and staged readings, and regional theater productions in depressing small towns. She was hoping the festival would expand her horizons. Even if *I Used to Know Her* failed to get distribution, she wanted to use her time in Utah to make connections and meet talented people with whom she could collaborate on other indie films like the one they had made, films that didn't speak down to their audiences.

"We're not going to win," he said, taking his hand away so he could type. "Dramatic will go to the one about the suburban New Jersey boy whose stepmother comes on to him. Or *Rap Sheet*. Anyway, distribution is way more important than awards."

"Well, whatever happens with *I Used to Know Her*," she said, rubbing his belly, "I'll still think you're the most talented man in the universe."

She had met him three years ago, during her final year of grad school, at an Irish dive bar after a performance of *The Importance of Being Earnest*. He'd come up to her while she was waiting for her drink and said, "Best Gwendolen I've ever seen." She'd thought the bump in his nose was cute; she had always been drawn to Jewish guys, maybe because they reminded her of her father.

Her dreadlocked classmate Sal, who had played Algernon, said, "You're the only Gwendolen he's ever seen. He's a movie snob. He's complimenting you because he thinks you're pretty." Dan had directed Sal, who'd invited him to the play, in a short.

"That is not true," Dan said. "I love Wilde. I'm wild about Wilde."

"Oh my God, he's lying," Sal said. "Maddy, stay away from this guy. He has a thing for actresses."

"Is that true?" she asked, aware that she was flirting.

Dan said, "I'm trying to rehabilitate myself. I had a bad breakup with one a couple years ago and swore I'd only date civilians. Then I dated a ballet dancer, and now actresses seem like a pillar of sanity."

The three of them sat in a corner by the window. After an hour Sal cut out, giving them an accusatory look before he left. As they watched people's feet pass above the window, they talked about movies. Dan was a movie buff the way Peter Bogdanovich was, his knowledge obsessive, exhaustive. He told her about Ernst Lubitsch's musicals, Godard, Fellini, and Truffaut. He told her about his favorite Fassbinder film, *Ali: Fear Eats the Soul*. He said theater would be irrelevant one day. She made a great show of being offended to mask the fact that she was offended.

Still, there was something in his ambition that appealed to her, and when he said he would ride the L with her to East Williamsburg, where she lived in a graduate-housing loft, she said yes. In front of the steel door, he kissed her, murmuring, "I'm afraid of what I might do if I come up." When he headed off, she had to shout to him that the subway stop was the other way. He called the next morning to say he couldn't stop thinking about her. She moved into his Fort Greene apartment a few months later.

In the condo now she delicately removed the phone from his hand

and placed it on the bedside table. She planted her knees on either side of his hips and kissed him languorously. "I think I'm too distracted," he said, putting his palms against her shoulders. Maddy's sex drive had gone down the first months after her father died, and then something strange had happened: She wanted it all the time. It confused her, because she worried it meant she wasn't properly grieving.

"That's a great reason to do it," she said, grinding herself against him. "It'll focus you." She was an inch taller than he was, five-ten to his five-nine, and she had broad shoulders and ash-blond hair that she wore to her chin. As a teenager, she had been self-conscious about her height, but in acting it was an advantage; it allowed her to measure up to men during dramatic scenes.

Dan pushed her away gently. "I feel like I shouldn't let any go before we screen."

"My boyfriend is Muhammad Ali," she said, rolling off.

"It worked out pretty well for him," he said, and reached for his phone.

The opening shot of *I Used to Know Her* was a bus coming down a high-way with MONTREAL on the top. When Maddy saw it on the enormous screen, she felt a mix of pride and dread. Pride because they had worked so hard to make the film, and she was seeing it for the first time in a theater. And dread because the theater was only a quarter full. Ed Handy and Reid had tried valiantly to chat up the critics (*The New York Times*, *L.A. Times*, *Variety*) before the screening, but they had looked morose nonetheless, hungover and reluctant.

Maddy had fantasized about watching it here, in Mile's End, with her father beside her, but he had never seen even the rough cut. The shoot had taken place the January before, in Potter, a small town on the Vermont/Canada border, famed for its majestic Yarrow Lake. Her dad, on vacation from his teaching job, was the production's unofficial mayor — doing carpentry, cooking big spaghetti dinners. Friends offered meals, homes, and locations for free, thrilled to have a movie shoot in town, no matter how low-budget.

The last time she had seen her dad was at the end of the shoot. He had hugged her tightly and pronounced, "I've said it before, but watching you up close, I really got it. This is what you were meant to do." Though she thanked him, she wasn't paying attention; Dan was worried about traffic and wanted to get on the road. She had since replayed that goodbye hundreds of times, wishing she'd said "I love you" or told him it was his faith that had made her dream big.

Maddy tried to focus on the screen, the second-unit shots of the Potter cornfields, the gas station, the country store, and a couple of old guys (real Potterians she'd known her whole life) smoking cigarettes on a porch. Finally, she saw herself, not herself but *Alice*, looking out the window and listening to headphones. It was bizarre to see her face blown up so big. All those moments spent in front of the camera—crying, inhabiting her body, fighting with Kira in character—were about to be made public and about to be judged.

It was amazing that the film had gotten written, much less made, given Dan's mental state a year and a half ago. His most recent film, *Closure*, had been his third not to get distribution. He would complain about his day job, pouring beer in a Gramercy Park sports bar that he said catered to date rapists. He would stay up late watching European films, and he lost interest in sex. One night Maddy came home from her restaurant, La Cloche, to find him drunk on Jameson, watching Rohmer's *Claire's Knee*.

"You should write a movie we can shoot in Potter," she said, squeezing next to him on their weathered green couch, "and I'll act in it."

They had been dating two years by that point but had never worked together. He hadn't wanted to cast her in his other films, even though *Closure* had a well-drawn, troubled female lead; he said a collaboration could create stress in their relationship. Though hurt, she had decided not to fight him.

So she was surprised when he turned away from the TV and said, "What would the film be about?"

"What about the time I went to Lacey Rooney's wedding?"

A childhood friend of Maddy's, a girl up the road, had married a jerk. Maddy had gone home for the wedding, and the two friends had argued at the rehearsal dinner. Lacey thought she was a snob for wanting to act, and Maddy worried she was marrying a dangerous man. (Maddy had wondered what would happen when word got back to Lacey that they would be in Potter filming a movie based on their story, but Lacey, by then divorced, came to the set and posed for photos with Kira, joking that she herself was better-looking.)

As Maddy told Dan about Lacey that night, he listened, though he didn't seem very excited. But when she came in the next night, he said, "I wrote eleven pages." They read them aloud and Maddy talked more, gave some notes on the scenes. They continued to work this way until one night she arrived home from work and he handed her a thick sheaf of pages bound by paper fasteners. When she read it for the first time, with "story by Maddy Freed and Dan Ellenberg" and "screenplay by Dan Ellenberg" on the title page, she got giddy, thinking it could be a turning point for both of them. After an early reading of the screenplay, a former classmate of Dan's commented, "It's about that moment you realize the person you love most in the world is a stranger."

For the first ten minutes, the Alpine Theater was quiet. She glanced down the row at her fellow actors. Ellen Cone, who played Maddy's mother, clutched her own breast, an affectation that was either a reaction to the film or a result of living alone a long time. A snuffle emanated from one of the front rows. Maddy feared it had come from the *Variety* critic. As the movie went on and Kira had a funny bit with a dog, Maddy began to hear more laughs. Later, when the emotional pitch rose and the women had their big fight, the audience went silent.

When the end credits rolled over an indie-pop song, there was a long beat, and then the moviegoers began to applaud, a few at a time. The reviewers dashed out. Maddy tried to read their body language. Were they rushing to call long-lost childhood friends, or running late for their next screenings?

The house lights came on and the *Know Her* team went to the stage for the Q and A. Each chair had a bottle of water on it, and Maddy drank gratefully, feeling dizzy and hoping not to faint from the mountain altitude. Sharoz had informed Maddy that you had to be clever and witty at the panel discussions if you wanted people to spread the word about the film.

The moderator introduced the panel and Dan began fielding questions. A grandmotherly woman raised her hand. "Maddy, I was so impressed by your performance," she said. Was she an agent? A financier? "What kind of training do you have?"

"Um, I studied at the New School," Maddy said, and noticed, next to the woman, a young man nodding vigorously. It was Zack Ostrow. He had come. At ten in the morning. He was a man of his word. Maddy squinted to see if he was with his mother, but on his other side was a blond guy in a bulky parka. "I mostly do theater," she continued, "but of course, Dan and I watch a lot of movies at home, so I had a good film education. I always tell people I studied at the Dan Ellenberg School of Filmmaking."

"So you two are a couple?"

"Oh. Yeah," Maddy said. "The film was shot in my hometown in Vermont, and Dan and I came up with the story together."

Someone else asked if Dan considered it a women's film. "Not at all," he said. "I want my work to resonate with all kinds of people. I'm interested in human stories."

Kira spoke into her mike. "Dan gave us a gift. He writes women so well, it's almost like he has a vagina." Everyone laughed. "And in a sense, he does. Maddy's vagina." They laughed harder. Maddy stiffened. She knew Kira wasn't trying to upstage her, but Kira was easygoing and goofy, and Maddy knew she'd seemed remote by comparison. Or maybe the oxygen deprivation was turning her paranoid.

Kira had arrived late to her audition for *I Used to Know Her*, in a rented rehearsal room in midtown, just as Dan, Maddy, Sharoz, and their casting director were packing up to go. Kira said she had subway problems, and Maddy noticed that her makeup was smudged, either artfully or accidentally. Dan had already read sixty girls for Heather, the character based on Lacey, and was beginning to lose hope that he would be able to find the right actress.

Maddy had been turned off by Kira's lateness, which felt unprofessional. But then they played the scene in which Heather and Alice argue on the rock where they used to go as children, and she was so brilliant and compelling that Dan cast her on the spot.

Another hand shot up, an overserious bony guy. "I'm wondering what the acting process was like for the two of you. Was there any improvisation?"

Maddy started to answer, but Kira jumped in. "You know, the script was really tight, so Dan discouraged any improv. It was hard for me, because I have a more fluid way of working than Maddy does. She comes from the thee-ah-tuh, where the script is God. I'm more moment-to-moment." The audience murmured appreciatively, and Maddy felt that Kira had scored yet another point.

On the street after the screening, as Dan and Maddy headed up Mountain Way, a voice came from behind them. "Maddy, you were sensational." Zack Ostrow.

"Thanks for coming, man," Dan said. "We needed every audience member we could get. Was your mom there, too?"

"No, I'm sure she'll come to another one," Zack said, clearly accustomed to people using him to get to his mother. "Dan, I don't represent directors," he said, "but if you'll let me, I'll put you in touch with one of my colleagues. And Maddy, I would love to get a coffee with you and discuss career possibilities. BHA has incredible reach."

Maddy was flattered that he was thinking on those terms—she hadn't come in search of a new agent, but Dan had said there would be hundreds at the festival, seeking new discoveries. "Absolutely," she said.

"Come to think of it," said Zack, "my mom is having this dinner at her lodge tomorrow. You guys should come. I'll help you drum up audience for the other screenings."

"We'll be there," Dan said, so quickly that Maddy was almost embarrassed.

"Do you have a car here?"

"No," Maddy said. "We ride El Cheapo. The festival bus." Dan glared at her, as though not wanting Zack to know they were losers, but she didn't understand the accusation; it had been *his* decision not to ask the backers to cover a car rental.

"Then we'll send one to get you," Zack said. After he headed away, their condo address in his phone, she wondered who "we" was. Zack, his mother, or his agency?

It didn't make a difference. They were going.

———

Having been to many films and bad Off-Broadway theater in his time at
Bentley Howard, and countless premieres with his mother as a teenager,
Zack was not easily impressed by actresses. But Maddy was different. Her
performance had been luminous, thoroughly unself-conscious, and he
was intrigued by her figure, which was un-Hollywood, with its small, natural breasts and enormous shoulders.

Zack had been at Bentley Howard since right after graduating from
Skidmore. His primary responsibility was to serve the needs of his boss's
clients. George Zeger was a sloppy, corduroy-wearing man who had been
at the agency nearly forty years. As an assistant, Zack had listened in on
George's calls and heard him negotiate, manipulate, and rage when dealing with employers, but speak softly and gently to his clients.

In addition to George's clients, Zack had a handful of his own, most
referred to him by Bridget, but he had come to the festival in search of
more. George had said Zack could go if he paid for his own lodging. Re-
luctantly, he had asked his mother if he could crash. He made $49,000
a year at Bentley Howard, which meant that his mother paid the rent
on his loft in Tribeca and thus kept him under her thumb, inasmuch as
she could from Brentwood. He would not have access to his trust fund
until he turned twenty-eight, four long years away. For his entire childhood, the contingency age had been twenty-one, but at Skidmore he'd
run into problems with coke, and when he wound up at Silver Hill, she
changed it.

Zack was dizzy as he headed up the street, dialing his phone. He had
stayed till five A.M. at the *Rap Sheet* party, playing foosball and doing
tequila shots, and then a young, dorky network-comedy star offered him
a few bumps, and because of the bumps, he couldn't sleep. By the time
nine A.M. rolled around, he'd decided to get a coffee in town and see the
movie.

When his mother answered, he told her about the extra invitations.
"I'll have to redo the seating arrangement," she said with a sigh. "Who are
they again?"

"The girl from that Vermont movie. Maddy Freed. You met her at the
Entertainer. And her boyfriend. He's the director."

"Was she the blonde?"

"Yeah."

"Are you trying to sleep with her?" she said.

"I am not trying to sleep with her, Mom," he said. "I want to sign her." It was scary, what she picked up on. Zack had always had an intense relationship with his mother. As his many shrinks had reminded him, it was a by-product of his father being out of the picture. There were lots of nannies, and he had resented her absences. Lately, he was working on resenting her less. He had been in therapy on and off since he was ten, for being antisocial and later for doing drugs, and he was enjoying not being in therapy for the first time in many years.

"Just let me have them over, Mom," he said. "You won't have to do anything. I'll make sure they have a good time."

"Not too good a time," she said. "This is a classy party."

"You need to watch this right now," Bridget told Steven in his suite at the Niels Lundtofte Lodge. "*I Used to Know Her*, it's called." They were standing in his kitchen, and she was holding the DVD in its clear case.

She had called Ed Handy, immediately after hanging up with Zack, to request the screener. When Ed said Maddy had been at the opening-night party, she remembered Steven watching her with an odd, intent gaze. That look, then Zack's call. Bridget had been so transfixed, she didn't stand up until the film was over.

"Never heard of it," Steven said from the kitchen island, sipping a green smoothie. "What's her name?"

"Maddy Freed."

"What makes you think she's right?"

"She can handle the material."

"The material is very sexual," he said, "and it needs extreme commitment. A lot of the girls have had trouble with it."

"It will make her career. Come on, now. How could any bright, talented actress turn down the role of a lifetime?"

"I'll watch it tomorrow," he said, noticing a ring of water that the smoothie had left on the countertop, and wiping it with his fingers.

"She's coming to my dinner party. With her boyfriend. He directed it.

I want you to see it before they come." Bridget knew not to push him too hard. A manager's job was to walk in the client's shoes and guide him to the decisions that were best for him, like a therapist teasing out insight from a patient. If he watched this movie and didn't like the girl, they would be back to the drawing board. But it was his decision to make.

She looked at Steven evenly for a few seconds. Finally, he sighed. She smiled as she walked past him to the DVD player.

As *I Used to Know Her* began to roll, Steven prepared to be disappointed. He had been to many film festivals and seen a lot of atmospheric shots of toothless men, tetherball courts, and snow—and more than enough protagonist-toting vehicles. But as soon as he saw the girl, he remembered. He had noticed her at the Entertainer. She had a type of beauty that you took in slowly. Striking without being striking. Her eyes were open and widely set, her mouth turned down slightly. She had baby fat around her chin, untrimmed eyebrows, and a mole on one temple that he found fetching.

The girl greeted her mother. You could sense the ambivalence she felt about coming home for a visit. The mother was talking, the girl frustrated. She moved naturally, a little tomboyish, hunching her shoulders in an adaptation to being tall, and unlike many actresses of her age range, she didn't fry her voice when she spoke.

Around the sixty-minute mark, she wasn't speaking to the best friend, and after an ugly fight with her mother, she stormed out the door and peeled off in her mother's truck. She met up with a chubby former high school classmate, and they got drunk on bourbon and made love in his car in the parking lot. As she came, there was a hint of sadness behind her eyes, as though the orgasm brought her into contact with her disappointment. She was melancholy. Steven didn't know how much was the actress and how much the character. He wondered if the girl had the same depth in real life.

When the movie was over, he said softly, "I want Walter to read her."

"I knew you would," Bridget said. He could tell she wanted to say "I told you so" but was holding herself back.

He moved to the window, looked out at the mess of pine trees. They'd had several near misses for the role, but casting was ninety percent of a project, and he was unwilling to compromise. Ellie had to show sexiness, determination, and sadness. They couldn't cast just anyone. Audiences needed to feel there was no one else on earth who could play her.

It would be hard to make much headway at the party with the boy-friend there to distract her, but he was emboldened by the challenge. Though Steven Weller had many talents, one of his greatest was his ability to connect with men.

3

The car that ferried Dan and Maddy to Bridget's lodge was a large black gas-guzzling SUV. On the ride, Dan stewed about the competition. An NYU classmate, Bryan Monakhov, had already gotten his film acquired by Apollo Classics: *Triggers*, a Jewish-gangster crime caper set in Brownsville, Brooklyn, during the 1930s. Monakhov had won Best Dramatic Feature before, for a mother-son incest picture. Dan was worried the early deal would hurt *I Used to Know Her*'s chances, because the studio had only a finite amount to spend.

But that morning's screening had twice the audience of the first. The reviews had come out—in its roundup, *The New York Times* had called *I Used to Know Her* "a pitch-perfect study of the pleasures and pains of female friendship," and *Variety* had cited "two knockout performances and a spare smart script." The *L.A. Times* review was mixed, saying that Dan was "more comfortable as a writer than a director, framing his shots with little originality." Dan was furious, and Maddy felt protective, but she told him to focus on the other two.

With the reviews had come other firsts: Two agents had given her cards after screenings, and she was scheduling coffees. Nancy Watson-Eckstein was a self-assured, petite, African American woman who worked at Original Talent Associates. The other, Galt Gurley, was an anemic-looking older white woman at United Creative. Maddy couldn't believe that she could have a choice.

Reid had authorized a few interviews for the cast, and Maddy was taken aback when an indie-film blogger brought up the Special Jury Prize for Acting. Maddy laughed and said she had no chance because their film was too small. But then she couldn't help it: She imagined herself holding up the award at the Mountain Way Theater. It was a variation on the old Oscar-acceptance fantasy she'd had as a girl. Except in those fantasies, her father was in the audience, cheering her on.

Her dad was the reason she had grown up in Potter, which, in a way, was the reason the film had gotten made. A Jewish Philadelphian, Jake Freed had gone to Dartmouth, where he met Maddy's mother, née Dorothy McHale, in an Eastern Religion class. They discovered Potter on a road trip with friends, and Jake fell in love with the Northeast Kingdom. After graduation, he sent out his résumé for teaching jobs and landed a position as an English teacher at the Potter Ski Academy, a private school that churned out Olympians. Dorothy was a nurse in nearby St. Johnsbury before she got sick with breast cancer; she died when Maddy was seven.

Jake's memorial had been packed with all the friends and family members who were in such high spirits during the shoot. Many cast and crew members came, wanting to pay their respects. Neighbors stood at the podium and told stories of his generosity—letting kids crash at the Freed house when they were going through rough patches, caring for a fellow teacher who became ill. Jake Freed was a thinker, a teacher, a mensch. People like him weren't supposed to drop dead in their sixties. He made too many people happy.

The SUV ascended a steep hill and Maddy felt the familiar grief welling inside her. In the dark of the backseat, she reached for Dan's hand, but he was studying his phone. She tried to snap herself out of her reverie by imagining the dinner. Weller would be there, undoubtedly, and Cady Pearce. Probably other stars, too. It was one thing to hostess people like this at La Cloche, another to dine next to them.

The SUV pulled up to two stone pillars and a gate, which opened as if by magic. Maddy wondered who controlled the gate—a guard, unseen in a little booth behind the house, like the man in *The Wizard of Oz*.

A snaking driveway let them out at a parking lot where a dozen luxury cars were already stationed. She worried she and Dan were out of their league. At the door, a girl in a knee-length parka searched a clipboard for their names. The entryway had huge stone columns and picture windows with views of the forest.

They checked their coats—what kind of hostess had a coat check person in her home?—and made their way into a living area decorated with moss art and a slate fireplace. Tall steel candlesticks flickered on small finished tree trunks.

Dan edged over to the freestanding bar to get their drinks while Maddy took in the assembled guests: the star of *Triggers*, Munro Heming, the rising sandy-haired heartthrob who spoke like Marlon Brando; Ed Handy; Todd Lewitt, the director of *The Widower*, who dressed like a 1970s computer programmer; and Lael Gordinier, a redheaded late-twenties actress who specialized in femmes fatales. As Maddy accepted a glass of chardonnay from Dan, she felt like she was in a scene in a movie about Mile's End.

A handsome young guy with slicked-back hair came over and Dan introduced him as Bryan Monakhov. "Crazy to see you guys here," Bryan said. "I didn't know you knew Bridget."

"Well, we do," Dan said tightly.

"Congratulations on your acquisition," Maddy said, hoping Bryan wouldn't notice Dan's scowl.

"I'm going to try to catch your movie," Bryan said. "Good luck with the screenings. I'm rooting for you, man. That's why I come here. The brotherhood of celluloid."

"I think that was a gay doc here a couple years ago," Dan said.

"Good one," said Bryan. "You are one funny cat."

Bryan went to greet a partygoer, and then Bridget strode over and kissed Dan and Maddy, each on both cheeks, as though they were old friends. She was wearing a royal blue organza skirt that flared out at the ankles. "You are an absolute wonder," she said to Maddy. "It was so original and so moving. Dan, you are such an actor's director." Maddy was surprised; she hadn't seen Bridget at any screenings.

"I really appreciate that," Dan said, his voice steady.

Zack came over. "I was just telling them how great the film is," Bridget said to him.

"You went to a screening?" Zack said.

"Ed sent me a screener," she said. "Steven watched it, too." Maddy couldn't imagine why Steven Weller would be interested.

"So what did Steven think?" Dan asked shamelessly.

"Absolutely loved it," Bridget said.

"How did you get him to see a little film like ours?" Dan asked.

"He does whatever I tell him—though many years ago, I told him never to act in a movie with the word 'bombs' in the title."

Zack started to say something but was drowned out by Weller's loud chuckle. He was moving through the room as he had at the Entertainer, clapping guests on the back. Maddy waited for the girlfriend to emerge just behind him, but this time he was alone. Cadyless.

Weller appeared to be coming right toward them. Dan blanched. Maddy looked over her shoulder to see if there was someone famous behind them, but there was no one there. He extended his hand to Maddy and said, "I loved your performance."

His palm was warm and rougher than she expected, the hand of a man who might use a rowing machine without gloves. He kept his eyes on her for a long moment, and she couldn't decide whether he was flirting with her or was one of those people who flirted with everyone. Celebrity was automatic sexual charisma.

"And you, sir," he said to Dan, "are a very talented director."

"I, sir, am very uncomfortable right now," Dan said, and gave a nervous laugh.

"There were so many little moments," Weller said. "Like when Heather is at the bar and she kisses the one guy and then kisses the other. The rhythm. It was like a piece of music. And the subject matter—to me, it was about the futility of long-term friendship." Maddy was impressed that Weller had not only seen the movie but had insight about it. "And the fact that they're women," he went on, "but their breakup is not about sex per se, is all the more interesting. Usually in film, when two women have a falling-out, it's over a man. It was brave of you not to turn it into that."

"Wow, you really got our movie," Maddy said, immediately wanting to kick herself for saying "wow."

"I want to ask you about one of the scenes," he said, turning to Maddy. Other guests were glancing at them, curious that these nobodies were monopolizing his attention. It was embarrassing. She wanted to release him back into the fold of successful people, where he belonged. "You know the fight they have after the rehearsal dinner?" he continued.

"There was this moment when it looked like you were breaking. What was that about?"

Maddy knew the moment he meant. It was part of a long monologue, and she and Kira had done a few takes, but Dan wasn't happy. He kept saying that the scene lacked nuance. Maddy had been getting frustrated when she remembered a lesson from one of her professors: The best auditions contained an element of surprise. In the next take, she threw in a smile right after the line "You never cared about me." Almost as though Alice didn't believe her own words. The smile had enraged Kira, and the take had contained an energy that the other takes lacked. When they finished, Dan had said, "That's the one."

"I wasn't breaking," she told Weller. "I was playing the contempt instead of the hurt."

"I hope everyone's hungry," Bridget said, gesturing toward the dining room. Zack and Bridget walked ahead, leaving Weller, Dan, and Maddy behind. Maddy could see Zack whispering furiously at his mother, but when Bridget glanced back at Maddy, she smiled.

As they turned toward the dining room, Weller's arm brushed Maddy's through his soft blue sweater. Her whole body came awake, even though all she had touched was alpaca.

In the dining room, a long distressed walnut table was set for twenty. Maddy took Dan's hand and led him toward two empty seats, but Weller said, "Bridget had place cards made up. Dan is next to me." Dan glanced at Maddy anxiously. "Maddy, you're next to Lael."

Weller led Dan toward one end of the table, and Maddy spotted Lael Gordinier at the opposite end. Siberia. She didn't like that Dan would be so far away. She wanted to experience the party with him. But Lael was a jury member, which meant she would judge the competition films. It could be useful to sit next to her. She could help their film.

After the two women introduced themselves, Maddy said, "I really liked your work in *Die Now*." It was a neo-noir in which Lael seduced her ob-gyn into killing her husband. Lael had a reckless bravado that she brought to all her roles. She also brought her voluptuous and much discussed figure.

"I was so fucking young," Lael said, staring ahead mordantly.

"Wasn't it, like, two years ago?"

"Yeah, but I was emotionally immature." Suddenly, Lael pivoted toward Maddy and said, "Your movie rocks. I'm very threatened by you." She said it like she could be either joking or serious. "It was brave how you didn't wear makeup."

"I did wear makeup."

"Oh."

At the opposite end of the table, Weller was speaking intently to Dan. Over the din, Maddy heard Weller say, "She's looking for what's best and what's next," and gathered it was industry-speak. She knew Dan didn't care about the business—or at least he hadn't before Mile's End—but now he seemed transfixed.

Weller caught Maddy's eye, and she turned toward Lael, not wanting to appear to gawk. On Lael's other side was a rangy model turned actress, also in her twenties, Taylor Yaccarino. The women were talking about some actor Maddy had never heard of, with whom they had both played recent love scenes. "He *always* pops wood," Lael was telling Taylor. "No one told you?"

"No!"

"Oh God, it's the worst. Then he spreads rumors that the sex was real. It's disgusting."

"You think he's telling people we did it?" Taylor asked, seeming horrified. "That's crazy. He had a cup."

"He probably put Vaseline in there to excite himself," Lael said.

Soon the women had moved on to industry gossip and a film for which they had auditioned. Maddy thought she heard Taylor say *"Husbandry."*

"I didn't know you went in for that," Lael said.

"Yeah. I thought I would just put myself on tape, but he only does face-to-face, so I flew to London."

"Me too," Lael said. "I heard they've been casting for a year. I don't think it's going to get made."

Servers were coming around with the amuse-bouche, a creamy squash soup. The table had gotten quiet. Weller was telling a story, and the guests wore the same hyper-alert expression Maddy had seen on the faces at the opening-night party. The story was about a television star named Clay Murphy who had been mocked several years before for having written a novel that became a *New York Times* best seller despite its abysmal reviews. "So Clay had to give a speech at a book fair," Weller was saying. "And he asked me for help with his speech. He said he wanted it to be about his love of reading. He told me his favorite writer was Ayn Rand." The group chuckled snarkily. "So he says to me, 'Steven, I think I'm going to lead with the story about buying my signed first edition of *Atlas Shrugged*. What do you think?'

"Well, Clay is a sweet guy," Weller continued, "and I don't want to hurt his feelings, but I know if he says that, he's going to look like an idiot in front of these literary types. So I say, 'Clay, I'm not sure that's a good idea.' He says, 'Why not?' I think for a second and I say, 'It's still so controversial.' He pauses a second and goes, 'I understand.'"

Everyone howled with laughter. It was a funny story, obviously delivered many times before. Maddy watched Dan sit higher in his seat as though soaking up adoration by association.

After the four-course dinner, guests mingled in the living room over liqueur and dessert wine. Maddy grabbed a glass, and after spotting Dan alone on a couch, she went to him. "So tell me all about Taylor and Lael," he said. "That sounds like a folk duo." He was sipping from a glass of something green.

"Horrifying," Maddy said quietly. "They spent half the time talking about how awful it was to do sex scenes and the other half talking about every famous guy in Hollywood they've fucked. But Lael loves our movie."

"Seriously?"

"Yeah. What did Weller talk about?"

"Oh, the glory days of the Hotel Bel-Air, his antipoverty work, and the history of his beaux arts mansion in Hancock Park."

"What's Hancock Park?"

"Some tony part of L.A., I guess. I think I have a bro crush. I've never had one on a gay guy."

"You said he wasn't gay."

"I changed my mind. I think he had a thing for me. That's why he wanted me near him. Gay men like me because of my feminine fingers." Dan seemed drunk. He always got Pinocchio circles on his cheeks when he imbibed.

Maddy indicated a backless bench across the room where Weller was chatting with Munro Heming. "You should lower your voice," she said. "He might hear you."

"I'm sure everyone at this party knows it," he said. "That's why he didn't bring Cady. She flew back to L.A. He said they broke up weeks ago. I said, 'Why'd she come to Mile's End?' He said she loves indie film. Obviously, she was just arm candy."

Dan went off to find the bathroom, and Maddy sat alone for a moment, sipping liqueur, before Zack Ostrow plopped down beside her. "My mom's going to pitch herself to you tonight," he said.

"What? I don't think so. I'm not famous." Though Bridget's words about the film had been kind, that didn't mean Bridget wanted to work for her.

"She'll tell you not to consider me," Zack said, ignoring the interruption. "Say I'm volatile and young. I'm not. Well, okay, I'm young. But you should consider me. Bentley Howard has been around since the eighteen hundreds, and you'll be in very good hands." Maddy wasn't sure she trusted him. Who knew if he was even a full-fledged agent? Maybe he worked in the mail room. While he talked, he kept glancing around the room and flicking his eyes back at her. It seemed an affectation designed to convince her he wasn't overly interested, which seemed strange for a man pitching his services.

"My mom and I do things very differently. She's interested in setting up projects that make money. I'm interested in setting up projects that are good."

"Can't something be both?" she said.

"That's my hope. That's why I do it. If you really want to build a career, long-term, you should be with someone like me. I take time with my clients. With my mother, you'd get lost in the shuffle. Who've you met with here?" She told him about Nancy and Galt—it was important to let him know that other agents were interested. Immediately afterward, she regretted it, thinking two wasn't enough to seem impressive.

"I know them both very well, and you'd be fine with either one," Zack said. "But they'll want you to move out to L.A." Dan always said he would never live in Los Angeles, and though Maddy was open to it, she couldn't imagine being apart from him. "You don't have to move," Zack added. "Better to be that intense, really good actress who lives in New York rather than another dime-a-dozen in L.A."

"Did you just call me a dime-a-dozen?" Maddy asked, grinning.

"No. That's the point. You have the goods." As he said it, he gently clasped her forearm. She couldn't tell if he was hitting on her. If he was, it seemed a stupid way to go about getting her as a client.

"If you're right, and your mother is going to make me an offer," Maddy said, extracting her arm, "why couldn't I—I mean hypothetically speaking— sign with both of you? Since she's a manager and you're an agent?"

"Because I only work with people who are moving the needle."

"Bridget isn't?"

"You don't have to whisper. She knows what I think. She operates under the old business model. Nothing wrong with that, except she thinks it's still viable."

"What's the old model?"

"Where you put a star in a movie and it makes hundreds of millions of dollars. That was the '80s. These days stars don't sell movies."

"What does?"

"Stories. That's the future of entertainment. If an audience can dig in to a story, they'll come out to the theaters. Mile's End has created a world in which directors can be household names. Moviegoers are finally beginning to follow the storytellers. If you sign with me, I'll pair you with them. She doesn't even know who they are." He stood up and crossed the room to the bar.

She sat there for a moment, dazed. It was a good pitch, although she didn't know how much of it was true; Weller was clearly working with storytellers, such as Todd Lewitt, and surely Bridget had something to do with those roles.

Maddy stood up to find a bathroom. As she moved out of the living room, she ran into Bridget, coming out of the kitchen. "Are you enjoying yourself?"

"So much," Maddy said. "Thank you for having us. I think Dan is still getting over the fact that he was next to Steven."

"Steven is such a fan of the film." Maddy smiled, needing to pee but not wanting to offend Bridget Ostrow by ending the conversation. Bridget continued, "So has Zack pitched himself yet?"

"I'm not sure. I think he wants to sign me, yeah." She was curious as to what Bridget would say.

"Of course he does. Listen, he's my son, and I want nothing more than for him to succeed, but he's very green. And he's ambivalent about agenting. He's trying it on for size. I wouldn't put money on him doing it in five years." Maddy was surprised by how openly Bridget was undermining her own son. Then again, Zack had just done the same thing. "Maddy, I think you're very talented, and in case I haven't made it clear enough, I'd like to work with you."

So Zack had been right. Bridget Ostrow wanted to work with her. And she didn't even know if *I Used to Know Her* would be released. It felt like a huge gesture of faith, to think she could have a career. "I—I don't know what to say," she stammered. "Thank you."

"Now, I know it gets a little confusing, the manager-versus-agent thing. Managers produce their clients' projects and guide their careers. Agents can't. I think you should relocate, because L.A. is where the work is. I believe in you. I don't have a lot of clients. Currently seven. A small shop lets me work harder. I don't do volume. Like that old Robert Klein DJ routine. 'How do I do it? Volume!' " Bridget smiled at her for a beat, and then rested her hand on Maddy's forearm, near where Zack had. "Anyway, I'm an absolute warhorse, I've been doing this forever. You can ask anyone. But you don't have to decide right now, honey. Think it over." She slipped her a card.

After Bridget left, Maddy headed for the bathroom. It was occupied, and the half-bath was, too, so she climbed the stairs to the second floor. Upstairs, she wasn't sure which door led to the bathroom. She pushed against one that was slightly ajar, but when she peered inside, she was startled to see Zack on a huge bed across the room, having sex doggie-style with a shorthaired girl. Neither Zack nor the girl turned, and Maddy shut the door quickly, not sure if he had seen her.

When she found the bathroom, she locked the door and leaned against it. Bridget had been right—he wasn't serious about being an agent. It wasn't the sex, it was the flaunting of it. The door open, as though he was broadcasting that he had come to Mile's End to party. She thought back to the way he had touched her arm.

Downstairs, she couldn't find Dan. She wanted to tell him about Bridget. She felt light-headed from the wine and liqueur.

She got her coat, slipped out the front door, and went to the side of the house, hoping the cold air would clear her head. She sat at a cedar patio table, crossing her arms. It was snowing lightly. She remembered being eight or nine, her dad coming into her bedroom one morning, opening the curtains so she could see the thick white clumps.

She heard footsteps coming from the house, and a moment later, Steven Weller was sitting opposite her. She had no idea what to say. "Hi," he said.

"Hi."

The silence was uncomfortable. He just looked at her, so she pointed at the sky and said, "That's the Little Dipper."

"I know. And Orion. And that's the Big Dipper. I'm from the Midwest."

"Oh." Silence again. She had known he was from the Midwest. She'd known his entire bio since she was a teenager: One of two sons. Polish family. Weller wasn't his birth name, but she couldn't remember the real one. "Kenosha, Wisconsin," she said, trying to recover.

"Yep. On Lake Michigan."

There was a matchbook on the table, and Weller tore off a match. He held it up between his fingers and said, "One, two, three." On three, the match vanished.

"How did you do that?" she asked, impressed.

"A magician never tells."

"Please? One more time!"

He did it again. She puzzled over it and then took the match, fumbling with her fingers, unable to figure it out.

"I meant what I said about your performance," he said. "You were stellar. Truly."

"I can't believe you're saying that. Thank you so much."

"How'd you get bitten? By the bug?"

"I was a shy kid," she said. "My mother died when I was young, and it was hard for me. My dad got me into acting. I think he realized it could help. When I acted, I didn't feel shy. There's this Danny Kaye movie I saw as a kid. *Wonder Man*. He's escaping from gangsters, and he winds up on the stage of an opera, mistaken for one of the performers. Every time he looks in the wings, he sees the gangsters waiting to get him. He's only safe as long as he's onstage. That's kind of how I felt."

She told Weller that when she was nine, her father had told her to audition for Elmer Rice's *Street Scene* at the Potter Players, their local theater. A small role, just a few lines, but she loved every moment of the rehearsals, the blocking, the lights, and later, the period costume. When she walked onto the bright stage on opening night, she got a rush. The thrill of the moment, the potential for mishaps, the breathing of the audience, whom you could see. There was a murder toward the end of the play. Backstage, she could smell the smoke.

After the show closed, she asked her father if she could take acting class. He shuttled her to a children's theater in Lyndonville, where she did improv drills, Shakespeare scenes, theater games, and original monologues. He suggested she try an arts camp in upstate New York. The other kids had names like Masha and Pippin and did unironic productions of Agatha Christie. In the company of these weird precocious kids, she wanted to be better.

Throughout her childhood, during school vacations or over long weekends, Jake would drive her the long six hours into the city, where they would check in to a hotel and see plays. Shanley, Ives, Albee, Wasserstein, Durang. Stephen Schwartz and Jonathan Larson, A. R. Gurney, musical revivals. Actors could create worlds out of nothing, summon real tears. They could turn psychology into behavior.

"What does your father think of the movie?" Weller asked on the patio.

"He died right after we wrapped. A heart attack." He had been cross-country skiing alone. A guy on a snowmobile had found him.

Weller reached forward and put his hand on top of hers. "Maddy, I didn't know. I'm so sorry."

"It's all right." She didn't like saying that, but she didn't want to talk about it.

The day she got the call from Tanya O'Neill, their next-door neighbor, she had been on her way to an audition for a regional *Room Service* revival. She was walking in midtown when her cell phone rang. Tanya said only, "Your daddy . . ." Maddy knew immediately. The word "daddy." Maddy felt like she had been shot. Because her mother had died young, it had never occurred to Maddy that her father could go early, too.

To change the subject, she said to Weller, "How did you get into acting?"

"Tenth grade, I got a knee injury during a football game," he said. "Had to quit the team. Started getting into trouble because I had too much free time. My English teacher suggested I try out for the school production of *Our Town*. I read George's monologue to Emily in the soda shop. I was blown away by the writing. That was it. I auditioned. I got George. Later, when my knee got better, I tried to do both football and acting, but I kept having to miss practice. My coach said, 'Steve, you gonna play football or you gonna do that fag acting?' " Weller laughed. "I said, 'I think I'm gonna do the acting, Coach.' It was no contest. Acting marshaled me."

Marshaled. Acting had marshaled her shyness, and it had marshaled his energy. He understood. Acting could save you from the pain of being yourself.

"I love acting," he said, "but I hate most actors."

"What's wrong with actors?"

"Aside from the falsity and braggadocio? Most of them lack person-hood. They're stunted. And prone to illeism."

"Illeism?"

"They speak about themselves in the third person. People who do that are missing an 'I.' They don't know who they are. I prefer people who know who they are." He was looking at her like he wanted to eat her. She looked down and then up again so she could catch her breath.

"Bridget offered to sign me," she said. She wanted to know everything about Bridget. Whether he felt he owed his career to her.

"And what did you tell her?" he asked. His smile had deepened.

"I haven't made up my mind. Maybe Bridget's too big for me."

"She wouldn't want to work for you if she weren't committed to help-ing you."

Work for you. It was so easy to lose sight of this simple truth: If Maddy signed with her, Bridget Ostrow would be working for her, not the other way around. "Bridget was the one who discovered you, right?"

"Yep. It was the 1980s and she was one of the few women in the talent department of OTA, and she saw me in *Bus Stop* at the Duse Repertory Company on El Centro. That was where I got my start. We used to do eight shows a year. I learned everything from Shakespeare to Beckett to Inge. She waited by the door, and asked me to have a drink. I said no, since I was supposed to be meeting a bunch of guy buddies to watch a Tyson fight, but she went along with us. Spent the night at a sports bar. When the last friend left, she said, 'I want to work with you.' "

"And what did you say?"

"I said, 'You're a woman. How do I know you'll be aggressive?' " He chuckled. "She loves to remind me of that. I was young. I had no experience with powerful women. She said, 'I'm twice as aggressive as any man,' and I signed with her a week later."

Though it seemed the kind of thing a 1980s Steven Weller would say, Maddy didn't like that he had been so openly sexist. Maybe he enjoyed the story because it had an arc to it, or maybe he'd never said it. Celebrities told the same stories again and again, in interviews, to mold the image they wanted. At a certain point, they probably couldn't even remember what was fact and what was fiction.

"Anyway, I hope you go with Bridget," Weller said, getting out of the chair.

"Because you think she's the best?" The moon made a halo around his head.

"Because then you and I might work together one day. And I'd like that." His gaze held hers. It was an expensive gaze to put in a movie and one that looked very good blown up a thousand times.

He went inside. She turned the matchbook over in her hand but couldn't get the trick.

In the living room, where Maddy finally found Dan, he was talking to Todd Lewitt about a tracking shot in *The Widower* and nodding at the answers the way Cady Pearce had nodded when Weller spoke. Maddy stood there silently, waiting for Dan to pause so she could tell him she had to talk to him, but there was never a pause. She noticed Zack enter the room, alone. She turned quickly to Dan and said, "We should be getting back," but he shook his head.

The girl Zack had been with, now wearing a tube skirt and a sweatshirt with a print of a cat, came down a minute later, as if Zack had instructed her to delay. Zack went to the bar for more liqueur. Maddy caught herself staring at him, blushed, and turned away.

"I'm leaving," she told Dan.

He nodded and said to Todd Lewitt, "I love Antonioni."

She took the car back to the condo, and the driver said he would return to the party to get Dan. She went to the bathroom and rinsed her face.

And I'd like that. That look. Steven Weller seemed to have been flirting, but maybe he was playing elder statesman. Though the two weren't mutually exclusive.

She lay on the bed and closed her eyes, but the room was spinning. She didn't want to throw up. She paced in the living room and called Irina to tell her about Bridget, if not about Weller. It was two A.M. in New York, but Irina was a night owl. When the phone went to voice mail, Maddy hung up.

Sharoz would have advice about Bridget Ostrow. Sharoz took the Hollywood stuff in stride. She would be able to say whether Bridget Ostrow was legit or just a vanity manager for a famous man. Maddy glanced out the window at Sharoz and Kira's condo. A light was on.

Kira opened the door in a cutoff Bad Brains T-shirt, a whiskey glass in her hand. She seemed to be weaving a little. "Hey, is Sharoz around?" Maddy asked.

"She's at some party," Kira said.

"Oh. Can you have her knock on my door if she comes back in the next half hour?"

"Yeah, sure." Maddy turned unsteadily toward the door. "So how were the beautiful people?" Kira called behind her.

Dan had told Kira about the dinner invitation, and if she had been jealous, she had hidden it well. Now she seemed too tipsy to be cool. "It was a good party," Maddy answered.

"And was the son there, the midget boy?"

"He's not that short."

"Oh my God, he is. I saw him in the theater for that first screening, and I was thinking how inappropriate it was that someone brought a child to our movie."

Maddy didn't know why she was knocking him. She was irritated with Kira for being haughty, for always undermining her. "The midget boy wants to work for me."

"Of course he does. Did you say yes?"

"No. I don't know what I'm going to do. You know, since you brought up the screenings, I've been meaning to ask you why you've been so obnoxious at the Q and A's."

"I have no idea what you're talking about," Kira said, her hand on her hip.

"Those comments about me being Dan's girlfriend. You always find a way to work it in. Like I only got cast because we're sleeping together."

"I never said that. Is that why you think you got cast?"

"You imply it. And you're so dismissive of my MFA. You were obnoxious during the shoot, but I never said anything because it was good for the movie. Now we've been lucky enough to make it here, and it's like you have it in for me."

"I don't have it in for you, Maddy."

Maddy wanted to scream. "Sure you do," Maddy said. "You think I'm a snob."

"God, I've never seen your cheeks this red except when you were doing that fucking in the movie."

When Maddy reconstructed the moment later, it was like she was watching from a corner of the room. She shoved Kira hard, and Kira stumbled back a few steps and then strode toward her fast, like she was going to hit her. Instead, she put her face right up against Maddy's and glared.

Without thinking about it or knowing why she was doing it, Maddy kissed her. Then she stepped back, shocked at herself and what she had done. Kira moved toward her, slowly, and touched her face. She kissed Maddy gently and with affection that seemed completely incompatible with the rudeness. Maddy's tongue began to move in Kira's mouth, and

Kira's hands were on Maddy's back, pulling her closer. She could feel Kira's breasts against her own, so much bigger than hers, these strange soft boobs in a place where until now she had encountered only hardness.

Kira was kissing her neck and her chin, and then she was unclasping Maddy's bra and her hands were on her. Maddy cupped Kira's breasts over the T-shirt, imagining the size and shape of her nipples. Kira lifted Maddy's sweater and shirt over her head and went for the bra strap, and that was when Maddy realized this was happening. Dan would be home soon, wondering where she was. He might see the light on. She pulled away.

"I should go," Maddy said. She picked up her sweater and began to put it on.

"Yeah, it's really late." She said it like Maddy had overstayed her welcome when only seconds ago, she had been kissing her.

Maddy felt both guilty and embarrassed. Now she had done it and she couldn't undo it and it was her own fault, she had kissed first.

Dan didn't get back to their condo for another hour, which gave Maddy time to shower and get into bed. It had been an otherworldly night. The dueling pitches from Bridget and Zack; then Zack with the girl; then Weller on the patio; then Kira. Maddy had never made out with a woman, not even kissed one. In the theater scene at Dartmouth, a lot of the women students got drunk and slept together, but at parties, when Maddy observed them drinking heavily and groping each other, aware that the boys were watching, it had seemed like an act. She didn't want to do something like that just to turn on guys. Despite the occasional erotic dream about women, she believed she was ninety-five percent straight.

Tonight she was less sure. With Kira being such a good kisser, she had been turned on. Maybe it was actually Steven Weller who had turned her on, and Kira was just a substitute, a nearby body. Or maybe it had nothing to do with Weller at all.

When Dan slid into bed next to her, she asked if he'd had fun. "Best party of my life," he said. His eyes were starting to close.

"Bridget wants to sign me," she told him.

"I knew she would," he murmured. "You should go with her. She knows everyone."

"She wants me to move out there."

"Maybe we should. We could rethink it." Soon Dan was sleeping and she was lying awake, feeling Kira's hands on her body. What if Kira told Dan what happened, just to spite her, to cause trouble in the relationship? The post-screening panels would go from bad to worse, Kira feeling she had something on Maddy. Maddy wished she had never knocked on the condo door. It was all Steven Weller's fault. He had made her crazy, turned her into someone else.

An hour into the third *I Used to Know Her* screening, on Tuesday night, distributors began to leave the room. In the theater, when people walked out, it meant they hated it. But Maddy learned later that the executives had been rushing to put in offers on the film. Four different companies made bids, and after a whirlwind night of negotiations involving Dan, Sharoz, and Ed Handy, Apollo Classics bought world rights for $4 million and first look at Dan's next screenplay.

When Dan came home in the middle of the night and gave Maddy the news, she was half-asleep and could make out only bits and pieces: He would be able to pay the actors their prenegotiated back salary; Maddy's was $25,000. On top of that she would get $15,000 for her shared story credit. Each fee was more money than she had ever made for anything creative. Sharoz and Dan would get a quarter of a million each, plus more if the film made any money. It wasn't a mammoth deal, but it was mammoth in relation to her life with Dan, their dumpy apartment, their service-industry jobs.

He got on top of her. "I have flop sweat," he said. "I smell disgusting." But he didn't make a move to stop.

So now he wanted to make love, after becoming a big man. He wanted validation. That was all right with her. Sex could serve many purposes. She had been trying to forget what had happened with Kira, even if it was only a makeout, even if Kira was a girl. In the three days since then, Kira had been distant with Maddy, terse and breezy. At the Q and A's she stopped lobbing her half-insults, as though she had lost interest in raising Maddy's ire. Maddy was ashamed of the lonely part of her that had kissed Kira. Her conversation with Weller had excited her, and then Dan wouldn't leave the party. If you were lonely, there were other things you could do, like buy cigarettes or listen to Tom Waits.

Dan was inside her now, though it felt clinical, like he was a surgeon doing a procedure. He came on her stomach and looked down at it with the hint of a smile. She was on the pill, so he usually finished inside her, but sometimes he didn't. He got a towel from the bathroom and handed it to her, and she dabbed at herself.

He was asleep a few minutes later, his body turned away from her. She stared at the ceiling. They would have to get cracking on *The Nest* now that he had a first-look deal. After he had finished *I Used to Know Her*, but before they shot it, they had started a new screenplay together. *The Nest* was a comedy about a Brooklyn girl who can't move out of her parents' apartment even though she's engaged. They wrote about sixty pages, but then Jake died and Maddy had stopped sleeping and hadn't been able to work on it. Maybe now they would finally finish.

Maybe she would start getting writing jobs of her own, since she had a story credit on *I Used to Know Her*. Her career would advance right alongside Dan's, the two of them in step like in that Atalanta story on *Free to Be . . . You and Me*. She was still holding the sticky towel in her hand. She set it down on the wall-to-wall carpet before turning to Dan and pressing her front against his back.

In the morning Maddy called Irina to share the good news. "Oh my God, I am shitting," Irina said. She had grown up in Bay Ridge and hadn't completely lost her accent. "I knew this would happen. How is Dan?"

"He's happy, but he almost seems like he knew it. It's weird. He was so squirrelly the first couple days, and now he's Mr. Cool."

"I knew you were going to get a deal," Irina said. "Can I throw you guys a party when you come home?" She and her sound-designer boyfriend lived in a loft in East Williamsburg.

After the festival, Maddy explained, they were going to L.A. to take meetings with agents and managers; they had decided that morning, before Dan went off to meet the head of Apollo Classics. "But definitely after we get back."

Maddy told her about Bridget Ostrow, and Irina said, "She's huge."

"I know. She might be too huge." Maddy told her that Steven Weller had been at the party, and had urged her to sign with Bridget. "We talked for, like, twenty minutes. Alone. It was so bizarre. I feel like I hallucinated it."

"The fact that he's her main client is not the biggest endorsement of Bridget Ostrow."

"You don't get it," Maddy said. "This new role is a tour de force for him. *The Widower*. He's getting better, Irina, I'm telling you."

Irina cleared her throat and said, "How many clients does Bridget have?"

"She said seven. She says she doesn't do volume. Like that Robert Klein routine."

"Who's Robert Klein?" asked Irina.

"The idea of a jury giving an award for acting is ridiculous," Lael Gordinier was saying from the podium of the Mountain Way Theater. "There is no objective way of judging actors in comparison to each other."

It was the closing ceremony for the festival. After the acquisition, every screening of *I Used to Know Her* had been sold out, with a line snaking around the block. Maddy and Kira were stopped for autographs wherever they went, and Victor was in talks to be a cinematographer on a cable comedy series about Staten Island secretaries.

Every seat in the Mountain Way was packed, and IFC was airing it live. "But sometimes there is a performance so unique," Lael continued, "that it deserves to be recognized. This year the Grand Jury has awarded a prize for such a performance. The Special Jury Prize for Acting goes to Maddy Freed for *I Used to Know Her*."

"You bitch," Kira said, but she was smiling. She leaned over to Maddy, and their eyes locked. For a moment Maddy feared Kira would French-kiss her, but she planted a wet one on her cheek.

Maddy registered very little of the next five minutes—the award, the way it was shaped like a mountain and made of something that looked like steel. Thanking Kira, Sharoz, Dan, and a dozen cast and crew members. Stammering something hokey about her father, then beginning to weep. Backstage, she did a press line before weaving back to her seat.

Dan hugged her. "I sounded like an ass," she said.

"A little bit," he said. She took out a tissue and dabbed her face, still unable to think past the moment when Lael read out her name.

Best Director went to the director of *Rap Sheet*, a portly white British guy, and Bryan Monakhov's *Triggers* won Best Dramatic Feature. When Bryan's name was announced, Maddy was afraid to glance over at Dan, who was sitting very still in his seat.

Bryan was high-fiving people, shouting jubilantly. He made a big show of getting Munro Heming and the other stars up to the stage with him and said in an exaggerated hoodlum accent, "I don't know what to say, man. This movie is about doing anything you have to do to make it, and it's a message I believe in. Peace out."

"I can't believe they gave it to him twice," Dan muttered.

"People are going to see our movie no matter what," said Maddy. "Remember, we have distribution. And we could still win Audience."

But the Audience Award, given out a few minutes later, went to a coming-of-age in a Lower East Side housing project. The director was so impassioned, it was hard to hate him. Maddy wanted to trade her award for Dan's. This was the injustice of her win: It helped their film, but only marginally. An award for Dan or the film would have helped them all.

The closing-night party was at the Entertainer. Maddy wanted to enjoy her prize, but Dan was cranky, and she felt too sorry for him to enjoy the many compliments and the fans who made her pose for photos. Around midnight, as they trudged to the festival bus stop, she asked, "Are you mad at me for winning?"

"Stop this," he said.

" 'Cause you seem sad."

"This is everything I wanted for you. It's going to get you real auditions. Bigger parts. You're a real actress now." But his tone was hollow.

The bus was full of drunk, exhausted filmmakers. Maddy and Dan stood near the front. After a moment a Japanese film crew approached, asking for her autograph. She handed Dan her award to hold while she signed, which gave her a little thrill. To them, she was a star, even if no one would recognize her the moment she returned to New York and to La Cloche.

At their stop, they walked silently in the snow toward the condo. She realized he was still holding her award and wasn't sure whether to ask for it back. But then he cast it away from his body and said, "Here," and the shape of his mouth was odd and ugly. She walked a few steps ahead of him so as not to see his face.

4

The sushi restaurant where Maddy went to meet Bridget in Hollywood turned out to be at a strip mall, two doors down from a Domino's Pizza. When Maddy pulled up, she was certain she had the wrong address—it was so grungy-looking, she couldn't imagine Bridget would eat there. But then she saw her waving from a back table. Sitting next to her was Steven Weller. Bridget hadn't mentioned that he was coming.

Maddy had already gone to Bridget's office in Beverly Hills and been impressed by the small staff, just one assistant and a constantly ringing phone. Though she was planning to meet Zack in New York as a courtesy, she was leaning toward signing with Bridget as her manager and with Nancy Watson-Eckstein at OTA as her agent. She had not expected to see Bridget again before she flew home to Brooklyn and had been surprised by the lunch invitation.

Maddy and Dan had been crashing at the Laurel Canyon home of a film-school buddy of his, driving to meetings with executives and prospective reps. (Kira had opted not to come to L.A. just yet, which was a relief to Maddy, who needed a break from the awkwardness.)

Standing over the restaurant table, she shook Bridget and Weller's hands, immediately feeling overformal. Weller looked her up and down, making her self-conscious. He was at a point in his career where he could leer openly and women didn't get offended. It was the license of having been voted the Sexiest Man Alive. Twice.

"This place looks like nothing on the outside," Bridget said as they sat, "but it's the best sushi in L.A. I came here years before it got written up. Yuki takes very good care of me." She gestured to a man behind the sushi bar who was wearing a folded bandana around his head and working intently.

Maddy suspected the sushi would be phenomenal, but the place was such a dump that she wondered if Bridget brought people here to show them she didn't need to impress them. Only someone at her level could lunch in a place like this.

"Congratulations on your Jury Prize," Weller said, tossing back a shot of sake.

"I was totally taken aback," Maddy said.

"Were you really?"

"Of course. Our acquisition was ultimately pretty small potatoes, even though it's still completely amazing, and there were so many buzzy performances at the festival. I just—I didn't think anyone would notice my work."

"They always notice what's exceptional," Weller said.

There were no menus. Bridget told the waitress to bring whatever Yuki wanted, and soon there was a spread of sashimi, sushi, and grilled octopus tentacles, which sounded disgusting but turned out to be delicious. It was the best sushi Maddy had ever tasted. Midway through the lunch, Bridget took a sip of sparkling water and said, "The reason I wanted to see you again is this. In a few weeks, Steven and I will be going to the Berlin Film Festival with *The Widower*. Walter Juhasz is going to be there. Steven is doing his next film and coproducing with me. Walter is interested in you for the female lead, and we'd like you to come with us, so you can meet him."

Maddy couldn't believe it. Juhasz was a famous Hungarian director who had been big in the 1970s in the States but now shot entirely in Europe. He was said to be reclusive and agoraphobic. He lived in London, and all of his films had a strange, dislocated feeling, theoretically set in America but totally un-American. His actress wife had left him in the late 1970s for a famous music producer, and Juhasz had a crack-up and flew to London, never to return to the States.

"How does Walter Juhasz even know who I am?"

"We sent him a DVD of *I Used to Know Her*," Weller said. "He was bowled over by your performance."

"The film is called *Husbandry*," Bridget said.

So this was the movie that Lael and Taylor had talked about at Bridget's dinner. She remembered Lael saying that they'd been casting for a year. Was it possible? How could Bridget, Weller, and Juhasz think she was at the same professional level as Lael?

"It's about a woman, her husband, and his troubled younger brother," Bridget went on. "Steven will be playing the husband. The brother will be played by Billy Peck." Peck was a notorious English bad boy who often got into bar brawls. "The lead role, Ellie, is unlike anything I've seen for a woman. She's complicated and alive. Every major actress in Hollywood has read for her, but none was right."

"I'd love to read the script," Maddy said. "Absolutely." She could be face-to-face with Walter Juhasz in less than a month. Every time she felt her life could not grow stranger, something happened to make her think she had been wrong.

"I'll try to get it to you before Berlin," Bridget said, "but he's doing a polish, so you may have to wait to read it until the festival."

"It will be a useful trip," Weller chimed in. "All the European companies will be there, and you can talk up *I Used to Know Her*. It's an unusual city. The art scene is fantastic, and the youth culture. We really hope you'll consider it."

"Of course I'll consider it," Maddy said. "It's Walter Freaking Juhasz."

Dan and Maddy were in his rented Prius on their way to see a friend's indie feature at the ArcLight. "I definitely think you should go," he was saying.

"Obviously, you don't," Maddy responded. "What's going on?"

Dan kept his eyes on the road, unsure whether to tell her what he really thought: that there might be something more to the offer. The girlfriend, Cady, was kaput, and a guy like Weller couldn't stay single for long. He needed new arm candy, an attractive female for all the Berlin premieres. Maddy fit the bill: pretty, independent, young, and most important, buzz-worthy. Dan's theory was that Weller wanted her to act like they were together but was smart enough to realize Maddy would say no if he asked her outright. So he and Bridget had come up with an "audition." Walter Juhasz went five years between movies these days; he was not known for being prolific.

"It's just . . . What if Steven's looking for a date?" he said. "For the festival."

"You think they're inviting me as some kind of . . . whore?" He glanced at her quickly in the passenger seat. She was pouting.

"Not a whore, no. A date, for appearances. Think about it. What are the two things Weller lacks? Heterosexual legitimacy and intellectual credibility. You bring him both."

"Jesus. You think Steven Weller needs me? I don't even have a career yet. I've won one award."

"He knows you're going to pop. I just don't want you to be upset if you go to Berlin and Walter Juhasz never shows up."

"He'll show up, okay? I heard Lael and Taylor talking about his movie. They both auditioned."

"Well, there you go. I figured I was reading it wrong. You know I don't have the greatest faith in the Hollywood machine. You should go."

She put her feet up on the dashboard, wishing Dan hadn't said what he'd just said. If he were right, it seemed a sick proposal. To be a red-carpet escort for Steven Weller—that went against everything she was about.

Maybe Dan was only pretending to think Weller was gay to convince her they were using her and give her a reason to say no, because he was jealous. She had felt it bubbling up between them after the awards ceremony. Maybe he didn't like the idea of her landing a Walter Juhasz film on the tails of I Used to Know Her, and despite all his lip service over the years about wanting her to succeed, he wanted her to succeed only at the same pace as he did. If that was true, it meant their relationship had been built on nothing. She felt a wave of carsickness and cracked the window. It vibrated loudly on the freeway. No one opened the windows in L.A.

5

The hotel-room phone woke Maddy at five-thirty in the evening. Her suite at the Hotel Concorde in Berlin was clean and spare, bigger than the entire apartment in Brooklyn. She couldn't imagine what it cost—a thousand dollars? Two? Walter Juhasz's UK production company was picking up the tab, but the room seemed exorbitant for an unknown.

The last few weeks had been surreal. The return home from L.A., the decision to sign with Bridget and Nancy Watson-Eckstein, and the white gardenias Bridget had sent to the apartment hours later, the card reading, "To successful collaborations. —B."

And then Steven Weller's private plane, with its overattractive stewardess and real flatware. There had been a handful of others on board besides her, which made Maddy feel the trip was wholly aboveboard: Todd Lewitt, plus two publicists from the studio, and Flora Gerstein, Weller's fiftyish personal publicist.

That morning Maddy had walked around one of the gallery districts, planning to look at art, but she was so exhausted, she'd headed back to the hotel. She'd managed to watch a few minutes of Juhasz's *Body Blow*, from the stack of DVDs that Bridget had given her, before the jet lag caught up with her and she drifted off in the king bed.

It was Bridget on the phone. The premiere of *The Widower* would be that night, she explained, and they would go in two cars, Maddy, Bridget, the publicists. They would enter the theater before skipping out to have dinner while the movie played. Evidently, stars did not watch their own screenings.

Maddy dressed in a simple sheath dress she wore for hostessing, and put her hair in a sloppy bun. In the mirror, with the lavish splendor of the hotel room behind her, what had looked classy and risqué at La Cloche now looked cheap and a little slutty.

As she was starting to do her makeup, there was a knock on the door. When she opened it, a bellboy handed her a garment bag. Inside was a stunning strapless red silk dress with gold woven vines on the bodice. The label said Marchesa. The material was puffy and gathered at the bottom, and in the back was a two-foot train. The note said, "Thought this would be perfect for tonight. —B." Along with the dress was an elegant black wool cape.

Maddy tried on the dress and admired herself in the mirror, both thrilled and ashamed to be thrilled. It was beyond classy. There was a pair of designer velvet heels that no one would see because of the train. For a brief moment she recalled her conversation with Dan in the car in L.A. He had been so skeptical about the trip, and now there was this knockout dress. But she was among Steven Weller's friends, and she was an Ostrow Productions client; she would have to be dressed appropriately. The phone rang. "Can I help you get ready?" Bridget asked.

When Bridget saw Maddy in the dress, her fingers quivered. It wasn't until you saw a girl properly costumed that you could imagine the potential. Her frame was hearty, but somehow Steven had picked a gown that worked for it. He'd had Marchesa send over a few samples and selected this one. Bridget had signed the card so as not to frighten her. They had to be delicate. Maddy needed to trust him in order to make the choice to collaborate.

Steven would be floored when he saw her. What made a true star was less beauty than mutability. Newman, Brando, Streep, Clayburgh all had it: the liveliness, the ability to show the slightest shift in emotion on their faces.

When Steven laid eyes on the dress, he would know she was right for the role, which required that Ellie be mousy at first but emerge into a sexually voracious adulteress with incredible will. "I knew it would be perfect," Bridget said. "Turn around."

Maddy twirled in the dress, barely hiding her glee. Bridget had brought along a makeup kit, noticing that Maddy favored minimal cosmetics and thinking something more intense was in order for the evening. "May I?" she asked, indicating the case.

"Of course," Maddy said. "I hate doing makeup. That was my least favorite part of acting school."

"Well, you seem to have done well with the costume part. You know how to walk in a train." Bridget had seen so many freshly arrived girls stumbling in their trains at the ceremonies, year after year, past the point when they could have hired someone to teach them. "I wasn't always a manager, you know. When I was alive, I went to acting school." She set up two chairs by the window.

Maddy looked at her and laughed. *When I was alive.* "Where did you go?"

"The American Academy of Dramatic Arts. That's what brought me to L.A. This old hag had dreams."

"You're not an old hag! I hope I look like you when I'm your age."

"Oh, stop it. I've lost my looks because I refuse to do anything. It's not vanity. I just don't like people touching my face."

"How did you go from actress to agent?"

"After grad school, I was booking a handful of things, but it had been a couple years, and nothing was catching on. At the time, my agent was Jack Keil at Original Talent. One day Jack called me into his office. He said, 'I know this may not be what you want to hear, but you don't have the talent to be a star. You have two choices: Find another career you're passionate about, or take a job in the mail room and work your way up to being an agent. I have a feeling you'd make a good one.' That Monday I started in the mail room."

"It didn't hurt you to hear that?" Maddy asked. She could hear the clacking of a room-service cart in the hallway.

"Only at first. I went home and thought about it all weekend and realized I was too much of a control freak to be only an actress. I never liked the aspect that requires you to be given work."

Maddy wondered if Bridget had slept with Jack Keil. As if sensing the question, Bridget said, "Everyone thinks I fucked him. But he was a mentor. They're very hard to find. An older man, with a young woman, who sees her as a person first, and wants to help her. There are two ways for women to move ahead in Hollywood: to mentor their way to the top or to be one of the guys. I chose the former. A lot of my friends chose the latter."

"What was it like, being one of the only women back then? Were you getting harassed all the time?"

"The things said to me, you don't want to know. All the men who mistook me for the secretary. I was always being asked to fetch coffee. I had to sit under the desk to cry, this little embroidery pillow over my face so no one would hear me. They still haven't figured out a good system for women crying at work. I've always felt there should be a special room. The newer girls, the ones rising up now, they have no idea what it was like. Maybe that's good. It's changed so much. The men in your generation aren't threatened by female success."

"Some are," Maddy said, thinking of Dan in the Prius.

"But the fearful ones won't get far with strong, self-assured women. When I was dating in the '80s, it was very difficult. I would go out with high-powered guys and tell them about deals I'd closed or stars I had signed, and their faces would just cloud over. They wanted wives. Los Angeles is a very sexist city, much more so than New York. I tried dating down, like with Zack's father, but that poses its own challenges."

"Who is Zack's father, if you don't mind my asking?"

"His name is Grant Mulaskey," Bridget answered, lining Maddy's eyes. "He was an actor, a client of OTA, though not my own. From Kentucky. Oh, so handsome. A goyishe. I was burned out on these movers and shakers. When I got pregnant, we tried to convince ourselves we had a future. But he was unhappy in L.A. and didn't want to be tied down. He's a general contractor in Arizona now. You know, Zack's here. He'll be coming with us tonight."

"He's here?" Maddy asked, surprised. She hoped it wouldn't be uncomfortable to see him. Before she left for Berlin, she had gone in to meet with Zack and his boss, George Zeger. The George guy, though complimentary about the film, didn't seem that passionate about Maddy. On top of that, she couldn't shake Bridget's warning about Zack—that he wasn't going to be agenting in a couple more years. Maddy emailed Zack to tell him she had signed with Ostrow Productions, and he wrote back a bland two-liner wishing her well.

"He has some clients in the festival," Bridget said, squinting at Maddy's face to regard her handiwork.

"How come he wasn't on Steven's plane?"

"Bentley Howard paid for this trip because he has meetings. He was staying with me at Mile's End because they wouldn't pay, but he's very practical. Only schnors when he has to."

She passed Maddy a hand mirror. Her eyes were smoky, sexy. "Wow," Maddy said. "You're really good at this."

"Now stand up and look in the mirror."

Maddy rose in her heels and moved toward the mirror on the wall. The makeup and the dress were perfect together. She felt like a princess, elegant, even regal. She had never been all that interested in clothing, beyond the way the right outfit could help her book a role, but now she was curious about the fabric, the cut, the way a dress could change the way you felt.

When Maddy arrived in the lobby at seven, she found Zack waiting on a couch. "Nice dress," he said. She had the cape on her arm, not sure whether to put it on at the hotel or at the theater.

"Thanks. Your mother got it for me."

Zack rolled his eyes, and she wondered if he was feeling competitive with his mother for having signed Maddy. "She has impeccable taste. So I hear you have an audition coming up."

"Yes, Walter Juhasz will be here on Monday." He nodded. "I don't even think I have a serious chance at a Juhasz film, but they say I do, so . . ."

"How's Dan? He didn't want to come to get publicity?"

"That's what *I'm* here for. He's busy working out the contracts and stuff." It was hard to read Zack's tone. Was he implying there was something improper about the trip, just as Dan had? "So how've you been since Mile's End?" she asked, sitting down beside him.

"Really busy, actually. I signed three new clients. Did she tell you?"

"Who?"

"Kira. She signed with me just last week."

"Really?" asked Maddy. "That's fantastic. She didn't mention anything about . . . I didn't even know you guys had met in Mile's End. I mean after the opening-night party." In the condo, Kira had mocked him. But maybe it was all a decoy. Maybe they'd already had a meeting by then, and she didn't want Maddy to know.

"Yeah, we had a coffee the afternoon of your first screening. I was so impressed with her performance. I knew I could help her, and luckily, she felt the same way." The last Maddy had seen of Kira was a few days before, at Irina's party. Cast and crew, plus Maddy and Dan's circle of friends, all trekked out to fete them, but the night had been so hectic that she and Kira had barely spoken.

Bridget, Weller, and Flora came off the elevators. Zack and Maddy stood to greet them. Weller examined her in the dress as though she were an expensive cut of steak. She blushed. "You are wondrous," he said.

"Thank you," she said, self-conscious again. What kind of man said "wondrous" who wasn't gay or eighty?

Maddy and Weller were put inside a car. In the front passenger seat was an enormous bald man who Weller said was a bodyguard paid for by Apollo Classics. Maddy was amazed by all the ways the rich and famous really did live up to the clichés. It was like the bodyguard was part of the swag.

She could see the Berlinale Palast rising high as they approached, the big red bear, the festival mascot, standing up on the side of the atrium. On one side of the car path, forming a T with the red carpet that led into the theater, hundreds of fans were packed tightly behind stanchions. A sea of people with no apparent end.

When their car door opened, there was an intake of breath as the fans waited to see who would emerge. Maddy stepped out, and a few seconds later, Weller followed. That was when she heard the roar. Weller took it in stride, smiled, pivoted to wave. The cries were hysterical and continuous, and then Bridget was beside Maddy, whispering, "Come." She ushered her to the foot of the red carpet, beside Zack. Todd Lewitt and Weller's costar, Henry Berryman, had already arrived and were posing for pictures. Berryman was a gracious English actor pushing eighty-five, a known life-long alcoholic.

As Weller and the bodyguard headed straight to the stanchions, fans thrust things at Weller—festival programs, head shots of him—and he signed them with a Sharpie. Those lucky enough to receive autographs clutched them to their breasts like boys at baseball games who had caught foul balls. Others held up cell phone cameras. All the while, Weller indulged them, as if they were friends, equals. She wondered if he was speaking German; a guy like him probably spoke half a dozen languages. The German fans seemed more grateful and less hysterical than American fans, admiring but not cloying.

After fifteen long minutes, Weller crossed to the red carpet. He embraced Berryman, clapping him on the back a few times, and the two men worked the press and photo lines, thrusting their arms around each other's backs and posing with and without Lewitt. Then Weller turned and came toward them as though he had something to ask Bridget.

"You enjoying yourself?" he asked in Maddy's ear.

"Very much," she said, nodding enthusiastically.

She felt him slip the cape off her shoulders. He handed it to Bridget and led her toward the press. Henry Berryman was facing the photographers on the opposite side.

As Steven laced his fingers through hers, everything went into slow motion. She felt a combination of horror—that Dan's prediction was coming true—and arousal. Steven had taken her hand, like she belonged to him. And yet the gesture didn't feel smarmy or inappropriate. It felt correct, and his palm was big. She remembered the way it had felt that night at Bridget's lodge, when he had greeted her.

He was looking over Maddy's shoulder, and when Maddy glanced in the same direction, she saw Bridget give a tiny nod. Maddy instantly understood. It was Bridget who had wanted this for Maddy, this moment. Bridget was managing even when she did not appear to be.

The voices were deafening, the camera flashes like a strobe. "Turn this way, please!" and "Over here, Mr. Weller!"

Maddy heard Steven saying, "This is Maddy Freed. M-A-D-D-Y F-R-E-E-D. She just won a Special Jury Prize at the Mile's End Film Festival. Keep your eye on this one, she'll be a lot more famous than I am soon. And she takes a much better picture."

She began to feel less intimidated, to relax. As her confidence grew, she turned her face this way and that. "Ms. Freed, Ms. Freed! Here, Ms.

Freed!" She was high. It was different from her feeling when she'd won the Jury Prize. That had been about her work. This was about her.

From the foot of the carpet, Zack stared at the V that Maddy and Steven's hands formed. He didn't like that V.

Zack was familiar with a certain cynical type of girl. He met them at premiere parties or nightclubs, the models/actresses—anoractresses, he called them. At first glance, they would blow him off, but when they found out he was an agent, everything changed. His diminutiveness was no object. Suddenly, they were touching his arm, moving their lips near his. Shameless.

In his first year as an agent, he had enjoyed the attention—it was a trip to walk into a Michelin restaurant with a knockout on his arm—but at the end of the night, it was just him and the girl in his loft. Because none of the girls was interested in talking, it felt a lot like bringing home dolls. Coke helped, but eventually that bored him, too.

He didn't know Maddy well, but he never would have put her in that category of girl. Now he wasn't sure. She was vamping, hamming it up in that ridiculous dress, a dress you wore only if you had a movie in the festival, not if you were someone's date. Berlin wasn't the Academy Awards; there were different rules. He couldn't reconcile the girl on the carpet with the girl he had seen in *I Used to Know Her*, the serious dramatic actress. Who could not only act but write. Maddy was smart. What was she thinking?

"It seems like a lot of trouble to bring her to Berlin for one audition," he murmured to his mother.

"Not when your director refuses to leave the continent."

"That's a very fancy dress."

"This is a very important premiere."

"What's your plan for her?"

"To break her in. Zachary, please. I don't need to educate you on the value of advance publicity. You're an *agent*, for God's sake."

He shook his head and watched the V grow tighter.

Maddy could hear a woman calling her name in a thick accent. The woman was in a parka, standing next to a guy with a videocamera. "Ms. Freed, I am Gisela Moor. I'm from a German television show?"

"Hey there," Maddy said. Steven had released her hand and was talking to another reporter a few steps away.

"What is your film in the festival?" the woman in the parka was asking Maddy.

"Oh, I don't have one. But I'm in a movie that just premiered at Mile's End, in the U.S. It should be out by Christmas in the States, and we're hoping for a release in Europe. It's called *I Used to Know Her*. By a great new director named—"

"How long have you and Mr. Weller been involved?"

"Oh, we're not—he isn't—we just met. My boyfriend is the director of my movie, and he's actually named Dan—"

Bridget was there, standing next to her. "That's all for now," she said. She ushered Maddy inside the theater. Maddy was flushed from the adrenaline of the past ten minutes and embarrassed that the press had misunderstood Steven's gesture. She wished she had gotten more time to talk about Dan and the movie. "You did very well," Bridget said, smiling warmly. "You're a natural."

When the rest of the cast finished their interviews and came inside, they all climbed the stairs to the theater. With Steven beside her, her hand still tingling, Maddy wasn't sure what to say. "Thank you for doing that," she tried. He said nothing but smiled at her briefly, paternally, before moving a few steps ahead.

At the after-party, held at a hot nightclub, she and the *Widower* crew sat a banquette in a roped-off private area. Zack had come to dinner with them during the screening but decided to skip the party.

Maddy's cell phone rang. It was a number she didn't recognize, with a strange area code, and not knowing any better, she answered. A man from the *Daily Mail* said he was calling for confirmation that Maddy was dating Steven Weller. "No, that's not true," she said. "I don't know where you got that. I have a boyfriend."

Bridget indicated that Maddy should give her the phone. Bridget took it, listened for a moment, and said Maddy was not going to comment on the rumors. Then she clicked off.

"But that makes it sound like it's true," Maddy said.

"No, it's always better not to comment," Bridget said, "or else it sounds like a false denial."

"Maybe I should issue some kind of statement. Flora could help me. I want the press to know that Dan and I are together. I want to get his name out there, too."

"Don't take any of this seriously," Bridget said with a wave of her hand. "The legitimate outlets won't report anything without attribution. As for the illegitimate ones, I try to give them as little attention as possible." A moment later, the phone rang again. Bridget silenced it, returned it to Maddy, and said, "We're going to have to change your number."

Maddy hoped no one else bothered her. She'd had too much wine at dinner and didn't want to answer by accident and say the wrong thing. That it had been exciting to hold Steven's hand. That she loved feeling his blood next to hers.

Maddy heard Chrissie Hynde singing "I'll Stand By You," and began to sway in response to the music. She was sixteen again, at the Potter High School prom. Steven saw her swaying and asked if she wanted to dance. "Yes, Mr. Weller, I will dance with you," she said, realizing she was verging on drunk. At the banquette, someone had ordered cranberry and vodka and she'd already had a glass.

He held her closely as they rocked back and forth. It was intoxicating to be close to him. He smelled like cedar or musk.

His wrists were heavy on her shoulders. In her velvet heels, she was three inches taller than he. "Your real last name is Woyceck, right?" she asked.

"Yeah. Polish. Way too hard to spell, so I changed it early. Why do you ask?"

"I was just thinking about how I used to know everything about you. When I was a teenager, I clipped articles about you from teeny-bopper magazines. Isn't that stupid?"

"Not at all. Even at a young age, you had good taste." It was classic

Steven, pretending to be full of himself as a way of pretending not to be full of himself.

He was cocking his head and closing one eye, and then he ran his hands down Maddy's hair. "What are you doing?" she asked.

"Imagining you with a shag. I think it would be a good look. I used to do women's hair, you know."

"You mean like Warren Beatty in *Shampoo*? The one based on Jon Peters?"

"Yes, but Jon Peters is sixty." His eyes were bloodshot. She wondered if he was drunk, too. The way he acted all the time was a little bit drunk, the hoarse voice, the ever-present whimsy.

"Can I ask you something? What exactly happened with you and Cady Pearce? Dan told me you guys broke up, but—he didn't say why."

"We didn't want the same things."

"Then why was she at that party at Mile's End?"

"Because she's a good friend. I try to maintain good relationships with all my exes."

"Does that include Julia Hanson?"

His face went dark. "Are you really asking me about this?"

"Sure I am. I appear to be slow-dancing with Steven Weller. I might never have this opportunity again." She put on a British-journalist voice and set her fist below his mouth like a microphone. "Tell me, Mr. Weller. Why did you and Ms. Hanson get divorced?"

He smiled at her, but the smile had lost some of its warmth. "When we married, I was very frustrated professionally. This was before *Briefs*. She was doing well, she had a film career. I was competitive. It was just a bad time to get into a marriage, especially so young."

He wasn't giving her anything. Maddy didn't blame him. It was inappropriate for her to ask about a near-stranger's divorce. Especially a celebrity.

"It also ended because she was insane," he continued, surprising her. "We had a bad fight one night, and I knew if I stayed, she would pull me into the abyss. Never sleep with someone who has more problems than you."

She smiled at him drunkenly. "Nelson Algren."

"What?"

"Nelson Algren. A *Walk on the Wild Side*." Dan had turned her on to Algren soon after they started dating. " 'Never play cards with a man called Doc. Never eat at a place called Mom's,' " she went on, speaking more loudly as the music rose. "Weren't you quoting him?" The music was blaring, and she couldn't quite make out his response, but it sounded like "Of course I was!"

Dan was at the kitchen table on his laptop. It was Friday night in New York and he had dinner plans with Sharoz and their lawyer. If he didn't leave soon, he would be late. But he was surfing. He browsed through his usual liberal news sites, pretending he wasn't looking for anything in particular, and then he typed "Maddy Freed."

Dozens of items popped up from entertainment and gossip sites describing her as Steven Weller's new girlfriend. He clicked on "Images." Rows and rows of photos appeared. Maddy in a glamorous dress, standing close to Weller. There was one where she was looking at him, not the cameras, and her eyes were so adoring Dan closed his laptop. His mother in Silver Spring would see these. And all his friends. People would think they'd split up. He would have to explain that it was a misunderstanding, that she was there on business.

Maybe he should have told her not to go. But she never would have listened. She wanted to meet Walter Juhasz. And maybe she would.

Weller was gay. Not a sexual threat. He was a master of this. Clearly, he'd been doing it all his working life.

Dan dialed Maddy's cell, even though it was two A.M. in Berlin. "There are pictures of you on the Internet," he said. "A lot of them."

"Oh God," she said. She had come home from the party and was hanging the Marchesa in her hotel-room closet. "I haven't gone online yet, but I should have expected it. These journalists have been calling me, and you wouldn't believe how many photographers there were. Did they print anything about *I Used to Know Her*?"

"No. They just call you an actress. These articles say you're Steven's girlfriend."

"Seriously?" She kicked off the heels, lay on the bed, and massaged her aching feet. "But I never said that. I specifically said—I mean—I told the reporters I had just met him. I told them about you, but then I got interrupted and—I didn't have time to explain."

"It's fine, Mad," he said. "You don't have to tell *me* he's not your boy-friend."

Dan squinted at one of the photos on his screen, blew it up as big as it would go. His girlfriend was not falling for Steven Weller. What Dan had with her was deep and important, the intimacy they had built. The look in her eye wasn't love. It was intoxication: the cameras, the attention.

He had to think like a director. These photos were golden for *I Used to Know Her*. The shots would run in the American tabloids, and the tabloids were more influential to the entertainment industry than every film festival combined. No matter how much that fact bothered him. What piqued audiences was backstory. And a romance, even a fake one, was just that.

Since Dan had signed with the OTA agent Jon Starr, he'd been reading scripts for directing jobs. He wanted to keep working, maintain momentum from the acquisition. Maddy was momentum. "This is exactly the kind of publicity we need going into our release," he said on the phone. "We couldn't have planned it better if we'd tried."

"But we didn't plan anything. I told you, I'm here to meet Juhasz. It was *Bridget's* idea for me to go on the red carpet, like an introduction to the media. The handholding thing just happened. He pulled me onto the line, and they—they drew their own conclusions. It's a sexist world. People expect any woman who's in public with a movie star to be sleeping with him."

"Where'd you get the dress?"

"Bridget sent it. It's her job to advance my career. You're reading this all wrong. You don't know anything about it."

"Are you saying he tried something?"

Her mind flashed back to the slow-dancing at the club. But Steven hadn't tried anything; she'd been the drunk one. She'd asked him a tactless question. "Of course not. He's been a total gentleman."

"I *told* you that he's gay."

Maddy stood with the phone and went to the window. There was a couple fighting below, in front of one of the luxury shops on the Kurfürstendamm.

"I don't care if he's gay, and you shouldn't, either," she said. "It isn't relevant. Grow up."

"It *is* relevant, because if I thought the guy was going to make a move, I wouldn't have wanted you to go. I'm not worried. Just have fun. Play it out a little. Look at Steven like you're into him. It'll be easy. Think about it as a role. You're an actress."

6

The next day Maddy slept till one in the afternoon. After ordering room service, she finished watching *Body Blow*, taking notes. All of Juhasz's work dealt with outsiders who could not figure out how to fit into society. *Ruth's Kiss*, about a young waitress in Los Angeles who slowly becomes unhinged, was a great example; at first Ruth just seems a little lonely, and soon it becomes clear she's insane. In Juhasz's films, madness could afflict anyone, given the right set of circumstances.

Maddy decided to go for a walk and get a coffee. On Kurfürstendamm, she passed the designer shops and department stores, the theaters and cinemas. At a newsstand piled high with magazines she was startled to spot a photo of herself and Steven. The magazine was called *Bundt*. His arm was around her waist and she was staring at him. The caption read, *"Steven Weller: Er ist seit Jahren in Maddy Freed verliebt!"* The only piece of it she could translate was *verliebt*; she knew *liebe* was love.

She lowered her head so the newsman wouldn't see her and hurried along to a café. She drank her coffee quickly, feeling exposed. She kept seeing her gaze in the photo. It was as though it had been Photoshopped; she looked like a woman in love.

If Steven was gay and using her as arm candy, then he was either a master seducer or a deeply gifted actor. When he'd touched her on the red carpet, he had made her feel that he liked her. And then he'd danced with her at the club, his body hot and near.

That evening at five, a quirky heist film by an Austin, Texas, director would be premiering. Steven and Bridget had said they were planning to go, and Maddy had been looking forward to it. Now, after seeing the tabloid, she felt it might be better to stay home.

That morning, her cell phone had rung several dozen times, all reporters, so she turned it off until Bridget could change it for her. At the premiere, they would be there again, flocking around her. If she mentioned
Dan, who knew if they would print it?

She went to the VIP restaurant in the penthouse, which Bridget had
told her about, and ordered a late lunch. It was a totally private area with
wraparound windows. After lunch, she started watching another Juhasz
film, and then four o'clock came, and four-thirty, and there was no call
from Bridget. Wanting to make dinner plans and not sure what was expected of her, she dialed Bridget's cell. "Are we seeing that movie?" she
asked.

"Oh my goodness, I forgot to call you," Bridget said. "I've been running around like a chicken without a head. We're not going. Steven's in
London."

"What? When did he go?"

"This morning. He went to meet Walter about the script."

"But you said Walter was coming here."

"He is. They'll come back together. Either Tuesday or Wednesday."

"Oh," she said quietly. "Well, did *you* want to see the movie with me?"

"I have a phoner I can't get out of. I'm producing a film in Sofia, and
our director is going over budget, it's a disaster. But you should go. That's
why you're in Berlin. There's a ticket for you at will call. Why don't you
take Zack?"

Maddy found the news of will call slightly disappointing and then was
shocked at herself for being so shallow. Steven's trip to London was good,
not bad. It proved that Dan had been wrong about him. If they had truly
invited her to Berlin to act like she was dating Steven Weller, he wouldn't
very well take off when the festival had just begun.

She dialed Zack but didn't get him and decided to see the heist movie
alone. She wore her sheath dress and a dingy gray coat and walked to the
theater. As she was approaching, a short bearded man darted in out of
nowhere, snapped her photo, and disappeared. She was shocked. She had
never felt watched before, used in this way. It was violating.

She took the civilian entrance to the Palast, a long walkway under a
temporary roof that ran parallel to the red carpet. From the glassed doors
inside the theater, she could see the director and two of his actresses pos-

ing on the red carpet, just as Maddy had the night before. It was as though she had hallucinated the *Widower* premiere, even the cover of *Bundt*. Except for that one strange photographer, it was as though the night before had never happened at all.

The next afternoon Bridget took Maddy to the European Film Market to meet international distributors and talk up the film. The distributors were exceedingly polite and couldn't wait to see *I Used to Know Her*. A few of them wanted to know how long she had been dating Steven, and she kept having to correct them, tell them about Dan.

In the car back to the hotel, Bridget took a call. When she clicked off, she said, "There's been a change in plans. Walter can't make it here after all. Steven is bringing back the script with him tomorrow. We'll all fly to Venice on Tuesday, and you'll read for Walter there."

"Where would I stay?"

"Palazzo Mastrototaro, of course. Oh, honey, did you think we would just drop you at a *pensione*?"

They were inviting her to his palazzo. This was turning into a European tour. She had already taken a week off La Cloche.

She had a bad feeling about *Husbandry*. So many delays, so many "issues," and now, a new city. She wanted to talk to Dan but was worried he would say, "I told you so." He would say Juhasz was Godot and wouldn't come to Venice. And if Juhasz was Godot, she would have to fire Bridget, because no actress in her right mind would employ a manager who had no intention of getting her cast.

Dan was having trouble reaching Maddy, and he was nervous. She had texted him her new number, and he had tried her a couple times, but it went to voice mail. Once, when she called him back, he had been on the subway and missed it. He had a vision of her holed up in a suite with Steven Weller, fucking him around the clock. He had been certain Weller was gay, but maybe he had it all wrong.

On Sunday he finally caught her. He was on his way to his attorney's office above Barneys on Madison Avenue. "What have you been doing the last couple days?" he asked.

"I went to the Film Market with Bridget. Visited a couple museums, walked around. And I've seen a couple screenings."

"With Steven?"

"No. Alone. Steven's in London."

"Gone?"

"London. To meet with Walter Juhasz. He's coming back today, and on Tuesday we're going to go to Venice. I'll audition for Juhasz there."

As soon as he heard her say Venice, he felt a chill. She would be staying in Weller's palazzo. In the most romantic city in the world. Dan had a premonition, however irrational, that if she made it to Italy, he would never see her again. "So it's happening," he said.

"I wish I had more time with the script. Not just to prepare, but what if I hate it? If I hate it, I'm not going to read."

"It's Walter Juhasz. It's all in the execution, anyway." He was quiet a second and then added, "I miss you."

"I miss you, too. I wish you were here. I went to the Brecht House. You would have liked it." As she started to tell him about the rooms, he had an idea. There was no reason he had to stay in Brooklyn just to go back and forth on deal points with Apollo Classics. Though he hadn't yet told Maddy, he had quit his bartending job, in anticipation of the on-signing money he had coming to him.

What if he surprised Maddy in Venice? If they were together, he could stop worrying about Weller. They would work on *The Nest* in the palazzo. She knew how to motivate him. She was the lead in *The Nest*. She was his muse. He imagined the words popping up on his laptop as if he were a stenographer, which was what had happened when he started *I Used to Know Her*. The atmosphere would help him, the atmosphere and the sex, and being in the company of Maddy. All Americans wrote better in Europe. They crossed the ocean, and every word they wrote was brilliant.

"There's someone at my door," Maddy was saying. "I have to go."

When she opened the door, she found a bellboy holding a brown envelope. Inside was *Husbandry* with a Post-it note: "At long last. Call when you've read.—SW." She wanted to dig right in, but she walked to a café a few blocks away. Old ladies with violet hair sat and ate cakes. She ordered a hot cocoa and opened the script, which was in blue-and-white binding that said OSTROW PRODUCTIONS on the front.

Ellie is a young housewife in an unnamed American suburb. Her husband, Louis, is an estate lawyer who makes love to her regularly and without passion. One day Louis's younger brother, Paul, who has just gotten out of jail, comes to visit. Paul and Ellie, who have never met, are instantly and wildly attracted. That night on the porch, after Louis goes to bed, Ellie tells Paul about her loneliness. They kiss.

Paul moves in temporarily. During the day, when Louis is at work, Paul and Ellie make love in her bed. Something is awakened in her, but Paul has problems. He owes money to bad guys. One night he gets in a bar brawl and is hauled off to jail. After bailing him out, Louis demands that Paul move out. Paul finds a motel in town. Louis goes away on business. The affair continues, in the bed, in the motel. When Louis returns, the lovers can't tell if he suspects.

As she keeps her affair secret, her paranoia grows. She gets confused and fearful. She tries to break it off, but Paul stalks her, unable to admit that it's over. Confused, she confesses everything to Louis. He calls her a whore and puts his fist through a wall. Convinced that she must end the affair, she goes to the cops and gets a restraining order against Paul. She cries as she fills out the paperwork. The couple returns to their sad life, Paul now living in a trailer on the other side of the tracks.

Louis guilts her every day about the affair. She becomes numb. He speaks to her coldly, like a robot. She discovers she is pregnant. She knows it is Paul's. She sneaks out to see Paul and tells him. He begs her to leave Louis. She resumes the affair. One day Louis follows her to Paul's trailer and comes through the door with a gun. A struggle ensues and the gun falls. Ellie grabs the gun and Louis jumps her. Trying to shoot Louis, she kills Paul.

After she has the baby, Louis and Ellie throw a party. The night of the party, they make love, Ellie unable to look at Louis. The baby wails in the night. When she goes to hold the baby, a boy, she realizes he cannot be consoled.

Maddy closed the script, deeply moved. Everyone around her was speaking German, which allowed her to think without distraction. The film reminded her of great French films from the 1960s in the way it dealt with female sexuality, and it contained the best of what Juhasz brought to the cinema: the dread and alienation of being human.

Maddy was intrigued by Ellie's dread. And she thought it was good that Ellie got to stay alive. Too often in movies, strong or adulterous women ended up dead.

She wished Dan were here with her. It was the kind of screenplay that made you want to talk about it: what it meant to be a woman, to be in a relationship but feel lonely. It was about someone who woke up one morning and realized the life she'd built for herself was a prison.

She had to get this role. The reason she had gone to grad school, the reason she greeted Eurotrash at a hostess station for $21 an hour, was so someday she might play a role like this: strong, complex, layered, and undeniably the center of the film.

From the café, she tried Dan. Voice mail. She walked down Kurfürstendamm, past the glittery designer shops with their blank-looking mannequins. At the hotel, she went straight to the VIP restaurant, ordered venison and pinot blanc, and read the script again, liking it even more the second time.

Back in her room, she called the front desk. She asked for Steven by name, and the clerk said he wasn't staying there. She remembered Steven had told her on the plane that his pseudonym was Gerber Stan, an inversion of his *Briefs* name. She called back. "Gerber Stan's room, please."

"Just one moment, miss."

His voice was husky when he said hello. "I read it," she said.

"And?"

"I love it."

"I knew you would." She started to say something, but she was so excited, it came out sounding like a Swedish vowel. She tried again. This one was more like a French vowel. "Do you want to come up for a minute to talk about it?" he asked.

His suite was twice the size of hers. The windows met at an angle, and she realized that they were in the penthouse, in the wedge-shaped apex of the building.

He poured two glasses of red wine, and they sat on a white couch. "So you liked it," he said.

"I liked it and it terrified me. I wish it could have had a happier ending, but Juhasz doesn't do them."

"No. He's interested in the way we create our own hell. Louis thinks he's getting Ellie back by cutting Paul out of their life, but instead he has the baby to live with forever, the ghost of his brother."

"Exactly," Maddy said. "In constructing a jail for her, he winds up constructing one for himself."

"Are you okay with all the sex scenes?"

"I don't know if I would say I'm okay with them, but I mean, the way they would be shot, the nudity, that could all be negotiated, right?"

"Yes, and Bridget will be there as producer. So you would have a wonderful advocate in her." He swirled his tan fingers around the rim of the wineglass.

"How is it possible you haven't cast Ellie yet?" she asked.

"Different reasons. The younger, edgier actresses had trouble with Walter's language. We read some girls who were great with the material but didn't have the right look. He wants Ellie to look real. He wants someone without plastic surgery."

The wine must have been going to Maddy's head because she said, "Are you trying to say I'm right for it because my breasts are small?"

"I didn't say anything about that. You're the one bringing your breasts into the conversation."

She blushed, unsure whether he was a gay man doing an impersonation of a straight man or the most heterosexual man on the planet. "So does it bother you that Louis is a cuckold? You're not afraid to play that?"

"You know, when I first read it, Walter and I discussed my playing Paul. The two men were written as closer in age. But I thought it would be more interesting if she had married someone older and the brothers were ten years apart. And then we found Billy Peck and it was perfect. It's a great triangle in cinema. Young woman, young man, older man. Walter loved my idea. He thought it would make the affair more motivated. I'm getting older and I want to use that in my work. And I don't want to do the same things I've always done."

"You're definitely not."

"Yeah, these new films are different, aren't they? What did you think of *The Widower*? You never told me."

"You never asked." It excited her that he wanted her opinion. He probably surrounded himself with people who said what he wanted to hear. "I liked it. Especially that walk you did after you kissed that woman. You seemed totally defeated but trying not to seem defeated."

"I put a lot into that. Todd and I worked on it together."

"You're very physical as an actor. I like that about you." He grinned, and she felt like she had passed some kind of test. She hadn't been vague and she hadn't been dishonest.

"So do you think you're up for playing Ellie?" he asked. "It's dark stuff."

"I really think I am. It—the whole thing—just feels right. But I'm going to have to convince Walter Juhasz."

"I'm sure he'll be as charmed by you as I am," Steven said, flashing his black eyes.

The word "charmed" was like a pat on the head. "Charmed?"

"Yes, you're charming. And brave. And beautiful, of course. But I think what I like most about you is your ambition." He was blinking at her slowly. The room felt very close. He was staring at her the way he had on the patio in Utah. His gaze was confident and cool and this time unmistakably sexual. She looked back at him, wanting to kiss him but not wanting to be unfaithful to Dan. She trembled, more frightened of herself than of him.

"What's going on?" she finally asked.

"What do *you* think is going on?" he asked, his smile impermeable. He was making her feel she was delusional to think he was interested. Her discomfort mixed with her disappointment that he had made no move to touch her, and then she felt guilty for being disappointed. What was she thinking? She had a boyfriend. A live-in boyfriend.

"I have to go," she said, her cheeks burning. She strode purposefully toward the suite door, but it turned out to be the bathroom. She opened it to see a gleaming marble tub, and embarrassed, she spun around, not knowing where to go.

"It's to the right," he said. He didn't get up. She pulled open the door and turned her head to see if he was following her. But the hallway was empty and quiet.

Maddy's hands were shaking as she slid her card in her door. What she'd felt in that room had been electric and irrefutable.

Or maybe she was just being self-centered. Maybe when he said *What do* you *think is going on?*, he was letting her know he was gay and had no interest. She barely knew the man.

She lay awake awhile before drifting off into a deep sleep. She had an old recurring dream in which she was in the backseat of a car, behind an empty driver's seat, trying to reach the steering wheel. It was hard to control from a distance, and the car went faster and faster, some unseen force gunning the gas. This time there was someone in the front seat. Steven Weller. As she struggled to reach her hands around the wheel, he turned to her with that fake-innocuous grin, and there was a terrible screech, and she woke up.

The next morning Zack called to see if Maddy felt like visiting Marlene Dietrich's grave. She said yes, curious about him, about Bridget, their relationship. And after what had happened in Steven's penthouse, she felt Zack might be able to shed light on him. Zack must have known Steven most of his life, which meant he'd seen things other people hadn't.

Maddy and Zack got off the U-Bahn at the Friedenau stop and headed in search of the cemetery. Dietrich's grave was simple and dark gray. It read, *"Hier steh ich an den Marken meiner Tage."* Beneath it was MARLENE and the dates of her life.

Maddy looked down at her guidebook. " 'Here I stand upon the border of my days,' " she read. "It's adapted from a sonnet by Theodor Körner. It says he wrote it after he got a head wound during the Napoleonic Wars and thought he was going to die in the forest. That's awful."

"Obviously, the guy lived," Zack said, "or he wouldn't have written the poem. So he was wrong."

"But he never forgot the fear, the hours he was in the cold, waiting to go."

She thought again of her father lying there in the snow. And no one coming to save him.

Right after she'd gotten the news, she'd found herself unable to sleep. She would lie awake, replaying the last moments of his life, as though she could rewind and bring him back. The insomnia continued in Vermont, where she and Dan drove to make arrangements. She became convinced that if she had been with him the day he died, she would have skied with him and he wouldn't be dead. It had been the weekend of Presidents' Day. He had invited her and Dan up to visit, but she was working extra hours to make up for her time off during production, so she'd said no.

By the time they held the memorial a few days later, she was a basket case, not having slept one wink since she got the news. She'd made Dan do the driving because she was so frayed, she thought she'd have an accident.

She told Dan about the insomnia, and when they got back to Brooklyn, he made her see a Fort Greene psychiatrist named Larson Wells. Larson helped Maddy realize that her father's death hadn't been her fault. The lorazepam and Zoloft she prescribed had helped, too. Soon she could sleep, and after a week, when the Zoloft had kicked in, she became less obsessive. Instead of lying awake, replaying the end of Jake's life for hours, she would do it for a few minutes and it would cease to engage her.

But while on the antidepressant, she went on a few auditions and felt off her game, unable to access her emotions. There was a part of her that felt she was cheating herself of the very valid agony caused by his death. She stopped the drug and terminated therapy, against Dan's wishes.

As she and Zack walked down the paths, they talked about films. Zack had always liked art films but when she asked if his mother had gotten him into moviegoing, he said, "God, no. Bridget likes mainstream stuff.

She can't stand anything with subtitles or anything more than eighty-five minutes long."

Clearly, he was trying to carve out a separate career, but when you worked in opposition to someone, it meant that person still controlled you. "Was she one of those working mothers who doesn't miss a school event?"

He let out a high-pitched laugh, and lit a cigarette. "She missed a lot. I don't think she ever really wanted to be a mother. She wanted to have a child. They're not the same thing."

"I'm sure she wanted you."

"It always seemed like there were places she would rather be. She was always on the phone. I must have had six nannies by the time I was ten. Polish, Tibetan, Mexican, there were even a couple of hot au pairs from Scandinavia."

"Did you ever feel resentful of her work?"

"No."

"You didn't think Steven was pulling her away from you? Any boy would have felt rivalrous. It's very Oedipal."

"You sound like the shrink I went to as a teenager. It's funny you ask about Steven. When I was, like, ten, I had this fantasy that Steven was my real father. My dad had remarried by then and had two other kids, and I was angry about it. Steven was the biggest force in my mother's life, and I thought how great it would be if he were my real dad. I used to stare at pictures of him and tell myself we resembled each other."

"Did you ever ask Bridget?"

"I remember we were out at an Italian restaurant. She had just won some 'women in business' award and dragged me along. I burst out with the question and she doubled over laughing. 'I can promise you Steven is not your father,' she said. I got so pissed, I ran out of the restaurant. Later she apologized, said she hadn't meant to hurt me. She said my dad had taken a test proving that he was my father and she could show me the results. I said no. I didn't look at them till years later." He shook his head bitterly. "It's weird to think about that. I can't believe I wanted Steven to be my dad, but the thing about Steven is, everyone wants him to fill the hole we have in our lives."

"Do you guys get along?"

"Not really. He's a seducer. It's why he's so successful. He manipulates people, and he's so skilled at it that they don't realize they're being manipulated." He began to talk about *The Widower*. He had hated it. He said Steven's performance was phony and thin. As he delineated everything he disliked about the characterization, she saw his face grow hard. "So what did *you* think?" he asked with a hint of a sneer.

"His performance wasn't perfect, but I guess I feel like he doesn't get enough credit as an actor because his work is very subtle. To me, that's the essence of great film acting. When it doesn't feel like a performance."

"Maybe you just have a thing for him. I saw you holding his hand at the premiere."

"He took mine," she said, her cheeks growing hot. She was no longer sure what had happened on the press line, not after what he had said in his suite.

"Whatever," Zack said. "I saw the way you looked at him." They had stopped under a tree covered with snow. A gust of wind moved through, and little flakes fell on their shoulders. "Maddy. You probably think I have a problem with Steven because of some unresolved anger against my mom. But I don't. I'm not angry. And I don't hate him. So when I say what I'm going to say, I want you to listen and not ignore it because of the source. I have known this guy most of my life, and this is not a role you want to play."

Maddy was confused. "What role?"

"Girlfriend of Steven Weller."

"I'm in love with Dan," she protested.

"I know. But with you and Steven both being Bridget's clients, you're going to run into each other, whether or not you book this role. And if someday your situation with Dan changes, I wouldn't want . . . How can I put this? Steven doesn't respect women."

"He has a woman as his manager. How can he not respect them?"

"She's the only one. And that's business. In his personal life, he likes his women pretty, dumb, and quiet. And he doesn't like any for more than a year."

She nodded slowly, trying to read Zack's eyes. *Doesn't like any for more than a year.* Maybe he was warning her that Steven was gay because he guessed she had a crush, and he didn't want her to develop feelings. He was being protective. Or maybe he was just calling him a womanizer.

"Can I ask you something?" Maddy said.

"Sure."

"Promise not to tell your mother?"

"I have no problem keeping secrets from my mother. I do it all the time."

"Dan has a theory that Bridget and Steven invited me here so he'd have someone to see movies with. Because he's gay."

Zack had lit another cigarette and was examining the tip. "And?" he said.

"Well, there must have been parties at your house, I figure you saw people. Friends of his. I mean, it's not like I care one way or the other, I'm just curious."

"What are you asking?"

"Did he ever, like, come to your stuff at school?"

"You mean when I was in *Peter Pan* at eleven, playing the dog, did he bring some muscular guy with a Tom of Finland tattoo and a handkerchief hanging out of his jeans pocket?"

"So he brought girls, then?" She felt like an idiot as she was asking it, classless, overeager.

"The times he came to see me in plays, he was with my mother."

Zack began walking more quickly, and she had to run to catch up despite his stubby legs. Not only had she failed to get anything out of him, but it seemed she had offended him with her questions. Whether he was being dense or merely protective of his mother's star client, she could not tell. They walked in silence for a while, and when they neared the cemetery's exit, he said, "If you're so sure you're not interested in him, why do you care if he's gay or straight?"

"I don't," she said. Her cheeks reddened and she was ashamed. He knew her interest in his sexuality had more to do with her than with Steven. Whether Steven slept with men or women made no difference, because nothing was going to happen between them, except an audition. She would read with him and do everything she could to get the role. That was what she needed to focus on. In one day's time she would be in Venice, preparing to meet Walter Juhasz.

7

Venice was like a fairy tale, with the thick February fog hovering over the Grand Canal. They flew from Berlin to Marco Polo Airport on Steven's plane, and to Palazzo Mastrototaro by private motorboat. Steven greeted the grizzled captain with enthusiasm and introduced him as Giorgio.

They sat inside the boat because it was so cold and windy. As they made their way through the lagoon, Steven pointed out the island of Murano and the legendary Harry's Bar. The palazzi were pink and decayed. Maddy was excited to see the city, which she knew only from movies. In film, Venice always represented love, death, or both. She could see why: It was a city of decay.

"Venice is 'the most beautiful of tombs,'" Steven said, as though reading her mind. "Henry James wrote that. He was more astute on this city than anyone else." It was a little pretentious, but his passion seemed genuine.

"Henry James is Steven's favorite writer," Bridget said. "Bores the fuck out of me. Some of it's okay, but mostly, I'm like, skip, skip, skip."

"How'd you get into Henry James?" Maddy asked Steven.

"I was in my twenties. A friend gave me a copy of *The Ambassadors*, and I went crazy for it. That's my favorite of all of his novels. Since then I've read everything he wrote."

"All I've read is *The Heiress*, for grad school, plus *Washington Square*. What should I read next?"

"Definitely *The Portrait of a Lady*. You in particular would like that book."

They coasted to a stop in front of a grand yellow-white building, its windows shaped like suns. Young, handsome butlers collected their luggage as Steven greeted them in Italian. Everyone seemed happy to see him, as in a scene from a Victorian costume drama where all the servants loved the masters. They went up the stone stairs to the door.

"Would you like a tour?" Steven asked Maddy inside, after Bridget disappeared to make some phone calls. Maddy was overcome by the majesty of the palazzo but also found it spooky. She nodded.

"This is the *pianterréno*," Steven said, "but it's really the cellar." They climbed a flight of wide marble stairs to a spacious main room. "This is the *mezzanine*, where the kitchen is, and the servants' apartments. I've converted some of them to guest rooms, because most of my staff doesn't live here."

They climbed another flight. In the wide hallways, colorful chandeliers hung from beamed ceilings. It was glittery and otherworldly. The walls were done in marigold. "The *piano nobile*," he said, "where the noblemen lived." He led her down a wide hall to an enormous ballroom with marble columns.

"Do you have parties here?" she asked.

"I'm having one tonight."

"Who's coming?" she asked, getting excited despite herself. As anxious as she was about the audition, there was something magical about a party at a private Venetian palazzo.

"A cross section. Some writers, some painters, some actors. You'll enjoy it."

They left the ballroom, and he showed her a library with bookcases containing a mix of bound first editions of English classics, including several volumes of Henry James, and hardcovers of 1960s and 1970s American novels. He offered her a black copy of *Portrait* whose pages were so thin she had no idea how she'd be able to hold them between her fingers. The walls were covered with monochromatic modern paintings and photographs, a lot of squares and lines, no people. She approached one of them. "You like that?" he asked from behind her.

"Yeah."

"That's by Ed Ruscha." He pronounced it "RooSHAY." When she had seen the name in print, she had always read it as "ROOSH-a." She was embarrassed by her mistake.

"Are you a serious art collector?" she asked, pivoting around.

"I would never call myself a collector," he said. "I just know what I like. Why don't you unpack, and then we can go to L'Accademia? I always visit *La Tempesta* on my first day."

Her bedroom had an adjoining living room. A fire roared in the fireplace. She had brought the Marchesa from Berlin and hung it in the closet. Bridget had not asked for it back. It might be the most beautiful piece that Maddy ever owned, and she felt it was her duty to keep it, for if she and Dan ever had a daughter.

Out the window was a private garden that she imagined was resplendent in summer. Her father and mother had honeymooned in Venice. She had seen pictures in their album. They had probably passed this very palazzo, maybe posed in front of it for a photo. And now she was inside it. She imagined her father watching her from up above. (She always imagined him looking down on her, even though he had been a secular humanist who didn't believe in God or heaven.) He would want her to soak up everything, the fog on the canal, the cold air, the Academy. She *would* soak it up, for him. She had to appreciate everything wonderful that happened to her.

Her theatrical adventures had been thrilling to him, the quirky film actor who came backstage to compliment her after a production of *the dreamer examines his pillow* or the famous guest lecturers at The New School. He salivated for all the details, and she relished sharing them. He had been practical so she could be impractical, and because she was impractical, she was here.

Giorgio, the captain, was waiting in front with the motorboat. Bridget was busy, Steven said, so he and Maddy took off on their own. The Academy was only a short ride. No doubt they could have walked, but she guessed that Steven wanted her to experience the water.

As they entered the Academy, she noticed a few American tourists. They recognized Steven and whispered to each other. He walked past them casually. She waited to see if they would swarm him for autographs, but they watched from afar, pointing and gesturing. He acted like he wasn't aware of it, but he had to be aware, he had to be used to this, it was his life.

La Tempesta by Giorgione was a startling, confusing image. A naked woman breast-fed her baby. The baby looked one way; the woman looked at the viewer. To the woman's right, at a distance, a dandyish man stared at her, leaning on a staff. Behind them were a white city and a bolt of lightning in the midst of clouds. "What do you make of it?" Steven asked.

She was struck by the expressive sexuality in the work. The Peeping Tom. The dark woods. "There's a lot going on," she said.

"Yes," he said. "Nothing is as it seems. A Madonna who is not a Madonna. A voyeur whom she may or may not know is spying. It's quintessentially Venetian."

"Why is that?"

"Because everything about Venice is a trick." As Maddy stared at the painting, Steven glanced at her to observe her reaction. She felt self-conscious being watched, and then he was saying something: "In Berlin . . . in my suite . . ."

"Yes?" She stared at the painting, unable to face him.

"I'm sorry if I made you uncomfortable." She turned. So he was admitting there had been something for a moment. It was a relief to know she hadn't imagined it.

"It's okay." She didn't want to talk too much about it. If she did, it would be more awkward, and she didn't want to sully her chances of booking *Husbandry*. "I was just—confused." He nodded and turned, moving swiftly toward the next gallery.

Back at Palazzo Mastrototaro, she sat in her living room and reread the *Husbandry* script, trying to unlock Ellie. Maddy wanted to make the character bolder and braver than she seemed on the page. She remembered a mantra from school: "Be interested, not interesting." It was about the importance of listening, not doing. With Ellie, Maddy felt the key was to play not the lack of sex or the boredom, but the interest in Paul. Ellie had to come alive when she was with him.

She was so engrossed in the script that when her phone rang, she jumped. "I miss you so much," Dan said.

"Oh God, I miss you, too. I can't believe I'm in Venice without you."

"So you made it."

"Yeah, we got here a couple hours ago." She didn't want to tell him she had gone to the Academy with Steven alone. It didn't sound right. "I wish you were here with me." She wanted him nearby, so she could remember everything she loved about him.

There was a knock on her door. "Hold on a second," she said, "there's someone at the d—"

When she pulled it open, she was face-to-face with Dan, his skin smudged and sweaty, a duffel bag slung over his chest. "What's going on?" she cried out, kissing him. "How did you get here?"

"I flew. Just like you did. Probably not as nice a plane, though."

"But how did you find the palazzo?"

"I went online to find the address, and when I got here, I said I was your boyfriend, and one of the guys got Steven. He was really cool about it."

She kissed him again. The handholding in Berlin and Steven's strange looks were meaningless now. Dan would stay for her audition, help her prepare. They were "partners on screen and in life," read the headline of a blog piece about them that had come out during Mile's End.

He wanted to take a bath. She went into the bathroom with him. Matching marble columns connected the ceiling to the tub and on one wall was a framed etching of an egg.

"What made you decide to come here all of a sudden?" she asked from the tub ledge, stroking his hair.

"I missed you, and I just didn't see the point in staying in Brooklyn. We can write here. I quit the bar. I don't need it anymore. I'm a director now."

She climbed into the bath with him. Held his cock in her hand. It was like the finger of a musical man. Pale and long. It stiffened in the water.

She soaped his body, massaged him. They kissed and then rose, wet, moving to the bed. Their sex at Mile's End had been strange, not connected. Now he was present and she was, too. He got on top of her. She had a fantasy of Steven taking her on the window seat of his suite in the Hotel Concorde and pushing her legs up into the air. She imagined the cleft in his chin and the feel of his stubble as it rubbed against her mouth, turning it raw.

When she came, she cried out loudly. Dan came soon after. "That was intense," he said.

He dozed for a few minutes and then woke up and said he was wired. "I want you to read this," she said, handing him the *Husbandry* script.

She moved around the room anxiously, unpacking his things, while he read it on the couch. When he finished, he breathed in deeply through his nose and closed the script. She darted over and sat next to him. "So?"

"It's really good," he said.

"Do you really think so? I know the language is poetic, and it's not a real American city. You don't think it's too . . . Euro? Pretentious?"

"It's sexy, it's dark, it's Juhasz's European take on an American marriage. He's going to turn this small town into a horror show."

"So you think I should read?"

"Of course you should. You're going to nail this. You have that combination of sadness and raw sexuality." He bit her earlobe playfully.

"I feel like I get this character. But Juhasz might hate me."

"He already loved *I Used to Know Her*. Just do what you always do. Prepare, be confident, and show him who you are." He kissed her. There was an ornate mirror across the room, and in it she could see them nuzzling.

"How do you think I would look with a shag?" she asked, angling her head so she could better see her reflection.

"What?"

"Nothing."

In the library Steven was lying on a couch, his head facing away from Bridget as though she were his shrink. She was in a dark blue armchair. The light from the canal made patterns on the ceiling.

She had to keep Steven on task. Focused on the future and not the present.

The boyfriend had been an unexpected hitch in the plan. It took balls to crash at Steven Weller's palazzo. Maddy and Dan had come down for a late lunch, both with wet hair. Steven had been gracious with Dan, asking about his flight, the room. Now the couple had gone on a walk, "exploring the town."

"Maybe she's too complicated," Steven said. In Berlin, in his suite, he had been beguiled by Maddy, certain she was the one they'd been looking for. The frisson between them would enliven the project. But now the boyfriend was here, and he felt as though he were running a youth hostel.

"It's good that she's complicated," Bridget said. "We already know that not just any pretty face will do. You need a costar who can be an equal."

"He's probably read the script. All the sex scenes. It could be a problem for him."

"He went to NYU! He's not a Mormon! You're forgetting the sex scene in his movie."

"Even if he encourages her to do this, I'm not sure I feel the requisite . . . passion for her. I need to feel that the girl is the only one who could possibly play the part." He sat up and adjusted a stack of architectural and art books on the table so they were lined up perfectly. One was a study of eighteenth-century German coins.

Bridget crossed her left leg over her right so her body was facing him, and bounced her foot up and down slowly. "I know I don't usually talk to you this way," she said, "but we've been in each other's lives a very long time."

"Yes."

"And I have to—I'm frustrated with the way you're handling all this. I watched you fight so hard to do *The Widower*, and I don't know what happened to that spirit. Don't you want this to happen?"

"I'm not sure. My enthusiasm has waned."

"Why give up now?"

"This has been a long process, and I'm tired."

"And now it's going to pay off, all the work we've done to get here. You've been persuasive. She wants to do this. I saw the way you two connected on the patio." He glanced at her sharply. "You know I see everything. Now stop. You cannot be so fear-based."

"You're forgetting that I'm the one who has to work with her."

"I'll be working with her, too. And she is right for it. You've been doing such a good job. Let me do mine."

"What can you do about this situation?"

"Well, I was thinking." She had a vein that ran down the center of her forehead that throbbed when she was excited. With age, it had gotten bluer. "Dan is such a skilled director, particularly with female-friendly material. That was an unusual film he made."

"And?"

"He's responsible. Obviously professional. Well trained. He wouldn't need to learn on the job."

"What are you talking about?"

"*The Valentine*. My film in Bulgaria. They've been having so many problems. Patrick Fitzsimmons is a disaster. It's a serious love story, and I'm getting reports that this guy has no facility with actors. The cast is miserable. And Dan wants to work. I want to go out on a limb for him, the way I always do for people I care about."

There was a kind of love you could feel for your manager that surpassed even the love of a child for his parents. "He does want to work," Steven said, smoothing the jacket of one of the art books and examining his palm for dust. None.

"I want to help the boy. I like matching talented people with important projects."

"Of course you do," he said, patting her on the knee. "It's what you do for a living."

"It's more than a living. It's who I am."

For the party Maddy chose a black wool boatneck dress. Dressy but not too much. She wanted to be herself. Dan had noticed the Marchesa in the closet and fingered it, wolf-whistling. "This must have cost ten thousand dollars," he said. "More."

"You know rich people get everything for nothing," she said. "I'm sure they gave it to Bridget for free."

When the couple arrived in the ballroom, they found a dozen or so dinner guests, all in expensive sweaters, speaking accented English. A handsome Spanish actor was there, and a man she recognized as a Soho art dealer. A British memoirist with prematurely gray hair was talking to a 1970s-era comedian whom Maddy's father had loved.

"Oh my God," Dan murmured as they came in together.

"I know," she whispered. "It's like every subset of the creative world."

She took in the details of the room, the incredible sparkling chandeliers (*ca'rezzonico*, Steven had told her they were called), the live chamber quartet—all the things she would have mentioned to her father if she could have called him.

A server offered Maddy and Dan colorful drinks. They took glasses, clinked. The drink was sweet and refreshing. "What is this?" Maddy asked.

"Venetian spreetz," the server said. "Prosecco, Aperol, and sparkling water."

Bridget swooped over, accompanied by a thirtysomething woman with dark eyebrows. "I wanted to introduce you to Rachel Huber," Bridget said. "Rachel is the head of production for Worldwide Films. We're working together on *The Valentine*."

"I just saw *I Used to Know Her*," Rachel said to Dan. "I loved it."

"Thank you so much," Dan said.

"You know, even though I work for the devil now, I actually started in indie film myself." Rachel dropped the names of a couple of now-defunct New York–based companies.

A server was calling them inside for dinner. There was a long handcrafted table, with place cards that indicated Maddy was next to Dan. Rachel was on his other side. Steven was bracketed by a tall, glamorous Italian woman and the old comedian. Steven was in his element, his skin luminous in the candlelight.

Throughout dinner, Rachel asked Dan a lot of questions about *I Used to Know Her*, and several times Maddy noticed that she tapped him on the arm for emphasis. He mentioned some names of NYU classmates, and then they began gossiping about indie-film people. Dan drank Prosecco, and the Pinocchio circles began to appear. He would say something funny, and Rachel's gray eyes would glint. Maddy felt something greater than irritation and less than jealousy.

Throughout the meal, Steven told show-business anecdotes. One was a famous story that he attributed to Gore Vidal, which required him to imitate Vidal imitating the characters. Jack Kennedy and Tennessee Williams had met at the Kennedy estate in Palm Beach in 1957. JFK was shooting a target and offered the gun to Williams. Williams took the gun with great confidence and got three bull's-eyes in a row. "'Very good,'" said Steven, as a Boston-accented Kennedy. "'Yes,'" said Steven, in an exaggerated Southern drawl, as Williams. "'Considering I was using my *blind eye*.'"

For after-dinner drinks, they moved to the sitting room, and Bridget, Rachel, and Dan got into a detailed discussion of how a seminal 1992 Mile's End film had come to be acquired and distributed. Maddy was not quite bored but ignored. Steven came in and beckoned to her. With a glance at Dan, she went to him. "He seems happy here," Steven said, eyeing Dan as he laughed at something Rachel said.

"Oh God, he's going to be on cloud nine for weeks. Thank you for having him. I know it was unexpected."

"Please, it's nothing. He's welcome in my home. As are you. I take my hosting duties very seriously."

She saw the tall Italian woman light a cigarette, her fingers long and elegant. "Who is that?" she asked.

"A friend. Albertina. She's a princess."

"If you didn't like her, why did you invite her?"

"No," he said with a laugh. "She an actual Venetian princess."

Maddy spotted Bridget, Rachel, and Dan stepping outside to one of the terraces. Bridget had her arm around Dan. "Come with me for a second," Steven said. Maddy hesitated and then followed.

He led her downstairs and down a long hallway to a kitchen, where men in white aprons did dishes. Through the kitchen was another, smaller room. More men in white ate and drank. They rose as Steven entered. He said something in Italian. They were pulling out seats for them and smiling, laughing. Pointing at her, Steven said, *"Permettete che vi presenti la Signorina Freed?"* He said each word with a perfect Italian accent except *Freed*, which sounded hard and Wisconsin. *"Un giorno sarà più famosa di me."* She recognized the word *"famosa,"* but when she asked him what the rest of it meant, he wouldn't tell her.

One of the men, who had thick eyebrows and a handsome stubbled face, had a bottle of something dark and shimmering. Two extra glasses were produced, and Steven poured for Maddy and himself. It was some kind of wine, strong and sweet. She took another sip and her body grew pliable. She didn't want to go upstairs and try to hold her own around all those important people. She wanted to stay down here and learn dirty jokes in Italian, smoke unfiltered cigarettes with men. "What am I drinking?" she asked.

"An old recipe. It's Vito's grandmother's. He could give it to you, but then he'd have to kill you." The men laughed again, and one of them said something in Italian she didn't understand.

In the bedroom later that night, she was flipping pages of a coffee-table book of photography and essays called *Venice Observed*, by Mary McCarthy, when Dan came in. He tossed her a screenplay. "What's this?" she asked.

"Rachel Huber asked me to read it, and I already did. But I want to know what you think."

The title page said *The Valentine*. "What is this?"

"The movie Bridget's producing in Bulgaria."

"Why does she want you to read it if it's already in production?"

"Can you just read it? And then I'll tell you."

"I'm tired," she said. "Too many spreetzes."

"Okay," he said. "But read it in the morning."

She drifted off within seconds and awakened to find sunlight streaming through the partly open drapes. She could hear Dan in the bathroom, in the tub. She picked up the screenplay.

It was awful. Each scene was engineered to produce maximum tears. A young couple in the South, the girl rich, the boy poor, separated by their families. She had finished by the time he came out of the bathroom, a towel around his waist.

"It's horrible," Maddy said. "Why did Rachel want you to read it? She wants a rewrite?"

"She wants me to replace the director," he said, and began to put on his clothes with his back to her.

So this was what all the quiet talk was about the night before, out on the terrace, while she was in the kitchen with Steven and the cooks. "And what are you going to tell her?" she asked.

"I'm going to do it. I don't think it's that bad. There's a lot of potential."

"But this isn't your brand at all. *I Used to Know Her* was an honest movie. This is just—schmaltz. Worse than schmaltz. Dreck." She couldn't understand why he was so eager to take the job, no matter how much they were offering. He had just gotten a distribution deal. The two of them were going to finish *The Nest*. He had a Hollywood agent sending him scripts. This was the kind of job some washed-up has-been director would take when no one else would hire him.

He put on his sweater, sat on the edge of the bed, and named the two young stars who played the leads, both on the rise. "It's a chance to make something a lot of people will see," he said. "You're being a snob. You get an audition for Walter Juhasz, and all of a sudden you're an elitist."

"I'm not an elitist. I just know how to read. I get that you want to work, but you have a quarter of a million dollars coming to you. You don't have to take the first offer."

"I think you're jealous," he said, going toward the sitting area. "You want Hollywood success, but you don't want me to have any." He stared at the fireplace, though the fire had gone out the night before.

"That is not true. Since I met you, all I've wanted was for you to be successful."

"So you understand why I'm going to take this. Mad, I can make an entire independent feature with the money she's offering. I won't see most of the Apollo money for a year."

"Slow down a little, okay?"

"You just want a fixer-upper."

"What?"

"I was a failure when you met me. Now this good stuff is happening. I've been supportive of you signing with Bridget. Auditioning for Juhasz. But now that I have an opportunity, you're being a bitch about it."

"I only want what's good for you!" She went to him, to touch him, but he turned his body away. "Why don't you ask Rachel to find you something else?" she said. "I'm sure Bridget would help."

"Because they need someone now. A huge part of working in Hollywood is getting someplace first."

"You never used to say things like that."

He left the room. Downstairs, she found him in the dining room eating Venetian biscuits and drinking cappuccino with Rachel Huber, Steven, and Bridget, plus the comedian and Albertina. She wondered if Albertina had spent the night in Steven's room.

A server put a cappuccino in front of Maddy. She took one sip. It was perfect, but she couldn't enjoy it. All the breakfast talk was about Dan and *The Valentine*. He had already said yes while she was upstairs. Or maybe the previous night, before she'd even read a word. Somewhere between Mile's End and Venice, he had stopped seeing the two of them as a team.

A few hours later—after Dan, Bridget, and Rachel sped away on a boat toward the airport, and the other guests had left, too—Maddy stood on a terrace overlooking the Grand Canal. Steven came out. "Are you all right?" he asked.

"I don't know. I will be. It just happened so fast. He just got here, and now he's left." She wasn't sure how much Steven would want to hear about her missing Dan.

"This is a good city to be in when you miss someone. Now come with me."

"I need to prepare for my audition. I only have two more days."

"You need to get out of your head."

A half hour later, they were on a private boat in the canal, with a captain named Marcello. Steven said he wanted to give her a tour of the Lido. "You don't get seasick, do you?" he asked.

"Of course not. I love boats. I grew up on a lake. We were more into canoeing, though. My dad was an old hippie."

"There's nothing I enjoy more than being on water. The wind. The quiet. On my boats, there're no casting problems or production delays or infighting."

They stood on the deck of the motorboat. She wore a cable-knit sweater he had lent her. Here she was in frigid February, in the Venice lagoon with a movie star, wearing a borrowed sweater like a girlfriend, when a month ago she had been trudging from the Atlantic Avenue stop in a hostess dress, counting the blocks till home.

The Lido was deserted and gray. Steven took the wheel, Marcello next to him, and pointed out the various hotels, including Hôtel des Bains, where Visconti had shot *Death in Venice*.

"You have a sailboat in L.A., right?" she asked. He was always talking about his boat in interviews.

"Yeah. When I need to get away, I take her out."

"What's she called?"

"*Jo.*"

"After *Little Women?*"

"After Jo Van Fleet. I saw *Cool Hand Luke* when I was starting out as an actor and she blew me away. She and Newman were only ten years apart and she played his mother. I got the boat after Bridget booked me my first commercial. Now I realize it's corny to name a boat after an actress, but it's bad luck to change it."

He said his father had taught him to sail on Lake Michigan; his only happy memories of his dad were from the boat. His father had been a depressive auto-parts factory worker who got laid off and became a big drinker.

"Is he still alive?"

"He died when I was a teenager. Heart attack."

"And your mom?"

"She died three years ago. She was eighty-two when she went."

A *vaporetto* came at them, veering dangerously close. Marcello cursed at the other captain through the glass as he steered out of the way. "He has good instincts," she said.

"Everyone who works for me," Steven said, "has better instincts than I do."

Over the next three days, Maddy and Dan communicated mostly by text, about work—her audition and his movie. He was overwhelmed with production details. He said it was a good cast, and they seemed to like him, but his days were long. When they spoke by phone, it was brief. He would begin to describe a scene in the movie, then add that he was boring her because she had hated *The Valentine*. "I didn't hate it," she said during one talk. "I just didn't understand why you wanted to do it."

"It's a woman's story, Maddy, just a different kind." She wondered if she had been too hard on him, not understanding the toll of all those years of struggle.

Whenever Maddy wasn't preparing her scenes, she toured Venice with Steven. He took her to Santa Maria della Salute and the Guggenheim. They walked backstreets of the city and dined in small trattorias. He translated snippets of the newspaper aloud for her, explaining that the Italian penchant for exasperation was apparent even in the construction of sentences.

At first she was uncomfortable spending so much time with him, but he was so gallant, she told herself he was merely being a good host. If she allowed herself to believe that he wanted to sleep with her, then she had to believe that the audition was somehow illegitimate. And she had to believe that it was legitimate in order to want to get it.

As she came to know him better, she realized she *enjoyed* being with him, as a person, not a movie star. He was witty and theatrical, observant and intelligent. At Caffè Florian, he told her a story about the Canadian actor Joe Wiseman. In the late 1950s, Wiseman had starred in *Viva Zapata!* on Broadway opposite Marlon Brando. "Every night the cast was mobbed for autographs," Steven said, setting down his espresso with a smirk. "It was the hottest ticket in town. One night on the street, this boy calls out, 'Mr. Wiseman, Mr. Wiseman!' Joe just wants to go home, so he walks away. The kid follows him up the block. Wiseman's walk becomes a run. He circles the block. The kid's on his heels. Finally, he ducks into an alleyway, thinking he's lost him, but the kid comes in. Joe's trapped. He figures he'll just give an autograph and get out of there. He approaches the kid. The boy says, 'Mr. Wiseman! What's Marlon Brando like?' "

She laughed. A young Italian couple walked by, and Steven murmured imagined conversation between them, a lover's spat.

"I love this city," he said. "The press leaves me alone here." He told her about the many intrusions over the years. The magazine that got a shot of Cady Pearce sunbathing naked on the deck of *Jo*, and the one that reported Steven and a prior girlfriend were seeing a sex therapist. Once, a gay bodybuilder had told the supermarket tabloid *The Weekly Report* that Steven had paid him to have sex. He claimed to know Steven's identifying characteristics. Steven had sued and settled with the magazine, which retracted the story. He had donated the settlement money, $500,000, to a children's charity. "It's important to send a message," he told Maddy at the café.

Maddy had always been skeptical when she read actors' tirades on the paparazzi. Though she had found it jolting to face the press at the Berlinale Palast, she felt that acting was a public career, and if you chose it, you had to be willing to sacrifice some privacy.

"But papers have always printed lies about famous people," she said. "Why not just ignore it?"

"Because the lies get reprinted until they become a sort of truth," he said, leaning intensely over the table. "They become the story. I want to tell my own story."

"What kind of lies bother you the most?"

"That I'll never marry. That I'm a womanizer. That I can't commit. That I'm a playboy or gay."

She peered closely down into her own espresso as she asked, "Why do you think—why do you think they say that about you?"

"Type in any male actor's name on the Internet, and the word 'gay' pops up right after. Type in any actress's name and you get 'divorced.' Think about who's doing the searching. Women are pessimists and men are optimists. Maybe it's because I collect art, or have a strong hairline, or own property in Italy. Or because I'm divorced and haven't remarried."

She was watching his face, trying to figure out what he was saying. Was he denying the rumors or acknowledging them?

"Well, what do you think?" he asked.

"About what?"

"You asked about my marriage to Julia, so obviously, you're curious. Do I seem gay to you?" His smile turned the question into a flirtation.

"It's none of my business," she mumbled.

"You're being clever now," he said.

"I'm not clever," she said. "I'm an actress in need of a job."

The morning of the audition, Bridget called from Bulgaria and told Maddy, "I have no doubts about you." When she clicked off, Maddy felt a little abandoned, but she decided to take it as a sign of faith that Bridget didn't feel the need to be there for the reading.

She ate lunch at Florian alone, and when she returned to Palazzo Mastrototaro, Steven said Juhasz had arrived and was resting. He said to meet them in the sitting room on the *piano nobile* at four.

At five minutes to four, she went down. She was wearing a flowing white blouse over jeans. She was as confident as she could rightly be, given the limited time she'd had to prepare. She was completely off-book, which she tried to be for every audition, because it freed her up to take direction.

The two men were standing and talking. Juhasz wore a black button-down shirt and black flat-front pants. He was short with white hair and a long nose with a dent in its tip. He had merry wrinkles around his eyes that made him appear to be laughing all the time. He kissed her on each cheek, then held her hands. "Lovely," he said. Did he mean her or the moment?

"It's an honor to meet you, Mr. Juhasz," she said.

"What did you think of my script?" He had a mild Hungarian accent and a higher voice than she had imagined.

"Extremely gripping. Thank you for writing such a rich female character."

"I am sorry I couldn't get it in shape before Berlin, but I hate Berlin anyway. Venice is a much more scenic place to meet."

"Well, I'm honored to have a chance to read for you."

"I have a terrible track record with women in real life, but not in my films. Perhaps it is because in my scripts, the women cannot talk back to me." She wasn't sure she liked this and said nothing. He slapped his thighs and said, "I can see that you are ready to work. Let us begin."

There was a digital camera set up on a tripod in the center of the gigantic room. Juhasz and Steven sat in two chairs behind the camera, and Maddy sat in the straight-backed wooden chair facing it. Steven had a copy of the script in his lap. "You two will do the Louis-Ellie scene in the car," Juhasz said, fiddling with the camera. "Steven, you can begin with 'You look tired.' " Maddy had the pages on one knee for safekeeping, just in case she drew a blank. "Whenever you're ready," Juhasz said.

A red light was glaring at her. She breathed in a few times, then nodded slightly at Steven to let him know she was ready. In the scene, Louis tells Ellie he's disappointed in her because she has stopped putting effort into her appearance, and she tells him she no longer respects him.

Steven read in a flat tone—maybe he was trying to be neutral—that made it hard for Maddy to know how to play her response. The scene culminated in a short monologue from Ellie: "I was a possession. You wanted to show me off. To add me to your collection. You're angry because you can't do that anymore." She looked up at Juhasz. The red light went off.

"Excellent," Juhasz said. "Let's move on to the scene after Ellie and Paul make love for the first time. Just the monologue. Since Billy Peck is not here with us."

"You don't want us to do the scene again? You don't want to see it any other way?" She had come all this way for one take. Maybe he had hated her and didn't see the point in wasting more time.

"I liked your choices in the scene. I wanted to get a sense of the chemistry between you and Mr. Weller. Now, for this monologue, we need to feel that Ellie is constantly afraid of the feelings. I want you to show me the vulnerability. She is almost like a child. Like Laura in *The Glass Menagerie*. Start with 'The sky is so dark.' Whenever you're ready."

"Good," said Juhasz, when she finished. "Now I want you to take it again from the top, and this time play the grief and not the euphoria. I see that you can play the high of the new feelings. Now I want to see that you can play the pain."

She was relieved to get some direction. She loved the way you could transform the meaning of a scene with how you played it. She tried the monologue again. By the end, she was crying. She had learned to do it in school, with relaxation and breath work. She hoped the tears would make him think she was a professional, but then feared it had been too show-offy.

Juhasz came toward her. She thought he might hug her or hit her. He opened and closed his fists by the sides of his face like a Bob Fosse dancer. Was he rendering his verdict? Had she been cast or not? In New York they just said "Thanks so much," but he seemed to be communicating something of great importance without words. She tried to see Steven's face, but it was blocked by the camera.

"Shall we eat?" Juhasz finally asked.

She had no idea if this meant she had booked it or if she would find out in a few days that she hadn't. Maybe he would call Bridget, and Bridget would call her. She was supposed to fly back to New York in the morning and couldn't face the possibility that she might go home not knowing if Ellie was hers.

"Absolutely," Maddy said, pretending everything that had happened so far was ordinary, that she went on auditions this strange all the time. "I'm famished."

The boat trip was cold and quiet. Steven had said their destination was a surprise. They rode about forty minutes before Giorgio docked the boat. "Welcome to Torcello," Steven said. "This was the original Venice. It was wiped out by malaria. Now almost no one lives here year-round." He pointed out a small cathedral. "Santa Fosca."

They walked underneath a green awning into a yellow building. Inside was a warm-toned room with low ceilings and a fireplace. At their table, the waiter brought menus that said LOCANDA CIPRIANI. "Steven knows it's one of my favorite restaurants in all of Italy," Juhasz said. "Many luminaries have dined here, Kim Novak and Charlie Chaplin. Most famous was Ernest Hemingway. This was his inspiration for *Across the River and Into the Trees*. Widely considered his biggest failure." Maddy giggled. "Even so," he went on, "I would rather have a Hemingwayesque failure than a Juhaszian success."

Soon there was food on the table: the famous carpaccio; risotto alla Torcellana; and lagoon shrimps. Steven had ordered Prosecco for all three of them, and though she was wary of getting tipsy, she liked it as much as she had at Steven's party.

"Do you mind if I ask what inspired the screenplay?" she asked Juhasz, hoping he would give some indication as to whether he had cast her.

"As I age, I keep returning to the subject of women. And jealousy. It is the most destructive of human emotions because it has no utility." He had to be talking about his first wife, who had made him so jealous that he'd left the country.

"I disagree that it has no utility," Maddy said. "It crystallizes feeling."

"For whom?" Steven asked across the table.

"Well, both people. I was thinking of the Bardot character in *Contempt*. To me, it's about a relationship that ends because the man wasn't possessive enough. A woman needs to know she is wanted."

"And what about your boyfriend?" Juhasz asked. "Is he a jealous man?"

"How do you know I have a boyfriend?"

"He directed that Vermont movie, no? If he were a jealous man, he would not have abandoned his girlfriend in a palazzo of a major motion picture star, and taken her matronly chaperone along with him." Maddy was surprised that Juhasz knew so much about the situation.

"Dan wants me to succeed," she said. "He believes in me."

"I feel the film is less about jealousy than triangles," Steven interrupted cheerfully. "Louis loves Ellie even though he doesn't know how to make her happy. Ellie loves Paul. And Paul, in a certain way, loves his brother. He wants the approval of his brother but can't figure out how to live in the world. The triangle is a really interesting place of human interaction."

"I love triangles," Juhasz said. "The three of us are a triangle right now."

"How so?" Maddy asked.

"Mr. Weller needs me to legitimize him, I need you to challenge him, and you need him to make love to you."

Maddy blushed. She was struck silent, momentarily, by the accusation, and could not summon the words to protest. How had Juhasz gotten this in his head? Had Steven said something? Was her attraction so obvious?

She realized she had focused so much on the "make love" part of the sentence that she hadn't paid attention to the rest: *I need you to challenge him.*

"Mr. Juhasz," she said, "what did you mean about challenging Steven?"

"I want your Ellie to really draw out the best in him."

"I have a callback?"

Juhasz looked at Steven, his mouth wide and delighted, and back at Maddy. "You have the part. You did not know?"

"How would I know? You never said it." She was so relieved, she wanted to cry.

"I am sorry, my darling," Juhasz said, patting her hand. "I thought it was clear this was a celebratory meal. We've read many major actresses for Ellie, but none of them was right." Maddy got a strange feeling when he said it, as though her Prosecco had been drugged. "The role is yours. Congratulations."

She could feel herself floating to the ceiling of Locanda Cipriani and over the island of Torcello, above the spirit of Ernest Hemingway, who was cheering as if at a boxing match.

She had gotten it. A real, legitimate feature role, shooting with one of the greatest living directors opposite a Hollywood icon. And she was the lead. It was Ellie's movie more than Louis's or Paul's. If her Jury Prize had been the equivalent of putting her foot on the pedal, now she had pressed it down.

The men held up their glasses by the stems. "To the birth of new talent," said Juhasz.

"To collaboration," said Steven, looking at Maddy.

8

Maddy was on the stairs of the palazzo. Juhasz had retired to his room, and she had started up to her bedroom to call Dan when Steven, tending to the fire, said, "Stay with me a little."

"I was going to make a phone call."

"Not even a few minutes?"

She came down a few steps. Sat next to him on the couch. She kept flashing back to the moment when Juhasz had said, *And you need him to make love to you.* It was embarrassing that he had said it, out in the open.

Steven rang a bell, and Vito brought two glasses of a dark brown liquid. "Cynar," Steven said, moving toward her. "It's made from artichoke."

She sipped. "I like it." They sat in silence, watching the flames. "This has been the oddest evening," she said. "I feel like Walter's going to come down those stairs any minute, and I'll find out I was on a candid-camera show."

"I told you he would love you."

"I never thought this would happen. Any of this, not Mile's End or this. Until now, the biggest job I'd gotten was a Foxborough revival of *Barefoot in the Park.*"

"Pay attention to what you're feeling right now. You're so open. Try to remember this moment."

He was close, his face inches from hers. She could smell the Cynar on his breath. His eyes were gleaming. The light on the irises, the way they always seemed alive, no matter what emotion he was playing. Steven had an abundance of personhood. This was why he was successful. He lived too fully not to do so on screen.

"I wanted to be alone with you tonight," he said. "I'm sorry it wasn't possible."

"No, it wasn't," she said carefully.

"I wanted to take you around the island. Show you the Basilica. I love being alone with you. You make me selfish. When I saw you at that party at Mile's End, it was clear."

She saw her hand trembling before her face. "What party?"

"Opening night. I knew I would fall in love with you." So he had been looking at her. She hadn't imagined it. She had been strapped into a roller coaster and the car had started to move. She could hear the irreversible clacking on the tracks. "The past couple of years, I've had a feeling something was about to happen for me," he said. "I didn't know what it was, but I was waiting. When I saw you, I understood that you were what I'd been waiting for."

His breath was hot as he leaned in and kissed her. She had never been kissed like this. His lips were soft but deft. And then he was on his knees, his body between her legs, his strong arms moving up and down her back. She touched the hair on the back of his head, so much softer than it looked from far away. The kiss went on through entire decades of cinema: She was every actress who had ever kissed Steven Weller in a movie, and she was Audrey Hepburn and Katharine Hepburn and Lauren Bacall and Rita Hayworth, and the kiss was nothing like the ho-hum kisses Dan had given her lately; it had personality and confidence, and she offered her whole mouth, her self, to him.

When she finally opened her eyes, he was scooping her up without a grunt. He carried her up the grand marble stairs.

His bedroom was dim and huge. On the bed, she could feel his hardness against her and it thrilled her, his desire for her. She had done this to him.

He kissed her for a long time, moving above her. She craved life and Steven was life and she would be doing this even if Dan had not left for Bulgaria, even if he were sleeping in her bedroom in the palazzo right now.

She felt powerless. She was Steven's. She had been avoiding this truth since he looked at her at the Entertainer, but now it was unavoidable. He had enraptured her with his mind and his notorious grin and she was as unable to resist him as the millions of American women who had tuned in on Thursday nights to see him arch his eyebrow in close-ups or who had cheered in cineplexes when he appeared shirtless from the heat in his Louisiana law office.

He moved his mouth down her body, sighing loudly when he unclasped her bra and her breasts came free. It defied rationality that a man with the undoubted sexual experience of Steven Weller could caress her body with an expression of such wonder. He moved his hand on her belly and hip bones. His mouth was on her, what was he doing, fingers inside and wetness, and she was coming. His pants were off and his nakedness rubbed against hers. There was a question in the air and she said, "I'm on the pill," and with that she took him in. Things were as they were supposed to be, there was nothing between them. She was not making love to a movie star, there was no world but this, it was only Maddy and Steven, not Steven Weller but Steven. As he rocked, he hit a place deep within her, and they were like this for how long she couldn't guess because there was no time, there was nothing, there was no room and no place, just them.

She was coming again and he kept moving and his warmth was inside her and he kissed her as she cried out, and made a strange noise, touching her tongue. He would never soften, she was made to have him inside her. Then his expression changed, it didn't cool, exactly, but he became separate again, and she felt the tragedy of the moment being over and he was out, examining her features, moving his finger along her mole.

It was too much for her that it was over, and she cried and was embarrassed by this, and he took her nipple in his mouth and she had to have him and they were turned this way and that. This was something she had never liked, she found it confusing, too much at once to be wanted and wanter, receiver and giver, but this seemed natural and soon he was very hard. This time his orgasm in her mouth brought on hers, his taste in her so thrilling and illicit that it set off an eruption. She stroked it and it shrank. He moved so his face was near hers, and this time she didn't cry, because he would be in her again many other days and nights. There was no need to rush.

And when he said, "Be with me," she knew he wasn't asking her to make love again. He was asking her to be his, and there was no question in her mind that she would.

She was with him now, and she would be with him, here in Venice or Los Angeles, wherever he wanted, he could take her anywhere and she would go, because the sex was the punctuation for the feelings she'd had since he first looked at her from across the room at the festival. She was his.

In the morning, when a text came from Dan, three words, "How was it?," she did not hesitate before using her thumbs to type out three of her own: "I'm leaving you."

Act Two

1

Maddy and Steven stayed in Venice another week, making love, eating in his bedroom, and occasionally seeing the town. Dan called her several times a day to beg her to change her mind. They had brief, tortured conversations in which he alternated between screaming and crying. He said Steven was using her because he was gay, that he didn't love her and never would. Steven told her not to answer the calls, but she couldn't just turn her back on the man she had been with for three years, a man she still loved, even if she could no longer envision a life with anyone but Steven. She told Dan that Steven wasn't gay, but she knew it would hurt him too much to learn how she knew it: Steven made love to her in a way no man ever had.

Soon Dan changed tactics, sending long emails about her opportunism and duplicity. He called her "a shallow whore." He said all she had ever cared about was fame. She wanted to scream back that no one who cared about fame would pursue theater, but he wasn't being rational; there was no point. The emails grew so abusive that she had to block him, email and phone, which made her feel worse.

When Steven had to return to L.A. to shoot a film, they first flew to New York and checked in to the Lowell so she could have a day to gather her things. When Steven came to the apartment on South Portland with her, a few guys on a stoop recognized him and made him pose for pictures. As professional packers separated her things from Dan's and boxed them up, she took her last glimpse at the posters of Dan's student films and her Samuel French plays, their stained Mr. Coffee, the IKEA spice rack, wondering if she would ever see them again.

She was reminded of those fevered weeks when Dan wrote *I Used to Know Her* and she had felt proud. Even after they'd gotten into Mile's End, he hadn't been that person. Brooding, selfish, and phony—and then he had gone off to do *The Valentine*. Maybe someday he would remember who he was.

Before she took off on Steven's plane, she went with Irina to an Indian place in the East Village that they used to frequent. Irina sat with an expression of disbelief mixed with dubiousness as Maddy spilled every detail, from the slow attraction to the audition and the first night together at the palazzo.

"I know I sound like the dumbest girl in the universe," Maddy said, looking down at her food, "because he's famous and old and he's dated a lot. But I don't care. I want to be with him no matter what."

"I thought you liked 'em poor and skinny."

"So did I."

"Are you guys going to have a live-in maid?"

Maddy laughed and shook her head. "He has housekeepers but no live-ins. Except the cook." He had told her he employed a private half-German chef named Annette Kohl, who had gone to Le Cordon Bleu.

"I knew it! I bet you'll eat sashimi for breakfast. I read that Steven Spielberg does. You know you're really rich when you eat savory in the mornings." Maddy giggled but felt an undercurrent of hostility from her friend.

As they wolfed saag paneer and drank bad red wine, Irina told Maddy about some recent auditions and a grant she'd gotten to develop an experimental dance-theater piece on Cape Cod. Maddy told her about the *Husbandry* script, and Irina seemed supportive, though she said Juhasz's work objectified women.

After the dishes had been taken away and they were lingering over wine, Maddy mentioned the strange homemade wine she'd had in Steven's Venetian kitchen. "So that's what you really want?" Irina asked. "Italian wine, and your own palazzo, and a mansion in L.A.?"

"It's not about any of that," Maddy answered. "It's about Steven."

"You don't have any regrets? After all those years with Dan, you just wash your hands?"

"You know, I think I was in denial. He was so loving after my father died that I convinced myself it wasn't already over." As she said it, she started to believe it. "He wasn't as into sex as I was. And he was in a bad mood all the time. Steven's nothing like that. I've never met anyone who enjoys life the way he does. Food and drink and art. He has this incredible collection. Ed Ruscha."

Irina narrowed her eyes, a look Maddy remembered her giving right before she gave a scathing critique of a classmate's work in *Blood Wedding*. "What?" Maddy asked.

"Nothing."

"Just say it."

"It's—I always thought creative respect was the most important thing to you. In your relationships."

"It is!"

"But how can you respect Steven Weller?"

"I do respect him. *You're* the one who doesn't."

"Is it possible you're in such a sex haze that you're deluding yourself into thinking you like his acting?"

Maddy tensed up. "No. It's not just about sex. He cares what I think about his work. Like, he wants my feedback. I want to sleep next to him every night and wake up looking at him."

Irina gave her another long, level gaze. Maddy knew she would feel the same way if the roles were reversed, and yet she wished Irina could be the slightest bit happy for her. Steven Weller wanted her.

But Irina saw the world in terms of hacks versus artists, and to her, Steven would always be a hack. "You promise to come visit," Irina asked, "even after you're making a million dollars a movie and you have a stylist, a hairdresser, and a personal publicist?"

"I don't know about all that stuff," Maddy said, "but of course I'll visit. I'll be back and forth all the time." From Irina's look, Maddy could tell her friend thought she'd never see her again.

Bridget and Steven were in the backseat of Steven's Highlander, where they conducted most of their business. Steven had a vintage Arcadian-blue

Mustang for pleasure, but his everyday car was the Highlander. Usually, Bridget would join him on his way somewhere, and during the hour they spent in traffic, they would get more business accomplished than they did at her office.

It was a sweltering late-April Thursday, and Steven's driver, Alan, was taking them to the set of *Jen*, a network comedy about a single girl living with her brother. Maddy had booked a guest spot, and Steven had taken the afternoon off from his own film, *Declarations* (about an unhinged underwriter), so he could watch her on set.

Bridget had been surprised when Steven told her he wanted to watch Maddy; usually, his shoots overtook every aspect of his life, including romantic. But she was pleased to see him taking such interest. It was a good sign for *Husbandry* that he was engaged by her process.

When Bridget left them alone in Venice, she had wondered when it would happen, but she had not been sure. One morning in Bulgaria, after Steven had phoned Bridget to update her, Dan arrived on set in a rage. "You did this! You drove them together!" the boy screamed in front of the *Valentine* crew, who were readying a complicated crane shot. Bridget whisked him away, explaining to him that she had done nothing of the sort. People loved whom they loved. "Try to see your work as an escape," she had counseled him. "It's a gift to have this job to keep you busy."

The next few days, he had been distracted at work, but he soon regained his focus, though he was visibly colder to Bridget, which she didn't mind. She preferred him blaming her to blaming Maddy. She was used to taking the fall for clients; it was part of being a manager. Rachel Huber spent a lot of time talking to him, which Bridget felt was kind of her, looking out for him in a time of need.

In the Highlander, Steven and Bridget had been discussing the upcoming DVD commentary for *The Widower*, and he was glowering. It had gotten its theatrical release a few weeks before, and it wasn't performing. She had been convinced it was one of Steven's best performances, but reviewers had called him "stiff" and "miscast as a loser." She had reassured him that it took time to reinvent oneself as an actor, to make risky choices. He had to keep being brave; they were reshaping an almost fifteen-year-old image.

She was confident that *Husbandry* would establish him, once and for all, as an actor and not just a star. Juhasz and Weller were a collaboration for the ages, old Hollywood and new. Whenever Walter made a film, critics rewatched and remembered all the great movies he had made in the 1970s. Louis was a braver role than the lead in *The Widower*. A husband with rage and erectile issues. Anger and ED were practically guaranteed Oscar bait.

When her phone rang, she hesitated. She never liked to take calls while conducting business with Steven. But he was looking down at an email and nodded for her to answer. "Tim Heller," her assistant said. Bridget and Tim had been trading calls.

"I just saw the screener for *I Used to Know Her*," said Tim, an officious Brit. "And I was dazzled by Maddy Freed. My next project is *Freda Jansons*, and I want her to read for me."

"Tell me more," Bridget said, though Nancy Watson-Eckstein had sent her the screenplay a few days ago to pass along to Maddy. Bridget had taken a quick glance at it—it was a long and long-winded biopic—but when she saw that the shoot dates conflicted with *Husbandry*, she had tossed it.

"It's based on a true story in the 1950s about an autistic scientist," Tim continued, "who figures out how to cure a senator's son." Steven had finished his call and Bridget put Tim on speaker. "It's a biopic with a lot of freewheeling elements."

"You know she's doing the Walter Juhasz in June, July, and August."

"We go into production in July," Tim said.

"Well, there you go. She's unavailable."

"Has she read the script?"

"Not yet."

"She should. I'm sure Walter would accommodate—I mean, he's known for a lot of production delays."

"You know, Tim," Bridget said, "I'll certainly take you up on a general, but I can't put her in two places at once. Besides, she signed the contract. There's nothing I can do."

After she hung up, Bridget looked at Steven. He had changed so rapidly since he'd met Maddy. None of the other girls had affected him like this. His hair seemed thicker and his complexion was ruddy. What those two had together, it wasn't just sex. When he was in Maddy's company, he gave her his full attention. He leaned in when she spoke.

"There's something different about you these days," Bridget said.

"What?"

"You're more playful. And you seem healthier. It's in your step."

"I cannot tell you how lucky I am to have such a bright, talented woman in my life."

Bridget inspected her nails and turned to Steven. "It makes me happy to see you so happy. You're less . . . tethered."

"I used to think all the time about what other people had to say about me," he said. "Not now. When you have someone who loves you unconditionally, the less important things fade away."

"Yes," Bridget said.

They rode in silence until Steven typed something into his phone. Without looking up, he said, "I didn't think she signed her *Husbandry* contract yet."

Bridget shrugged. "That doesn't matter."

He smiled. "You did the right thing. But sometimes you make me want to take a shower."

"You just said how much she's changed you. We need to keep her focused on what's important. And nothing is more important than working with you."

Maddy was surprised to find that there was a reserved parking spot for her right outside the soundstage. She got out of her Prius, and a production assistant was already coming out to meet her. Had the guard called, or was there someone whose job it was to stare out a window of the building, waiting for the cars to roll up?

The role on *Jen* was the second she had booked since moving to L.A. and into Steven's mansion. The first was a psychological thriller, a supporting role as a shrink. Another girl had backed out at the last minute, and Maddy had stepped in. It was only a week's worth of work, but she got to join the Screen Actors Guild, and when she deposited her $20,000 paycheck in her new Los Angeles banking account, she felt she was building her future. Even if Steven wouldn't let her help pay for living expenses, and insisted on giving her the Prius and a black credit card, the money from work helped her feel she wasn't completely dependent.

Maddy's role on the comedy was Jen's brother's new girlfriend—it had a lot of physicality, plus half a dozen great zingers. Less confident in comedy than drama, Maddy was only so-so on her audition and had been shocked when Bridget called to say she'd booked it.

After she walked inside, Maddy was introduced to the costume designer, show runner, makeup, hair, director, assistant director, and a bunch of PAs. A PA took her to her trailer, which was elaborately decked out—it even had a flat-screen TV. On the dining table, she found three beautifully wrapped packages: gifts from the show runner, the director, and the star. A gorgeous black-and-white Hermès scarf, a funky red leather watch, and a basket of expensive bath salts. Each had a tasteful note wishing her luck.

She suspected not every day-player on a rising sitcom got this kind of attention. Such things happened to her frequently these days, expensive gifts from executives, cosmetic companies, and designers coming by messenger to the house.

On set, as the director had shaken her hand, she'd sensed him looking at her too closely. It was a glance she had become accustomed to in her short time as Steven's "new girl," a glance she saw at the charity balls and premieres and dinners out. It was a glance that said, *Why her?*

She had no answer. They just loved each other, that was all. Maddy knew she wasn't the prettiest or even the youngest girlfriend he had ever had. She couldn't pinpoint what made her worthy of his love, and yet she believed him when he told her what she meant to him. She didn't care if she was delusional to think it would last. She felt she would follow him anywhere.

During a long rehearsal, Maddy was shocked to see Bridget and Steven slip into two directors' chairs by Video Village. She was both honored that he had come and concerned that he might distract her coworkers.

Maddy hurried over on her next break. "How'd you get off the film?" she asked him, pecking him on the cheek.

"I'm a very powerful person," he said, drawing her close. "Or did you not know that?"

"You're doing great, honey," Bridget said. "We're having such fun watching you."

"Thank you," she said, loving his hands on her, getting turned on. "But Steven, you're causing a fuss." She nodded toward the set, where the other actors were staring and pretending not to stare. "It's not fair to those guys."

"I won't stay long," he said. "I just want to catch a few minutes. I love to watch you work."

His compliment made her feel like a balloon. She realized what it meant to her that he had come. Not only because it showed the cast and crew that he cared, but because he did care.

Back on set, she did her next few takes with elevated energy. Later, when she looked out to see that Bridget was alone again, she felt a twinge of disappointment.

On her lunch break, Maddy went to her trailer and ate a walnut-and-chicken salad that had been prepared by Annette. Bridget, who had come in to sit with her, said, "Your physicality is fantastic. You remind me of Jean Arthur." Maddy and Steven had watched *Mr. Smith Goes to Washington* in the screening room of his house, and it had helped her prepare. She wondered if Steven had told Bridget they'd watched it. Then she decided there was a simpler explanation: In two decades of working together, they had a common vocabulary of stars, living and dead. Steven seemed closer to Bridget than anyone else in the world.

"Honey, what is it?" Bridget said, patting her arm.

Maddy set down her fork. "Do you think I got this part because— because of him? So they could bill Maddy Freed as their special guest star? My audition was not that good. I got some of the comedic beats, but the girls in the hallway, they were *really* funny. They'd all done improv in New York."

"Maybe it is because of Steven."

"You say it like that's okay. How can I know, from this moment on, whether any job I get is deserved?"

"You won't. Everyone knows you're Steven's girlfriend when you

walk into an audition room. But you knew you were talented long before you met him. You have range, you can handle different kinds of
material, you can use your body as an instrument. If you continue to do
everything you do naturally, for most roles, it'll come down to you and one
or two others. At that point, when it's just a few, *anything* can tip the scales.
The color of your hair. The shape of your mouth. Your chemistry with a
costar. If a director likes you because of Steven, that's no different from
another girl booking it because she's curly and you're straight. Your talent
will get you ninety percent of the way. What gets you the last ten percent
of the way is out of your control. Why think about it?" Bridget opened
her purse and pulled out a manila folder. "While I have you, you need to
sign this. The contract for *Husbandry*." Bridget, Nancy, and Maddy's new
lawyer, Edward Rosenman (who was also Steven's lawyer), had negotiated her a salary of $200,000, far more than Maddy had expected for her
first professional feature. Maddy had agreed to full nudity with a merkin,
a pubic wig. Bridget had explained that they used merkins on shoots to
avoid X ratings; prosthetic hair was an R, but real hair was an X. It sounded
ridiculous to put fake hair on top of real hair, but as Bridget liked to point
out, that was only one of many ridiculous things about the film industry.

    "I can't believe my first big movie is going to require all this sex,"
Maddy said.

    "The sex is important to the character," Bridget said, "and I'll be there
to protect you. And Steven will, too." After Maddy signed, Bridget said,
"Congratulations, my darling. You've just signed the contract that is going
to make you a star."

    "How do you know that?"

    "I knew it the moment I saw you on that horrible bus in your movie.
Give me some credit. I've been in the industry longer than you've been
alive." She put the contracts back in the folder and plopped it into her
handbag. "Now don't let me keep you another second," she said. Maddy
started to say she didn't mind the company, but Bridget was already gone.

"How come you're not ready?" Steven asked, stepping out of the walk-in
they shared. "We have to leave in five minutes." He arrived everywhere

at least twenty minutes early; he became agitated in the back of the car if there was traffic, even though Alan knew every obscure shortcut in greater Los Angeles. He and Maddy were going to a Housing Project USA house-raising in Oxnard. Steven was on the board.

"I'm almost ready," Maddy said from in front of the Biedermeier vanity table where she was sitting naked, doing her makeup.

Steven's mansion was intimidating, a 1920 beaux arts. He had bought it while he was still on *Briefs*, then spent five years restoring it to its original splendor. It was ten thousand square feet, with eight bedrooms, columns in front, and a wide iron gate. Maddy was hopeful that one day she could convince him to move someplace smaller, warmer, and more *heimish*, as her father would have put it.

"Don't wear a lot of makeup," Steven said, kissing her neck and looking at the two of them in the mirror.

"But when I go out without makeup, the photographers put me in that spread."

"Fine, but only a little," he said. "You hardly need it, anyway."

A few days after she'd moved in, a tabloid had snapped a shot of her exiting Yuki Sushi with Steven, looking bedraggled. Bridget had sent over a makeup artist to give her a tutorial. But it was hard to know how "natural" to be when there would be camera crews at the event.

Aside from makeup skills, Maddy had learned other rules in the time she had been living with Steven: Don't read tabloid magazines, don't Google your boyfriend, and don't Google yourself. Though she tried to adhere to them, on occasion she would be at her laptop in her study, watching a comedy clip, and begin to surf, and spot an item on the side or bottom that said "Maddy and Steven in Lover's Tiff" or "The Shocking Truth About Weller's Girlfriend!" Feeling sheepish, she would click and read a complete fabrication, and it would upset her so much that she'd vow never to go on again.

Bridget had also gotten Maddy a stylist who'd brought a mix of designer dresses for evening events and casual, high-end pieces for every day. Steven helped her select items, watching as she paraded around. It was clear the bill would go to him; there was no way she could afford the pieces.

If their time in Venice had been a world that consisted solely of the two of them, Los Angeles was the two of them in the world. Every night, it seemed, was a different event. And everyone wanted to be near Steven. Women ogled him openly. Gay men were no better. At a fund-raiser at the Pacific Design Center, she had seen two effeminate guys whispering to each other when they passed. If Steven noticed all of this, he hid it well. She tried to follow his lead: He let it all roll off of him, the good parts of celebrity as well as the bad. People could speculate and gossip as much as they wanted, she told herself, but she was the one who shared his bed.

From the walk-in, she selected a gray James Perse T-shirt and dark jeans and a baseball cap of Steven's that said GREEN BAY PACKERS. When she emerged, he was sitting on the edge of the bed, putting on a pair of designer high-tops. He reeled her in and kissed her. "God, I love you," he said.

Maddy's body softened. How was she supposed to be on time for the event when she wanted to take off her clothes and make love? When she was around him, she wanted to be touching him all the time, his forearms, his hair, his ears. When he came home after a long day and she heard the beep of the alarm system, she got woozy. "I love you, too," she said.

As Steven pushed her hair behind her ears, he realized that he never got tired of hearing her say "I love you." With Maddy in his life, he was less pessimistic. He felt that Maddy knew him, and this made him see the world differently, made him less glum about the business and his role in it.

The most miraculous thing about his new relationship was its completeness. He liked to hear what she had to say about his scripts and was impressed by her close reading. And she was making him a better actor. On the set of *Declarations*, for a heavy scene with the actress playing his wife, he had been struggling. In the fight, he said she didn't understand him, and he was coming off very heavy-handed. After six difficult takes, he took a break, and while he sat in a director's chair, he remembered that Maddy had played a similar scene in her Mile's End film. For the next take, he tried laughing maniacally in the middle. The director loved it and complimented him. It was a special thing to carry with you the person who made you complete, to take what she gave you and bring it into your work. That was the essence of love.

So far Maddy was holding her own in her new lifestyle, with everyone from rising directors to studio execs to Beverly Hills doyennes. She had a way of bringing out genuineness in the least genuine of people. Sometimes the two of them would be out at a fund-raiser, mingling separately, and he would sense that she missed him. He would cross the room and place his hand on her back and she would sigh happily. He loved that she needed him.

Downstairs, Alan was waiting to drive Maddy and Steven to Oxnard. He was in his mid-sixties, large, and had been a bodybuilder at Gold's Gym in the 1970s, and Maddy liked his easy, low-key manner. When they arrived at the work site, she instinctively grabbed the door handle, but Steven said, "Alan'll do it." Of course she had to wait. Everything had to be timed just right.

Alan opened it and she stepped out. The cameras went off, but this was all authorized press, so it wasn't as jarring as the paparazzi. The paparazzi had been one of the scariest things about her new life in L.A. One evening she and Steven were coming out of a northern Italian place they liked on Beverly Boulevard, and she saw dozens of them outside, flashing madly. "Don't say a word," Steven whispered, ushering her swiftly to the car door. Later, he explained that if she said anything, even "Leave me alone" or "I don't want to talk," they could put it on an evil television show and make it seem like she was drunk or unstable. "Think of it as the fourth wall," he said.

In Oxnard, Flora and a Housing Project USA publicist led Steven to a podium where folding chairs had been arranged. While Maddy sat in the front row, Steven said a few words about homelessness in Ventura County. He wasn't reading from notes, yet he was completely eloquent. Then the organizers led them to the construction area, where they were given hard hats and aprons.

Her job was to pry nails from two-by-fours with a hammer, which disappointed her because she'd thought she would be doing real construction. Her father had taught her woodworking, and she knew her way around an electric saw. She knelt and began the work, depositing the nails in a plastic can. They were working next to teenagers from the community, mostly Mexican, and Steven joked around with them.

While they worked, camera crews roved and interviewed the celebs. When Maddy saw a young female journalist approaching with a videographer, she got nervous. "Can you tell us a little bit about why you're here?" the woman asked.

"Um, homelessness is a serious social ill, and I grew up in a community where there was a fair amount, in rural Vermont, and I guess the way I feel is that if you can give people houses, you can empower them in a lot of other ways. That can help them get control of their lives. Because without a home, there are so many things that you just don't have access to. It can be hard to get a job and also—"

The journalist was striding away, her videographer trailing behind. A network-television star had arrived, and the woman was going after him to get a shot.

In horror, Maddy watched them leave. "Oh my God, I feel like such a loser," she said.

"They never want more than a sound bite," Steven said. "But I liked what you said. It was very heartfelt."

"Did I just make a total fool of myself?"

"No. It takes time to learn this stuff." But she felt humiliated. She had wanted to make him proud. "The important thing," he added, wrenching out a nail, "is that you're here. Making your presence known."

After they'd been working about an hour, Maddy saw a figure coming toward them in the distance. He was burly, and when he got behind Steven, he put his hands over his eyes. Steven flipped him over and they rolled around like wrestlers, chuckling deeply and swearing.

"Maddy Freed, Terry McCarthy," Steven said as they rose to their feet.

"The famous Terry, at last!" Maddy laughed and shook his hand. Steven's best friend. Terry was a bearish Irish-American guy with blue eyes who had befriended Steven in the mid-'80s on the audition circuit. They had done walk-ons for the same sitcom and had been close ever since. For a brief period they had shared an apartment on Sunset Boulevard. Terry had long ago given up acting and become a top screenwriter.

Though Maddy had never met Terry, she had gone to lunch with his wife, Ananda, a few times. Maddy liked her. Ananda was a half–African American, half-Korean former actress with high cheekbones who spent most of her time caring for their three kids. At one point Ananda had confessed that when she first started dating Terry, she was jealous of Steven, because of the rumors that their friendship was more than a friendship. "These men were so close," Ananda said. "They lived together in this tiny place."

"So you wondered?"

"Of course I wondered! It took me a long time to accept that straight men could have friendships as rich and rewarding as those between women."

As Maddy worked next to Terry, she asked him about his early days as an actor and his shift to screenwriting. He told her about all the embarrassing sitcom walk-ons he had had in the 1980s, the pizza delivery boys and jocks. The men started to talk over each other, laughing and mocking.

After Steven left to do more press, Maddy said to Terry, "I have to tell you, I am such a fan of *Marginal*. I saw it when I was at Dartmouth. A whole group of us. That scene in the garage gave me nightmares."

"You saw it in *college*? Oh, God, you're making me feel old."

"Writers have so much more creative freedom than actors," Maddy said. "You must be happy you made the transition."

"I don't know, most of the time the studios destroy anything good that I put on the page. It's like when Mervyn LeRoy optioned a novel and said to Spencer Tracy, 'This book has everything. Great characters, an element of surprise, a sophisticated theme, beautiful writing. But I think I can lick it.' "

She laughed. She could see why he was Steven's best friend. Terry seemed wholly genuine and funny. He was more politically active than Steven was, lobbying frequently on behalf of Rwandans and working as a World Children's Welfare ambassador.

"It's a relief to finally meet you," she said. "I was worried. Steven told me about the time you met a girlfriend of his and pretended to have a limp."

Terry chuckled. "Yeah, he told her I was faking, and she was looking at him in horror because she believed me. That was a long time ago. But you shouldn't have been nervous to meet me. I've never seen him so happy."

"Really?" she asked coyly.

"Dating Steven isn't like dating other men," he said. "It's hard, I think. There will be people who think they can tell you who he is. What he's about. They'll pretend to know him, but they don't. A successful relationship has walls and windows. You need to let the world in a little, but not too much. For Steven's sake and your own, make sure there aren't too many windows."

His eyes were close and very serious. She wasn't sure what he meant but nodded intently. She was relieved when he resumed his nail-prying and added, "And don't forget to give him shit. He's got too many people kissing his ass already."

Early the next morning Maddy woke up from a bad dream. It was about her father. In this one they were on a canoe on Yarrow Lake, and the canoe toppled and she was a very little girl screaming for him, but he was gone.

The clock by the bed said two. She wandered down to see if Steven was in the kitchen. He wasn't.

She moved through the living room, past the eighteenth-century *faux marbre* columns. A soft voice was coming from Steven's study. He always kept the door closed; he had said he didn't want her going in there without him. It was the only room of the mansion that she'd never been in alone.

One of the double doors was ajar, and through the crack she saw him. The desk was in the center of the room, facing the arched windows that overlooked the patio, garden, and pool. He was leaning back in his chair, talking on the phone, and one of the desk drawers was open. While he talked, laughing so quietly it was almost inaudible, he pushed in the low drawer, inserted a key, and locked it. Then, very casually, he took a framed photo on the desk, removed the backing, and inserted the key behind the photo. "Don't be ridiculous," he was saying on the phone. His voice was husky and affectionate.

She pushed the door open. He jumped a little, but when he turned to her, he did it slowly.

"Who are you talking to in the middle of the night?" she asked, coming in. She had joked, a few weeks after she arrived, that his study was like part of the west wing in Manderley. He'd said, "Men need space to be alone. Howard Hughes had an entire wing barred to his family, where he would sit for hours, reading aviation books." She had laughed and said he shouldn't point to Howard Hughes as a paragon of male virtue.

"Someone in Italy," Steven said, angling the mouthpiece away from his mouth. The photo on the desk was black and white. It was his mother, standing in front of a house, hand on hip, smiling.

"Who?" Maddy asked, trying not to sound worried. Her voice quavered on the "who."

Steven sighed, said something inaudible into the phone, and hung up. He went to her, near the door. "What's going on?"

"Was it Albertina, that woman from your party?" she asked. "The princess?"

He expelled a rush of air through his mouth. "It was Vito, from the palazzo." His head butler. "There was a problem with a fireplace."

"He couldn't handle it himself?"

"I tell him, when it comes to Palazzo Mastrototaro, to call me day or night."

"But I heard you say, 'Don't be ridiculous.' "

"So? He's my friend. He dialed me on my cell but I didn't want to disturb you, so I came down and called him from the landline."

She had to try to remain calm, but it was difficult. To date Steven Weller was to date Warren Beatty. She was in a constant state of nervous tension. When he left, she often worried he would never come back. He would just pick up a woman more beautiful and cultured, and tell Maddy it was over. He had gone off to D.C. for meetings about Darfur, and when she'd asked to come, he'd said she would be bored. A few times he had taken out Jo alone or with Terry, to Catalina or San Diego, but he hadn't invited her. She hadn't pressed him, but it bothered her that she had never been on the boat.

She often obsessed over the girls who had come before her, like Cady. They were bustier or better in bed. She wanted to be a better lover than every woman he had been with before, and she thought about it during sex, which made her worry more, and that made it hard to relax.

Sometimes she imagined his life with Julia Hanson. Wondered whether what he had said about her was really true, that she would have pulled him into the abyss. Julia's TV show was advertised on billboards all over L.A. Maddy would stare up at Julia in her crisp white pantsuit and wonder what secrets this woman knew about Steven.

"I just need to know that you're loyal," Maddy said in the study, hating the needy pitch of her voice.

"I am loyal," he said in an exhausted tone. "But I'm older than you, and we do things a different way. We don't vomit everything up like your generation."

His tone was hostile and defensive. It reminded her of the arguments she used to have with Dan when he was in a funk about his career and took it out on her.

All this time Steven had seemed too confident to be hypersensitive, but perhaps men were all alike. It was as though Venice had been a hundred years ago. "I'm not asking you to vomit everything up," she said.

He walked over to the couch and sat. The moonlight was flickering on the pool out the window.

She sat in an armchair adjacent to the couch. The study had built-in bookshelves holding dark, monochromatic volumes. On one of the walls was a de Kooning painting of an angry, naked woman. Maddy didn't know if it was original. She wasn't sure how wealthy Steven was and didn't want to be sure. She didn't like the things about him that made him different from her, like his modernist Catalan portraits and antique urns. She liked the things they had in common: his devotion to acting, his attention to scripts, his belief in the power of art.

"I think I'm lonely," she said. "I feel like we're not alone enough."

"We're busy people."

"I'm not busy yet. It seems like every night you're free, we're at an appearance. It makes me worry that I'm not . . . special to you."

He came over to the armchair, got beneath her, and lifted her so she was on his lap. He stroked her hair. "Is that what this is about? How long have you been feeling this way?"

"A while. Don't you want to be with just me sometimes?"

"These commitments are for causes I believe in. But you're right. It's not fair. I haven't made enough room for you."

"I left my whole life for you."

He began to kiss her. You couldn't know, in a relationship, whether you were being lied to, she thought. She had a study, a converted guest room, and she was trying to make it her own, but it wasn't yet. A desk, a chair, some paperbacks, and her books and plays from The New School. She wanted independence, but she didn't escape into it in the middle of the night to take private phone calls or lock things away in drawers. She didn't have drawers with locks. She had a shoe box of mementos given to her by different boyfriends over the years, cigarette-filter flowers; wallet-sized photos of boys, taken in grade school; Valentine's cards. But the box was in storage in Steven's garage, and she hadn't looked at it in years, not until she'd found it in the back of the closet in Fort Greene.

Steven carried her to the desk, so strong, as if she were nothing in his arms, even though she was sturdy and tall. When he touched her like this, there was no frustration, no discord. When he held her, she believed him.

After they finished, he left the room first. Like a dare. She picked up the phone on the desk and placed her finger above the redial button, and then she felt a chill and put the receiver in its cradle.

2

The next morning she woke up alone. Steven had left for his set. The clock said ten-fifteen. Annette was out shopping. The house-keepers didn't come until eleven.

Maddy made herself a cup of coffee, and homemade Greek yogurt with fresh berries and granola, and took it to the patio with that morning's *New York Times*. She flipped through the Arts section, reading play reviews. There was a rave for a new Off-Broadway play about a deaf brick-layer, and Maddy was surprised to see that Irina was in the cast. They had exchanged a few emails after Maddy's move, and then they'd slowed down, and eventually, Irina hadn't written back.

She wasn't in touch with anyone from New York, not in a sustained way. She had heard through Sharoz that Dan had wrapped *The Valentine* and moved to Venice Beach. Sharoz said he was dating Rachel Huber, the executive on *The Valentine*. Maddy wondered if the affair had begun during the shoot but Sharoz said she didn't know.

She had not yet run into him in L.A. and wondered when she would. Though she wasn't sorry their relationship was over, she was nostalgic for the nights they had stayed up late hammering out the story beats. Maybe someday she would collaborate with him again. Ananda McCarthy said Hollywood was like a big summer camp in which exes were constantly forced to work together, making the best of it.

The sun was bright. She could hear a house sparrow. She read the paper and did twenty laps in the pool. She never swam in New York, but now that she lived in a home with a pool, she felt an obligation to take advantage. After one of Maddy's film auditions, Bridget had reported that the casting director had commented she was "healthy." Maddy had been shocked and wounded; in the theater world, they weren't as picky about weight. She was aware that in Los Angeles, the trend was super-slim with fake breasts, but she'd hoped that in the eyes of the casting directors, if not the tabloids, her Special Jury Prize would set its own expectations.

"Do you think I need to lose weight?" Maddy had asked Bridget on the phone.

"It might not be a bad thing for *Husbandry*," she said. "Especially with what Ellie goes through in the movie." In response, Maddy began swimming every day, telling herself it was for wellness, not appearance.

After her swim, she headed inside with the vague plan of taking a yoga class in Santa Monica. No auditions today. She preferred the days when she had them. The days when she didn't feel like a bored housewife, like Ellie in the movie. Alone in the house when Steven was working, she tended to worry, pacing the rooms, leaving him voice mails that said "I love you," that she was embarrassed to have left, taking walks in the neighborhood, then racing home when a paparazzo caught her. She had discovered the Wilshire branch of the public library, one of the few places where no one seemed to know or care who she was. She had been reading for pleasure, a mix of modern fiction and the classics that she felt Steven would want her to read. After finishing *The Portrait of a Lady* (a great hook, a slow middle, and a conclusion too ambiguous for her taste), she had decided to check out *The Wings of the Dove* from the library. But she was making her way through it painstakingly, afraid that Steven's adoration of James might be something she could never completely share.

In the house she started toward the stairs, but when she passed the door to Steven's study, she stopped.

She turned the knob, pushed the door open. She flipped the lights, not wanting to open the drapes in case the housekeepers came early. Though he had a burglar alarm, she had once asked him whether there were hidden video cameras and he'd said only outside the house, not in.

The furniture was all 1930s, shiny blond wood tables with silk skirts. There was a crystal bowl filled with yellow apples and an iron vase with fresh pink azaleas.

She ran her hand across one of the shelves. Eliot, Flaubert, Turgenev, Sand, Proust, Wharton, and James. She examined a copy of *Middlemarch* that appeared unread. She wondered if he kept the books here for show. Clearly, he had read James, whom he quoted often, but she had seldom heard him talk about the others.

She went to the desk and lifted the photo of his mother. She pulled out the key and inserted it in the bottom drawer. Steven would be furious if he found out she was here. She glanced up at the ceiling but saw no camera domes.

The drawer was deep, and when she pulled it open, she found hanging files. Inside them were folders containing receipts, articles on Darfur, Christmas cards from studio executives. Nothing interesting, nothing juicy.

Why would he lock a drawer that had nothing important in it? Maybe he knew she'd seen the open drawer and had moved whatever had been in there. But if that was true, why hadn't he moved the key? Was he taunting her because he suspected she would snoop?

She closed and relocked the drawer, put the key back behind his mother. Shut the lights. She checked the bookshelf one more time to be sure all the books were even, then darted out.

"It's time to tack," Steven was calling. They were aboard *Jo*, on their way to Catalina for a long weekend. He had proposed the trip spontaneously a couple of days after his two A.M. phone call. He was taking time off from *Declarations* just to be with her.

She helped him pull the sail and they ducked as the boom moved. *Jo* was a beauty. White sail. Regal, with two gorgeous cabins and its own showers. Maddy squinted up at the mast, which seemed enormous against the bright sky.

She was sitting across from Steven, her feet propped up next to him. "Okay, your turn," he said.

She took the tiller. "Where are we going?" she asked.

Steven pointed to a distant mound of brown. "Aim for that," he said.

"I've sailed before," she said. She had been on friends' boats on Yarrow Lake in summer, and she'd always enjoyed the thrill of moving fast, as well as the constant work that went with having a boat, the tying and moving and switching sides.

"You haven't told me enough about where you're from. Tell me all about your father."

"People always said we were similar. Whenever he was thinking hard about something, he would run his hands through his hair. Both hands over his head, crossed. I do it, too. It's eerie. He loved the crossword puzzle. He could do it in, like, five minutes. But he also had a really bad temper. He was a complicated guy. Hair-trigger temper, but he wept at Hallmark commercials. He taught me to play chess. He read me *All-of-a-Kind Family*."

"I wish I had met him."

"He would have loved you. He was an English teacher. But he loved mysteries. Total Anglophile. He watched those BBC shows, which was probably why he wanted me to be an actress."

Steven was wearing a blue-and-white-striped button-down shirt, and his hair billowed in the wind, his sunglasses shielding his eyes. This was how she wanted it, away from everyone else. It was what she had missed these months in L.A.

He came to her side, put his arm around her, and raised his sunglasses to the top of his head. "Has any woman loved a man as much as I love you?" she asked.

"Many have asked themselves that very question."

"Shut up," she said, swatting his arm. She closed her eyes and felt the wind on her face. "I wish we could be like this all the time. I feel selfish about you. It can be hard to be your girlfriend, you know. Intelligent, respectable women make eyes at you like teenagers."

"It's the fame. They don't know me. Don't read too much into it."

"Men, too. At these parties, gay men, they look at you and whisper."

"I'm not the only one they whisper about."

"I'm sorry I got so upset the other night," she said.

"I've already forgotten it."

"I shouldn't be so jealous. I'm just getting used to being with you."

"I know you are," he said. "And I don't envy you. There are times I wish I could go back to being Steven Woyceck."

"What do you mean by that?"

"Just be alone, like this, on the water. With someone I love. Not have to worry about long-lens cameras or tabloids or blogs."

She felt a surge of love for him and guilt that she had mistrusted him. She had been brazen the other night. Not believing him. A sophisticated girlfriend wouldn't have harped on him. She wanted to be one of those cool, confident girls who didn't need to pry. She feared that she had soured things between them that night.

"You can be Steven Woyceck with me," she said.

"I want to be."

It had been disingenuous to act like she needed to know everything. He didn't know everything about her. "There's something I want to tell you."

"And what's that?" he asked, positioning his hand over hers on the tiller, adjusting the angle slightly, his eyes on the distant island.

"I was with a woman once."

"Oh yes?" he asked with a smile.

She told him what had happened in Kira's condo at Mile's End. "I feel really weird about it."

"Because it was good?"

"Yeah, and because—I never told Dan. He still doesn't know."

"If I had a cell phone on this boat, you could call him up right now." Steven didn't allow phones on *Jo*; he liked to be at one with the elements. He said there was a radio for emergencies. "I think it's good you experimented," he said. "Sometimes I worry I'm not enough fun for you."

"But you are!"

"I'm not too old?"

"Stop saying that."

He kissed her. She felt safe and invincible against the world.

As they approached Catalina, she started to sing "26 Miles," which she had learned at summer camp. Steven joined in, but their voices were off-key.

That night after hiking, and dining on the island, they made love in the cabin twice. He was so good at touching her; the way he made her come was unlike the way Dan had. He was focused on her, picking up on the tiniest gradations of pleasure. She loved his hands on her, wherever he wanted to put them. Afterward, the boat moved gently in the current. He ran his finger around her nipple and said, "You'd look good nursing."

"How do you know I plan to nurse?"

"You have arms that were made for it. You could hold twins in those guns."

"What about my boobs? You didn't say I had boobs made for nursing."

"I like that they're small. Big ones scare me." He kissed her and pushed her hair from her face. "Do you want kids?" Her body tingled, less at the prospect of being a mother than at the prospect of him loving her enough to make children with her. Which he had never done, not with any woman. "How do you feel about it?"

"Oh, Steven," she said, and began to cry.

He put his thumbs on her cheeks to blot the tears. "If you want to wait, that's okay. If you don't, it's okay. Don't you understand, Maddy? I want to make you happy."

"Do I not seem happy to you?"

"I want you to have whatever you want. Feel taken care of. I want to take care of you, whatever that means to you."

"You do," she said. "You already do."

"So has L.A. gotten the better of you?" Zack asked Maddy on the phone. She had said she was in her car, on the way home from spinning class. He had never imagined her as the type of girl to spin. It was for gerbils.

"I'm not sure what you mean," she said.

"Weekly mani-pedis?"

She laughed. "Only twice a month."

Zack swiveled in his chair and looked up at the painting on the wall behind his desk. He had recently moved into a bigger office, and though it was only slightly larger, it was a symbolic victory. After attending an art opening on Hudson Street with a colleague, he'd sprung for a small painting of a Jewish English boxer from the 1930s, Jack "Kid" Berg. Berg had Hebrew letters on his shorts and was posed formally, fists up, small but tough.

Zack's actors were working consistently, some getting second and third leads in big-budget movies, the kind that garnered entire-paragraph digressions in reviews. Kira had already shot a pretty decent indie drama. For the first time, he was feeling like an agent and not a servicer. But he had called Maddy because an agent had to think constantly of all the clients he was going to sign, not just the ones he already had. If his fervor for her was greater because she was his mother's client, he tried not to think about that.

"You'll go weekly soon," Zack said. "Most *men* in L.A. get their nails done. One of the reasons I can't stand it there. Seriously, how has the transition been?"

"The hardest part is the driving," she said. "The GPS makes it simple, but I have no conceptual sense of the layout. I read Steven's old Thomas Guide at night, and he calls me a Luddite. I tell him I want to have a sense of east and west."

Zack had not been surprised when he'd learned about Maddy and Steven. His mother said the two of them were "blissful," but Bridget massaged the truth for a living. He wondered what Maddy's day-to-day life was like in that creepy mansion, which seemed like the kind of place where you would be murdered in your sleep with a pillow.

"So do you know what second position is?" he asked her.

"No."

"The second-position agent is the one who's waiting in the wings. The one who didn't get the client. I'm yours. Which means you can call me and talk about anything you want, your roles, your jobs, your representation, and I'll listen. You don't have to worry that I'll blab, and I'll always tell you the truth because I don't work for you."

"You mean that the people who do work for me lie to me?"

"Absolutely," he said, running his hand over the surface of his desk. He liked to keep almost nothing on it. He had always been neat, even as a child. When his mother gave him presents, he would fold the opened wrapping paper into squares before giving it to her to throw out.

Work was the most important thing in his life. That wasn't to say he couldn't enjoy other things, like the yoga he took regularly at a studio in Tribeca or the occasional lecture at the Open Center on being present. He wanted to be a good businessman but not a bad person. To that end, he hadn't done coke since he'd been at Mile's End.

Sometimes his mother could be a bad person; as a kid, he'd hear her screaming on the phone, and afterward she would say something innocuous about what she was making for dinner. She was like two different people.

"As second position, I have a question for you," he said to Maddy on the phone. "I was talking to the casting director on *Freda Jansons*, and he said you hadn't come in to read. I was surprised because it seemed right up your alley. They've been searching all over the country. Kira auditioned here. What happened? Did you not like the script?"

"I don't know anything about it. I've never heard of it." Her voice was tinny and afraid.

"It's directed by Tim Heller, who did *Grande Dame*. The screenwriter, Erin Hedges, is going to be one of the top"—he started to say "woman" but stopped himself—"screenwriters in Hollywood in another year or so. It's about an autistic scientist and her relationship with a little boy. Kind of a *Miracle Worker* set in the 'fifties. I couldn't understand why you weren't seen."

"Maybe Bridget's going to send it to me," she offered.

"It's already been cast. Lael Gordinier is Freda."

"What? Well, maybe the problem was Nancy. Maybe she never got the script."

"Nancy had to have gotten it. Everyone saw this." It was exactly as he'd suspected. Bridget was withholding information from her own client. Representatives did it all the time, but not the ones who really cared.

"I'll call Bridget," Maddy said.

"Don't tell her we spoke, okay?"

"Why? You don't want her to know you're trying to get me as a client?"

"No, I don't want her to tell George. You see, I'm helping you, and the number one rule of agenting is 'Don't work for anyone who isn't paying you.'"

It was a lie, of course. Bosses loved employees who wooed clients from rivals. But he wanted to make Maddy feel that he was putting himself out in order to call her. If she did, she might become loyal, and loyalty would get him halfway to his goal.

After Maddy hung up, she couldn't shake the jumpy feeling in her chest. She couldn't fathom why Bridget hadn't told her about such an important role. Wasn't Bridget's whole job to be her client's eyes and ears?

She tried Nancy first. "What can I do for you, Maddy?" she asked. They had seen each other only a few times since Mile's End; most of their interaction was by phone. Nancy had a well-modulated voice, like the ones you heard on yogurt commercials.

"What do you mean you never read it?" Nancy asked after Maddy told her.

"I just heard about it now, from a friend. Steven doesn't like me reading the trades."

"I sent it to Bridget, God, it must have been last month. I can look it up. She said you loved it, but it conflicted with *Husbandry*. I'm sorry for any miscommunication." This was a classic Hollywood coping mechanism, Maddy had learned. CYA. Cover your ass. She couldn't tell whether Nancy was being honest and it occurred to her that she might need a new agent. But before she could make a decision like switching agencies she needed to know what Bridget had to say.

"Honey, I didn't send it because the shooting dates conflicted with your commitment to Walter's film," Bridget said.

"But maybe we could have figured it out. I mean, at least if I'd seen it."

"Not really. You had signed the contract by the time I got the script."

"Can't contracts be broken?"

"No, it's more difficult that you would think. Look, the last thing in the world I want is for you to dwell on this. There will always be projects you lose because you're too busy. Hollywood history is made on the basis of who's available when. Frank Sinatra almost played Dirty Harry. And Steve McQueen was going to be Butch Cassidy."

"That makes me feel worse. Lael Gordinier might make history doing that role, and I didn't get a chance to go in."

"You'll make history doing *Husbandry*."

"Why did you lie to Nancy?"

"Huh?"

"Why did you tell Nancy I loved the script when you knew I hadn't read it?"

Bridget had handled these situations before. The key was to be calm and never admit you'd done something wrong. "Honey, I just didn't want to get into it with her. I'm sorry. I was only trying to protect you from being disappointed. One thing you should understand is that you can't be two places at once."

"Don't lie to my agent, Bridget. And don't hide scripts from me. Are we clear?"

"Of course."

Maddy hung up feeling uneasy. She wanted to trust Bridget, she had to, but this was not the kind of thing a manager was supposed to do. Especially not in the beginning. Bridget had encouraged her to do the psychological thriller and then *Jen,* and both had worked out well. Now she wasn't sure she had an ally. She thought she heard a call coming in on the dashboard phone, but it was only a horn beeping from far away.

As she and Steven were lying in bed reading, she told him she'd heard "from a girl I see at auditions" that Tim Heller was casting a movie called *Freda Jansons,* and Bridget hadn't sent her the script because her *Husbandry* contract was signed. "I thought a manager was supposed to relay all the phone calls," Maddy said.

"Bridget knew you were booked," he said. "I was with her when she got the call. She had the executed contracts in front of her."

"Why couldn't I delay?"

"We don't want to hold up Walter. He's taking a gamble on you. Delays can be more dangerous to the actor than the director."

"You mean he would fire me, when he's been trying to cast Ellie for a year?"

"Bridget's not perfect," he said. "We've had our conflicts, but don't dwell on this. She only wants the best for you." He closed the script he was reading, a much buzzed-about drama about the 1968 New York City teachers' strike. "One thing you have to get used to is that it's impossible to be two places at once."

"That's exactly what she said."

When Maddy walked into the restaurant in West Hollywood, for a moment she didn't recognize him. The man waiting for her at the table was so tan and muscular, his hair grown out, his biceps visible in his T-shirt, that she thought he was an actor. But then he waved eagerly, and she realized it was Dan. As they hugged, she said, "You look fantastic."

He had called to ask her to breakfast, saying he wanted to catch up. "Thanks," he said. "This climate's actually good for me, despite everything I thought about L.A. before."

"So what have you been doing to get this buff?" she asked.

"Well, surfing."

"You? Surfing?"

"I know. I go to San Onofre. I have all these new buddies. I feel like, if I made the choice to live here, I should take advantage of the the water and get in shape."

She thought about her own nascent L.A. social life—Ananda McCarthy's friends, mostly ex-models and ex-actresses. All of them had used their looks and sexuality to get money, jobs, or men. Most were housewives, with full-time nannies. Maddy felt young around them and bored by their anecdotes. She wondered if Dan's surfing buddies were real friends.

"You look like you've lost weight," he said. "Please don't tell me you've been dieting." Through yoga and swimming, Maddy had dropped from a size ten to a size six. "Just eating better. I want to be a little smaller for *Husbandry*."

"Don't get too small."

They ordered food, and before it came, he reached for her hand on the table. "Mad," he said. "I'm sorry about those emails I sent when you were in Venice."

"It's okay. It was sudden. You were angry. You don't have to apologize." Delicately, she moved her hand away, not wanting there to be any ambiguity. This was a friendly coffee, not a relapse date. Since Catalina, she and Steven had been making love at least once a day, even on nights when they came home late from events. She had decided that the key to her happiness was to trust him and give him his space. When she did that, he was not only warmer but hornier, which made her more confident and certain of his love.

"I want you to know that I forgive you," Dan said.

"Uh-oh," she said with a smile. "Did you join A.A.? Are you doing the steps?"

"No, but I started therapy. I've been seeing a female shrink who's helped me a lot."

Watching her swirl her spoon in her coffee, Dan couldn't believe how much he had hated her once. For months he had been furious, convinced that she was a sellout. In his bleaker moments, he had told himself the online rumors were true: She had been offered a contract to become Weller's wife and draw attention away from the fact that he was gay: $1 million a year, with a five-year minimum and a $1 million bonus for each baby.

But even if he believed such contracts existed, he couldn't believe that Maddy would agree to such a thing. She had too much pride. And too much craft, as she would call it. She never would take money to be a prop.

More recently, he had come over to the less interesting, more depressing version of the story, the one that Rachel favored: Steven was straight and Maddy loved him but had subconsciously chosen him because he could help her career. Dan couldn't blame her. On the screen, she was a natural. He had been a yutz for not casting her in one of his films before. He had told himself it would harm their relationship to collaborate—but it was mainly a cover for his fear. He had been afraid that if he put her in a movie, she would overshadow him.

If Maddy was with Steven for her career, then she was no more cynical than most people he had met in L.A. Everyone in the entertainment industry was an opportunist; they all just had different standards for how far they would go. He was an opportunist for taking the directing job in Sofia, and for dating Rachel Huber—even though the sex was only so-so, and she was too svelte for his taste—because he felt she could get him more jobs with Worldwide Films.

"Anyway," Dan continued, "I spent all this time being angry with you. But now I understand that . . . we love who we love."

"That's true," she said.

The food came—she got a spinach-and-goat-cheese omelet and he got oatmeal, both of them so healthy now—and they talked about her recent acting jobs. He said she'd been right about *The Valentine* being a bad script, but he expected it to do well at the box office because of its stars. He was renting in Venice Beach and doing the color correction on *I Used to Know Her*, and he said it was going to be really good when it came out. "But honestly," he said, "even if all it does is earn back the advance, I'll be fine with that. Even if it plays a couple weeks, then dies."

She was surprised to hear him say this. The movie had been his heart and soul, and now he didn't care how it did? "You don't want it to die," she said.

"No, I want you to get good reviews. And Kira. But I've moved on from it. It was a stepping-stone. Now I'm ready for studio jobs."

This was the opposite of the Dan Ellenberg she once knew. "You don't want to alternate—one for you, one for them, one for you?"

"It's funny you should say that. I've been thinking about *The Nest* lately."

"Are you working on it by yourself?" She hadn't thought about the script in months. The part of her that had written *I Used to Know Her* with Dan seemed so young. When she remembered writing it, she had to think about the breakup, which made her feel guilty.

"Sort of. I showed it to this screenwriter buddy of mine. His name's Oded Zalinsky. He wrote *Hazing*." He coughed a little into his napkin. "And *Butterface*."

Maddy had not seen either one, but the posters had been enough for her. They were misogynistic screeds about idiotic horndogs. "Why would you show *The Nest* to Oded Zalinsky? It's a subtle, feminist, character comedy."

"He was over at my place, and I mentioned the script, and he said he wanted to read it. He went crazy for it. I mean, he was so impressed by what we came up with. The idea of a girl who loves her parents more than she loves her boyfriend. So he and I were just riffing, kind of spitballing, and we reconceived it as a more adult comedy. A relationship comedy. With a male lead instead of female. He wants to collaborate with me on it, cowrite it, because he already has a vision for how he would direct it. But because you and I had started working on it together . . . um. It's a little complicated." He took something out of his jeans pocket and handed it to her.

"What is this?"

"Kind of a release. Basically, it says that for a small consideration, you'll let me do whatever I want with *The Nest*."

"I don't understand." She scanned the page. She saw the phrases "all of my rights of every kind throughout the universe in and to the Work" and "sum of one dollar." She lifted her head slowly. "You want me to give up my rights to *The Nest* for a dollar?"

"Well." He coughed again. "It sounds like you're focusing more on acting these days, and there's no use having those pages just sit there. I didn't think you'd care about the money since, you know . . . Steven . . . This way Oded and I can take the grain of the story, the concept, and develop something new from it, without having to worry if you'll—"

"Sue you?" So this was what their friendly breakfast was all about. It was sneaky to do it here, one-on-one, instead of through her manager or lawyer. Dan had been trying to appeal to her nostalgia, her affection for him, all to get her to give up her intellectual property.

She had a copy of *The Nest* on her laptop but never looked at it. If he had rewritten it without consulting her and the movie had come out, she wouldn't have sued; at least she didn't think so. But he had played his hand. Dan had always been a terrible businessman.

"I have to show this to my attorney," she said.

"Oh, sure," he said, swallowing some water. "No problem."

"And I'm sure he's going to say no way."

Dan nodded and chewed his lip, which he always did when he was chagrined. She'd been feeling generous toward him, like maybe he still understood her, but he'd just wanted something for nothing. For a buck.

They were quiet, looking down into their bottomless coffees. Finally, she said, "I guess we've both gone totally Hollywood, huh?"

"Why is that?"

"We get together for the first time since we broke up, and you ask me to relinquish my rights."

3

It was two weeks into the *Husbandry* shoot, and Maddy was removing her costume in her dressing room. It had been a long day. She had shot a difficult sex scene with Steven. She had been nervous at first, but because the sex was meant to be bad, she was able to focus on her character, so it went relatively smoothly. It turned out it was easy to play bad sex.

Which was why she was nervous about the next day's call sheet: good sex. She would be doing her first bedroom scene with Billy Peck, the English actor playing Paul. Bridget would be there, with the skeleton crew: Walter; Jimmy, the director of photography; and Stu, the boom operator. Wardrobe would be supplying Maddy with a nude-colored G-string, a nude bandeau, and her merkin, which had been dyed to match her own pubic hair.

There was a knock. "Just a minute!" She hung up her dress and put on a robe.

Walter. He came to her dressing room from time to time to talk about Ellie, and he had a playful Platonic style. He was a sharp observer, which gave her confidence that in his hands, she would give her best performance. There were times he could be difficult, though. He would stand on her mark and pantomime: "Do not scratch your nose like this. Do it like this!" But she respected his desire to have things be just so; in film, the director had to be a dictator.

He was wearing a white linen shirt, unbuttoned farther than usual. "May I come in?" he asked, though he was already in the room. She had decorated it with photographs of her parents and postcards of Jim

Jarmusch, Liz Phair, John Garfield, and Eleonora Duse, the great Italian stage actress known for blushing on cue. Even with the attempts to personalize it, the room still felt too fancy and too generic.

Walter sat on one of the couches. "You were excellent today," he said. She sat on the opposite couch, pulling her robe more tightly around her body. She should have dressed before she answered the door but had been expecting a wardrobe girl. "I am proud of the work you have been doing," Walter went on. "It has great integrity. I could tell when you wept that you weren't afraid to be ugly."

From anyone else, she would have taken it as an insult. From Walter, she didn't. She was ugly when she cried; most people were. It was the chaos taking over the face. He spread his knees and leaned forward. "What's amazing to me is that you carry yourself with no awareness. Most beautiful women know it from an early age, and it ruins them. You carry yourself like someone who doesn't turn heads."

This was the longest conversation they'd had alone. "Steven has excellent taste," Walter continued, gazing distantly toward Maddy's picture window, the one that overlooked Woodmere's Victorian gardens, which were often used for period films. Woodmere was the famous postwar soundstage where they were shooting the film, half an hour from London. "What a refined man. He has great appreciation for attractive things. And yet I wonder whether he appreciates you the way he should."

Not sure where he was going with this line of talk, she stood and walked to the window. She looked out at the gardens. "Walter, is this about the scene tomorrow?" she asked, keeping her back turned.

"You are a young woman," he said from the couch. "You have a promising road ahead of you professionally and personally. If you'll forgive my playing for a moment the role of sage old man, you'll let me give you a piece of advice. A woman's job is to be where she's most appreciated."

Be where she's most appreciated? He was trying to get inside her skull by maligning her boyfriend. Didn't he see how counterproductive it was? "Steven appreciates me," she said, spinning around to face him, "if that's what you're trying to—"

"Not in the way you think he does." He stood and moved to the other side of the window so he was facing her. "You may love him," he said, enunciating carefully, "but I can say with confidence that he does not love you."

He took a few steps toward her, his hands extended, and she jumped back. "Walter!"

His face seemed to soften, and after a moment he retreated. "I am so sorry, my dear. I do not know what came over me. I feel protective of you, but sometimes I am not the best communicator." He moved swiftly to the door, and it closed behind him without a sound.

As she went to the town house in the chauffeured car, she kept hearing Walter's words. The most logical explanation was that he was trying to make her vulnerable for her lovemaking scene with Billy. Nicholas Ray had famously manipulated James Dean and Sal Mineo by whispering "He hates you" to each of them on the set of *Rebel*.

Or maybe Walter was just an old man who didn't get that younger American actors worked differently from older ones, and liked their sets PC, their boundaries clear. He probably didn't remember half the things that came out of his mouth. The entire moment could have been chalked up to senility.

But it irritated her that Walter had known Steven longer than she had, that he had visited Palazzo Mastrototaro several times. Steven had said that he and Walter were not friends but friendly, and yet she couldn't shake the fear that Walter knew something about him that she didn't: There was another woman in his life. Cady. Or Albertina. Maybe the person on the phone that night; she still didn't completely believe it was Vito. Or someone else, some English model whom he visited in the black of night while she slept. Maybe Walter knew, and like a grandfather, he had been warning her not to trust him. Just because Walter seemed crazy didn't mean he didn't speak the truth.

The Regent's Park town house rental was furnished in a sleek, luxurious style, with views of the park's rowing pond, but because of the paparazzi, Steven and Maddy never opened the drapes. She was even less at home there than she was in Hancock Park, where at least she was beginning to build up things of her own, clothes and music and books.

At dinner that night, Maddy picked listlessly at her paella; Annette had come with them to London for the duration of the shoot. She wanted to ask Steven what Walter might have meant by his comment, but she was afraid he'd get angry with Walter and disrupt the production. Either logical interpretation of Walter's words was discomfiting: Walter believed Steven was unfaithful, or Walter had been trying to seduce her.

"Are you nervous about tomorrow?" Steven asked, as though reading her mind, swirling his glass of Bordeaux. He liked red wines all year, even in summer.

She was terrified. As a producer, Steven would be in the production office while they were shooting, but she didn't want him to come to set, and she didn't know how to tell him. She would be fucking another man all day. "A little. It'll probably be the longest stretch of time I've ever spent naked," she said, forcing a smile, "except for Venice, with you."

"I wouldn't have wanted you in this if it were exploitative," he said.

That night in bed, long after he had fallen asleep beside her, she tossed and turned. *He does not love you.* There was someone else in Steven's life. Walter's eerie pronouncement was keeping her awake, the night before the most important day in the shoot.

It was two in the morning. She went into the bathroom to fetch her anti-anxiety pills and deposited two under her tongue.

Before they had left L.A., Maddy had gotten a bad cough, and Ananda had recommended her general practitioner, who turned out to be a dashing Frenchman named Thierry Chataigne. (Steven didn't trust doctors and didn't have a general physician of his own.) Dr. Chataigne had diagnosed Maddy with bronchitis and put her on antibiotics. A few days later, after a bout of insomnia brought on by the missing *Freda Jansons* script, she'd made an appointment and he'd prescribed her lorazepam, the same drug that Dr. Larson Wells in Fort Greene had given her after her father's death. She had brought the pills to London but hidden them from Steven, who would disapprove. He didn't even take Advil for a headache. She didn't like the idea of relying on them, either, but she had to work in the morning, and if she could not sleep, she could not deliver.

The pills under her tongue, she went back to bed. She'd had intermittent insomnia as a child. She would become anxious for no reason, then fixate on lying awake. This would go on for two or three hours, and she would go into her father's room and stare at him sleeping, envying him. Sometimes she'd wake him and he would take her into her room and rub her back until she drifted off. On the soft sheets in Regent's Park, the lorazepam began to work, and she fell into a dreamless sleep.

In the cafeteria at Woodmere, Maddy took a bowl of Irish oatmeal and milk. Usually, she ate at home, but today she wanted the extra time to get her thoughts in order. She had driven over with Steven, who had kissed her on the cheek and gone into the office.

Walter sat next to her and asked how she was feeling. "Like I'm at the ob-gyn's waiting room," she said, casting her food aside.

"We'll get through it."

"Where's Billy?"

She heard a voice over her shoulder. "I was just having a session with my fluffer," Billy said.

She liked working with Billy. He was cute, with reddish hair, and friendly, and so far didn't seem like a diva. She had been attracted to him when Steven first introduced them at a premiere in L.A. She had felt it at rehearsal and in the cafeteria and at the first table read, and she had been telling herself the attraction was good because of the plot. He was wearing a blue oxford shirt with the collar cut off. "Have you done any sex scenes before?" he asked her, plopping down beside her.

"Yes, just one. It was a really low-budget shoot, and we didn't have any merkins."

"You'll be fine. It's the first that's the most painful. Just like life." He was staying in his American accent around the clock, and when he spoke, the R's were harder than they should have been.

On the bedroom set, Jimmy was behind the camera. The set had a New England feel, with wainscoting and Shaker furniture. Out the windows were flats of green mountains. It was deliberately fake, Juhasz's stylized idea of small-town American life.

"Have a seat, my pets," Walter said.

"When he said 'pets,' he was talking about my balls," Billy said. Maddy elbowed him hard.

"This is the most important scene in the film," Walter said. "We must believe that Paul and Ellie are meant for each other. The sexual chemistry must be otherworldly."

"All my sex is otherworldly," Billy said.

In the scene, Ellie and Paul stumble up to the bedroom. From there, Walter's stage directions read:

```
They kiss as they move into the bedroom. Paul kneels by
the bed and puts his hand on Ellie's breast. She unbut-
tons her blouse and removes her bra. He puts his mouth
on her nipple. She unbuckles his pants, holds him. He
pulls her skirt off. Eats her. She cums. He mounts her.
She raises her legs to her ears and then moves to ride
him. He lifts her in the air. She maintains her mount.
She cums again. He explodes.
```

Maddy had been uncomfortable with Walter's spelling of "cum" when she first read the screenplay but had figured Walter was trying to show that the sex needed to feel real, and hot, and urgent. "So here's how we're going to work," Walter said. "We'll rehearse it once. I'll tell you how to move. You'll both be dressed. This is just for the blocking, for camera. I want you to kiss. Everything else, you can suggest."

Suggest. The death knell to the actor. Often "suggesting" was more uncomfortable than doing it. Bridget had come to the set and was standing near Walter. "The two of you will enter the room here," Walter went on, indicating the door. "You'll be kissing while you enter. Maddy, you'll come in first, your back to the camera. So—just go for it."

Billy and Maddy stood on the other side of the door and closed it. "Action on rehearsal," Walter called. Billy leaned in and kissed her. It felt illicit because no one could see them doing it.

She hadn't expected him to use tongue. His kiss was different from Steven's, so much more welcoming. It was strange to be kissing Billy when Steven was in the building, a few hundred feet away. What if he had sneaked onto the closed set? The PAs wouldn't stop him. But there was no time to worry, because Billy was pivoting her so her back was to the door, and then he pushed it open, moving with her into the room.

They shot the scene over several hours, in portions and out of sequence. Shortly before the lunch break, Walter began to get frustrated with her. She wasn't sure what she was doing wrong, but he kept saying the sex felt "stagy." He sat on the bed and said to Maddy, "I want you to play more. Not so serious. We need this to feel spontaneous, the first good sex she's ever had. This time keep going until I say 'Cut.' We'll get out before your first orgasm."

"That's always a good idea," Billy piped up.

They got into position. Walter called action. Billy's hands were rough on her nipples. She didn't want to be responding, but she was, her nipples perking up. For this angle she was wearing the merkin, and he had on a nude jock cup, and as she rode the cup, she realized she was wet.

She rocked above Billy and saw something new on his face: surprise. Did he know? She had always heard that sex scenes weren't sexy, but this *was* sexy, and maybe all sex scenes were, and she was conscious of the muscles on Billy's body. Remembering Walter's direction to keep going, she tilted her head, leaned down, and kissed Billy. Her tongue entwined with his. She was not herself, she was Ellie with Paul, and she had been unhappy in her marriage, and now this frightening man was making her feel things she hadn't felt. They kept going, simulating the sex, and she wasn't sure whether to continue, but it was a no-no to cut before the director did, so she kept riding Billy and she pretended to come, her back arching, her nipples exposed and alert, her mouth widening as Ellie cried out.

Finally, she heard "Cut." She pulled up the covers. A wardrobe girl handed her the robe, and she slipped into it and sat on the bed.

Walter approached the two of them, a strange smile on his face. "Did you not hear me?" he asked Maddy.

"What do you mean?"

"I said 'Cut' a few minutes ago."

"No!" Maddy spun to Billy. "Did you hear it?"

"Yeah," he said. "But when you didn't, I figured Walter would probably want us to keep going."

"Bridget, did you hear?" she called.

Bridget nodded. "It's okay," she said. "That was the best one." Maddy couldn't believe she'd been so wrapped up in the scene that she'd lost her hearing, lost her sense of space.

"Please do not be embarrassed," Juhasz said. "It's good that you continued. You two were electric."

Alone in her dressing room, she sat in a daze. She was not the kind of actress to lose her senses in performance. During plays she would hear sneezes, candy wrappers. She was always aware of her surroundings even in the moment. It was as though they had played a monstrous trick on her, wanting to embarrass her.

Steven worked late at Woodmere that night, a production meeting involving Bridget, Walter, and other key staff members. She crossed paths with him a few times, but he said he didn't have time to talk.

When he arrived in the town house bedroom past midnight, he undressed silently, turning his back to Maddy. She put her hand on his shoulder and he jumped. "What is it?" she asked.

"I saw the dailies," he said.

"Yes?"

"I could hear Walter saying 'Cut,' and you kept going. You were overheated to the point of deafness."

"I was acting. It's what I do."

"You looked unprofessional."

"I was just in the scene. You have to get past it, Steven. There's a week more of sex scenes to go."

"And I'm sure you're looking forward to them."

"What's that supposed to mean?"

"Are you attracted to him?"

"He's a good-looking guy. But I'm in love with you."

"Maybe you should be with Billy instead of me."

"I don't know what you're saying." Out of all people, he had to understand what it was like to do a sex scene. "Come on, Steven. I shouldn't have to explain this."

"You disrespected me." His lips were thin and old and she could see the shine on the lower one as she had at the Entertainer, when Kira postulated about his sexuality.

"Why are you being like this?"

"Because I care! You should know that jealousy is a sign of that. You said it on Torcello."

"I know, but there's nothing to be jealous of here—"

"Why did you do this to me?" His jealousy was so insecure and boyish. It wasn't befitting of a powerful man. It seemed almost like an act. "Your only job was to get through the day professionally. And you failed."

She dashed into one of the guest rooms and she sobbed into a pillow. She had imagined him leaving her many times, but not because she had performed too well in a role. Now he was going to end it, and when people asked what had happened, she would have to answer, "I didn't hear Walter Juhasz call, 'Cut.'" And they would laugh.

The irony was that she had no desire to be unfaithful. Their sex life was great, attentive, and playful. For a middle-aged man, his appetite was big; he was always hard and ready to go a second time. He said no other woman had turned him on this much. Whatever attraction she had to Billy, she didn't want to act on it. The arousal had been chemical.

After she had finally stopped crying, she went downstairs, got her cell phone, and took it back into the guest room, closing the door. She held the phone in her hand as though not sure whom to call, but she knew she was tricking herself.

"Hi," she said when Dan answered, and her voice must have been sniffly, because he said, "Are you okay?"

"Yeah. It was just a hard shooting day. I'm under too much stress, I think."

"What happened?"

"Steven got jealous after a sex scene."

"That's moronic," Dan said.

"It was maybe too much for him. It wouldn't have been as bad if he weren't producing."

She fluffed up some pillows behind her head, remembering the long phone calls she and Dan used to have at the beginning, when he was courting her, when she fell asleep with the phone in her hand, or he did. "Are you sure you're okay?" he said.

"I guess it's a lot at once. First movie, starring opposite Steven, tons of sex. If it were one of the three, it would be enough."

"I'm sure he'll get over his jealousy," he said. "He's a professional."

"Anyway," she said, "tell me what's going on with you. Are you in Savannah?" She had read in the trades that he'd signed on for another romantic weepie, *The Inscription*, also produced by Worldwide Films.

"Yeah," he said. "It's actually crazy that you caught me. I'm on a break right now."

"I should let you go," she said.

"No, I'm glad you called," he said. "I thought we might be communicating through lawyers from now on."

After her ill-fated coffee with Dan in the spring, she had taken the *Nest* assignment of rights to Edward Rosenman, who had worked out a collaboration agreement with Dan's lawyer, the one he had hired after he fired the one who drafted the assignment. She would get costory credit on any version of *The Nest* that got made, and a third of any purchase price. She felt that the deal was fair to generous, but worried that Dan felt she had been greedy.

"No need to," she said. "We came to terms. Did you guys finish the screenplay?"

"We're getting really close."

"Do you have a new title?"

"Yes, but it's not locked, so I'm going to keep it secret."

"Never say 'locked,' " she said. "You sound like a real operator."

"Never say 'operator.' You sound like you're in a Rosalind Russell movie."

"Right now I wish I was in a Rosalind Russell movie."

"Good luck with the sex," he said. "And tell Steven he's not allowed to give you a hard time about fake coitus. The guy's fake slept with hundreds of women." After they got off the phone, she cradled it in her hand as if Dan were still there.

———

"I told you she was young," Steven said. He and Bridget were walking side by side in the gardens of Woodmere.

"You're making too much of it," Bridget said, removing a silver cigarette case from her purse. She lit the cigarette and blew the smoke out of her nose.

"How could she do that? 'Cut,' 'cut,' and 'cut' again. Even Billy didn't break."

"He was going along with the scene."

"I can't have these shenanigans on my film."

"Are you taking care of her the way you should be?" she asked. They had stopped at a fountain. In the center was a naked girl with no arms, water spitting out of her mouth.

"Everything is fine in that department. Better than fine."

"I'm taking your word for that," Bridget said, "but put yourself in her position anyway. She's without her family, without friends, carrying the movie. This is an incredibly masochistic role. And you're her support system. When she comes home at night, she needs to be taken care of, like a princess. Bathed, massaged, loved. Rise above this. Remember how old you are and the things you've seen."

He thought about her words, angry at what she was implying. If the sex with Maddy wasn't nightly, it was often. It was difficult for him at times to satisfy her. She wanted it every day. He was not a young man. And the pills, he didn't like what they did to his system. He didn't like taking pills for anything. The congestion, which lasted until the next day and affected his vocal style, his adenoids. He had his own needs, the responsibilities of producing, and his lines and scenes, his body and health. He didn't have time to take care of her the way Bridget was suggesting.

"Is it possible she's the wrong girl?" he asked.

"What do you mean?"

"It's not too late. There might be other girls who would come with fewer . . . hairs."

"She is the one," Bridget said. "Just be a good partner. And keep Billy at arm's length. No socializing outside of production."

"We haven't. He's never been over."

"Well, keep it that way. We don't want life to start imitating art."

"But it already has," he said.

For the next few days, Steven was on set during Maddy and Billy's sex scenes, making everyone else miserable. He would have long conferences with Bridget and Walter while Maddy and Billy sat around in their robes. The tension between Steven and Walter rose with each hour. Billy told Maddy privately that she needed to take control of Steven because he was turning *Husbandry* into an unhappy production.

One morning Maddy came downstairs to find Steven at the dining table, a half-eaten omelet beside him, the *Daily Mail* on the table. The headline was "MORE THAN JUST A PECK?" There was a shot of Maddy talking closely with Billy near the gate of Woodmere. Their heads were angled so it looked like they were kissing, though in reality, they had been two feet away from each other.

> According to a source close to the production of *Husbandry*, Maddy Freed has been stepping out on Hollywood hunk Steven Weller with her costar Billy Peck. "Billy and Maddy got overheated during one of their scenes and started an affair," said the source.
>
> Weller is a producer on the film and plays Freed's husband. According to the source, "Steven wants to fire him, but Walter loves the chemistry between Maddy and Billy." Ironically, *Husbandry* focuses on a woman who begins cheating on her husband with his brother.

"Oh God," Maddy said. "How can they print lies like that?"

"They do it all the time." He was looking at her as though some part of him believed she was having an affair.

"What does Bridget say?" she asked.

"Bridget says we ignore it. That it'll die. But I think she's wrong. This is why I wanted you to be professional. You gave them an opening."

"It's not my fault! You're playing a cuckold. Of course they're going to gossip."

"I think this was Walter," he said, frowning over the newspaper. "It wouldn't be Stu or Jimmy. Walter planted this to draw publicity to the film." She didn't think Walter was capable of it. He wouldn't play games with the press.

The rest of the week, Steven was even more hostile to Walter. There were long producer meetings and whispered conferences among Steven, Bridget, and Walter, usually after scenes involving Billy and Steven. Crew members stormed off. Jimmy snapped at his guys. Everyone was abusing someone else; it was a classic example of the mood flowing from the top down.

Maddy was anxious about her ability to work with Steven over the next five weeks, much less live with him. They had most of their Ellie-Louis scenes left to shoot.

The paparazzi, already irritants, seemed to get worse. Each morning she found a new story in the tabloids open on the dining table. "Billy and Maddy Planning to Elope," "Maddy Expects Bundle of Joy—But Who's the Daddy?," and "Steven to Maddy: 'End It Or Else!' " Steven took long phone calls from his publicist, Flora, strategizing about how to respond. One piece had "someone close to Mr. Weller" saying Steven was gay and not having sex with Maddy, that she had fallen into Billy's arms due to sexual frustration. Each piece enraged him further. She was surprised that after all these years, he was paying so much attention to the tabloids.

In bed one night, Maddy was going over her lines while Steven thumbed through a book about the Malaparte house on Capri. "I think you have to be nicer to Walter," Maddy said.

He shut the book and regarded her, his face tortured and white. "Don't tell me what to do."

"I've overheard the crew. They think you're crazy."

"They can think whatever they want. I can fire all of them." He had drunk three glasses of whiskey at dinner.

"Is there a reason these stories are getting to you like this?"

"Yes, because they're insulting."

"And that's it?"

"I don't know what you're talking about."

"Have you ever experimented with men?"

He licked his lips. She had never seen him look at her so coldly. "This is some weird obsession with you. Why do you keep asking me? For God's sake, do you not think I'm attracted to you?"

"No, I mean, I know you are, of course you are, but the article that said I'm having an affair with Billy because you don't satisfy me—I thought maybe you've had gay experiences, and that's why these articles get under your skin."

"They get under my skin because they're not true and people read them and think that they are."

"I want you to know that if you've been with a guy, you can tell me. I told you about Kira. I believe sexuality is a spectrum, and—"

"Why would you think I was with men?"

"You did repertory theater."

"It's not my thing. I'm sorry if that makes me less exciting to you." He lifted his book in front of his face and the red lettering of MALAPARTE seemed to blink at her to stay away.

A week after the first item appeared, Billy, Steven, and Maddy were doing a scene where Louis tells Paul he has to move out. They did three takes, and after each one, Walter directed Steven to be calmer. "You are not the powerful person in the scene," Walter said. "When you tell him to move, it brings you pain."

Steven did it again, and Walter gave another version of the same direction. On the seventh take, Walter called, "Cut," then said to Steven, "It appears you are not listening to a word I am saying. I do not know if you are deaf or merely obstinate. Stop trying to prove your masculinity. This is a film set, not your life."

Before Maddy was fully aware of what was happening, Steven had lunged for Walter, and Walter was on the floor, screaming, "You're crazy!" and bleeding from his nose. Two crew members restrained Steven, though he was making no attempt to land another punch, while another rushed to take care of Walter.

Walter tried to sit up but couldn't move. The second AD and a couple of PAs were dabbing at his face. Someone called for medical help. Walter had never looked so frail. Maddy could not believe her boyfriend had slugged a septuagenarian.

The first AD announced a ten-minute break and, at the end of it, knocked on Maddy's dressing room door to say they were wrapping for the day. She realized she didn't need to go home and wait for Steven to return. She decided to see a movie.

The cabdriver let her off at the Curzon Mayfair. She didn't care what she saw, she just wanted to be in the dark. They were showing *The Apartment* with Jack Lemmon and Shirley MacLaine.

One of the reasons Maddy loved *The Apartment* was that it was about a person without morality finding morality. As she sat there watching the film, the first she had been to alone since before she met Steven, she imagined a life without him.

She would get through it. They would complete *Husbandry*, both of them too professional to sabotage the film because of a breakup. She would rent a modest flat, finish the shooting, and move back to New York. Or she could stay in L.A. and try to capitalize on the connections she'd made so far. It might be harder than it had been lately, as Steven Weller's girlfriend, but it had been hard before, in New York, and she hadn't given up. Maybe she could move back to New York.

Outside the cinema, she kept her head low and walked a few blocks unnoticed. She had turned off her phone. She went inside a pub, ordered a pint, and found a table in the back, taking a deep pull.

She wouldn't stay with a rage-filled man. If they built a life together, inevitably, there would be disagreements, but she could not live with someone who hurled words at her unfairly, who made her feel flattened and worthless. His anger was like that lightning cloud rising above the dome in *La Tempesta*.

Maybe she had made a terrible mistake in leaving Dan for Steven. She had been so hasty to tell herself, and Irina, that it was love. It had been love, but she was also Steven's fan, as she had been since she was a girl. Just because you admired someone didn't mean he was your soul mate.

She bought another pint and realized she could not remember the last time she had gone to a bar and had a drink by herself. What an easy pleasure. In L.A. she was often alone at home, but rarely alone in the world.

After she finished her beers, she got the idea to go to a fancy restaurant. She took a cab and walked into one unannounced, but the hostess recognized her right away and she was taken to a table tucked into a back corner. She had been eating carefully throughout production but one decadent meal would make no difference. She ordered a seven-course dinner that included lobster and salmon ravioli, foie gras, and suckling pig. There was beautiful deliberation in every course, and she sat and enjoyed her food and the fame by association that had allowed her to walk into a three-star Michelin restaurant without a reservation. When the meal was over, she paid with her own credit card and not Steven's.

By the time she got back to the house, it was dark. The bedroom was empty, but the light was on in Steven's study. She brushed her teeth, changed into an oversize New School shirt, and got under the covers.

Steven came in and lay next to her. "Where did you go?" he asked. "I was worried."

"It doesn't matter." He seemed about to say something, but his face was pained and feminine and nothing came out. "I was appalled by what you did today," she said.

"I was, too," he said quietly.

"Even if Walter was goading you, what you did was unconscionable. He's an old man. You're rude and hateful. Is that who you really are?"

"No, no, it's not."

"You're like a different person. You know I'm not sleeping with Billy. If I were going to cheat on you, do you think I would do it with my costar, on the set of a film we're both in, that you're producing?"

"I know you're not having an affair."

"Then why are you treating me like this? If this is what you want, some kind of sadomasochistic relationship, I'm the wrong girl for you. This doesn't turn me on. I don't hate myself that much."

He nodded, sat up against the headboard, and folded his hands in his lap. "I don't think you hate yourself at all."

"Maybe we jumped into this whole thing too fast. We don't really know each other."

"Maddy," he said, looking afraid.

"Maybe it's better to break up now. Before it gets more complicated. I can't be with someone who treats me like shit."

"I don't want you to go. I'm so sorry I've been cruel to you. The way I've been treating you—it's not right. Please don't leave me. I promise you, it's going to be different." He was weeping, and the tears seemed so genuine and pained, it made her think the tears in *Beirut Nights* had been real, too. "I can't lose you."

She pitied him a bit. Who was this small, crying man? What had made him turn from a monster into a trembling boy? She couldn't tell if he'd been acting before or was acting now, or if he knew the difference. She thought Steven Weller might be a better actor in real life than in his films.

"I want you to stop," she said. "Be the old Steven again, the man I fell in love with."

He kissed her face and neck. "I love you so much," he said. "I don't want to be like this."

"Then stop."

"I will. I already apologized to Walter. We had a long talk. The set's going to be different starting tomorrow." He took her hands. His face was close, and she could feel his warm breath in the cool room. "When those stories came out," he said, "they made me feel like the world didn't respect us. The papers were trying to say our relationship wasn't real. They've said that about me before, about Cady and others. And maybe on some level, they were right, that I only wanted to have fun. But—I can't have them saying it about you. It is real, what I feel about you, and I want people to know. I want everyone to know. I don't want to be in this in-between space. I'm older than you, and I'm tired of it not being clear."

"Tired of what not being clear?" she asked, and her hands began to shake.

"I want to live! I wasn't living. Live all you can. It's a mistake not to. It doesn't matter what you do in particular, so long as you have your life. You're my life. Don't you see?" He caressed her cheeks, his fingers behind her ears.

"See what?"

"Madeline," he said. "I want to marry you."

4

The Yellow Room of the Old Marylebone Town Hall was elegant and understated, with a small chandelier, marigold drapes, and a few artfully placed vases of orchids. Maddy wore a belted, off-white, flower-bedecked dress, a replica of the one Audrey Hepburn wore to the 1954 Oscars. "Maddy," Steven was saying, slipping the ring on her finger, "as I take you to be my wife, I promise to love, honor, and respect you." His eyes were moist, and she felt she was about to go on an incredible adventure.

She had not been certain a few weeks before, but now she was. The night of *The Apartment*, she told him she needed to think about it. He said he understood it was a big step for her, she was young, he wanted her to be certain. They made love before falling asleep in each other's arms.

The next morning she called Irina, who told her it was a mistake. "You don't get engaged after a fight. The fighting is a sign that something's wrong."

In search of a second opinion, Maddy called Sharoz, who said she should do what felt right. If she truly believed that Steven and she were meant to be together, there was no point in delaying it. Then she added, "He's going to want a prenup, so you'd better think about whether that's okay." Maddy scoffed but privately worried that she was right.

Ananda McCarthy started crying as soon as Maddy told her over the phone. She said she had never seen Steven so besotted with anyone. Maddy told Ananda about the fights they'd had about Billy Peck, and Ananda was certain it was a sign that Steven loved her. She said, "He wants you to belong to him. He's older than you. He wants a family."

During Maddy's breaks from shooting, she walked on the grounds of Woodmere and tried to decide what to do. On the set, he was a different man. He became deferential to Walter, protecting him when Walter disagreed with Jimmy. When Maddy had important scenes with Billy, sexual or not, Steven didn't come to set. On nights off, when she asked him to take her to restaurants or plays, he said yes, even though the paparazzi were always there.

She began to forgive him, began to feel that those two weeks were just a blip. And so one night, while they were making out in bed, she took his cock in her hand and said, "Yes," and in her palm he got hard. She couldn't believe marriage could turn a man on, and she felt all the more certain about her choice.

They went to the registry office to give their intent to marry, and found out they had to wait sixteen days before the ceremony. They picked Marylebone because it was simple and historic; Paul and Linda McCartney had married there.

Steven had his grandmother's engagement ring shipped to England from Hancock Park, and he and Maddy went to Cartier to select bands. They had agreed to write their own vows but hadn't shared them with each other in advance. Now, in the Yellow Room, it was real.

The only guests were Terry and Ananda McCarthy and Bridget. "I will be your partner," Steven said, massaging her hands with his thumbs. "I will be true to you and loyal. I will care for you, laugh with you, and cry with you. I cannot wait to build a family with you. Whatever life may bring, I will be there for you. I am the song, you are the melody."

She slipped the ring on his finger. "Steven, as I take you to be my husband, I promise to love you and take care of you. I will be kind to you and support you in your creative endeavors, your work, your art. I am your biggest fan, most loyal advocate. You are my companion, my partner."

She thought of her father not being here to watch, not being able to witness one of the most important days of her life. The guests were all from Steven's circle; she hadn't been comfortable inviting Irina or Sharoz. Bridget was there for both of them, but Maddy had known her only half a year.

"I will take care of you when you are sick and cheer you on when wonderful things happen," Maddy continued. "Whatever life may bring, I am yours."

Steven had wrapped a glass in cloth to represent the Jewish tradition, and with one stomp, he smashed it. The guests cheered.

As he kissed her, Maddy felt the room swirl. She was beginning her life. When someone was right for you, there was no point in waiting. She felt grateful for the strife that had come before, because it had crystallized what she felt for him, caused him to step up and be a man. In her ear, Steven whispered, "I feel like everything's about to begin."

Bridget was very still as the new couple embraced. It was incredible to see the leap of faith they were taking when they had known each other only several months. Steven was stubborn and did things at his own pace. It was one of her favorite qualities about him: that he was not beholden to conventional ideas about men. It had been thrilling to see the changes in his personality, especially after he realized he might lose Maddy and became a better producer, a more attentive costar.

But in that historic room, Bridget knew her relationship with Steven had changed. They had never been deep friends but their intimacy surpassed friendship, it was a meeting of the minds, sometimes an ESP. All that would change. Maddy was the marker between the present and the future.

Bridget had never wanted to marry; as a child in 1950s Flatbush, she had been bored by her friends' endless wedding enactments. As a teenager, she had visited Coney Island with her friends, and they'd all written with sticks in the sand their plans for their future. Every other girl wrote about the man she would marry. Bridget wrote, "I want to work."

For almost twenty years, singlehood had been something she'd shared with Steven. "Maybe both of us were meant to live alone," he had said after one breakup. She had been the most important woman in his life. She had even been his date when he needed one, and many times he had stepped up to assist her. Now he would no longer need her escort services. He had a booster, acting partner, and consigliere in one package.

Someday these two would have children, and Bridget would know these children forever, even if she could not say the same of Maddy. (Bridget had been urging him to get a prenup, but he'd refused. He wanted to marry quickly, he said, and he wanted there to be no doubts. She was holding out hope for a postnup, which was better than nothing.)

She could imagine the baby's face. A girl. The baby would be good-looking, for sure, and one of the most photographed in entertainment history. Maybe they would make Bridget a godmother and she could bring presents and take the baby to the parks, though God save anyone who mistook her for Grandma. She liked the idea of being a beneficent aunt. Not the mother. She had no desire to be a mother again.

For a while she had dreamed of another baby. When Zack was ten, she was dating a college math professor named Clark who had silver hair. He had been scarred by his divorce, and he thought Bridget was beautiful and powerful, and in bed he wanted to bury his face in her.

They dated on and off for about a year. She loved the sex, but he didn't feel comfortable at industry events, and sometimes it was easier to leave him home. They spent much of their time together at his house, because she didn't want Zack to get too close to a man who might not stay. And then one month her period never came. She had been forty-six. Clark wanted her to keep the baby, but by that point she had made her peace with having only Zack. It was already difficult enough to be a good manager and try to be a good mother, see his school plays, check his homework, be home in time for dinner on weeknights.

And she had been old, and she didn't want to go through all the testing just to find out there was something wrong, then have to end it. She didn't tell Clark until after she had gone to the doctor, after it was all over. He was stunned and hurt. "You should have talked to me," he kept saying. They tried to make a go of it for a few more months, but when he broke it off, saying she had betrayed him, she was relieved.

So Zack had been the only, and now he was ungracious and he blamed her for his problems. It started when she changed the contingency age in the trust and now it was continuing, with his jealousy regarding her client. He avoided one-on-one time and refused to live in L.A., despite or perhaps because of the pain this caused her. If Steven and Maddy had a child, the child wouldn't resent her. Children only resented the mother.

If it was a girl, they could go out to lunch and get their hair done and Bridget could visit her in college and tell her she could be whatever she wanted to in life.

Maddy and Steven were exiting the room. Bridget remembered the rice—she had brought rice for everyone—and she threw it at them, beaming at Terry and Ananda on the other side of the aisle. As they passed, Steven smiled at Bridget, and the smile took over his face.

5

After the newlyweds returned to L.A., they were eating dinner one night when Steven wiped both corners of his mouth and said Edward Rosenman had been nagging him about a postnup. Maddy shuddered, remembering Sharoz's warning. They had just spent a week at the Ritz, mostly staying inside the room, and Steven had been so warm, so gallant. Now he was talking about this cold, ugly document.

"Those are for people who don't love each other," she said. "People who are using each other." She had lost her appetite and pushed her lamb away.

"I've always felt the same way. I told Edward I had no interest in it. I said I was going to be with you until death and knew you weren't marrying me for money."

"Of course I'm not marrying you for money. How could anyone think that?"

"Because there's such a discrepancy between us, in terms of earning, he thought it was a good idea to put some stuff on paper. He keeps saying it's good for both of us."

"No, it's not. It would be good for you. Don't you trust me? I would never try to take you to the bank. Never. Even if you got tired of me one day."

"I'll never be tired of you," he said, placing his palm on her neck. "But what you just said isn't true. These agreements actually protect both people. Someday you're going to be making more than I am. I really believe that. I'll be old and poor and unemployed. You don't want to protect the money you'll make when you get really famous? You want me to come after it?"

"Yes, if you were unemployed," she said. "I'd let you have it." She shook her head at the ridiculousness of the conversation. How could they be thinking about the end of a marriage when it had just begun? "I don't want to think about any of that stuff. I'm in love with you. I'll never leave you."

"If you don't want to do it, we don't have to," he said. "That's what I told Edward. In the end, it's up to us."

But later that night, awake in bed, she found herself worrying. Though she wasn't some chippie after his money, she liked the idea of protecting herself as a creator, an earner, an artist in her own right. A few days later, she made some phone calls and spoke with a family lawyer, a pretty, middle-aged woman who had photos of her kids and husband. Lisa Burns Miller. She said, "You have just married someone who has a lot more money than you do. If you had called me earlier, I would have recommended a prenup, but at least this way you'll have something. You need to protect yourself."

"From what?"

"From a marriage that leaves you with nothing."

"But I don't want his money. And it's not going to end."

"What if you have children and you stop working to care for them, so he can make movies, and your earnings go down and then it's hard to work? Wouldn't you want to be compensated for that? You know how brutal your industry is on women. A postnup doesn't mean you're planning to divorce. It means you two are being mature adults who have a plan for if things change between you. No one can be certain of anything in life."

With a large dose of ambivalence, Maddy retained her, and over the course of a week, Lisa and a matrimonial lawyer hired by Steven went back and forth, negotiating language. The basics were: In the first year, only ten percent of Steven's wealth was community property, but each year it bumped up, until after ten years, it was a hundred percent community. Maddy's income would never be considered community even if she became wealthy, and it didn't get factored in to compute support. If they divorced, she would get $1 million a year of spousal support for each year they were married, and $50,000 a month of support per child, which would be adjusted according to the visitation schedule.

The day they went in to sign the documents, there were video cameras set up in the attorney's office. Her lawyer said they were for documentation, to show that there was no duress, but they made Maddy feel like the whole thing was a grand performance. After they finished, she cried in the elevator.

"Don't feel badly about this," he said. "We decided this together. It makes us stronger."

"I know, but I don't ever want to look at those papers again," she said.

"We don't have to. Not once. I love you so much more that you did this."

"Why?"

"Because it means you believe in yourself as much as I believe in you," he said, and they walked in the bright sunlight from the building to the car.

One of the biggest social events of the L.A. fall season was the World Children's Welfare ball. The guests were a combination of star-studded Hollywood and charity circuit: Steven always insisted that the key to progressivism was to make it sexy. He was devoted to doing his part to eradicate poverty, both domestic and international, and through his fame, he had gotten a number of young actresses and actors involved with WCW.

The ball was at the Beverly Wilshire Hotel. The newlyweds shared a table with Terry and Ananda, Bridget, and others in Steven's circle. Steven was shooting a remake of *The Friends of Eddie Coyle*, and Maddy had begun production on *Line Drive*, about the relationship between an Iowan sportswriter father and his daughter. It was strange to make all these movies that no one would see for close to a year, which was why she was looking forward to the release of *I Used to Know Her* in October. Dan would be there, and Kira, though Maddy was more nervous about seeing Kira. She and Dan emailed from time to time and she considered him a friend.

The live auction was interminable, the auctioneer making entertainment-industry jokes, testosterone-jawed men in tuxes drunkenly raising paddles as their wives hooted. Forty-five minutes in, Maddy excused herself to go to the ladies' room.

She passed women doing their lipstick at the mirror and adjusting the implants in their redundant bras. "I was just talking about it with my shrink," a platinum blonde was saying to a friend, "and I finally get that my father's money issues come from his Jainism and his age."

Maddy went into one of the stalls, and when she emerged to wash her hands, she noticed that someone was next to her. A woman. Staring at her in the mirror.

Julia Hanson. From the billboards. She was striking, with shiny dark hair, and she wore a high-necked burgundy gown and long diamond earrings. She was more beautiful than Maddy had thought, and there was something overly and frighteningly intense about her.

"You're the new wife," Julia said.

"I . . ."

"Are you lonely yet?"

Maddy looked at Julia's reflection and said, "I don't think I—"

"When I look back, I remember the loneliness. During his sailing trips on *Jo*. The guys' nights. Whenever he was off with Alex."

"Who's Alex?" Maddy asked, unable to stop herself.

"From the theater. The repertory company."

Maddy had never heard Steven mention an Alex from the Duse. She didn't want to know about this person, didn't want to know the details of Steven's time with Julia and why it had gone wrong. She thought about the postnup and felt she had been wrong to sign it. Julia seemed cynical about marriage and Maddy had signed a document outlining what she would get if it ended.

"I have to go," Maddy said. Why were they the only two in the ladies' room? There had been half a dozen women a few moments ago.

"He needs you more than he needed me," Julia said. "Because he's older. It was time. The entertainment community is so narrow-minded. He must have felt pressure. He'll say you're his one true love. But you can't be. Alex was the only person he ever really loved."

Alex. Why, oh why, did it have to be a name like that and not Janine or Melissa?

"What do you mean by that?" Maddy asked hoarsely.

"The one he still dreams of years later. The one he can't get out of his head no matter how hard he tries. We all have someone like that."

Maddy went to the door and Julia followed quickly, gripping her arm. Maddy could feel her nails digging into the flesh. "I hear you're very good," Julia said. "Keep working. Even when he tells you that you should be home. He calls himself a feminist, but it's a lie. I've never met a man who hated women more. And I've lived in Los Angeles twenty-five years."

Instead of returning to her table, Maddy made a long circuit around the room. She scanned the crowd for Julia, but didn't see her. She had disappeared among the throng or left. Feeling faint, Maddy stopped at one of the bars and drank a glass of water slowly, as the auctioneer sold a kiss from a premium-cable star.

She walked slowly back to the table so her breathing would return to normal by the time she arrived, but when she reached for her wineglass, she saw that her hand was shaking. "Everything okay?" Steven whispered, squeezing her tightly.

"Fine," she said, and took a large swig.

When they got back to Hancock Park, Steven went to bed, and Maddy went into her study and closed the door. On her laptop, she began to type: "Alex Duse Repertory Company Steven Woyceck." Without pressing enter, she moved the mouse over to the images tab. Then she stopped herself.

Even if Alex from the theater was a man, what did it matter? Steven had been in the company in the mid-'80s. Even if there was some man back then, it didn't mean they were in touch now. Steven had married her. He was capable of getting hard, fucking her, and ejaculating in her night after night. Why make herself paranoid? Julia had probably wanted her to do just this, had wanted to sully Maddy's marriage because she was jealous.

He was sleeping when Maddy went back in the bedroom. He often got bone-tired after these balls and charity events, where he was always drinking whiskey, and fell asleep as soon as they returned. Sometimes they would make love in the morning, after he had showered. He said he was more of a morning person.

She reached for him, wanting to feel close, to feel his body near hers.

His skin grew warmer. She kissed his chest, his belly. Moved down below his navel and took him in her mouth. She felt it get big inside her, big because of what she was doing. She waited for him to stop her and pull her on top of him, but instead he held her hair and moaned and she let him, and as she bobbed above him, his eyes closed. She rose up and down and realized she was sore on her upper arm. She couldn't figure out what it was from until she remembered that it was the spot Julia had grabbed.

In the morning, Steven left before she awoke. She had a late call time that day, ten A.M., a blessing because she wanted to be alone. She went down to the kitchen, drank a smoothie standing up, then went to his study. She had not gone in since before England, before the wedding, but she felt there was a connection between her talk with Julia and that open drawer. She darted in and shut the door swiftly behind her. The room was flooded with light; he had left the drapes open.

The key was still wedged in behind the photo of his mother, and Maddy's fingers trembled as she used it to open the bottom desk drawer. Inside were the folders, but behind them, this time, was a wooden box. So there *had* been something that night he was talking on the phone. She shoved the folders forward with her hand and lifted the box. It had a treble clef painted on it. It was ugly and looked like the kind of thing he would laugh at if he saw it at a store.

She lifted the lid. Inside was a sterling silver man's ring in the shape of a greyhound dog; a note on a napkin that said "Went to watch the sun rise"; and a weathered, glossy, three-by-five photo. It showed Steven and a handsome, tan, blond man, both in their twenties. They were carefree, the wind in their hair, and they were on *Jo*, she recognized immediately. The man was looking at the camera and Steven was looking at him, an arm draped casually around him. The date on the back said August 1986. She flipped it over. Steven's eyes hypnotized her. Dancing and full. What kind of man named his boat after Jo Van Fleet?

She wondered if Steven thought of that hairless youthful body when he was in bed with her, that strong jaw, those noble cheeks. Maybe they were just friends, it was too hard to tell from a photo. Maybe she was connecting dots she wasn't supposed to.

She put back the items, replaced the box in the drawer, closed and locked it, and stashed the key behind the photo. She went to one of the windows. She could see a hint of her reflection, the pool and the azalea bushes beyond. She stared at her face and said, "Don't be homophobic."

Of course the blond boy had been his lover. He had to be.

So long ago. It didn't mean Steven was gay. Dan had done a circle jerk at Jewish summer camp where they raced to see who could come first; that was about as homo as you could get.

It would be unusual if Steven *hadn't* had same-sex experiences. He was an actor, after all, and half the men in her grad school had been gay. But in bed in London, during that awful time, he had said, "It's not my thing."

She stepped away from the window to the middle of the room, imagining what it was like to work in here, read in here, think in here. To be Steven Weller. The Steven Weller who talked on the phone late at night to his staff, or maybe not his staff but exes and friends she had never met. The Steven Weller who read classic literature, or pretended to, who displayed books like trophies, none of them dog-eared or stained by use.

She stared at the floor-to-ceiling bookshelves. The Henry James books were arranged alphabetically. She stopped at *The Ambassadors*, remembering the first boat ride in Venice when he had said it was his favorite book. She flipped open the cover, and the book opened to the title page. "Steve—Live all you can; it's a mistake not to. Love always, Alex."

The room felt chilly, like a morgue. The phrase had sounded strange when he'd said it in their bed in Regent's Park, but she had never asked him. If only she had started her James education with *The Ambassadors* and not *The Portrait of a Lady*. She would have recognized those words when he spoke them. And then she would have known.

Alex loved these words and Steven had recycled them to propose to her. It was Alex whom he loved, Alex whom he loved still, Alex to whom he had wanted to propose. Whether a man or a woman, the man in the photo or another, there was someone in Steven's past whose love coursed through him and governed everything he did. Someone she could never replace, a Rebecca de Winter. She replaced the book on the shelf and fled from the room as though from a fire.

When Steven came home from the lot that night, she was by the pool. She wore a long beige cashmere sweater and held a du Maurier collection in her hand. She had bought it in an English-language bookshop in Paris on their honeymoon and had been reading it in small doses. She had started a story called "Split Second," about a middle-aged widow who gets a feeling of foreboding as she's eating her lunch. The woman goes out for a walk and almost gets run over by a van, and when she returns to her house there are other people living there.

The French doors opened, and she could hear his steps on the patio. She buried her nose in the book. He sat on the chaise next to her. Kissed her on the cheek.

"How was your day?" he asked, lacing his fingers through hers.

"Tell me about Alex," she said, pulling her hand away. She would have to bluff a little.

"Alex who?" he said, his face betraying nothing.

"From the theater."

"Where did you get this?" he asked. He seemed to be working hard to see just what she knew.

"Julia was at the ball. She said you used to go off with Alex."

"The ball? I didn't see her. What did she say to you? She was in an institution. You can't trust a word out of her mouth."

"She told me about Alex. So I know. He was at the Duse Rep, and there was something between you."

She waited for him to correct her, say Alex from the theater was a woman, but he said nothing, only sighed, stood, and paced by the edge of the pool. Then his shoulders slumped and he straddled the chaise, facing the water.

"When I was in my mid-twenties . . ." He drew in a breath and started again. "When I was starting out in my career . . . there were a lot of gay men at the Duse. There was no line between work and fun. We were all passionate about what we did and about each other. Alex was in the company with me. I knew he was gay, and he knew I wasn't. We were friends. I went to gay bars with him as a lark, and sometimes he came to straight bars with me, trying to guess which women I would hit on. He'd had a difficult childhood, too, and we talked about it. We were very close. And then one night we had been out late, drinking, and we were back at his apartment and . . . we slept together."

She was almost relieved that he had finally told her; she was getting to it at last. All day she had heard the inscription in her head. The words he had taken from another lover and used on her. To seduce her. This was what shook her more than Alex's gender: the idea that the proposal hadn't been genuine, that she was a stand-in for someone else.

"Was he the one on the phone in your study?" she asked.

"I told you, it was Vito."

"I don't believe you."

"Well, you should. I don't even know where Alex is these days."

"How long did it go on?"

"It didn't. It was just that one night. It was confusing. He understood that I was straight. That it could never be. It messed with our friendship. We didn't speak for a while, but then we made up. After I married Julia, sometimes he and I would hang out. She thought I was still seeing him. I wasn't. He was my friend."

"In London I asked if you had been with men. And you said no."

"I thought if I told you, you wouldn't get it. You'd— Most women think if a man has been with one man, he's gay."

"*Are* you?"

"No, Maddy." He said it like she was stupid. "Are *you?*"

"No!"

"You slept with a woman."

"We made out a little! It was mostly kissing."

"And you enjoyed it. And I didn't judge you. You're a hypocrite."

"You lied to me, and now you're calling me names?"

She raced up the lawn toward the house. He followed and pivoted her toward him roughly. "Maddy. It was only Alex. One night and one man. I'm not gay. The line between friendship and attraction—it's—it can be complicated. You know that."

She wondered where Alex was now, even if he wasn't the one in the photo. Maybe he was dead of AIDS and Steven missed him. Or maybe she was being stupid to think any gay man in the '80s must have died of AIDS.

He put his hands on her shoulders. "It was a youthful indiscretion. I was going to tell you about him. I was just afraid of how you would react. And now . . . I feel like I was right to be."

"I went into your study," she said. She waited for a lecture on the importance of privacy, the terrible invasive thing she had done, but he was listening, as though he understood that Julia had shaken her. "I was so upset last night. I felt like I didn't know you. I went to your bookshelves, and I was thinking about how you love Henry James, and I took out *The Ambassadors* and there was an inscription . . . from Alex."

"Yes, yes. A quote from the novel."

"But you used that quote when you proposed to me!"

"Because I believe it. Alex did, too. I want to be someone who embraces life. For so many years I've been about work, and that's something I've wanted to change. To soak up the world, to appreciate my good fortune. Even though he gave me the book, we had discussed those lines before that, the words Strether speaks. You should read it, you would like it. When Alex wrote that, he knew the quote had meaning to me, and it still does. It's not about him, it's about Henry James."

"Henry James was a closeted fag."

His eyes widened. "Is that the way you think of gay men? You won't get very far in this industry."

"You weren't proposing to me. You were proposing to Alex. I don't even know if you love me. Why did you have me sign that agreement?"

"The postnup? I thought it was what you wanted."

"It was your idea. I was afraid you'd leave me if I didn't." She hadn't admitted it to herself, but she had believed if she fought him, he would end it. She had wanted so desperately to please him. "Was it because you don't love me, because you don't think we'll last? Was it because you still love Alex?"

"Of course I love you. The books a person gives us, they last longer than the relationship itself. Alex was a very important person to me. He introduced me to James, and now James is mine, like he belongs to so many others."

"But it wasn't just a friendship," she offered.

"Are you going to be haunted by this man whom I literally have not spoken to in decades? Dan was important to you. You said he turned you on to Walter Juhasz. And to Lubitsch and Sturges. I'm not angry about that. It doesn't make me love you any less."

He was right. You took words and poems from one lover and shared them with another. It wasn't wrong, it wasn't deception.

He knelt on the grass as though proposing all over again. "You have all of me now. There's nothing hidden. If you want me to, I'll tell you everything I did with Alex."

"That's the last thing I want to hear!"

"I just mean I won't hide from you again."

"I've never kept secrets from you."

"But you're so much younger than I am."

He stood and cupped her face. She was afraid of his power. She needed space. "I think I want to be alone for a little while," she said, going to the lounge chair and fetching her book.

"What are you reading?" he asked.

"Daphne du Maurier," she said. "It's a collection. I was reading it on our honeymoon."

"I didn't notice you reading," he said.

"I did after you were asleep. You always fall asleep before I do."

"Tell me about one of the stories."

"A woman arrives home and finds these strange people living in her house. She tells them she lives there, but they won't believe her. They act like she's insane, when they're the ones who are acting crazy."

For the next few nights, they saw little of each other. Both were working long hours on their films, and at night Maddy would retire to one of the guest rooms, trying to make sense of everything. She was more hurt that he had lied than that he had slept with one man.

Surprisingly, Steven gave her space. He didn't ask if she'd forgiven him. He seemed to want to allow her the room to be hurt.

And when she took a pill each night at ten P.M., or sometimes earlier, because it was better than lying awake for three or four hours and then taking it, she came to feel she was being too hard on him. She understood why he hadn't told her about Alex, and she even understood why he had used the line from *The Ambassadors* to propose. She didn't want to let Julia Hanson put a spear through her marriage. Terry had warned her to have walls and windows. She hadn't built enough walls.

On the fourth night, around eleven o'clock, she went into the master bedroom. Steven was reading a script about James Earl Ray. He put it down beside him and pushed his glasses to the top of his head. "I tried not to love you," she said, "but it didn't work."

He pulled her toward him, held her face. "I feel lucky," he said.

"Promise you'll never lie to me again."

"I won't," he said, kissing her. She looked in his eyes while he moved in her and got on top. She wondered what he was thinking about.

But he didn't have to tell her. Not now that she knew. If he thought about men, that was all right. She thought about Kira sometimes and didn't feel the need to tell him. They were closer now. Wedded. She felt a surge of love. The man inside her was more complicated and thus more real than the one she had known before.

6

The premiere for *I Used to Know Her* was held in September at the Chinese Theatre. Zack, Kira, and the other cast members did the red carpet, along with all of the VIPs Maddy had asked Steven to invite on her behalf. Sharoz was in Austin on an independent thriller, but Kira had flown in from New York with her new girlfriend, Reggie. Reggie wore cat's-eye glasses and a geisha dress, and Maddy liked her immediately. Dan came with the screenwriter Oded Zalinsky; he and Rachel Huber had broken up.

Maddy walked the press line with Steven, less nervous than she had been at the Housing Project USA event that spring, now that she'd had more practice. She wanted the film to do well because she believed it deserved to, and she knew Steven's presence would ensure maximum publicity. All the reporters wanted to see her engagement ring and wedding band. The press had dubbed them "SteMad," and some reporters even called out the name, which she found bizarre. Steven was game on the press line, indulging but never overshadowing Maddy, standing behind her. The questions about the movie were the usual idiotic ones, but Maddy had learned how to answer them. You had to be brief and positive, and you had to act like each was being asked of you for the very first time.

The after-party was at a club called Havana, on Ivar, in Hollywood, a big, decadent place with multiple levels and banquettes. There was a table reserved for the cast, and Maddy found herself sitting opposite Dan and next to Steven. She kept waiting for Steven to show hostility toward Dan, but he was so convivial that if you didn't know she and Dan once lived together, you never would have guessed.

Kira couldn't keep her hands off Reggie. They kept nuzzling and smooching and petting, which seemed inappropriately showy at first, but it was clear Kira was besotted and it soon became cute.

At the table, the cast reminisced about the shoot. Bridget and Steven were uncharacteristically quiet, unable to chime in. Since moving to L.A., Maddy had been socializing in Bridget and Steven's world. Now they were in hers. For the first time, they seemed old to her, too rich, too successful, and too smooth.

Dan asked Maddy if she had liked working with Walter Juhasz, and she said quickly, "Walter was amazing to work with. He hasn't lost a step."

"That's what I've heard," Kira said. "But *you* didn't like him, did you, Steven? I feel like I read that somewhere."

His face was unyielding. "It was one of the best professional experiences of my life," he said. Maddy was shocked to see the ease with which he lied. It was as though he did it professionally, which, in a sense, he did. "The press likes to make movie sets seem more exciting than they are. As I'm sure you're aware."

"This is the first film I've done that's gotten press," Kira said evenly, "so I really wouldn't know."

"Do you guys have a release date yet?" Zack asked.

"Next fall, in time for the awards circuit," Bridget said. "Maddy is unbelievable in this."

"I think you mean she's believable, Mom."

Bridget pursed her lips at him and went on, "I mean she is just stellar. Even though her character is unfaithful, you're rooting for her. You're going to be biting your nails and turned on at the same time."

"That reminds me of a hooker I once went to," Zack said, and everyone laughed. Maddy felt he was trying to make sure everyone got along, to bridge the gap between old and young.

"So what have you been working on, Kira?" Maddy asked, clearing her throat.

"I did a couple days on *Freda Jansons*. The Tim Heller film. I just had a small role. Lael was fucking awesome. I played a babysitter to the boy. A day's work, but supposedly, Tim Heller really liked me and wants to find me something more substantial."

"Kira just booked another movie, actually," Zack announced. "It's a

black-and-white indie called *Rondelay*. She plays a modern dancer with
a bad love life."

The title rang a bell. Bridget had sent Maddy the script, but the salary
was SAG minimum and Bridget felt strongly that it was too small for her.
Bridget had said that the director, Deborah Berenson, had a mixed track
record. She was said to be mercurial and to have trouble getting projects
off the ground. One of her scripts, a girl-girl buddy comedy, had been in
turnaround for ten years, Bridget said.

"My girlfriend's going to be very famous someday," Reggie said, running her fingers through Kira's hair, which had grown down to her chin.

"You're only saying that because I sleep with you," Kira said.

"No, I'm saying it because I think you're the most talented woman in
the universe."

"What do you do for a living, Reggie?" Steven asked.

"I work at a domestic-abuse crisis center?"

"She's the real deal," Kira said. "She couldn't give a shit about money.
She just wants to help women and girls."

"And how did you two meet?" Steven asked.

"At a bar on Avenue B," Kira said. She held Reggie's face and said, "Is
this not the cutest girl you've ever seen?"

A celebrity DJ had been hired for the party—it was possible that the
party had cost more than the film—and as a heavy bass cranked up,
Reggie and Kira got up to dance. Oded was already on the dance floor,
acting goofy. Zack followed the women, and Maddy was left with her ex-
boyfriend, her manager, and her husband.

"Why don't you stay here without me, sweetie?" Steven said. "I have
that six A.M. call tomorrow. You'll have more fun with just your friends."
She pretended to be disappointed, but she was relieved. It was complicated
to have to be Mrs. Steven Weller and Maddy Freed at the same time.

Bridget said she was going to walk out with Steven, and as she headed off
to the bathroom, Zack decided to seize the moment. When his mother
came out, he was waiting. "Have you had too much to drink?" she asked.
"Do you need a lift back to your hotel?"

"I wanted to talk to you for a second."

"Not near the restrooms. Never talk business near shit." She steered him to a back corner of the room. "This can't wait until breakfast?"

"I have to cancel. I'm going back first thing. I have a commitment in New York."

"But I was so looking forward to sitting down with you. I never see you. Why don't you move back here? You're wasting time with those theater people. It's a dying industry."

"I like it there. This isn't the only city where deals get made."

He was looking at her so heavily that she almost suspected he knew. She'd had only one meeting, sneaked off for a few days to Connecticut, but it was going to happen. A few weeks more and Steven would be catapulted to the top of the A-list. He was doing a good job of keeping it quiet, and she was, too. But it would be bad if it leaked. She was about to become executive producer on a multimillion-dollar franchise that would change everything for her client and for her.

"I want to ask you about Maddy," Zack said, and Bridget opened her mouth so her exhale wouldn't sound so loud. He knew nothing. He would read about it in the trades like everyone else.

"What about Maddy?"

"I heard you didn't send her *Freda Jansons.*"

"I knew it was you who told her. Spare me your guilt trip. The best thing I've done for my client since I signed her was not send her that script." Bridget lowered her voice. "I hear it's terrible. The screenplay was a mess, and Tim Heller was rewriting every day on set. The actors made up their own lines."

"That's not true. Not one thing you just said is true."

"Whatever you say." She was looking off in the distance, as if she saw someone more important. It was a look he had seen many times.

"You have a fiduciary duty to your client. Be careful, Mom. You don't want Maddy getting the idea that you signed her for self-interested reasons."

"What are you talking about?"

"*Husbandry* was a vanity project for Steven. Juhasz's last couple movies have tanked. He needed you more than you needed him. You told him to cast her."

"That's not true. He wanted her. It was his choice."

"I'm sure she'll be very good. But that's not why she got it. The film was just the hook. It was about Steven. You put her in his way."

"I haven't the foggiest idea what you're talking about. Zack, those two fell in love. I had nothing to do with it. I've never seen two people look at each other the way they do. Look, I understand you're frustrated. You're the one who invited her to my dinner in Mile's End. But she's mine now. Let it go. Build your own list."

"I saw her movie first," he said.

"I found you your first half-dozen clients. Consider it a trade. I shouldn't be so important to you. It's not healthy."

I shouldn't be so important to you. As though she didn't understand why she was.

She'd been dating the dorky math professor. Clark. Zack remembered that night she came into his room. It was past his bedtime and he was reading Jack London. Bridget sat down on the edge of the bed and rubbed his hair. "I want to talk to you about something," she had said.

He had been annoyed. He was deep into his book and didn't want to stop reading. He stuck his finger in the novel. "Yeah?"

"How would you like a baby brother or sister?" she had asked.

He was more confused than anything, unsure what she was asking. *Brother or sister.* His first thought was that she had reunited with Grant. His mom and dad had worked it out. He fantasized about it a lot. But that was impossible. His dad was remarried, with two other kids, in Arizona.

Then he remembered. That professor she had been dating. There was going to be a baby?

"I don't really know," he said.

"Well, if you could have one, let's say, would you be happy about it? Or do you like having me all to yourself?"

He didn't like that creepy Clark guy, found him phony and stiff. If this meant Clark would move in with them, Zack certainly didn't want it. "I don't know. I guess have you all to myself."

"That's exactly what I thought," she said, and gave a little nod.

A week later, he came home to find her already there, lying in bed.

His mother never lay in bed in the middle of the day. She worked through bronchitis and the flu. She was always at work. When he asked what was wrong, she said she had a stomach bug.

It wasn't until years later that he put the pieces together. He had never asked her, he couldn't know. But he didn't think the question had been hypothetical. And even if she had asked him out of pain and desperation, it had been wrong. He was *ten*.

"Just be careful with Maddy," he said to his mother at the club. A waiter was coming toward them with champagne, but Zack shook his head at him. "If you withhold quality scripts, she might fire you and hire me instead."

"I'm sure Steven would talk her out of that very quickly."

"And why is that?"

"Because he loves her. And when a man loves a woman, he only wants the best for her. Now walk me to the car, honey, will you?"

"What happened with you and Rachel?" Maddy asked Dan.

They had sat in silence for a moment after Steven and Bridget left. Maddy had been self-conscious, worried that people were watching them. But Dan was still her director and this was their premiere. It was all right to talk to him.

"She wanted to get married and have babies, and I think she realized I wasn't there yet."

"I liked her."

"No, you didn't."

"I thought she was smart, and good for you." She could sense he didn't want to get into it, so she changed the subject. "Hey, by the way, congratulations on your deal. Do you have a start date for production?"

"Congratulations to you as well."

Oded and Dan had gone out with their script based on *The Nest* in August, with Dan attached to direct. They had changed the title to *Hirshman's Mistake*. When Maddy first read the script, she almost called Edward Rosenman to have him take her name off, it was so lewd and immature, filled with fart jokes and frontal nudity. Oded and Dan wound up selling it for $1 million to Worldwide Films, of which Maddy got a third. She would be able to join the Writers Guild of America, and despite the questionable material that had allowed her to join, she was excited about it in case she wanted to write something of her own down the line.

When the film went to auction, she'd had mixed feelings. She knew that if she hadn't been with Steven, she wouldn't be represented by Edward and never would have gotten such a generous collaboration agreement. But Dan had been naive to think she would sign that ridiculous piece of paper. And if $333,333 was perhaps too much for the pages she had helped write, $1 was too little.

"I just hope they don't try to fire me from *Hirshman*'s when *The Valentine* comes out," he said, sipping from his tumbler. "I think it's going to suck."

"I'm sure it won't suck."

"I should have listened to you. If I had listened to you and stayed in Venice, then maybe . . ." He gave her an intense, longing gaze.

"Don't think that way," she said, and looked down at the table. She could feel him staring at her, and when she looked back up at him, his eyes were soft. She felt a rush of feeling for him, for what they had made together, for what she had left behind to be with Steven.

"Do you ever wonder what might have happened if . . . if you'd never gone to Berlin?" he asked.

"No," she said. "I loved you, but I was meant to be with Steven."

"Do you really believe that?" His tone wasn't cruel, but it was deeply doubtful.

"Of course I do. Why would I be with him if I didn't feel we were meant to be together?"

He nodded and gave her a wincing smile that she didn't like. And then he was gone, dirty-dancing with a couple of girls who didn't seem much older than twenty, all of whom were grinding against Oded. Who looked like a human teddy bear.

She tossed back her cocktail and went to dance with Zack, Reggie, and Kira. Maddy asked Reggie a little about her work, and she said it could get really depressing but she believed in it, because at night she went to sleep knowing she was helping people. Reggie seemed like the kind of person who wouldn't be competitive with Kira, who would be content to let Kira be her outrageous self.

After a while Maddy got dizzy and went back to her table to drink some water. She couldn't get drunk—if she drank too much and got sick, the story could get out and it would be a disaster. This was one of many new things she hadn't had to worry about a year ago. She spotted Kira making her way over from the dance floor. She was wearing high platform heels with ribbon straps that went around her ankles. She sat down next to Maddy and mixed herself a vodka cranberry from the bottles in the center of the table.

"Kira," Maddy said, glad to have a second alone with her. "Watching the movie tonight, you know, I was so impressed. I never told you how good I think you are."

"Thanks," Kira said with a sigh, as if she didn't enjoy the compliment. "I have this really good teacher in the East Village, and he's teaching me that process will take me a long way. I'm not a natural, but I work hard."

"I know you do. You and Steven are similar that way. You two work harder than anyone I know."

Kira seemed to have matured over the past year. She seemed less outrageous and more serious. "Steven works at a lot of things," Kira said.

"What do you mean?"

"I just mean that my goal isn't exactly to be compared to him in the hard-working actor department."

"Why not?"

"I have other idols."

Trying not to take her bait, Maddy said, "It's kind of insane that so much has happened to us since Mile's End."

"Yeah, who knew?"

She and Kira had never spoken of their kiss, which seemed like it had happened years ago and not months. Maddy felt the need to smooth things over. "When we were together," Maddy said, "I mean, that night at the festival, I just want to say—I'm sorry."

"Why?" Kira asked.

"Because I was lonely. And I—I used you."

"Huh. *You* used *me*."

"Isn't that what happened?"

Maddy could see Zack and Reggie approaching. Kira said, "I don't think so at all. I went for you, remember? I was drunk. You could have been anyone."

The other two had sat down. Maddy lowered her head, not wanting to talk about it in front of Reggie. "Don't be weird about it, Maddy," Kira said. "Everyone at film festivals hooks up. Reggie knows we sucked face at Mile's End. Zack, too. He's not just my agent. He's my friend."

Zack glanced away, evidently not wanting to embarrass Maddy further. On the dance floor, Dan and Oded were doing 1970s-style moves to the delight of all the girls. "You didn't tell Dan, did you?" Maddy asked.

"No, but I can tonight, if you want me to." Kira started to get up, bluffing or not bluffing. With Kira, it was impossible to know.

"No!" Maddy said a little too loudly. "What would be the point?"

"I want both of you to know," Zack said, raising his eyebrows Groucho Marx–style, "that I would have no problem representing two actresses who have sexual history. It's excellent publicity for the agent."

Maddy felt as though they were all making fun of her. She wanted to melt into the floor. "You know what your problem is, Maddy?" Kira asked, slurring her words. "You get all worked up over stupid stuff. It's because you think you're the center of the universe."

"I don't think I'm the center of the universe," Maddy said.

"Even before you married Steven, with your fancy French honeymoon, and your, like, fifty-bedroom mansion, you always thought you were better. Better than Sharoz and me and even Dan. You looked down on us."

"Kira," Reggie said, putting her hand on Kira's arm. Kira shook her off with irritation.

"I don't look down on any of you!" Maddy cried. "I just told you how good you were in the film." She looked at Zack pleadingly, hoping he could explain it, but he was examining the grain of the table.

"All you ever wanted was fame," Kira barreled on. "Don't get me wrong, I want to be famous, too, but there are limits to what I'll do. I'm not as cynical as you. No matter how much I believed someone could help me, I wouldn't do what you did."

"What are you talking about?" Maddy asked.

"The contract, of course."

Did Kira know about her postnup? Had it been reported on the Internet? Reggie was trying to whisper in Kira's ear, but Kira was dodging her.

"What contract?" Maddy asked.

"I *told* you it's not true," Zack said to Kira.

"Oh God, don't pretend you don't know," Kira exploded. "It's all over the Internet. The *marriage* contract. For appearances. The one that pays you a salary to be his wife. You have to go out with him to public events and smile for photos, but you don't have to fuck him. You get a million a year plus a million-dollar bonus for each baby, and you agree to do IVF with his sperm so the baby looks like him, too. And you get a bump to two million if he wants you to stay more than five years, but when it's over, you get nothing."

She didn't like that "million a year" figure; it paralleled the postnup too closely. But a payout to appear as someone's wife? Who came up with this kind of thing? Did people do this? She couldn't tell if Kira believed it or was pretending to believe it to provoke her.

All her friends were turning against her. Dan being crass about Steven, and now Kira accusing her of taking money, like some kind of high-class prostitute.

"I don't know where you read this," she said, "but just because something is on the Internet doesn't make it true," She looked at Zack for help. "There is no marriage contract. Zack, tell her."

"There's no contract," he said. "Kira, leave her alone. You had too much to drink." At least he wasn't rushing to defend Kira.

"Yeah, honey," Reggie said. "Let's go outside. Get some air." She helped Kira to her feet in the platforms.

"Steven and I love each other," Maddy said. "It was messy, I'm not saying it wasn't. But it's real. How could you not think it was real? What kind of person do you think I am?"

Reggie was guiding Kira away from the table. "Why don't you go back to your haunted mansion with your old man," Kira said to Maddy, "where you belong? Why waste one more minute with the riffraff?" And with that, she stumbled toward the door.

7

Maddy learned that Steven was to play Tommy Hall when she was driving to the set of *Line Drive*, flipping channels on the car radio. It was a few weeks after the *I Used to Know Her* premiere. She wasn't even paying attention, just wanted sound for the car, and then she heard a talk-radio guy mentioning Steven's name. Tommy Hall, who had been created by the novelist Jerome Roundhouse, was a legendary character with an insatiable appetite for sex and risk and a constant stream of bons mots. A divorcé with several ex-wives, he had a hankering for attractive women half his age. Roundhouse, a reclusive man in Connecticut, had written eight Tommy novels and for many years had refused to sell the rights, but the guy on the radio was saying Roundhouse had made a deal. The first adaptation was *The Hall Fixation*.

The radio sidekick, a woman, thought Steven was sexy, but the man, a shock jock with a nicotine voice, thought he was too old. Maddy had never heard Steven mention Tommy Hall. Her first thought was that it was a hoax, one of those radio gags they did to attract more listeners.

She pulled over and typed "Steven Weller Tommy Hall" into her phone. At least a dozen items popped up, all opening with some version of "Apollo Pictures has announced that Steven Weller is to play the iconic spy Tommy Hall in a three-picture deal."

So it was real. If all these outlets were saying so, it had to be. She dialed Steven but got his voice mail.

When she arrived on her set, the cast and crew were abuzz about the Tommy deal, congratulating her, asking her to send him their good wishes. She nodded faintly, the only saving grace that she had heard it on the radio so she didn't look like a complete idiot.

That night she was to meet Steven at the Italian restaurant on Beverly Boulevard. When she arrived five minutes early, he was already waiting in the garden. She could sense diners watching her as she paraded to the rear. As he stood, she felt her face crumple. She sat quickly so no one could see her, lowered her head, and said, "How could you not tell me?"

"The studio was going to announce it Thursday," he said, "but it leaked, so they had to move forward with it. I was going to tell you Wednesday."

"But why not before? You used to talk to me about your jobs. I tell you everything." She often felt she put too much weight on his opinion, delaying responses to scripts until Steven had a chance to read them.

"This wasn't an audition," Steven said. "Everything came together so quickly. Bridget kept it secret from me for weeks." He explained that Jerome Roundhouse had gotten director and actor approval and wanted only Steven for the role. He felt no one else could play Tommy.

"I thought you were into artistic films," she said. "This is a total one-eighty for you, and you didn't even want to share it with me."

"It was because of the confidentiality, Mad."

She wondered if it had something to do with their talk about Alex a few months ago. He must have felt violated to learn she had been in his study. She had snooped, and he was betrayed, so now he didn't trust her with his decisions. She had built a wall between them.

The waiter came, and Steven ordered them a bottle of her favorite Tocai. "Aren't you even a little bit happy for me?" he asked.

"I just didn't think this was the direction you wanted to go in. I thought you wanted to do projects like *The Widower* and *Husbandry*."

"I'm not sure those films were serving me. We'll see what happens when *Husbandry* is released, but you know *The Widower* wasn't what I had hoped. Anyway, I don't see *The Hall Fixation* as selling out on any level. High art can be low art and vice versa. The script is going to be incredible. We're trying to get Bryan Monakhov."

She winced. Dan would be insanely jealous. "I just didn't know you were interested in—a franchise."

He stiffened at the word "franchise," as if it were a slur. "This is a deeply personal project for me. I told you I read *The Hall Fixation* when things were bad with my dad."

"You never told me that."

"Yes, I did, you're forgetting. I told you in London that night we went to see the Pinter. I'm not even interested in the thriller elements. It's the father-son relationship between Tommy Hall and the boss, Richard Breyer. That's the crux of the films."

She was almost certain he'd never said anything about the books. She would have remembered. When he referenced books, they were usually by James or Wharton. It was as though he were spinning her, as he would spin the public. With a made-up story that Tommy was personal.

Lowering his voice, he proceeded to tell her the deal points: $12 million for the first film with a pay-or-play, and options on the next two Tommy Halls, with escalations.

"So you just want to be richer than you already are?" she asked. "It's about money?"

"It's about what the money means. This will give me longevity as a performer, and allow me more choice as I get older, which I'm going to need. It could lead to more producing. It's not just for me, Mad. It's for us. I want to have children with you. This will ensure that they're taken care of."

A family. He was trying to seduce her with talk of a family. But he already had money, which she knew from the net-worth statement he had had to prepare before the postnup. Their children would already be taken care of. He was speaking like a minimum-wage janitor who had just won the lottery instead of a man already worth tens of millions.

Later that night, as he was making love to her from behind, she told herself to forgive him. If he wanted to build a family with her, then he saw her as a partner. But if he saw her as a partner, then he would have told her about it. She had lost him in some way, and as he came in her and cried out, his face invisible behind her, she felt like she wasn't even there.

In mid-October, a few days after Steven's Tommy role had been announced, Maddy came home from a long day of complicated driving shots in *Line Drive*, wanting to eat a plate of Annette's roast organic chicken and go right to bed. Steven was at the dinner table—Annette was out—and though he'd already eaten, he had warmed a plate for her and poured her a glass of red. She was moved by how kind he was being, and they talked about their workdays. After a few minutes she could see that he was troubled by something. "What is it?" she asked, blotting her mouth with her napkin. "You seem upset."

He waved his hand. "It's— No, I told myself I wasn't going to do this."

"Well, now you have to tell me."

He let out a little sigh. "There's a story coming out, some guy came forward and said something ridiculous, but it's in a low-class publication and we're already on top of it."

She put down her fork. "Go on."

"Some lowlife took a payout from *The Weekly Report* to say he and I had an affair. They're running the story in a couple days. Edward's already on it, he's drafting up one of his famous Edward letters. Actual malice, reckless disregard for the truth. We'll get a retraction from the guy, but I wanted you to know because the paps are going to be worse than usual. Do you like the chicken?"

"Who is this person? Who said this about you?"

"He works at the yacht club. I've known his father forever, and we've met, but only dealing with the boat. He's a dockworker. Last name Bernard. I can't even remember the first, Chad or Charlie or something. Anyway, Edward's going to squash him. Kid must be desperate for cash, because the supermarket tabs don't pay as much as they used to. I think he has drug problems."

It couldn't be true. It was too perfect, too easy. A dockworker, the yacht club. It was only because Steven was famous that this was happening. And because he had signed on to do *The Hall Fixation.*

"You're supposed to do the press thing for Tommy next week, right?" she asked, no longer hungry.

"Yeah." He would be doing all the morning shows, the late-night comedies, choice entertainment-blog interviews, phoners with the international press, and a few trades. "But we know about the story early, which is good, and we're going to get him. The guy will retract it before anyone can blink, and the magazine, they never retract, but that doesn't matter. We'll get a letter from him, and Edward will leak the letter. Everyone will know it's meritless."

His cell phone rang, and he went into the study to take the call. From his tone, it sounded like Bridget, but she wasn't sure.

The first sign the situation had worsened was when Maddy pulled out of the studio lot, at the end of a long shooting day, and saw fifty paparazzi standing there. She wondered whom they were there for, and then one of the guys ran up to the window, the rest trailing behind, and said, "What do you think about the *Weekly Report* story about Steven? Is Steven gay?" She had to close her window, afraid that one of them would stick his hand or his face in the car. She drove so fast to get away that she ran a light.

At home, what looked like a hundred photographers were on the sidewalk corner. Maddy drove up the driveway and opened the gate, terrified that they would follow her in, and when she got out of the car, she ran in. Bridget was there. "Oh, my darling," she said, and hugged her.

Bridget led her into the study. Flora, their publicist, was there; and Edward, a wide-faced sixtyish man who resembled a young Ernest Borgnine; and Steven, each typing frantically on a device. Classical music was playing in the background. Their faces were alert but not happy.

Maddy took a high-backed wooden chair. Bridget went to the chair behind Steven's desk. She wore a big silver-and-opal vertical ring on the pointer of her right hand and stroked it periodically.

Steven cleared his throat. "I wish you didn't have to deal with any of this, Maddy, but unfortunately, it affects both of us. We were just discussing that we'll be hiring a temporary security team to deal with the situation outside the door. We'll also be getting bodyguards, and if need be, we'll relocate temporarily."

"Relocate? What are you talking about?"

"You may not have to move," Flora said, "but there are safe houses. Places you can go to get away from them. If they're following you around all the time, it's dangerous for you to drive. What you've experienced in your marriage is only a taste of how bad it can be."

"How can this be happening?" Maddy said, conscious of the chamber music playing in the background. "I thought you were threatening a lawsuit, Edward."

"I released my cease-and-desist today," Edward said. "We're saying it's defamatory and recklessly untrue and seeking a full retraction from this, this"—he looked down at a sheet of paper—"Christian Bernard."

"The problem," Bridget said, "is the Tommy Hall press tour. Steven was supposed to be on that plane to New York tomorrow. The studio doesn't feel it's advisable at this point. To expose him in this way."

"But it's not true. Shouldn't he be going on with business as usual, to show everyone it's baseless?"

"They want the focus to be on the role," Bridget said. "The franchise. This is a massive distraction. It's not responsible to put him out there in front of the press when he's so vulnerable. Any appearance he makes, he'll have to address this. Even the soft outlets. They still have a marginal obligation to what they consider newsworthiness. The studio is putting a lot of money on the line for him, and it's up to them, not us. Flora agrees."

Flora nodded. "I can't feed him to the wolves. The studio's doing the right thing. You type in Steven's name on the Internet right now, and this is all you get."

"When do you expect the retraction to come in?" Maddy asked Edward.

"We're having trouble locating the guy," Bridget said.

Edward said, "We'll get him. I'm working with a PI, and it's going to happen. This is no rocket scientist. If he were, he wouldn't have done this. But it may take a couple of days."

The meeting went on, with more and more news. Flora and Edward were running a campaign to discredit Bernard; they had done their homework and found out he had a criminal record (attempted assault in a bar fight, marijuana possession, reckless driving). The stories would come out, and he would be known as an unreliable, unstable money-grubber. Steven looked miserable even as they rattled off the details of how they were "countering."

A half hour later, Edward left and an enormous, muscled security guy came. He, Flora, Bridget, and Steven got into a detailed talk about cars, and schedules, and avoiding paparazzi. Maddy got so tired that she went upstairs and lay on top of the bed.

She could hear them strategizing downstairs. She wanted to be in control, wanted to do the right thing, but her curiosity overcame her. It was a masochistic curiosity in which the horror and the rush that the horror gave her were synonymous. She went into her study and opened her computer. Her first search was for the *Weekly Report* story. The headline was: "STEVEN WELLER CAUGHT IN GAY SEX SCANDAL." Alongside was a photo of Christian Bernard, and the first thing that struck her was how devilishly handsome he was, in his mid-twenties, brawny, in a gray T-shirt, with thick, defined arched eyebrows and lips that pouted. She started to read the story but got only a paragraph in before the words on the page jumped out at her: "cocaine," "poppers," "wrestling," "wanted to make a sex tape." These words had nothing to do with the Steven she knew, who didn't even like ibuprofen. What was the point of reading all this, why do it to herself? She was helping the enemies by giving them one more hit, driving traffic to their website. She could read it no longer, she had to stop. Only a woman who hated herself would keep reading.

When Steven finally came into the bedroom a few hours later, he looked twenty pounds lighter. "Come here," she said. She pulled him toward her. His gaze was so open that she knew he was scared. "We're going to get through this," she said. She hugged him tightly. She had to be the grounded one, the low-key one. If they both lost it, there was no way they could make it. As she held him in her arms, she could feel his heart beating desperately against her own.

Their routine the next few days was like nothing she had encountered in the marriage. A bodyguard had to get her to a private car, where a driver took her to the studio lot and straight home at the end of the day. There were no public appearances, no dinners out. Bridget, Flora, Edward, or all three were in the house almost every night, strategizing. She didn't want to know the nitty-gritty, though she understood that Steven's *Eddie Coyle* director was upset with him: There had been a *Vanity Fair* writer on the *Coyle* set doing a profile on Steven, but Flora had Steven pull out, and now the reporter was planning a nasty write-around.

Neil Finneran, the CEO of Apollo, had been spotted lunching with Billy Peck, and there were rumors that Billy would replace Steven as Tommy Hall. Steven had hundreds of thousands of supporters, too. There were hashtags on social-media sites like #letStevenWork, and #team-Weller. But Jerome Roundhouse had given a blog interview saying that if the *Weekly Report* story were true, he would boycott the movie because Steven was unsuitable for the role. The anti-Steven hashtags included #WellersDockworker and #tommyhallcruises. Though he had scheduled a handful of lunches and meetings with executives and directors to discuss other roles in the days following the Tommy Hall announcement, Steven was getting cancellations left and right. Suddenly, everyone was away. Meanwhile, Edward's PI could not find Christian Bernard.

After a strategy session at Flora's firm, it was decided that in the absence of a retraction letter, Steven and Maddy should do some well-placed counter-press. Flora arranged for them to dine at a sushi restaurant on Robertson Boulevard to look romantic and show the marriage was stable.

The restaurant, where they had never been, was chosen for its outdoor patio, easily accessible to zoom lenses. Flora's people alerted the paparazzi. When they got out of the car, Steven put his arm around Maddy. They kept their heads down and took a prearranged table on the patio. The entire time, they talked about the miserable past week, but they did so while smiling and tilting their foreheads together, as Flora had instructed.

That night in bed, Maddy listened to the sound of his breathing. It was shallow and came at odd intervals. She took his hand in the dark, thinking about the security guard stationed outside the front door and the other one in the dark car parked around the corner. "This is going to end soon," she said. "I don't want you to be so afraid. When Edward tracks down the guy and he says he made it all up, no one's going to remember this. They won't fire you."

"I just hate that it has to be like this," he said. "I chose my career, but I didn't choose this part of it."

She rubbed his arm, but he was still and robotic. Something dawned on her. She had been feeling trapped the past week, pained by watching her husband become so demoralized, so frightened. She sat up in bed in the dark. "I want to help you," she said.

"What can you do?"

She turned on the light next to the bed and looked down at him. His arm was cast over his eyes. "I can go out there and tell them who you are."

"It wouldn't matter. The studio can terminate me even if they have to pay my salary. The franchise is way more important to them than I am."

"It *would* matter. Flora wouldn't have asked us to go to dinner tonight if she didn't think that kind of thing could help. You can't do press right now, but I can. If I go out there and—"

"Go out where?"

The more she thought about it, the more excited she got. "On a tour, to tell everyone about the man I married. I mean, it's got to make some difference. Wouldn't it? It drives me crazy that there are people out there who want to ruin you. I want to help you. I want to tell them about the man I know." She felt the way she did when she booked a new role and began to mark up the script. She could—what was the phrase?—change the conversation. Neil Finneran would feel better about the deal, and if they tracked down the dockworker after her appearances, maybe Steven could do a belated press tour for *The Hall Fixation* and turn everything around.

"I'm going to call Flora first thing tomorrow," Maddy said. "She'll know where I should go." She clasped his hand. "Edward and Bridget and Flora, they're your team, but I'm your team, too."

"Okay," he said, nodding.

She wanted to believe she was giving him confidence. She wanted him to be strong and happy, to be *Steven*. "Can you sit up?" she asked. He slid up in the bed so their backs were against the gray headboard. "It's just us here in this room now. No one else. I am going to throw myself behind you. I'll be everything you need me to be. But this isn't just your life. It's ours, and I have to be clear. Did you sleep with this man?"

He was still and didn't touch her, as though he knew that anything he did would make her wonder. He stared at her, his gaze direct and strong, and said, "No."

And so she decided to believe him.

By the time Maddy went on *Harry*, she had already done a morning show, a prime-time, and a cover interview with *People*. Flora's strategy was "limited and well placed," targeting women. On the prime-time sitdown, Maddy showed photos from her wedding album and recounted the story of how she and Steven had met. The *People* spread (four pages, photo-heavy, including candids from her life with Steven) had broken records for Internet traffic and newsstand sales.

The PI had tracked down Christian Bernard, who had been in hiding in Miami Beach and was already scared about the repercussions of the story. His retraction letter, which was being written by his lawyer, was expected any day. It was just down to the wording.

It had been Maddy's idea to go on *Harry*. At first Flora said a comedy show would make a mockery of the story. It was the wrong forum for Maddy's audience. Maddy argued that it was the right forum for Tommy Hall fans, those coveted eighteen-to-thirty-four-year-old men, and so after half a dozen extended conference calls with one of the producers and Flora and Bridget on the line with her, the appearance was scheduled.

Maddy had gone on *Harry* twice already, the week before *Jen* aired, and when *I Used to Know Her* came out. She didn't particularly like going on the late-night shows because she didn't feel funny enough, but Harry Matheson, a charming, laconic redhead, was the most likable of all the guys.

When he eased into the question, Maddy was crossing one leg over the other and thinking that her dress was too short. It was electric blue and very slinky. Patti Young, a stylist she'd been working with the past year, had selected it. Though Maddy had practiced sitting in it, it seemed to be riding up more now. Her hair was loose around her face. Her English hair stylist, Gemma, who had come to the house to help her get ready, had used the word "postcoital" to describe it.

The first minute or so of the interview had been easy. Softballs about her current projects, jokes about New York versus L.A. But everyone knew why she was there. She didn't have a movie to promote. As she was tugging her hem down, Harry Matheson said, "We've all been reading a lot about your husband in the tabloids." The crowd got hushed. "As everyone here knows, you're married to Steven Weller." Faint cheers, a few titters. "Who's going to play Tommy Hall. Which is very exciting, by the way. I'm a huge fan of the novels."

"They're really great novels."

"Apparently, some guy, I guess"—Harry looked down at a card—"a dockworker down the coast a little, said he and Steven had a thing." As he spoke, she was careful not to nod—if she nodded, it would seem like she was agreeing—but she couldn't get angry, either. She smiled faintly, attentively, *Be interested, not interesting.* She knew the high-def video was getting the slightest nuance of her expression. "And he provided a lot of details. I mean, this would shock the pants off a lot of people here. I wondered if you wanted to comment on the story."

There were a few lone giggles, and then they died out. She could feel Harry feeling the silence; you weren't supposed to be quiet on TV. But Harry was tolerating it, letting it go on longer than he would with another guest. Because he knew, as they all did, that this was why she had wanted to do the tour. He knew this was television gold.

As she opened her mouth, she felt the stage fright that she had experienced when she did theater, which had abated now that she was doing films, where she didn't have to worry about dropping lines. The light obscured the faces in the audience but not completely: She was aware of the eyes and the mouths. On her movie sets, there was no audience, and now she was performing in front of an audience again, even if it was in Burbank and not on Theatre Row.

"I heard about that story," she said. The audience laughed at the understatement. Good, they were on her side, at least a little bit. "And you know, for legal reasons, I can't get into the specifics of what the guy is saying. But I can say a little bit." She was reminded of how nervous she had been at the Mile's End panel. The problem then was that she hadn't seen the panel as a performance of its own. This appearance was, too. "And I'm sorry if it's more information than you wanted to know, Harry, but I have to tell you, Steven Weller is the best lover I have ever had." Which was true. She and Steven did it a few times a week, when they were in the same city. However, the last ten days they hadn't touched each other, both of them too terrorized to make love. He had been remote, someone beaten and afraid.

The audience was guffawing. A few people clapped, they were eating it up, she felt that she might have them.

"Now, don't get me wrong," she continued. "I wouldn't want you to get the misperception that I've had a lot of lovers. Because I haven't. I'm from Vermont." Scattered giggles. "Based on my small but quality list, I can tell you that if Steven doesn't like women, that would come as a news flash to my clitoris."

She had memorized that line, which was all about the syllables in "clitoris." Flora hadn't liked the sentence at first, but Maddy had swayed her: She said the way to fight the ugliness of the Bernard story was to be blithe and confident. She said Harry's viewers would get this.

It must have shocked the live audience to hear the word "clitoris" spoken clearly, because they were screaming with pleasure. It took a solid five seconds for Harry to shut them up. When they finally did, he mugged and said, "I'd like to be the anchorman delivering the news flash to your clitoris," and the audience went crazy all over again.

Steven was waiting for her in the greenroom. Flora was there, Edward and Bridget, Terry. It was like a war room, with all his supporters. When Maddy came in, they all stood up. Terry said, "You were perfect," though his brow was knotted, as if it had been hard for him to watch Steven go through the past week and a half.

Steven was coming toward her. Later, she would remember the look on his face, a kind of gratitude that could be interpreted as love. He hugged her while the trio went on and on about how it couldn't have gone any better, how she was a natural. She put her face in his chest so as to drown out their voices. She didn't want to be around anyone else, she wanted to be alone with Steven, the man she loved, the man she knew.

In bed later that night, he kissed her cheek, her shoulders, and she was relaxing, feeling not precisely open, the way she had in Venice on her first trip, but getting there, getting there, and he pushed her back onto the bed and she softened.

He was making love to everything about her that made her female. There was no way he could have been with that man. He was going down, down, and he put his tongue in her, and her eyes rolled back. Her hips fell open, and then, on the verge of orgasm, she brought her pelvis down to meet his and he was moving against her until they came at the same time. The story would be retracted and everyone would know, but that wasn't the important part. They had won. They had triumphed over the press, and now his fans knew it and the studio knew it, too, and soon everything would go back to normal.

Act Three

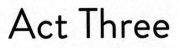

1

About a year after her *Harry* appearance, Maddy was eating breakfast by the pool when Steven came out and threw a pile of printouts on the table with a scowl. They were the reviews of *Husbandry*. The couple had attended the premiere the night before, a charmed night, and they'd had a happy reunion with Walter and Billy. The audience had loved the film, and Maddy had been proud of her work and her husband's.

She had been planning to read the reviews later. Though she told interviewers she didn't read her own press, that was a lie. She scanned them quickly, knowing from Steven's face that the news wasn't going to be good. The critics had loved Maddy and Billy, but Steven's reviews were almost universal pans. He was "out of his league in such a dramatic role." "Wooden" and "remote." "His perpetually downcast eyes make it seem as though he is trying to find his mark."

She thought the reviews were too cruel. Steven's performance had been a bit stilted, but it was because Louis was tightly wound. Watching the film in their screening room for the first time, she'd felt the three of them had created something magical, each character compelling if not wholly sympathetic. Her scenes with Billy were both arousing and arresting, and during the final confrontation she gripped the armrests, almost unsure which character was going to die.

"They're wrong about you," she said now.

"Walter sabotaged me in the editing room," he said, looming over the patio table. "He humiliated me. We never should have given him final cut. He deliberately chose my weakest takes."

"I don't think he did that."

"He was attracted to you and jealous of me for having you. He's a pig. And after I hit him, he never forgave me. He just pretended to. This film was his punishment."

She remembered consoling Dan about his pan at Mile's End, but back then there had been other positive reviews to focus on. The most innocuous of Steven's *Husbandry* reviews called him "not a detriment to the production."

Her reviews were as warm as Steven's were cold: "quietly brave," "operatic," "proof of the awesome power of female sexuality." It had been a triumphant year for her. After winning raves for *I Used to Know Her,* she'd begun fielding big offers—mostly dramatic roles, many of them period films or adapted from successful modern novels—and her quote was now $1 million.

The *Husbandry* pans were the third set in a row for him, following *The Widower* and *Declarations.* But he hadn't seemed upset about the other two. After *Declarations* was released in February, buried, and then savaged, he'd said the indie phase of his career was over—he was focused on playing Tommy Hall—so Maddy thought it was odd that he was worked up about the Juhasz. She didn't want to believe his anger stemmed from jealousy over her good reviews. He was too sophisticated for that, and too powerful.

Everyone was anticipating the release of *The Hall Fixation* the following March. After the Christian Bernard retraction, the studio decided to keep Steven on, and he did a belated press blitz. The production had wrapped in the spring. Everything Steven and Maddy had been afraid of hadn't happened. In her own way, she had gotten him to the place he was now. She felt she had changed the way the studio saw him. She had helped his fans, his employers, and the media regain confidence in him.

"It's going to be okay," she said, standing up and going to him. "You can't dwell on this. You're Tommy Hall. That's all anyone's thinking about. And you said the footage is great."

"The release is still five months away," he said. "Bridget and I had reservations about how Walter was assembling the film, but he kept reassuring us. Never again will I work with a director who wears Depends. Juhasz has set my career back decades." He started inside.

"Well, I don't regret doing *Husbandry* for a second," she called after him.

"Of course you don't!" he said, spinning around. "Because you got raves!"

"No. Because *Husbandry* was what brought us together." He nodded, but his face was white and cold.

A few days later, when she went to take her birth control pill in the kitchen, she noticed the pack wasn't there. Unlike her lorazepam, which she hid in the back of her nightstand drawer, her birth control was kept in one of the kitchen cabinets by the vitamins they both took.

Steven was doing laps in the pool. When he approached the side, she leaned over and grabbed his hand. He picked up his head. "Where are my pills?" she said.

"I've been thinking about it, and I don't want you to take them anymore." His goggles were on and made him look like a bug.

"But you can't just steal them. They're mine."

"Why don't you want to get started on having a family?" They discussed it every couple of months. She knew he knew her reservations. Lately, he hadn't brought it up, which she had taken to mean he was okay with postponing it.

"We've talked about this. I'm only twenty-eight. We have time. I want to be an involved mother, and I'm not ready to stop working now. My career just started."

She thought he understood. He had seemed happy for her, happy that she was becoming a star in her own right.

"Women work through their pregnancies," Steven said, gripping the edge of the pool. "We'll get you trainers to help you lose the weight. You can bring the baby to set. You'll be able to do it your own way. Let's get it going. Get those toxins out of your blood."

"Toxins?"

"The hormones. They're poison. I don't want to be fifty when we start. I want to know my children. Don't you get that? I bought a new house for you. You said you wanted something better for a family."

After her repeated entreaties to move someplace homier, they had closed on a new house a short walk away, an Italianate Mediterranean with a small guesthouse, warm-colored tiles, stenciled beams, and a family-friendly feel. But Steven was renovating it, consulting with contractors and architects, and he said it could be a year before they moved.

"I do want a family, but not yet. You can't just take my pills. It's a violation."

"If you don't want to have children with me now, you never will!"

"That's not true," she said. "Don't you want me to work?" Bridget's phone had been ringing off the hook since the *Husbandry* reviews; she said the film would take Maddy to a new level. There was already Oscar buzz on *Husbandry*, and Bridget said Maddy might get nominated for the many awards that came before the Oscars.

"Back of the spice drawer, underneath the cumin," Steven said, and took off, splashing angrily as he swam.

Out the window of the kitchen she watched him slice through the water, and hated him. He was guilting her for wanting to work. It had to have something to do with her raves and his pans. If he was jealous, she wanted him to rise above it. She didn't understand why he couldn't wait a few more years when he had waited half his life already. In the scheme of a lifetime, a few years meant nothing at all.

Later that week, Steven said he wanted Maddy to come away on *Jo* with him. To Cabo San Lucas and back. After the Christian Bernard story came out, he had moved the boat down the coast to Orange County. He had gotten a one-week break from the action thriller he was working on and wanted her to take a break from her own film, a cancer drama called *The Pharmacist's Daughter* that was being directed by Tim Heller, who had done *Freda Jansons*.

"I can't ask for that," she said. They were in the garden of the Italian restaurant on Beverly. "We're doing all the deathbed scenes next week."

"You can do whatever you want. You're Maddy Freed."

She thought she detected a sneer but said nothing about it because she didn't want to have a fight. "Even if they let me, I can't do it to the rest of the cast," she said. "It's not fair."

"I need you," he said. She remembered the way he'd needed her to do the press the year before, and how she had helped him. Bernard's letter had retracted every detail except that they had met at the yacht club.

"I just want to get away from the bad press," Steven said. "Clear my head. And I feel clearer when I'm with you." She wanted him to act this solicitous toward her all the time. "Please come with me."

Though she could have asked Bridget to speak to Tim on her behalf, Maddy felt obligated to do it herself. When she did, Tim said, "It's going to be hell to reschedule, but I'll make it work if it's what you want."

Maddy didn't want to abandon Steven when he needed her, but the truth was, she was enjoying the film; she liked her costars and didn't want to take a break. So she told Steven no, and the next day he said Terry would come along instead.

The night before he was to leave, Maddy was anxious. "Why don't you just postpone this till we're both free?" she said.

"Because I want to go now. And Terry knows me. Knows how to be there for me."

"I wish you weren't going."

"Maddy, you're not making sense. Do you want to come or don't you?"

"It's too late now. I'm sorry. I shouldn't be confusing you. Have fun. I'll miss you."

He turned over and shut off his light. As she lay there in the dark, she told herself not to be anxious. It was a male-bonding trip. The couple had dined with Terry and Ananda over a dozen times since getting married. Clearly, Terry was straight, and a loyal husband and father. On the boat, the men would do nothing more than talk trash, play poker, and cook.

But maybe he wasn't really taking Terry. There could be women, younger than Maddy, hookers. Or men. Alex. Maybe Steven had lied to her and he was still in touch with Alex.

The first three days he was gone, she was busy with the film, but then she began to think about him nonstop, and she became unfocused on set. By the time it was Steven's last day, she had a day off, and didn't know what to do with herself. When Steven was around, she often wished there were no housekeepers, no Annette, but now she wanted company. Annette was on vacation, visiting friends in Portland. Steven had told her to go, saying she needed a break.

In the morning Maddy sat on a chaise by the pool and tried to read *Act One* by Moss Hart, which she had checked out of the library, but she couldn't focus on the words and realized she had read five pages without absorbing anything. She decided to get a facial at the Four Seasons spa, where they always accommodated her and gave her full privacy.

Earlier that year she had been invited to the fashion shows in Paris. She had become interested in style, and she was enjoying working with Patti, the stylist. She had made other important hires, too: a nice Italian business manager named Craig; and the hairdresser, Gemma. She had built up a nest egg of her own from her movie roles, residuals, and a handbag campaign. She never paid for things with Steven's credit card anymore.

In the facial room, with her eyes covered, she got an itch and scratched her nose, and her knuckles got burned under the steam. "Ow!" she cried out. The aesthetician gave her a cold compress, but for the rest of the hour, her hand smarted and she found herself counting the minutes until it was over.

She stopped at a newsstand on her way home and bought a pack of natural cigarettes and smoked one out the window of the car before she started to feel sick. At home she swam her laps, and when she got out, she didn't feel tired. It was only three o'clock. If she could just talk to him, she would feel better, but he never took phones on the boat.

She sat by the pool and dialed Ananda's cell.

Ananda was someplace loud, and when she answered, she was laughing at something. "How's it going?" Ananda asked.

"All right, I guess." Maddy strained to hear if Terry was in the background. He had a deep, easily recognizable chuckle. "I was just calling to say hi. It's been a long day."

"Did you want to get together? Today, tomorrow? Is everything okay?"

Ask her. Just ask her.

But if she asked and Ananda said the men were on the boat, then Ananda would tell Terry and Terry would tell Steven. Steven would know she hadn't trusted him. He wouldn't like that. It would embarrass him, especially given how painful the Christian Bernard mess had been.

If there was some way she could ask Ananda without asking . . . "Yeah, everything's fine," Maddy said.

There was a loud giggle in the background, but it was a woman's giggle. "What?" Ananda shouted. "I'm sorry, my sister's in town, and we're having drinks and—"

"Oh, have fun with her. I have a really early call time tomorrow anyway. We'll talk soon." Maddy clicked off, listening to the awful birds, the birds that reminded her that it would be hours before it was dark.

She smoked five more cigarettes and felt nauseated and wondered why she had done it. In the kitchen, she ran the butts under the faucet and threw them in the kitchen garbage where he wouldn't see them; he hated cigarettes almost as much as he hated pills. On her way to the stairs, she stopped at his study door, but it was locked. He was pushing her out of his life and if she told him she had noticed it was locked, it would only prove to him that he had been right not to trust her.

Upstairs, she went into her study and shut the door, even though she was alone. Her fingers typed swiftly in the search field, "Alex Duse Repertory Company Steven Woyceck." She paused a long moment before hitting enter.

The first few hits were duds. A guy named Alex Duse who blogged about a theater in Kentucky. A mommy blog by a woman in Duse, Idaho, named Alexandra Woyceck.

She tried "Duse Repertory Company," and an amateurish-looking Web page popped up. The title was "Duse Repertory Company, 1965–1991." It had a gallery of photos organized by year, with all the different repertory companies. Production photos and candids. *Awake and Sing! Othello. Little Murders. Bus Stop.*

Steven was in a lot of the photos, looking young and confident, with longer hair and softer eyes. The last one, at the bottom, was marked, "1984–1985."

She enlarged the thumbnail. The actors looked attractive and hopeful, with large 1980s hair. She was able to locate Steven quickly. He had his arm around the blond guy from the snapshot taken on *Jo*. She scanned the caption, the names, "L. to R." "Casey Landis, Steven Woyceck, Alex Pattison, Mason Rose." The faces were so innocent and young.

In the search field she tried "Alex Pattison Duse." Nothing. "Alex Pattison theater Los Angeles." A listing popped up in seconds. Professor Alex

Pattison, Theater Arts, Los Angeles College. The page included a photo, his CV, his building with room number, office, and phone number. She grabbed her cell phone, stared at the page on her laptop, and back at the phone. What if the professor were there and he told her some version of events that didn't gibe with Steven's? If a journalist hadn't already hunted him down in the fifteen years since Steven had become famous, then most likely there was nothing to tell.

In the bedroom, she put two pills under her tongue and waited for them to work. It was only eight o'clock and she usually didn't take them this early.

She lay in the blackness, thinking about that Danny Kaye movie she had seen as a child, a video rental with her father, who had loved Kaye. *Wonder Man*. Every time he tried to go offstage, the thugs were waiting for him, so he stayed onstage, not for joy but for survival. Offstage was death; onstage was life.

She and Steven had talked about the film on Bridget's patio in Mile's End, the night everything began. She was afraid of Steven now, didn't trust what he told her. She had been reckless in her love for him. Leaving New York without a second thought, leaving the stage. Steven had been her stage. With him, she'd felt safe and protected, no matter how rash it had seemed to Irina or Kira. Now she thought of everything, everyone, she had left behind. She had been afraid that if she took things slowly, he wouldn't want her at all. All this time she had been thinking that Steven was the stage—when maybe he was the gangster waiting in the wings.

Steven was already home when Maddy returned from set the next night at eight-thirty. She bounded into the house. He called out to her from his study, and then he was opening the study door before she had a chance to try it.

She threw her arms around him. "You're back!" she said, going in for a kiss.

"You kiss so openmouthed," he said.

"You never had a problem with my kissing before," she said.

"I never said anything before. Your mouth, it's so open. I like it softer. Gentler. Like this." He kissed her, but she was self-conscious. His eyes looked different. His hair was sandy and his face was tan but unkind.

He sat on the couch. She climbed into his lap. "So did it fly by?" he asked. "Like I said it would?"

"No, it seemed like you were gone forever. I was so lonely." She kissed him again, trying to be conscious of how he said he liked it, and though he kissed back, he seemed distracted. She ran her hand down his cheek and noticed a small red mark near his carotid artery. Broken blood vessels.

"I've been doing some thinking while you were gone," she said, "and I want to move into the new place soon. I don't want to wait a year."

"It's not ready. I told you, it's hell to live in a place that's being renovated."

"But that house will be ours. This one is yours. I've never been comfortable here. When you were gone—I feel like this is haunted."

He lifted her gently off his lap, stood up, and went to the window, his hand on the drapes. He stood in profile as though looking at something very far away. "Maddy, I love you very much, and it's because I love you that I'm saying this." He was going to tell her that things would change. There would be no more boat trips, and he was sorry he had been cruel after the *Husbandry* reviews came out; they would take a trip to Palazzo Mastrototaro. He turned to her. "You don't seem well."

"I am well," she said, astounded. "It's just hard for me. We've been apart so much the last year, with you off in Prague all that time. I know you're busy, but sometimes it seems like you're avoiding me."

"This is our life. It's the work that we both want to do. No one said it would be simple. I love you very much. But you're not the woman I fell in love with."

The rage rose from her belly to her throat. He was accusing her of being crazy. The last few days, she had felt crazy, but before that, she hadn't been conscious of it. And he hadn't said anything about this before. They were separated more than they were together. If, on the phone, she often said she missed him, it wasn't unusual. It meant she loved him.

"You have something on your neck," she said.

He moved his hand daintily to his neck and went to a mirror on the side of the room. "This? We went swimming by a reef. I got stung by a jellyfish." He seemed cool, collected.

"It looks like a hickey."

"You think this is a *hickey*?" he asked. He said it as if he found the word hilarious.

"How am I supposed to know? The boat was where Christian Bernard said everything happened. And I think it's weird that you never take your phone."

"You're bringing up that gold-digger again? After a year?"

Every month or so, when she was feeling lonely or bored or some combination, she would go on her laptop and type in "Christian Bernard." He had become a celebrity in his own right, even though he'd gone back on his story. He had shot a porn video, and he had a manager, and you could book him for $350 a half hour for a private video chat. He appeared to be living in Vegas. She would stare at the gallery of photos, examining his dark eyebrows and full lips, and scroll through them, imagining him and Steven together in the main cabin. After half an hour or so, when she could no longer take it, she would turn off the computer and vow never to do it again, until the next time she got bored or lonely and did it again.

The day the retraction had come out, Steven had invited some people over, Bridget and Flora and some staff from Edward's office. It was festive, and in a quiet moment she pulled Steven aside and asked whether Edward had paid Christian Bernard. "Of course not," Steven said. "He threatened to sue, and that was enough to make Bernard realize he would lose in court."

"So no one bribed him to say it wasn't true," she had said.

"No. He knew it was all over."

Now, in the study, she felt she had been a moron to believe that no money had changed hands. "Were you really with Terry the last couple of days?" she asked.

"Of course I was."

"Are you having an affair with him?"

"You want to know what Terry and I did this week? Why don't you call and ask him." He went to the phone on the desk, picked it up, and held it out in front of his body as if it were a gun. "We played guitar, we cooked, we listened to baseball, played cards, and talked. Drank Scotch. Okay?

You want a minute-by-minute itinerary?" That nasty tone in his voice, that obnoxious, patronizing tone. He put the phone in its cradle but didn't come to her. "I wanted you to come with me on *Jo*. I begged you. But you cared more about your career than our marriage."

"That's not true. I just didn't want to break from production!"

"You see how angry you're getting? This is exactly what I mean. It's not good to be this angry. I've noticed a change in you. In Prague, when you came to visit, you were rude to Corinna." His love interest in the film was played by Corinna Mestre, a beautiful Spanish actress with a Jessica Rabbit figure and a thick accent. Maddy didn't like the way she looked at Steven during breaks. "I'm not rude to your costars, am I?"

"You don't come to my sets. You used to, but not now."

"Poor girl hardly speaks English, and you were glaring at her. And now, after everything we've been through together, this nonsense that I wasn't with Terry. What's going on? I'm concerned about you. You're needy."

"Needy" was a word filled with blame. If a person needed assurance, that didn't make her crazy. It wasn't a personality flaw to want your husband to be faithful.

She was in a terrible conundrum. If she continued to be herself, she might lose him. She pretended to trust him and she was loved, or she was herself and she was despised.

He guided her to the mirror where he had inspected his neck. There was a stone bust of a woman on the table beneath the mirror, and she had to squeeze next to it to see her face. Her eyes were white and her pupils were like tiny pins. "Look at yourself," he said. "You must get some help. I cannot do it for you. I'm sorry it's complicated—that we're apart so often—but you have to find a way to trust me. Otherwise this marriage will fail."

"Are you threatening me?"

"I am trying to paint a picture for you of what you are doing to us. If our marriage ends, you will have only yourself to blame. A marriage is very delicate. You have to treat it with care."

She wondered if he was threatening her. She thought about how she'd felt when he'd brought up the postnup. She hadn't wanted to think about the end, and now he was talking about the end.

"I'm not being careless about our marriage," she said.

"You need to get better. If you want to see a therapist, I'll give you a few names."

"Why can't we see someone together?"

"Because I am not the one with a problem. If therapy doesn't appeal, there are other modalities. You could benefit from more exercise. Those laps in the pool aren't doing much for you. You need an hour a day minimum. More yoga might help you get out of your head. Pick something, I don't care what it is. But commit to it." He guided her firmly to the door of the study. "Now let me be. I have work to do."

He closed and locked the door. It wasn't until she was up in the master, her head buried in three enormous pillows, that she allowed herself to cry. She had to make sure he didn't hear a sound. If he did, he would only be more certain that he was right.

2

Maddy called Dan from the car on her way home from *The Phar-macist's Daughter*. It was a few days after Steven's return from Cabo, and they had been avoiding each other. It seemed like he was watching her too closely. She was afraid and angry, a bad combination.

Tonight Steven had business dinners and drinks and wouldn't be home till eleven, he'd said. She had wrapped at eight and was on the 101, but she didn't want to go home. When Dan picked up, she was so relieved that she panted. "Are you in L.A.?" she asked.

"Yeah," he said. "What's the matter?"

She started to say "Nothing," but then she began to cry and had to cross three lanes and take an exit so she wouldn't get in an accident. She took him off speaker, held the phone to her cheek.

"What is it?" he asked. "What happened?"

"I don't know. I think I made a mess of my life. And I don't know how to fix it."

"Is this about your work, or . . ."

"My work is fine. It's the only thing keeping me sane right now. Can you . . . do you think you could meet me? I need to talk to someone. You have friends, but I don't. Just Steven's friends."

"Yeah, sure, sure. Why don't you meet me in forty-five at London House?" It was a private club with branches in New York, Dubai, London, and now in L.A. Maddy had no idea he was a member.

"Could we go someplace less sceney?" she asked. "I don't want anyone to see me. I'm kind of a mess."

"I'm sure you're not a mess."

"Please?" The makeup woman had commented that she seemed tired, and when Maddy had leaned in to her reflection, she had looked frightened, her skin pale, her hair thin.

"Meet me at my house, then," he said.

She thought about it a moment and then asked the address.

Dan's house in Venice Beach was small, on a quiet street about a ten-minute walk from the ocean. His movie posters were artfully arranged, along with vintage surfboards from the 1960s. It was neat and airy, wholly unlike their apartment in Fort Greene.

"Hey," she said at the door, hugging him hard.

"Hey," he said.

He had a brown couch with no arms and a brushed-metal base, and a kidney bean–shaped coffee table. There were coasters that looked like tiny record albums, and on one of them was a glass of whiskey. "Can I have one of those?" she asked, sitting in a cow-hair chair.

"You're not a whiskey person."

"Everyone is, under the right circumstances," she said.

He disappeared into the kitchen and set down a tumbler that said SO-CAL SPEED SHOP. He was wearing a crew-neck shirt with an artfully weathered collar. She realized he was starting to spend money on clothes. "This place is really nice. I didn't know you were so into decorating."

"I had a little help," he said. "I decided that thirty's too old to have shitty things."

"Success suits you," she said.

"I wouldn't be so sure. I feel like it's just made me more neurotic now that people are actually watching my movies. Anyway, let's not talk about me. What's going on with you? You don't look so good."

She took a sip of her whiskey and winced, it was so bitter, and then she took another one. Dan was quiet, watching her. The way he used to be when she came home from a bad audition and he sensed it hadn't gone well. He could be high-maintenance and melancholic, but he knew how to be silent.

"I feel like I married a stranger," she said.

"Anyone in a relationship feels that way sometimes."

She shook her head slowly. "I thought he would be my home, you know? And now I think maybe I was wrong and he was only using me. Maybe you were right. Maybe he just needed a girl and it didn't matter so much who she was."

"You really think that?"

"I don't know anything for sure."

He sipped his drink contemplatively. Behind his head was a poster of Cassavetes's *Husbands*: "A comedy about life, death, and freedom."

"Does this have to do with—that story about the dockworker?" he asked.

"Yeah, and other stuff, too. Stuff I can't talk about. I try to talk to him, but he makes me feel like I'm crazy. I can't tell if he's right. If I'm right, and I'm not crazy, then I have to . . ." She wanted to cry, but she was numb, cried out. The miserable last day when he was gone, with the hours ticking by. And the hickey. That badge, that stamp, that looked like it had been put there by a troublemaker. "I used to think that if I knew someone was betraying me, then I would have to end it, but it's not so simple. You can be in love and pain at the same time. I just feel . . . stuck. And I don't know how to get unstuck."

"You don't have to stay, you know. What's stopping you from . . . breaking up? You don't have any children."

"I don't know. Maybe I don't want it to end. I want it to be different. I want him to love me, just me. The way . . . he used to."

"I loved you."

"I know." She looked down into her whiskey. "I cheated on you. With Kira. At Mile's End. I think you're the only member of the production team who doesn't know."

"But you hate Kira."

"The night of Bridget's dinner party, I came home before you did. I kissed her and then we—made out a little." He looked more confused than angry, so she continued. "I was tipsy and it was a crazy night. Bridget wanting to sign me. And Steven and I had talked on the patio and I didn't want to tell you. And you didn't come back to the condo with me. I shouldn't have done it."

"It was almost two years ago. It doesn't matter anymore."

"I know, but I was a bad person, and I don't want to be a bad person." She drank some more.

"You're not," he said.

"Thank you for being there for me when my father died," she said.

"Mad, it's nothing. You would have done the same for me."

"You helped me take care of myself. Those nights of insomnia, I thought I was losing my mind. Like how I feel now."

"I was worried about you. I'd never seen you like that. I just wanted you to get well."

Get well. It could be a kind thing or a terrible thing to say to someone. When Dan said it now, it seemed kind, but when Steven had said it in the study . . .

"I think about your dad sometimes," Dan said. "I miss him, too."

"You were the Jewish son he never had. I used to imagine us getting married in Vermont under a chuppah. He would have been bawling so hard."

"Did you have a Jewish wedding to Steven?"

"Just the glass. We broke the glass. Supposedly, it's a symbol of the hymen breaking, but that's gross. To me, it's about pain. In every happy moment, there's sadness, too."

He was looking at her intently, and she was uncomfortable, so she suggested he give her a tour of his house. He took her to the back, where he had a porch and a yard with a trampoline and a hammock and a grill with some chairs. They brought out the tumblers and the bottle of whiskey.

When she put her third glass of whiskey down on the table between them, her hand brushed his and he looked at her. Instead of moving it away, she closed her eyes from exhaustion and drink, and just . . . felt. The warmth of his skin touching hers. To be with someone who cared about her. Who had been there during the most traumatic event of her life. Dan knew her, he had known her then, and he knew her now.

And when she looked at him, she could see the question in his eyes. He said, "I did love you. I had no idea you would leave me. I thought I would spend my life with you."

"I thought so, too, until I met him. It never seemed complicated to me then. It only got complicated later."

She stared at him over the table. Their hands were still touching, and he leaned in. His lips on her lips, the whiskey bitter, and the kiss different from the ones at the end. They kept kissing, and she stood and straddled his chair, and soon they were upstairs, his bedroom had blue walls and his bed was clean and made up, which he never used to do, and then they were under the comforter and he was on her, over her, she touched his long slender fingers. His body was different now, he had muscles that were never there before. It was as though he were a stranger, except this stranger knew how to touch her.

He was slower and less morose, and he seemed to appreciate her body, her smell, or maybe he had been appreciative when they were together and she hadn't wanted to see it because if she didn't see it, then she could leave. She let him take her, wanting to obliterate the feel of Steven on her body. She wanted Dan to stamp out any memory of her husband, the word "husband," she didn't want to think of that, didn't want to be Steven Weller's wife, just Maddy . . .

She came twice, the second time with him, and his eyes gleamed in the dim light. Afterward they lay there naked and said nothing. He went to the bathroom and got water for both of them. She drank gratefully. Her head hurt. They got under the covers, though she knew she would not stay. She could hear a party going on down the block, shouting and laughter.

If she told Steven what happened and he divorced her, she would not care. Right at this moment she would not care.

Dan seemed happy, too, and she curled up next to him, her nose against his. "Do you want me to make some food?" he asked. "I'm starving."

Ten minutes later, he came up with a tray filled with big turkey sandwiches, celery soda, and potato chips and put it on the bed between them. They sat and faced each other, eating naked and smiling.

"I missed you," he said.

"I missed you, but I didn't want to ad-miss it," she said. She wanted to stay here forever, but soon she would have to leave this room and leave this feeling of being open and free, and go back to the house with the iron gate.

"You always loved wordplay," he said. "You're a writer even if you don't think so."

"I'm more of an assistant."

"No, you helped me write that movie, and that's what started everything. I wouldn't own this house without what you did for me." He sounded nostalgic.

"You think you'll ever write anything like that again?"

"What do you mean?

"Respectful of women that comes from the heart?"

"Yeah, I do, actually. *The Valentine* was embarrassing, so fake and manufactured. All the crying and kissing. And then *Hirshman's Mistake*, even when we were testing it and the audiences were going wild, I was disconnected from it all." *Hirshman's Mistake* had become a huge hit over the summer, making a few hundred million dollars. Maddy had seen it in the screening room with Steven and been so embarrassed by it that she'd chosen not to attend the premiere.

"You didn't know that when you went out with the script?"

"I didn't realize it till I got on set. I mean, I tried to humanize the characters as much as I could, but in the testing, we cut all that stuff out because it was slowing down the film. Anyway, I've been thinking more about what it means. To have my name on something. I want to get back to directing my own work. You know, 'a film by.' The whole auteur concept. I haven't been feeling like much of an auteur. I want to make something character-driven. Something small."

"I think that's good," she said.

"Over the summer, I started writing again, just getting back into it. I haven't done anything myself since *I Used to Know Her*, and you and I hammered out the story beats together, so I don't even know if that counts. So it's really been three and a half years. I wound up writing this coming-of-age story about a kid growing up in Maryland. I mean, kind of obvious or whatever, but it's about me being a teenager, and my friends, and my mother. I wrote it in, like, nine days. I've never had an experience like that before. I wrote it really small, you know? I sent it to

Sharoz, and she wants to produce it. It wouldn't cost much. I'd do it with a really bare-bones crew. If I can find the right kid." He seemed to lift up as he spoke, and his face became more beautiful.

"I've never heard you like this," she said.

"I sat down with a line producer, and I think I can do the whole thing for a half-million dollars. I really want to shoot it on film because it's period, and I want to capture that flat suburban landscape."

"With the money you've made the last couple years, you could fund it yourself, couldn't you?"

"I'm going to put money in. People say never to invest your own money in your film, but that's bullshit. I mean, if you care about something, you have to. I'm going to put in a hundred grand." They sat in silence, and she'd opened her mouth to ask him something about the script when he jumped in. "To get the rest, I've been going to people, just a few people, who I feel know me and know what I'm about, and I'm asking each of them for twenty-five thousand . . . What do you think?"

She waited for him to say something else, but he was quiet and she was confused. "Are you asking me for money?" she said. Of course he wasn't; he was just telling her about his plans.

He looked surprised by her confusion. "Well, yeah. I respect you. And your opinion of my work. You have money now, and I need your help."

She got the same feeling she had when Steven told her about the Christian Bernard article. It was worse than dread, it was slow, heavy doom, and it started at her chest and moved down into the pit of her stomach.

"I can't believe you," she said. "You asked me to give you my rights and now you want my money. You don't care about me. Just what I can do for you."

"Of course I care about you."

She was backing away from him. She grabbed the sheet off the bed and held it to her front. "You just wanted to get me into bed to butter me up so I'd invest in your movie."

"*Get* you into bed? I had no idea this was going to happen. You think I planned this? You called me."

"But you invited me to your house."

"You didn't want to go to London House. I had no idea we'd wind up in this room. I was so worried about you when you came in. You looked like a ghost. I wanted to help you. I still do. You're going back to this jerk, and I'm sitting here knowing that moment's going to come, and we're naked and eating and I feel good and you feel good and I just . . . didn't see the point in waiting a week to send you an email."

"Are you asking me to pay you twenty-five grand for having sex with me? Because the sex was not that special."

"I thought it was."

She started dressing, quickly, turning her back so he couldn't see her breasts. He stood, still buck-naked, looking befuddled. "Maddy . . . what happened between us . . . I wanted it to. I'm sorry about the timing of my ask, but—"

"Your ask? Is that what I am to you? You see me as a backer?"

"You're confusing things. I loved what we just did. I'm post-orgasmically retarded right now, you can't hold my timing against me. It's because I feel so safe around you that I thought we could just . . . switch gears."

"I gotta get out of here," she muttered, crawling on the floor in search of a flat. When she had gathered all her things, he reached for her and she recoiled as if he were hot. "Leave me alone!" she shouted. "You're just like him. I thought you were different, but you're exactly the same."

In the car, her mind was racing. When she loved a man, made herself vulnerable to him, he betrayed her, and her father had betrayed her by leaving her so soon, leaving her when she still needed him, when she was barely an adult. She couldn't believe she had been stupid enough to go to bed with Dan. Steven and Dan were wheeler-dealers.

When she got home, it was around midnight. She found Steven in the bathroom, the door wide open. He was standing in front of the vanity mirror, using an electric clipper on his nose hair. His mouth was open slightly, his eyes intent and focused.

She waited for him to ask where she had been, but he said nothing. At first it looked like he was grinning, but he was only tightening his lips to get the best angle into his nose.

3

Over the next few days, Dan texted her ill-written apologies. After she did not respond, the texts stopped. She told herself this was a good thing, she could forget about it and pretend it hadn't happened.

But to forget was not so easy. Her body would come alive as she remembered the way Dan had touched her, and then the guilt would follow the arousal and she would resolve to tell Steven. A few times she opened her mouth to blurt it out, before shutting it for fear he would leave her if she did. Hoping that he would force her into a confession, she waited for him to ask about that night, but he never did. His lack of suspicion had the effect of making her feel less trusting than she already did. Any man who was faithful to his wife would expect fidelity in return. She became certain that he'd had sex on *Jo*, though with whom she did not know. Every time he went on the boat, she decided, dozens of times since they had met, he was fucking. Terry, another man, a woman, Corinna Mestre, many men, many women, the possibilities multiplied in her head until he was betraying her with half the industry. His directors, his trainers, his accountant, even Edward Rosenman of Rosenman Kogan LLP.

After his lecture about modalities, though, she was afraid to express her doubts, so her fear was accompanied by the pain of trying to hide it. Whenever he was gone for a long stretch but not on set—with his trainer or at meetings or dinners—she was careful to make it seem that she was not suspicious. Even so, he seemed to be waiting for her to attack him. Awaiting signs of neediness. As if he had decided she was a madwoman and nothing she did could change his opinion.

But her work was a distraction, a good one. After *The Pharmacist's Daughter* wrapped in October, her next film would be *Barry Hiller's Loins*, the new Elkan Hocky, in New York. Hocky was a famed Brooklynite director in his seventies, known for his witty dialogue, and *Loins* was an ensemble comedy about a young woman, played by Maddy, who decides to find her biological father only to learn that he's a mute homeless man. Maddy would be renting a furnished luxury apartment in Tribeca. She had thought about renting in Brooklyn but decided the commute to the Upper East Side locations would be too long.

A few weeks after she was cast she learned that Kira had been cast as her best friend—because of her work in *Rondelay*, which had had a healthy run in independent theaters and turned Kira into a hipster acting phenom. Maddy had watched a DVD of *Rondelay* with Steven in the screening room, and both agreed that Kira was magnetic. She seemed to be digging deeper than she had in *I Used to Know Her*.

Kira had been the subject of adulatory profiles in *The New Yorker*, *The New York Times*, *Entertainment Weekly*, *New York*, and *Out* in which she talked openly about her lesbianism. The op-ed page of the *Times* published a think piece on her called "The Non–Coming Out." The author, a gay-and-lesbian-studies professor at Harvard, said that many of today's twentysomethings had had same-sex experiences, or had friends who were gay, and weren't filled with the self-hate that had plagued earlier generations. "In today's entertainment landscape," the professor wrote, "homosexuality is no longer a liability to a career, something that must be hidden, as it was by Rock Hudson and Rudolph Valentino."

Maddy had been nervous when she'd learned that she would be working with Kira again, given their confrontation at the *I Used to Know Her* premiere, but Kira called a few days before shooting began. "I was drunk that night," she said, "and I was stupid. Your marriage is none of my business."

"Thank you," Maddy had said.

Barry Hiller's Loins turned out to be easy, fast-paced, and fun. Elkan was gracious and witty, and many days they shot on the streets, which Maddy loved—it was as alive as shooting on a studio lot was dead.

She went to dinner with Zack one night, and he told her he still wanted to work for her. Maddy said Bridget was helping her and she saw no reason to leave. Though he grimaced, he didn't call her again in New York. Maddy wasn't sure whether he hadn't truly wanted to sign her or was being tactical by not pushing too hard.

One night when she saw that she had an early wrap, she made plans with Irina to see a Polish production of *Waiting for Godot* at the Brooklyn Academy of Music. During the year and a half since she'd left Brooklyn she had been in only infrequent contact with Irina—mostly by email—and was excited to rekindle their friendship.

She had her driver take her to Irina's place in Williamsburg. With the sunroof open, they drove down the Brooklyn Queens Expressway to BAM and talked. Irina had booked a role in a Wooster Group production. Maddy told her how great Elkan Hocky was to work with, and Irina squinted at her and said, "You look really skinny."

"I lost some weight for *Husbandry*, and then, I don't know, I kept it off. We eat pretty healthy, and everyone in L.A. is low-carb, so it's easy."

"Is that Stella McCartney?"

Maddy was in a black knee-length dress with a poufy bottom and a double-breasted cropped jacket sewn onto the top. "Yeah, why?"

"I saw it in a *Vogue* spread." Patti had helped Maddy select it for an awards show.

When they arrived at BAM, Irina started to get out first, but she was on the street side and Maddy held her arm. After waiting for the driver to open the door, Maddy got out, Irina just behind her, and stepped onto the curb. Immediately, the press started flashing pictures. Irina emerged beside her and moved out of frame, waiting for Maddy to finish. Maddy felt bad and pulled her in, spelling her name for the photographers. Irina seemed to enjoy the chance to pose, but when they got to the lobby, she said, "You didn't have to do that."

"I wasn't going to let you stand there," Maddy said.

"They're not interested in me," Irina said. "They're interested in you. It was embarrassing."

In their seats, Maddy could feel the tension between them and was unable to enjoy the play. Afterward, they went to a small wine bar on Lafayette where she used to go with Dan. At the table, they dissected the production. She felt like they were reconnecting.

They began to laugh as they split a bottle of Valpolicella, and as they waited for their entrées to come, Irina said, "In August you and Steven will be married a year, right?"

"Yep."

"How old is he again?"

"Forty-seven."

"Does he want kids?"

"He does, but I'm not ready. He's older, so he wants to get started sooner."

"You should wait," Irina said. "You have time. Don't let him rush you into it."

The waiter brought their food. Maddy had ordered a large salad and a few sides, so it would appear she wasn't dieting, while Irina got pasta in a duck ragout. "He's not rushing me into it," Maddy said while Irina dug in. "I told him I really want to be there for a baby, take time off, and I'm not ready to do that yet."

"But you'll have nannies."

"Sitters, maybe. I don't know if we'd have a live-in."

"You'll definitely have live-ins. You guys are rich as shit."

"That's not very nice."

"Are you saying you're not?"

"No, but—"

"Why are you trying to pretend you're the same person you used to be? Nothing about you is the same. You dress differently. That dress cost, like, five thousand dollars."

"I got this dress for my career. If you were photographed all the time, you'd have to be careful what you wore, too."

"Why don't you admit that you like being famous? Standing on press lines and hiring private cars."

"I thought you would like the car, so we wouldn't have to take the train. I wanted us to have fun tonight."

"You had to impress me. Show off. I didn't have to go to an opening-night thing at BAM. I would have been happy to go to a bar. Just catch up with you. Or hang out at my loft."

Maddy realized she had botched it. She had brought Irina to her turf instead of the other way around. "I promise you, I wasn't trying to show off," she said, "but I can see how you would think that. I'm sorry."

Irina chugged her wine and wiped her mouth with the back of her hand. It left a mark by her lower lip, like a half-smile, except she wasn't smiling. "I don't know why you wanted to see me."

"I miss you. I thought we could talk. Maybe not pick up exactly where we left off—but—talk about things. You think my life in L.A. is so perfect, but it's not."

"What do you mean?"

"It's hard making new friends, and the women are sort of dumb, and I don't have anyone I can really talk to about my personal life, so—"

"What about your personal life?" Irina said, setting down her glass. "What do you want to talk about?"

Maddy wanted to tell Irina everything, about how hard the *Weekly Report* story had been on the marriage, and the boat trip with Terry, and the neck mark, and even her night with Dan a month ago. She wanted to ask if Irina thought she had made a mistake in marrying Steven. But she was used to having to keep everything close to the bone, for fear of the paparazzi and the Internet bloggers. She realized she wasn't sure she'd be able to open up to Irina even if she wanted to.

"I don't know, everyone's watching us so closely all the time. It can be stressful. The first year of marriage is hard enough, but then there's all this other stuff." The car with shaded windows. Private dinners in the mansion, so there would be no worries about the paps. She didn't want to be the kind of person who used the word "paps."

"Are you happy with him?"

"Of course I am. I'm very happy."

Irina scooted back in her chair, which made a loud noise as it scraped against the floor. "See? You don't really want to be friends."

"But I do!"

"You won't even talk to me. What's the point? I'm just some symbol of your authenticity. I'm your arm candy. You're different. The way you preened for the cameras, you were so into it."

"I wasn't preening. I was posing. You would understand if you . . . if you . . ."

"You've bought in to the bullshit. You pretend you haven't—'Oh, BAM, it's in Brooklyn, it's so edgy, so *authentic*'—but we might as well be in Manhattan. This neighborhood isn't even black anymore. You *have* changed. Even if you think you haven't."

Irina plopped some money on the table and dashed out, leaving Maddy alone. A woman at the next table did a double take when she saw her. Maddy got the bill and left. The car was waiting outside.

Back in the loft, she wrote a check for $25,000 made out to Dan Ellenberg and arranged for FedEx to pick it up.

She took her laptop into bed and got Steven on Skype. They'd been trying to Skype once a day. He had started a cop comedy, set in Boston but shooting in L.A., called *Booked*.

When he answered, she could see that he was in his study. "Hey," he said, but his eyes were flicking to the side.

"I had a fight with Irina," she said.

"Who?"

"My friend. From The New School. I've told you about her. We went to see this play at BAM and—" She heard voices in the background, followed by laughter. It sounded like women and men. "Who is that?"

"I'm having a little get-together. Some people from the movie." There were at least three or four voices. She was surprised he would let guests into the study, since nowadays he kept it locked.

"Oh. Anyway, I just wanted to tell you what ha—"

"It's not a good time. I'll try you tomorrow, okay?" The image froze. He had closed his laptop without saying goodbye.

Maddy was shooting a dinner-party sequence in a midtown restaurant known for its zebra-pattern wallpaper. Kira was in the scene, and two handsome comers playing their boyfriends. Maddy's was played by Jared Wilkinson, a bumbling comedic actor who specialized in Ralph Bellamy types.

It was a long talky scene that they had to shoot repeatedly so Elkan could get all the reaction shots. There were continuity problems, and the over-the-shoulders grew frustrating and tedious. There were parts of acting that were transcendent and others that made you feel like a prop.

When they broke for lunch, Maddy was relieved. Craft Services had taken over a church basement a few blocks away, and she went down the buffet line and then headed toward Jared and Kira's table. She saw Jared whisk something away and hide it on his lap. "What is that?" Maddy asked, sitting down.

"Nothing," Kira said quickly.

"Come on," she said lightly. "What is it? What were you guys looking at?"

"It's really nothing," Jared said, and the expression on his face was so mysterious that she lunged for the thing on his lap. The *New York Post*. She scanned the front page and then Page Six, which was on page twelve, till she got to the blind items. "Which A-list leading man holds all-male stag parties with his handsome 'bro-friends' at his home in L.A. whenever his wife is away on location?"

She left her food on the table and ran down the street into her trailer. It was humiliating to have her cast mates read this, mocking her marriage, when after this, she would have to go work with them.

Kira was pounding on the trailer door, calling her name. Maddy let her in, more to stop the commotion outside than to hear what she had to say. She shut the door but stayed standing so Kira wouldn't linger. "Maddy, I'm sorry," Kira said. "You weren't supposed to see that."

"You guys could not have made it more obvious."

"I wasn't even reading it. You think I would ever read that fascist rag? It was Jared's."

"You were acting like teenagers. Please just go."

But Kira walked to the couch and made herself comfortable. She occupied every space she was in as if she owned it. "Just listen to me for a second," she said.

"I don't want to." If only she hadn't grabbed the paper. You didn't learn who you were in a newspaper that left stains on your hands.

"I saw you on those shows last year," Kira said. "Defending your marriage. I felt sorry for you."

"He retracted it! The guy was a grifter."

Maddy didn't like the way Kira was looking at her, with horrified pity. "Just listen to me for a second," Kira said. "What if it's possible? What if all these rumors and blogs and blind items add up to something? And he cheats on you with men?"

"He doesn't." Maddy collapsed next to her on the couch. "You're not the world authority on homosexuality."

She could feel herself weakening. She hadn't been able to talk to Irina, and she couldn't talk to Bridget, and Ananda was Terry's wife. There was the loneliness of fearing you weren't loved and the loneliness of not being able to speak to anyone about it. She had tried to tell Dan, but he'd ruined everything.

"I know I'm not," Kira said. "But if you found out that he was cheating on you—with a woman or with a man—would you still want to be with him?"

Maddy couldn't take it anymore. She put her face in her hands and said, "He *has* been with a man." Kira sat still, saying nothing, as though she knew a single word might cause Maddy to shut her mouth. Then she told Kira about Alex from the playhouse, and the inscription, and her talk with Steven by the pool. She made her swear never to tell anyone. After Maddy finished, Kira shook her head. Her eyes were wide and knowing.

"It was just one night," Maddy said. "It doesn't mean he's gay now."

"He was so young then," Kira said, "and it was a different era. The mid-eighties? Do you know the stigma against gay men then? With AIDS, and the homophobia, and people thinking you could get it from touching . . ."

"So?"

"For a man to sleep with another man in the 'eighties . . . it means he had to really want it. Whether he cheats on you or not, whether he's closeted even to himself I don't know, but Steven is gay."

"You and I made out, and you never thought *I* was gay!"

"It's different for men."

"Come on."

"I'm sure he cares deeply for you, and I'm sure he wants to be straight, but what you just told me—I don't think he can be." Kira sighed and took both of Maddy's hands in hers. "Do you want to be married to a man who can never love you, no matter how hard he tries?"

"That isn't Steven."

"Things aren't perfect with Reggie and me, she thinks I'm hyper-social, she has a drinking problem and also a bit of a bread addiction, but I know she loves me. And I know she loves women. And it's a relief because I have this thing where I fall in love with women who aren't gay." Kira bent her head and then lifted it. "I've been exactly where you are right now. Which is why I know you're setting yourself up for a lot of pain. Don't you want to be with someone who loves you the way you want to be loved?"

"How do you know how I want to be loved?"

"Because I saw you with Dan when we were shooting the movie. I saw the way you looked at each other. Dan loved you completely."

Maddy thought of Dan's hands on her body at his house. He had asked for money, just moments later, and she'd gone home feeling miserable. "Steven loves me completely," she said.

"I know how much you want to be an actress. But you don't have to do it this way."

"What way?"

"You don't have to turn your work into your life. You made your life a movie."

"How many times do I have to tell you, *there is no contract?*"

"I know there isn't," Kira said. "If you had a contract, you'd be much less unhappy."

"I married Steven because I love him. Now would you please get out of my trailer?"

Kira went to the door, and when she got there she said, "I only want the best for you."

"That's not true at all," Maddy told her. "You don't even know me."

4

When Maddy returned from New York, Alan drove her straight to the new house. Steven had moved them without telling her. The house still had the beams she had loved on their first visit, the mural on the fireplace, and the loggia (a word Steven had taught her), but beyond that nothing was the same. He had stripped it of much of the very detail that had charmed her. There were severe angles, and everything was in gray, and it had a coldness that hadn't been there when they first saw it. It was covered with drop cloths. Drapes and dust. She had been in a rush to move in, but when she saw the plaster everywhere, she regretted that she had complained about the mansion. She needed a home that was peaceful.

"What do you think?" Steven asked after he embraced her in the loggia.

"It doesn't feel ready."

"Most of it is. The bedrooms are. I thought you'd be happy. We'll get it finished. I just want everything to be right. I wanted you to feel like this was a place we would have together." He came to her and held her face in both hands. "I'm so proud of you."

"Why?"

"For doing an Elkan Hocky. He's never cast me in a movie. Aren't you proud of yourself?"

"I guess so."

"The shoot was good for you. You seem much better. I think it was helpful for us to get some time apart."

She didn't feel healthy, but if he was saying it, she wasn't going to argue. He was being kind to her. She felt guilty that she had betrayed his trust by telling Kira about Alex. Maddy was anxious that Kira might unload it on the kind of person, some gay-rights activist, who would spill it to a tabloid. That was the last thing Steven needed after what they had gone through with *The Weekly Report*.

Annette was calling from the kitchen and Steven left the room. Maddy collapsed onto a couch and the plastic tarp crinkled beneath her. No matter which way she moved, it went on with its wretched sound.

Maddy had a two-week break before her next film, *The Cocktail Hour*, was to begin, so she was spending a lot of time doing yoga and reading. One morning she decided to jog to the Wilshire library. She was browsing in the literature stacks, which had a good selection of hardcovers from the '70s and '80s, when she heard a voice behind her. "Have you read Anita Brookner?"

It was Julia Hanson, dressed down in a gauzy top and dark jeans that showed off her fit figure. "No," Maddy said carefully, backing up a few inches.

Julia pulled out a slim paperback called *Hotel du Lac*. "You'll like this one."

"What's it about?"

"A romance writer who tries being alone." She pulled a few other Brookners off the shelf and handed them to Maddy.

Maddy didn't know what to say besides "Thank you." This Julia Hanson seemed completely different from the one she had met at the ball. Normal and nice.

"I've seen a few of your movies," Julia said. "You're very natural. That independent one about the two girls, that was a strong script. It's hard to find roles like that for women."

"I cowrote it," Maddy said. "I mean, I wrote the story."

"That explains it," Julia said. "You have to generate your own material if you want it to be any good. If I had done it, I wouldn't have been unemployed all that time. Now that I'm working, I'm grateful every day."

Maddy nodded at her. Not knowing what to say, afraid to go and afraid to stay.

"I watched that *Harry* appearance you did when the man came forward. You pulled off something nearly impossible. You were likable and genuine."

"I did what needed to be done."

"Steven must be grateful to have his wife go out there and defend him in a way he couldn't defend himself. People think he put you up to it, but I could see that it came from you. He never would have asked you to do that."

"It was my idea," Maddy said in a whisper. Then she pulled Julia deeper down the aisle, farther from the other people. "Julia," she said, "why did the marriage end?"

Julia smiled. A young woman came through, looking for a book, and took a momentary glance at them before landing farther up the aisle. Maddy knew Steven would be furious to know she was talking to Julia in a public place about him, but she felt she had run into her for a reason.

"It was all the fighting and the drinking," Julia said. "I didn't want to admit it was over, I wanted it to work. I loved him. He was my life. But in the end, he gave me no choice."

"So *you* ended it?"

"Of course I did. Did he say he did?"

"Not exactly."

"I'd never met anyone who got angry like Steven did. Before that, before it got ugly, there were many good nights. His humor and his love of life, his sensuality, the way he turned dinner and a movie into an adventure. The fact that he had his problems, problems that wouldn't go away . . . it doesn't erase the good moments. There's no one like him, when he's at his best."

Maddy wanted to ask Julia what had happened with Alex Pattison, whether Steven had cheated. Had she found them in bed together? Had he told her he was gay back then? Was that why they'd split up? What if Julia said he had come out to her? What then? Would Maddy go back to Steven and accept whatever explanation he gave, that Julia was crazy or still pining after him? Why ask a question if you didn't want to know the answer?

"I should go," Maddy said quickly, and darted out. She wanted to get out of sight before Julia could catch up, though she wasn't sure she was following. She was in such a rush that she cast the novels on a table on her way out.

December and January were filled with awards shows in both New York and L.A. Maddy felt honored by all the nominations she received for *Husbandry*: the National Society of Film Critics, the New York Film Critics Circle, the IFC, and the Golden Globes. Billy and Walter also netted a few, though Walter refused to travel to the States for the ceremonies.

Given Steven's poor reviews and lack of any nominations for his own work, he was surprisingly supportive of Maddy's accolades. He accompanied her to all the ceremonies and called himself her "arm candy." It was as though their terrible fighting after his trip to Cabo was a thing of the past. Every time she felt an instinct to question him about a late dinner or a long phone call, she forced herself not to. A discussion of fidelity could soon become an interrogation. The problem wasn't his behavior but her reaction to it. If he happened to be out late at night or away in D.C. on political business, she would just take pills to go to sleep, so she didn't have to lie awake and worry.

When the Oscar nominations were announced, she woke up at the crack of dawn to watch them on the TV in the screening room. Her heart fell when she didn't hear her name. When reporters called, she was gracious, talking up the other actresses, even though she was hurt to have had all that buildup without the most important nomination of all. Bridget said, "It was too sexual. The Academy is made up of ninety-year-olds. The women were offended, and the men had erection-induced heart attacks in front of their DVD players and died before they could vote."

Lael Gordinier had been nominated for *Freda Jansons*, which Maddy tried not to think about. Maddy and Steven were asked to be presenters for a costume award. For Steven, it was advance publicity for *The Hall Fixation's* release. Though the ceremony was long and less exciting than she had imagined it would be, and their intro was clunky, she liked presenting with Steven. When she stepped onto the stage and saw all the people, she hoped the next time she stood here it would be to receive an Oscar, not give one.

The Hall Fixation came out on March 15. All the entertainment journalists were on the red carpet, and most of A- and B-list Hollywood. Everyone wanted to see the movie. Maddy and Steven walked the red carpet together. The entertainment journalists didn't treat her like arm candy.

They asked about her projects and their plans for a family. She had become adept at dodging such questions with lines like "It'll happen when it happens." She was conscious that she was making no move to get pregnant. Steven had not mentioned it since the day he hid her pills, and she was coasting on his silence.

As Maddy stood just beside him, Steven discussed his Brazilian jiujitsu training, his pranking of Corinna Mestre, and his love of the Tommy Hall books. "I did not have the easiest childhood," he said, "and the books were an escape for me. That's what we were trying to do in the movie, just bring Jerome Roundhouse's vision to life."

Maddy had never seen the movie from beginning to end and enjoyed it about as much as she'd expected to. The action sequences elicited applause, and the scenes between Tommy and his boss, Richard Breyer, had real pathos (Billy Peck's father, Martin Peck, a 1960s screen star, had been cast as Breyer in a career-reviving turn).

The worst part of the film was the undercurrent of misogyny. Corinna had excessive frontal nudity and no funny lines. In one scene, her nipples were showing through her shirt. Her character's name was Cherry Rodriguez, with a long-running joke about whether it was actually Chevy or Cherry because she spoke with such a thick Spanish accent. Maddy hated that the sex was shot in fake blue light. In one of the scenes, Corinna's character came only after Tommy fucked her really hard.

The post-premiere party was held at the Hard Rock Cafe. After circulating briefly with Steven, Maddy found a perch by one of the bars, not too close to the DJ, so it would be quieter. She had learned from attending enough of these parties that sometimes it was easier to split up than be on each other's arm for hours on end. Steven was in his element, shaking hands, accepting congratulations, the prince of the night.

A photographer was making his way around the floor, and Maddy watched as Steven and Bridget posed together, both with blinding smiles. They looked like they were on top of the world.

"Now, why is a girl as beautiful as you all alone?" a voice said. She turned to see Billy Peck, and embraced her old friend warmly.

"Your father was amazing," she said. "He looked like he was having a great time on the press line."

"Are you kidding?" Billy asked. "People thought he was dead until Bridget rescued him. He can't believe he's making this much money in his old age."

A handsome early-thirties blond guy with broad shoulders came up to Billy, and they hugged and clapped each other on the back. "Have you met Maddy Freed?" Billy asked, gesturing to her. The guy shook his head. "Maddy Freed, Ryan Costello. Ryan and I are working on *Stick Shift*."

All she could remember was that it was a buddy movie. "Right, what's it about again?"

"I'm an uptight Brit," Billy said, "stranded in the Midwest because of a plane problem, and I have to hitch a ride with Ryan."

"That sounds hilarious," she lied.

"Ryan keeps making me break," Billy said. "If you haven't already, you have to watch *Bunk*. It's set at a summer camp in the 1980s, and Ryan plays the activities director."

"I hope *Bunk* isn't what I'm remembered for," Ryan said. His voice was deep and masculine, like a slowed-down record player.

"I've watched that goat-milking scene on YouTube like seventy times," Billy said, laughing.

"You're starting to creep me out, man," Ryan said. He came off as smug, maybe because he was new to Hollywood.

"So are you a Tommy Hall fan, Ryan?" she asked.

"Yeah, but they totally messed with the ending of the novel," Ryan said. "Where he begins to suspect that Richard is a mole."

"You read the novel?"

"Of course. It's all about Richard as the father figure for Tommy. Because he's always searching for his dead dad. Every guy in America with a shitty dad loves Tommy Hall. That's why this movie will be a hit."

A woman was coming toward them in a strappy black dress whose hem began at the knee and then rode up in a dangerous upside-down U before returning to the other knee. Maddy didn't recognize her at first, but then she saw it was Kira. Her breasts seemed smaller, and her hair had gotten longer and blonder. They hadn't spoken since they wrapped the Elkan Hocky.

"You must be so proud of Steven," Kira said, kissing her on both cheeks.

Maddy introduced her to the men. Billy and Ryan ogled her openly. "So what are you doing out here?" Maddy asked.

"I moved."

"Really? I thought you were going to stay in New York forever."

"I did, too. But there's more work here, and this was the right time to make the transition."

"Ah, you've crossed over to the dark side," Billy said. "For years I tried to live in London, and then I realized I was fooling myself."

"What about Zack?" Maddy asked Kira. "Is he still in New York?"

"Yeah, but he's moving out in a couple of weeks. He transferred to Bentley Howard's L.A. office."

Maddy was hurt that Zack hadn't called but didn't want to say so. "Is Reggie moving out, too?"

"We broke up. It was too stressful, I was never around. And she joined A.A., so she wanted to be with all her A.A. friends. She got super-neurotic about alcohol. I couldn't kiss her if I'd taken echinacea."

"There's alcohol in echinacea?" Maddy asked.

"Oh yeah," Ryan said. "A drop of echinacea is like a fifth of Maker's."

"I can't believe how different you look, Kira," Maddy said. "Did you lose weight?"

"Eight pounds. I did this cleanse. Don't worry, I'm not ano. It's just that after the shitting I've done the past week, there is nada in my lower GI. Later." She walked off, swaying her hips, and Maddy watched the men watch her go.

"I wouldn't mind getting a look at her lower GI," Billy said. Ryan whispered something to him, and Billy bent over laughing.

Maddy and Steven arrived home from the private after-party at three. There was plastic hanging from the bedroom ceiling, but these days she hardly noticed it. The renovations were never-ending. She was living in Roman ruins.

In bed, she said, "I'm proud of you," and pulled Steven close. "You were so good as Tommy. You've found your stride."

"Are you saying I didn't have a stride before?"

"I just mean you're a spy, and you do all this action, but it's like you're you at the same time. And everyone loves you."

"Do you?"

"More than all of your fans put together."

She felt close to him, connected. He was most pleasant to be around when he liked himself. If Tommy Hall made him feel relevant, funny, and strong, then she would support *The Hall Fixation* and the inevitable sequels.

When she got on top of him, she could feel his erection. He moved his hands on her and took his time, kissing her, sucking her breasts. Maybe it was the champagne at the party, but soon she was close to coming.

He moved her so they were lying on their sides, and then he pivoted her and lifted her haunches so he was taking her from behind. As he thrust himself in and out, she wondered if he was imagining that he was Tommy Hall making love to the girl in the movie, Cherry Rodriguez or Chevy Rodriguez. She still wasn't clear on the name.

One day in the early fall, Bridget took Steven to lunch. *The Hall Fixation* had taken in a whopping $58 million in its first weekend, continuing to build over the spring and summer. The nation and the world had been swept by Tommy fever. Business sections ran long stories on the long-lead marketing campaign and branding, Steven was swarmed by Tommy fans every time he went out. Critics extolled its performances and pacing; a *New York Times* reviewer called it "a postmodern action film." Over the past few years, the highbrow reviewers had taken to praising the occasional popcorn film. They would use words like "camp" and "entertaining" to show they knew they were going out on a limb. But even the good reviews made little difference to the box office; films like *The Hall Fixation* were critic-proof.

Apollo Pictures had already green-lit the next adaptation, *The Hall Surprise*, with Bryan Monakhov adapting and directing again. Bridget had read the first draft and liked it better than the first.

"I got an interesting call from Neil Finneran at Apollo today," she told Steven at the restaurant, after their salads had arrived. "Faye Fontinell in

The Hall Surprise? He had a really interesting idea about who could play her."

"Yes?"

She said the name and Steven jerked his head back in surprise, then bit a piece of arugula, chewing and not saying anything. She was anxious about how he would react, because she was already sold. The thing about these franchises was that you kept having to outdo yourself. Each Tommy Hall needed to be bigger, splashier, and better than the one before. And SteMad was the hottest couple in Hollywood. The mere announcement of Maddy's participation would get audiences primed.

"But when Tommy first sees Faye on that beach in Tulum," he said, "she's in a bikini."

"Maddy's a beautiful woman."

"You know what she'll say: 'I didn't get an MFA to wear a bikini.' She only did all that sex in *Husbandry* because it was Walter."

"If the bikini is an issue, I'm sure Bryan will be open to rethinking it. Neil feels Maddy will elevate Faye, and he thinks the two of you would make a fantastic combination. Like Andress and Connery. Bryan wants her. He knows her from Mile's End."

Steven wasn't sold on the premise. Maddy was carving out a niche as a dramatic actress capable of period films and English accents. The Tommy films weren't her brand.

"It's important for an actress to keep audiences guessing," Bridget continued. "When you played a small-town cuckold, you didn't think you'd be headlining an action franchise two years later, but it worked out. You know why? Because you adapted. Smart actors keep switching genres."

Bridget didn't want to have to spell it out to him, but it was important that she stay in the good graces of Finneran. She didn't want to be a manager forever. The effort-reward ratio was demoralizing, increasingly so in an era when costs were being cut. The list of stalled or dead projects grew longer each year. All the great representatives moved on eventually to do what they'd wanted to do all along: make taste. And the boldest way to be a tastemaker was to create entertainment on a global scale. By running a Hollywood studio.

"She'll be insulted if I ask her," he said.

"You have to present it to her the right way."

He was not sure he could. She seemed happy doing long, talky films based on unreadable six-hundred-page books. When she was happy, she was busy, and he liked her to be busy.

But *The Hall Fixation* had changed the way he thought of himself. He liked being on top again. It would help to have someone high-profile as Faye. "What's he offering?"

"Two million. For two weeks' work."

He leaned back in his seat, considering it. He and his wife were an object of fascination, due in part to that hellish Christian Bernard affair. There were infertility stories and constant items that one or the other was cheating with costars, or they were in couples therapy.

He had spent years hating the press but had never questioned the importance of public relations. If Maddy did Faye Fontinell, audiences would go nuts. The prurient thrill of watching them make love on screen. At all the press appearances, she would be by his side, in her own right, as a star and not just a supporter.

He brought it up over a quiet dinner at a four-star Italian restaurant inside a two-star Beverly Hills hotel. He waited until dessert. Tiramisu. Maddy had a bit of cake on the corner of her lip and was so unsuspecting that he almost felt guilty. He eased into it, telling her how excited he was about Monakhov's first draft. And then he told her about Faye Fontinell. He explained that they first meet on a beach, but she goes on to be a real sparring partner for Tommy, an intellectual equal. He chose not to mention that Faye was a stripper before she joined the NSA.

And then he landed it: "Neil Finneran wants you to be Faye."

"What?"

"Think about it. We'd get to work together. Be in the same city. The same home."

She shook her head slowly. "But Corinna's role was demeaning," she said. "I know you don't think so, but I do. Faye sounds like she's only in the script to give teenage boys boners."

"I can make you an associate producer. We can rework the scenes. I promise you. We can get it into the contract."

"They meet on a beach. So she must be wearing a bikini."

"We'll make it boy shorts. We're in a very strong bargaining position, with *The Hall Fixation* being such a success."

"How can I say it more clearly? I love that you're happy playing Tommy, but this isn't the kind of project I see for myself."

His face became cross. She hadn't seen this look in a while. The last time was after he went off on *Jo* and told her she had to get well. "If you loved me, you would do it."

"Steven." She sighed. "That's not what this is about."

"It is. Neil wants you, and I want to make him happy. It's important that I maintain a good relationship with the studio." He paused. "They're offering you two million. For two weeks' work."

"Jesus. All to prance around on a beach."

"You already have legitimacy. All those nominations and awards. There will be more when this awards season comes around. You can afford to play with your image. Audiences already have respect for you."

"So I can afford to lose some? Is that what you're saying?"

"This will be seen as meta, not desperate." He flashed her his Tommy Hall eyes. "Honey, don't you want to spend time with me while we're working?"

"You know I do."

"Then say you'll do it."

Maddy gazed at him as he placed his palm on top of hers. She had been feeling close to him since *The Hall Fixation* was released. He was happy these days. She was thinking about starting a family. She wanted him to stay happy and she worried he would become cruel if she said no. Maybe he was right about switching genres. No one thought of her as a comedic actress, and this film could change that, give her a chance to show she could laugh at herself. And she and Steven would be sleeping in the same bed. It could be like a working vacation. She wanted him to need her emotionally, but if he needed her professionally, that had to be a step in the right direction.

5

The moment Maddy peeled off the wet bikini in her trailer was the lowest she had experienced in her career. The bikini was orange, and underneath it there was elaborate padding and double-sided tape to keep it stuck to her boobs. She'd had to run down the beach, dodging machine-gun fire. Steven had been in jeans and a T-shirt because there was a running joke that Tommy Hall hated the sun.

The bikini had been custom-designed by a rising French designer whose name would be in the opening credits. The department stores would copy it so every woman in America could pretend she was Faye Fontinell. When Maddy did the scene, she could feel her breasts—or, more accurately, her pads—bouncing. In between shots, a bikini wrangler, a costume assistant, adjusted her tape and nipples. There were hundreds of fans gathered to watch. She had been working diligently with a personal trainer paid for by the studio, and she was muscled, svelte, and tan, but she didn't care.

She had ignored her professional instincts all because of Steven, and it was dangerous to do that. She wasn't some over-the-hill former ingenue in a slump. As Steven had predicted, the past winter she had received critics' nominations for both the Elkan Hocky and *The Pharmacist's Daughter*. She'd done the awards ceremonies on both coasts, scooping up three prizes. But as she thanked her directors and praised her screenwriters, all she could think about was playing Faye Fontinell. In February, when she had been passed over again for any Oscar nominations, she felt that Faye had jinxed her before shooting had even begun.

A wardrobe girl was at the door. Maddy handed her the suit, feeling like it was prison garb. She took a long hot shower, imagining that the water was a processing chemical spilling onto the film footage and bleaching the images.

Steven had two more months of work, but she would fly home. She wanted to be away from people, away from the industry, to hole up and forget she had ever done *The Hall Surprise*. The sex scenes had been nothing like the ones in *Husbandry*. These were scenes where the camera was the man, moving down her body lecherously. She could see it from her peripheral vision, with Bryan behind it, gleeful. It wasn't that the *Husbandry* scenes were candles and roses, but they showed her pleasure, they showed Ellie dominant and vulnerable, both. Nothing about her scenes in *The Hall Surprise* showed character.

She'd sold herself out to make her husband happy. Her only consolation was that the film wouldn't be out for another year, long enough to convince herself it had all been an awful dream.

Back in Los Angeles, Maddy had booked a female-oriented thriller called *Amnesia*. Two weeks before she was to start, the director was fired, and the new one wanted rewrites, so the project went into turnaround. She found herself with a hole in her schedule; her next job, a Mary Cassatt biopic to be directed by Tim Heller, was four long months away.

She was getting constant job offers, but because of Faye Fontinell, most were for action films, based on preexisting graphic novels or comic books, and the roles were as demeaning as Faye. Again and again she declined, even though Bridget urged her to take one, to capitalize on what she told Maddy would be the inevitable success of *The Hall Surprise*.

One night in August, Maddy called Dan, busy promoting his new film, *Silver Spring*, in New York, where it had opened in limited release. After receiving her check, he had written to thank her, saying he was "shocked but pleased."

"Do you think I should take one of these movies," she asked Dan on the phone, "just because I can?"

"Not if that's not how you see yourself."

"But what if that's what I'm meant to do and I just didn't know it all those years in scene study, memorizing my Fornés and Genet?"

"Do you really think it's what you were meant to do?"

"No. But I'm not working, and Bridget thinks I should be working."

"What about Nancy at OTA?"

"She doesn't give career advice. She lets Bridget handle all that."

"You can take some time to regroup. I never would have written *Silver Spring* if I hadn't."

She wasn't sure what it meant to regroup besides read, swim, and miss Steven. She thought about flying back to Tulum, but didn't want to be on that set again.

After Steven finished *The Hall Surprise*, he flew straight to Wilmington, North Carolina, to begin a buddy comedy called *Office Mate*, about the rivalry between two guys at a Web-design firm. His costar was Ryan Costello, who had been working consistently ever since *Stick Shift* did bonanza business. In that film, Ryan had gotten attention for improvising lines like "Hug it out" and "Walk it off," and some of them were printed on T-shirts worn by teenage boys.

At night Maddy would talk to Steven on Skype, but he seemed distant and disinterested. She would hear men's voices in the background, and he would say, "I'll be there in a minute, brah." His behavior was growing increasingly fratty.

Sometimes she would go online, type "Steven Weller," and wait to see what gray words appeared after his name. It was always "Steven Weller Ryan Costello" or "Steven Weller Tommy Hall" or "Steven Weller Office Mate." Though relieved that the first mentions were no longer of *The Weekly Report* or Christian Bernard, she had mixed feelings about the Ryan Costello hits. Articles said Steven and Ryan were having a "bromance." They had been spotted at a dive bar outside Wilmington, playing darts, and had bought drinks for the whole bar. Some of the entertainment-gossip sites said they were having an affair.

One night she was sitting by the pool, talking to Steven on her cell. She could hear Ryan's voice in the background. Steven laughed at something. "Do you miss me at all?" she asked.

"Sure I do. Oh God, I miss you a lot."

"Yeah?" she said.

"Honey, someone's calling me. I'm sorry, I can't talk anymore right now."

In the morning she went to take her birth control pill, and after she swallowed it, she threw out the rest of the pack. Maybe Steven had become this hyper-masculine man, this guy's guy, because he felt distant. And maybe he felt distant because he didn't believe she was committed—either because he suspected she had slept with Dan or because she hadn't gone off the pill after three years of marriage. The more she thought about it, the more certain she felt. The key to the Ryan Costello problem was to start a family. If she were pregnant, Steven would know she was committed and maybe, just maybe, he would come back to her.

Maddy went right from the Wilmington airport to Steven's sprawling eight-bedroom rental in Wrightsville Beach. She put down her luggage and drove to the soundstage.

A production assistant let her in, and she found Bridget by Video Village. "What are you doing here?" Bridget asked.

"I wanted to see Steven."

"Does he know you're here?"

"No, but he won't be surprised. He misses me."

"Honey, you should have told me you were coming."

"Why?"

"Because you don't want to interrupt the flow of things."

"I didn't come here to see you. I came to see my husband."

On the monitors, Maddy watched Steven rehearse a scene with Ryan. The two men were horsing around, and Ryan kept saying things under his breath to Steven, who would laugh raucously, as the director tried to walk them through their staging.

When Steven took a break, he spotted Maddy, frowned, and strode over. His expression was annoyed, not exuberant. He kissed her, but it was chaste. "What's going on?" he asked. "Is everything okay?"

"Of course. I wanted to see you. I loved being with you in Tulum."

Steven turned to Bridget. "Did she tell you she was doing this?" Bridget shook her head ominously.

"Aren't you happy to see me?" Maddy asked. She could see Ryan behind him, joking with a grip.

"Of course I am," he said.

Maddy stayed at the set a few hours. At lunch, Ryan greeted her but beyond that made no effort to include her in the conversation with the cast and crew, even though she was sitting right next to Steven. Her husband was his new best friend; it seemed in Ryan's interest to be decent. But Ryan's rudeness and Steven's obliviousness, real or faked, made her worry that Steven had spoken about her in a demeaning way.

That night Steven took her out to dinner at a fancy French restaurant. He was distracted and antsy. She asked if he was doing coke and he said, "No, Maddy," as if the question were ridiculous. "I haven't done coke since the 'eighties."

"Okay, fine, but what's going on with you? Why are you being so cold to me?"

"I don't like us to be on each other's sets. Not for more than a couple of days. Couples shouldn't go to each other's place of work. It's too distracting."

"I didn't distract you today," she said. "Ryan did. You wasted thousands of feet of film."

"I wasn't prepared for this."

"But you said you missed me, and I'm your family."

"Sometimes I don't like to mix family with work."

"I thought you'd like us being in the same city. You said if I did Faye, then we would get to be together, and I did, and we were."

"We were both working then. It's different when only one of us is."

"You're not making sense."

The waiter came to refill their wineglasses, and though he was gallant, the couple could not look at each other. Steven's coldness made even less sense to Maddy given the sacrifice she had just made for him. She had done *The Hall Surprise* to make him happy, and he was ungrateful. It was as though, in giving in to his wishes, she had made him hate her.

On the soundstage the next day, she sat by Bridget and watched. Ryan kept making the grips and gaffers laugh. Between takes, both men would rib each other.

While Ryan and Steven were doing a rehearsal, Bridget leaned over and passed Maddy a Tootsie Roll she had gotten from Craft Services. Maddy held her hand up to say no, then changed her mind and took it.

"It's beautiful here in summer, isn't it?" Bridget asked.

"I wouldn't know. I haven't spent much time outside."

"Why don't you go running? Or take a long walk by the beach? You don't want to sit here all day."

"I came here to see Steven. You're not trying to get rid of me, are you?"

"Honey, no. I just want you to enjoy yourself. You look bored."

As Bridget regarded her chewing on the candy, Maddy seemed almost childlike to her, her lips pursed insouciantly. All wives watched their husbands. That was not unusual. But Maddy was watching Steven with her entire being, and that was a dangerous thing.

"I'm not bored," Maddy said sullenly.

Bridget looked ahead at the men rehearsing their scene. It was a bit involving a stapler, and the director wanted the choreography just right. There was a stunt coordinator making sure no one got hurt. "Do you remember," Bridget asked, keeping her eyes on the men as they worked out their action, "when you were doing *Husbandry*, and you had those scenes with Billy, and Steven started coming to set?"

"How could I forget? It was horrible."

"Do you remember how you felt like you couldn't work?"

"Everyone felt that way. Not just me. I don't like to think about that time."

Bridget turned toward her. "I want you to listen to me very closely. I know I don't usually talk to you this way, but we've been in each other's lives a few years now, and there are times when I feel I cannot beat around the bush. On *Husbandry*, on that set, Steven wasn't giving you the freedom to create. You needed to have intimacy with Billy to achieve the wonderful things you achieved, and Steven wasn't allowing you any."

"What would he say if he heard you talking to me like this?"

"He would agree."

"I needed intimacy with Billy then, but that was a drama. This is a comedy."

"Even for a comedy, there is a rhythm, a mood on set. This is a comedy targeted toward men, and half the time *I* feel like an interloper, even though I'm one of the producers. Don't you wonder why Steven's acting the way he's been acting? These stupid pranks?"

"Yes, it's not like him at all. Steven said 'brosef' to Ryan this morning. I don't even know what that means."

"He's trying to get into character, just like Billy would stay in his American accent all day. It's not to be taken seriously, and it certainly won't last. You have to let it pass you. Observe it, take it in, but don't get involved. It's Method, pure and simple."

"It's not just the pranks. It's the way he acts around Ryan. They have all these secrets. It's like—the two of them against the world."

Bridget pitied the girl and at the same time was frustrated by her immaturity. She needed to be careful with Maddy, as cautious as she had been with Steven at the very beginning, in Venice. "This friendship won't last. It's a set friendship."

"I'm worried it will," Maddy said with a sigh. "Do you think it's possible that a man can have too many friends?"

"Not if they give him something he needs."

"What does he need from Ryan?" Maddy's eyes were wild. "You understand men better than I do."

"Sometimes it's easier for men to be around people like themselves."

"But Ryan's nothing like him!"

"He has a playful side. Steven likes that. He's enjoying the ability to horse around. Tommy Hall has freed him to be lighter."

"That's well and good, but Ryan's an asshole. You see that as well as I do."

"It doesn't matter what you and I think of the guy. He's your husband's friend. You need to let up on Steven or you'll ruin this."

Maddy wasn't sure what Bridget meant she would ruin: the film or something bigger. On the soundstage, they were about to roll. Maddy sat for a moment before walking out and driving to the beach. She watched the waves, hiding under a big sun hat. The problem was that she was looking to Steven to solve her frustration about her own career. She had come here to replace her emptiness with Steven, but he had no room for her now, just as she'd had no room for him on *Husbandry*. Even on a comedy, she had to respect his process, though she wasn't sure what it was.

That night he went out to dinner with Ryan and some of the other cast members, and she didn't ask to go along. She stayed in the house and went to bed early, and when he came back, she pretended to be asleep.

In the morning Steven left early for set, and as she was drinking coffee in the kitchen, she heard her cell phone ring. She trotted upstairs to fetch it. "Ms. Freed," the voice said.

She knew from the accent who it was. "Walter."

"I have something to discuss with you," he said. "I'm wondering if you can come to London."

"When?"

"As soon as you can manage it."

"Can you tell me anything more?"

"It involves a project. But please, do not tell Ms. Ostrow or your husband at this point. I ask only for the chance to discuss it one-on-one. Is there some way you can get here within the next week?"

She hung up but stayed at the window. You could feel stuck and then you could feel unstuck. It was as though Walter knew how depressed she had been after *The Hall Surprise* and wanted to help her.

She would stay at the Dorchester, do all the things in London that she hadn't had time to do when she was on *Husbandry*. Go to the theater alone. Walk around and shop, maybe eat at the hotel's new restaurant that everyone was talking about.

She wouldn't tell Bridget or Steven the real reason for the trip. Steven still blamed Walter for his poor reviews, and if she told Bridget . . . Bridget would never keep anything secret from him.

So she told Steven she was going to London to see a New School friend in a stage production of *Harold and Maude*. He didn't even ask the friend's name. There was a production of *Harold and Maude*, but she didn't know anyone in it. Maybe she would see it anyway. She hadn't been to the theater in a while, because there wasn't enough good theater in L.A.

Steven said, "That's fantastic that you're going. It will be fun for you to get away. It might help you get out of your head." She could tell he meant she was acting crazy again, but there was no need to argue now that she was leaving.

As the plane touched down in Heathrow, Maddy felt a sense of expansion. She had been off the pill less than a week but felt that she could hear more, smell more, taste more. She was looking forward to being in London in the summer again, this time alone. Out the window of the car, she scanned the faces on the street, reserved, pragmatic, some of them even grim. In L.A. everyone pretended to be happier than they were. In London no one did.

Her room at the hotel was deco, an homage to 1930s Hollywood, with a large terrace and its own dressing room. She took a bath, ordered room service, and flipped channels on the television. Then she stood on the terrace and looked out at Hyde Park.

The next day she went to Walter's Georgian town house in West London. It was decorated in bold colors, with an Italian feel. It had been just over two years since she had seen him, at the London premiere of *Husbandry*, but he did not look any older. In fact, he seemed younger, his cheeks fresh and pink.

He ushered her to the kitchen in the back, where he had set out tea and cookies. "Thank you for agreeing to see me," he said. "I have come across a very intriguing script. It's set here in London, in the early '60s. It is about a young schoolteacher who begins to suspect that her husband is leading a double life. As her mind expands, first in fear and later in shock, she begins to explore the counterculture of the time. She begins closed and becomes open. It's called *The Moon and the Stars*."

"When you say double life, what do you . . ."

"I'd like you to read the script. I know you have just completed an action picture, playing a siren with an alliterative name. Perhaps that is the direction in which you wish to take your career. But consider this. That's all I ask."

"I don't want to do action movies. I only did that because—because—that was just a onetime thing."

"Maybe you'll hate the screenplay. But I don't think so. I have realized I work better with material that I have not written. I want to do an homage to an older kind of film. They used to call them women's pictures. The screenwriter is Nuala Fallon. She's written for a popular television drama here. She wanted to meet you, but I said you'd have to read the screenplay first."

"When is it shooting?"

"October."

"That's in two months. You haven't cast yet?" He shook his head. "Walter, am I your second choice?"

"Another director was attached, and it didn't work out. He was going to cast his wife. When he backed out, she did, too. The financing is all in place, but now they want me to do it. When I came on board, I said I wanted you. Are you free?"

"I'm supposed to do this biopic," she said, "but I think I can find a way to delay it. If I like the script, that is." There were always out clauses, she knew, because she had gone in on other roles that other actresses couldn't do. It was all a big chessboard. She could push the Mary Cassatt a few months. She was big enough now that Tim would reschedule in order to keep her.

At the door, they embraced. "I know we had our ups and downs on *Husbandry*," Walter said, "and for that I apologize. There is nothing I would like more than to work with you again." She wondered whether he was referring to their exchange in her dressing room in Woodmere, the comment about Steven not loving her. She was about to ask him when she decided against it. What was the point? She had long ago concluded that he'd been manipulating her.

She read the script in bed that night. *The Moon and the Stars* was a slow, quiet drama with an upsetting revelation: The lead character, Betty, discovers that her husband is gay and sleeping with men behind her back. When Maddy got to the part where Betty first spies on him as he enters a gay bar, she threw her arm over her eyes.

She thought again of Walter's words in the dressing room. But Walter had not written this script. It had come to him. From a woman writer, no less.

Even so, she did not look forward to hearing what her husband would have to say about the script. He would hate the subject matter. Beyond that, there was the Walter factor, the hostility Steven had felt for him after the reviews.

But she liked the role of Betty even better than she had liked Ellie. She began to imagine how she would do it, flipping through the pages to reread her favorite scenes. It was a dangerous thing when you began to imagine how you would play a role.

The next morning Maddy went out to explore London on her own. She did some window-shopping and visited the Tate, then decided to see the Victoria and Albert Museum.

She stopped in the fashion gallery to examine the dresses, particularly interested in the ones from the 1960s. Her museum program said there was a special exhibit of photographs by Lane Cromwell, a name she had never heard before, and she decided to see what it was about.

She wound up staying in the exhibit for two hours, staring at the photos and imagining the woman who had taken them. By the end she had virtually memorized Lane Cromwell's life story.

Lane Cromwell was born Helen Cromwell in upstate New York, and her father, an amateur photographer, frequently took nude photos of her when she was a child. In her twenties, she had been plucked off a Manhattan street by a modeling agent and wound up posing for the women's magazines of the day. One of her photographers suggested she try photography herself. He sent her off to Paris, where she changed her name from Helen to the androgynous Lane and became a fixture on the Parisian scene, taking male and female lovers.

In the early 1930s, she returned to New York to pursue a career as a photographer and fell in love with a surrealist painter named Max Sando-val. When World War II broke out, she saw opportunity. Her black-and-white photos of men on the battlefield, many of them corpses, were stark and arresting. She went to Normandy, Paris, and Germany with the U.S. Army, even though women weren't allowed.

But after the war ended, she lost her sense of purpose. She had thrived on the danger and excitement and was adrift without it. She returned to London with Sandoval and had two children in two years. They moved into an old farmhouse in Buckinghamshire, and she became an alco-holic. She was bored as a housewife and mother, her life devoid of excite-ment. She died of liver disease in the mid-'60s. Her daughter and son had no knowledge of her past until they discovered a box of her photos and gradually learned the story.

Outside the museum, Maddy sat by the fountain, flipping through a biography she had bought in the gift shop. She fished her phone out of her purse and left a message on Zack's voice mail at Bentley Howard, knowing it was the middle of the night in L.A.

He called her back that evening when she was in her hotel room. "Have you heard of Lane Cromwell?" she asked.

"No. Tell me."

She rattled off the details of Lane's life. "She has an incredible story," she said. "It's filled with deep courage and, at the same time, intense pain. She was ahead of her time. She was a woman who thrived on danger, but when the danger ended, she couldn't find a way to be happy. I think I might—I might want to do something with it."

"Option it, you mean?"

"I want to find out if the life rights are available. And the rights to this biography I'm reading. Do you think you can help me?"

"Of course I can help you," he said.

Zack's instinct had been to keep his distance from Maddy when he moved to L.A., and he suspected it would soon pay off. If you were pushy, you didn't get what you wanted. Your goal was to listen. Just be.

"She was kind of unbalanced. Obsessed with men. She basically cheated on anyone she ever loved, and at the same time she wanted to be a man. When she realized she couldn't be one, she didn't know what to do with herself. If she had lived at a different time, her story might not have been so tragic. She was such a product of her era."

"I'll be happy to have our lit department look into this for you."

"Would you? And please don't say anything to your mother. I could ask Nancy and the OTA lit department, but I don't know, I'm just not—"

"You don't have to explain it. It's fine."

He could see that Maddy needed him. Her relationship with his mother had become dysfunctional; as soon as a client began keeping secrets from her manager, it was over. She obviously had no particular loyalty to Nancy Watson-Eckstein, either, and he guessed that she had chosen her because Bridget told her to. He thought of the Frank Sinatra song "Nice 'n' Easy." You could learn a lot about agenting from Sinatra.

"You mean you'll do it?" she said. "Even though I'm not a client?"

"Absolutely."

"How come you haven't called me since you moved to L.A.?"

"I thought you were happy with Bridget. I didn't want to bother you."

She thought about the night of Bridget's party, when she'd had that long talk with Steven, and she remembered what she had seen upstairs in the room. It came back to her, how shocked she had been, how the sex had changed the way she saw Zack. "I have to tell you something. You know that dinner your mother threw in Utah? I saw something kind of weird that night."

"My mother's utter phoniness and ruthless championing of her own causes?"

"I saw you having sex. I couldn't find the bathroom."

She waited for him to apologize, or get embarrassed, but he just said, "Annabel? Too bad you didn't get to meet her. She had a documentary in the festival on consent."

"Why didn't you lock the door?"

"I thought she did. I'm sorry you had to see it, but it doesn't change anything about how I work. I still feel that I could do excellent things for your career."

She thought back to how Bridget had encouraged her to leave Wilmington, when she could have defended her presence to Steven, made him understand why she had made the trip. Bridget was a woman but she hadn't been on Maddy's side. She remembered how, when she'd called to say she was uncomfortable with the idea of doing Faye, Bridget had sided with Steven immediately. She'd said Faye was comedic, wink-wink, her lines filled with wordplay and double entendre. She'd said "entendre" with a bad French accent. Maddy had allowed Bridget to convince her, because then she could tell herself it was good for her career, could tell herself she was doing it for her own good and not Steven's. But Bridget probably wanted Maddy only because Neil Finneran did.

She had never been convinced that Bridget cared about her career. Even at the beginning, there were signs. *Freda Jansons*. But Maddy had been moony over Bridget because of her power, and she'd believed that Bridget was doing her a favor by representing her. It had been as though she worked for Bridget and not the other way around. This feeling had continued past the point when it made any sense.

The two had never really clicked. All the period dramas, it wasn't just that Bridget didn't get them. She didn't *like* them. Lately all Bridget had been was a fifteen percent bill on top of the ten percent that went to Original Talent.

When Maddy had been sitting by the fountain earlier that day, it hadn't occurred to her to call Bridget about Lane Cromwell's life rights, or even about her story. Maddy had known that Bridget would be bored by it. It was too highbrow, and the adaptation would be way longer than eighty-five minutes. Zack had been the person who came to mind. Almost as though he already worked for her.

"Zack?" she said on the phone.

"I'm still here," he said.

"That's what I wanted to talk to you about."

Bridget was in the car when the email came through: "Dear Bridget, I have decided to seek new management. I've been wanting to do this for some time. I never felt you had my best interests at heart. I have already notified Nancy Watson-Eckstein as well. From now on I'll be working with Zack at BHA. Thank you for everything you have done for me. —Maddy."

Bridget read it at a stoplight on Avenue of the Stars and cast her device on the passenger seat. What the fuck? Maddy owed her entire career to her. You built them up and then they forgot how it happened.

Maddy was making a mistake. Bridget had been a good representative to her, steered the most appropriate work her way. If clients knew half the things said about them behind their backs, the things good reps withheld, they would have to institutionalize themselves. Maddy didn't realize that some producers saw her as strained. Inaccessible. Forced. Snobbish. Bridget had protected her from all of this.

If Maddy thought Bridget had been neglectful, she was wrong. She had introduced her to her husband, for one. Maddy didn't know how many strings Bridget had pulled for her. The guest spot on *Jen*. The psychological thriller right after she moved to L.A., so Maddy would feel confident in her ability to book. She'd needed that, just before *Husbandry*.

And now Maddy was on top, but there was no gratitude. Bridget had believed *The Hall Surprise* would be good for Maddy. Maddy didn't get that today's brightest stars went from big-budget to indie and back dozens of times.

Clearly, she was falling apart. When entertainers began firing their representatives for no good reason, it was usually an indication of a precarious mental state. Bridget hoped Maddy wouldn't do something stupid and leave the marriage, abandon everything she had built with Steven. Bridget hadn't liked what she had seen in Wilmington, the desperation, all brought on by boredom because Maddy wasn't working.

Bridget was furious that Zack had poached her. He'd been selling himself to Maddy from the start. It was personal for him. He had seen her first, he had said. So what? Bridget had a project for her. A lifetime's worth of work. Zack had nothing.

She pressed the button on the phone and dialed. "Zack Ostrow's office," said Natalie. Bridget had met her once when she went to pick up Zack at the office, a pretty Jewish girl with Japanese-straightened hair.

"It's Bridget," she said.

"Hi, Bridget," said Natalie, betraying nothing. A good assistant always acted in the dark. "Let me see if I can get him."

The phone went silent for several long seconds, and Bridget prepared her speech. She would remind him of the sacrifices she had made so she could be a manager and a mother at the same time. The business dinners she'd skipped for those excruciatingly boring parent-teacher conferences, the trips she hadn't gone on, the promotions that had taken years longer than they should have. As his mother, she wanted him to be aggressive, it would make him a good agent, but he had been wrong to pursue one of her clients.

"I couldn't get him," said Natalie. "Can he return?" Never before had the girl spoken these words to Bridget. He always took her calls.

"I know he'll take this. Try again."

"Just one moment," Natalie said, and Bridget detected a hardening of tone.

She was driving faster now, conscious of the trees passing, the seconds going by. She had been the agent on the other side of this call hundreds of times and could see the scene playing out: Natalie was reporting to Zack that Bridget wanted her to ask again. And what was he saying to Natalie in response? What words were being spoken during the silence? Was he wrapping up another call and stalling for time?

He was challenging her now, not to lose her cool. She had taught him to play Scrabble when he was about eight, and on vacations they would take a travel set. Back then she could make up words, and because he was so young, all he could do was believe her. She would devise long, complicated combinations of vowels and consonants to score bingos again and again, but by the time he was twelve or so, he'd begun packing a dictionary. From then on, he'd challenged her. Half the time she was right but the other half she was wrong, and she could still see his desperate, hopeful face as he thumbed through the pages, and she could always tell the result by his expression. Sometimes he didn't want to believe it; he would flip the page back and forth as though he had missed something, as though there was an entire colony of words between BI- and BIB-.

"Bridget?" Natalie said. "I just can't reach him right now."

She wanted to curse the girl out, but Natalie didn't work for her, she worked for Zack, and she wasn't insolent, she was being a good assistant, doing what she had been trained to do, what Zack had been trained to do by George Zeger, and Bridget before him with Jack Keil. Above all, it was important to remain professional: To yell at an assistant was to yell at a wall. And she didn't need Natalie reporting that she had become "hysterical."

"I understand," Bridget said. She clicked off, then slammed her hand against the dashboard and let out a sound that was anguished and macabre.

6

Steven was reading the last page of *The Moon and the Stars*. Maddy had left him alone, and forty-five minutes later, returned to the study. She was standing, too amped-up to sit, periodically glancing over at him at the desk.

It was late August, a week and a half after her return from London. He had wrapped *Office Mate* and flown home from Wilmington.

The layout in his new study was exactly the same as in the old. The Mediterranean house was finally beginning to seem finished, and though it was marginally warmer in color tone, his study was a replica. He had taken his creepy busts, ornate mirrors, and silk walls and transported them from one house to the other. She often felt as though she might as well be living in the mansion.

Steven looked up at her, his eyes narrow and angry. "If you do this movie, our marriage is over."

"But I did *The Hall Surprise* for you," she said.

"That film wasn't about our marriage."

"Of course it was," she said. "It was capitalizing on our marriage. The studio wouldn't have wanted me if I weren't your wife."

"This project is an insult," he said, rising from the seat. "It's a kick in the stomach."

"It's a role. It's fiction. You won't even be in it."

"It makes no difference. I can see the headline now: 'Maddy Freed Stars in Biopic About Own Husband.' "

"It's a strong role. It's period. It's Walter. It's by a really good screenwriter who's going somewhere. This is exactly the kind of thing I want to be doing."

"Do you remember our wedding vows? 'I am your biggest fan, most loyal advocate.' Did that mean nothing to you?"

"But this movie isn't about you and me. Unless you're saying it is."

"What's that supposed to mean?"

"What's going on between you and Ryan?"

"Oh my God, are we into this? What did I tell you about not trusting me? What did I say it would do to our marriage? I said you have the power to poison us. Do you want to poison us?"

"Of course not."

"I am asking you, as my wife, not to do this job. You saw what I went through with *The Weekly Report*. This would be low-hanging fruit for them. You don't want to do action films, fine. I'll help you do the movies you want to do. I was going to say Bridget will help, but she said you fired her. I can't believe you did it without speaking to me. You've gone off the reservation."

"It was my decision to make. I should have done it years ago."

"I don't know what's gotten into you. Firing your manager. Keeping secrets. And going with Zack, who is still so unproven that I don't know what you could be thinking. You know he's been to rehab."

"You didn't tell me about the Tommy movies until it was a done deal. You didn't consult with me. Why should I consult with you?"

"This is another level. I think you're unstable. Do you have your period or something?"

"I don't have my period! I went off the pill right before I went to Wilmington, and it hasn't come yet."

"You went off? But I thought you weren't ready."

"I thought if we made a family together that things would be better. But they're awful. You don't understand me. I would go back on it right now if it wouldn't mess up my system."

"I knew something was going on. It's the hormonal drop making you do this. Why do you want to have a baby with me if you don't respect me?"

"I do respect you."

"Then say no to this film. Walter hates me. He wants you to do this so he can make a fool of me again. And you're enlisting."

"You're wrong. This is a good role. I'm saying yes. Whether or not you want me to."

She had taken the script from his desk. It was the only copy she had, and she didn't trust Steven to hold on to it. He didn't stop her.

Steven wasn't her partner. Maybe he had never been her partner.

"I think I need to go away," she said, moving slowly toward the door.

"Go wherever you want!" he screamed, his face wrenched and ugly. "I don't give a shit anymore!"

"Good!" she cried. She ran upstairs, threw some clothes and the script into a bag. She went outside and got in the Prius. Her cell phone rang but she ignored it. She drove, with no destination.

Who was this man? How could he be so domineering when he *owed* her?

She made a few calls to get the number, and then Julia answered. "It's Maddy Freed."

"Hi, Maddy." Julia's voice was calm, indicating nothing.

"Did Steven ever tell you what jobs to take when you were married?"

"All the time. He was competitive with me, and he read my scripts more closely than I did. He hated me doing anything he deemed objectifying. Which, in the 'eighties, was pretty much every script with a woman in it."

Maddy was driving too fast; she had to be careful, her mind was racing with fear and excitement. "Did you listen to him?"

"Sometimes I did. Now I regret it."

"Why?"

"Because I was just beginning my career, and he had no right to make me suffer just because it was happening more slowly for him. Is everything all right?"

"I don't know yet."

After she clicked off, she kept driving, with no idea where to go. She could stay in a hotel for a couple of days, but the press might find out, and she wanted to be alone. She thought about calling Zack, but she was embarrassed. She was starting a business relationship with him; she couldn't have him thinking that she was nuts, that her marriage was on the rocks. After three and a half years in Los Angeles, she felt like she hadn't made any real, meaningful friendships. And then she had an idea.

———

Kira's house was a charming Tudor cottage in Silver Lake, on the East-side. Maddy drove up in the Prius and let herself in with the key in the planter, as per the instructions Kira had given her on the phone. In the living room, there was a poster from *Rondelay*, an indie-rock record collection, a flokati rug, and a tabby cat.

Maddy turned on the TV, and flipped channels. An action movie came on starring a young Steven. She stared into his eyes during an action sequence in which he ran from a moving train onto the roof of a passing SUV. She wanted the Steven in the movie to tell her whether to stay with him. Whether to do *The Moon and the Stars*.

When Kira came in from an audition, she fixed Maddy a vodka tonic from her 1930s-era bar in the corner, lay on the couch with her feet up, and said, "Tell me everything." When Maddy had finished, Kira said, "So basically, he doesn't want you to do it because it's about a closeted gay man?"

Maddy nodded bleakly. She was in a potato-chip chair catty-corner to the couch. "He says Walter hates him and wants me to do the movie because it will make a mockery of our marriage."

"That's an awfully expensive way to make a mockery of a marriage," Kira said. "Finance an international feature."

"Maybe, given everything he's been through, with the press and the whole thing with *The Weekly Report*, he's right to be concerned. And I'm being selfish to want to ignore him."

"I don't think you're selfish. It must be a good script. I mean, I don't know. Do you have it here?"

"I left it at home," Maddy said, though it was still in her bag. "Maybe I should just turn it down. If the roles were reversed—"

"If the roles were reversed, you'd send him off to London. Because you have respect for him as an actor. Though I have never been entirely sure why." Kira cocked one eyebrow.

"Come on," Maddy said.

"If you want to do this movie," Kira said, "I mean really want to, you have to do it."

"What if Steven leaves me?"

"Then you'll be a wealthy divorcée with a two-million-dollar quote and an awesome settlement."

"How do you know my quote?"

"It was in the *Reporter*. But thanks for confirming."

"Do you think I'm disgusting for doing *The Hall Surprise?*" Maddy asked.

"It's not out yet."

"It's pretty embarrassing. I say the word 'cockfight.' And the bikini, oh my God, the bikini. Kira, it's horrible, you should have seen the stuff they had inside it to try to make me look buxom. You should have done it, your breasts would have looked much better. But you wouldn't have played Faye Fontinell, not even for two million dollars. Because you're not a sellout. You're so much braver than I am."

"Are you fucking kidding? I'm wearing a push-up bra right now. I gave up chocolate. And I have hair down to my shoulders."

"But you don't pretend to be straight."

"You think this industry takes my lesbianism seriously? The young guys, the really hot-shit directors? To them, it's a turn-on. They just see it as a challenge."

"But would you wear a bikini in a movie?"

"Only if a woman ran the studio."

"There are no female studio chiefs right now."

"I know," Kira said. "It's so sad."

They got dinner at an expensive Japanese place in Beverly Hills, where the host found Maddy a table, and then they called a car to take them to Havana in Hollywood. The photographers called out Maddy's name as they entered. A few shouted "Kira!" and Maddy was startled by it, not aware that Kira was first-name famous. The press knew Kira because of her roles in *Barry Hiller's Loins* and *Rondelay* and two other mid-budget features that had been released in the past year. Maddy had been known since the moment she moved to L.A., because of Steven. Kira was known because of her work.

They danced by the banquette to the DJ's mix of Morrissey and Kanye West. She felt as though she were getting her spark back. Somewhere along the way she had lost it. It was the exhaustion of being with Steven.

Who hadn't made her feel beautiful in months, even though she had seventeen percent body fat from her training for *The Hall Surprise*. She and Steven lived like monks because Steven hated the press. He had been keeping her prisoner. And she had let him.

Maddy held a Seabreeze in one hand and waved the other above her head. She wasn't even drunk, just tipsy, but she was happy and free. They stayed a couple of hours, dancing with strangers. For so long Steven had made her feel that she was a drag, and maybe she was. She was insecure near him, and it turned her into someone she didn't want to be. A killjoy.

I am a joyous person who has been living joylessly. A husband was supposed to increase your pleasure, not decrease it. She had married Steven because she'd believed he would encourage her to live out her dreams, and now he wanted to squash them. All that talk about respecting her as an actress, and he was telling her what roles to take, like David O. Selznick with Jennifer Jones. Yes, the press had attacked Steven, but he had to be smart enough to know *I Used to Know Her* wasn't about him. Audiences could understand the difference between real and pretend.

Lael Gordinier came in with Munro Heming, whom she was dating, and Maddy greeted them. Munro got up to chat with some other Young Hollywoodites, and Maddy invited Lael to their table. Each congratulated the other on her recent films and gossiped about executives and directors. It turned out Zack was representing Lael now, too. Maddy was reminded of the friends she'd had at The New School, united by reckless ambition.

Lael and Maddy caught up about their projects, and Maddy remembered the dinner party in Mile's End, where Lael and Taylor had spoken about their own auditions for *Husbandry*. "You and Taylor went in for *Husbandry*, right?" Maddy said.

"I wouldn't call it auditioning," Lael said.

"What do you mean?"

"I didn't get to read. I got the sides and worked on them for days. They flew me out to London on the studio's dime, put me up in a really nice hotel, and summoned me to an audition room. For this ridiculously long time, I had to shmooze with Walter, Bridget, Steven, and some casting director I never heard of before or after that, and then they left. I never read the scene."

"What do you mean they left?"

"Everyone except Steven. I sat there and talked to him for about half an hour. I mentioned that I was into kiteboarding, and we wound up talking about different boards and where I had done it. It wasn't until Mile's End that I found out Taylor had almost exactly the same experience, except they talked about Brazilian jiujitsu. Every girl who went in had these long conversations with Steven about their hobbies or his art collection or, like, Kieślowski. Isn't that how it went for you?"

"Not at all," Maddy said. "I read two scenes. With Steven. On camera." She thought back to that strange audition in Venice, with Walter not telling her till the restaurant. As though it had been preordained.

"You know, that's really good to hear," Lael said. "Because I never believed the stuff people said."

"What stuff?"

"We all thought *Husbandry* was going to be bogus. Either put into turnaround or straight-to-video. A high-budget wife-finder. But when it came out and you were so amazing in it, I was like, *What?* And then I figured you guys must have fallen in love, which, you know, was a bit of a shocker. But anything's possible, right? I thought maybe Walter really *was* just trying to cast the best Ellie. In his own way. Maybe he was spying on all of us with a camera while we were schmoozing with Steven, to see about the chemistry. So no matter what people say about how it all went down, I think you deserve everything fucking awesome that's come to you."

Maddy nodded absently. It was stupid to put stock in anything that Lael said—she was nutty and probably competitive—but Maddy found it odd that they hadn't read Lael or Taylor. And then Kira was coming toward them and yelling that they both had to dance, and Maddy stood up and went to the floor.

7

"You need to get some perspective," Bridget said to Steven. They were lying on two of the chaises by the pool.

A separation was never good for a career, especially not one that made the man look cruel. It was one thing to play a womanizing asshole—you could win awards for that—and another thing to be one. *The Hall Surprise* would be released in just seven months, and Bridget didn't want any bad publicity before then. A film was like a baby. You had to be extremely careful until the birth.

"I have perspective," Steven said. "Walter wants to ruin me, and she wants to help him."

"That's not true. It was the wrong arena for you. We know that now."

"I won't have her working with him."

"She wants something meaty. Walter got a good performance out of her the first time."

"Why are you taking her side? She fired you."

"It doesn't mean I stop caring. But I'm not saying this because of her. I'm saying it because I still represent you."

"How could she think I would okay this? Are we living in a world where women are no longer expected to show deference to their husbands?"

When he said things like this, Bridget always felt like smacking him. She had to wait a moment before responding so as not to yell. In over two decades of working with Steven, she had never raised her voice at him, and now was no time to begin. Not when *The Hall Fixation* had done so well, not when Neil Finneran was looking upon her with such favor.

"Of course a wife should show deference to her husband," she said. "But a husband must also show deference to his wife. She did Faye Fontinell. Doesn't that mean anything to you?"

"You say it like she was a victim of torture," he said. "Two million dollars. And you wanted her to do it. *The Hall Surprise* will be good for her, too, not just me."

"Yes, but now it's time to support her in her choice. If it gets out that she's left this house, that you fought over Walter's next film, maybe she says something to a friend who talks to the press, you know how they'll spin it. 'Steven Weller is domineering.' 'Abusive.' 'Sexphobic.' Worst of all, 'Steven Weller has a secret.' They're already watching you closely because of your friendship with Ryan. Which, I advised you, has become a distraction. Given all you've been through. If you want to quiet the noise, the proper thing is to let her do it. Show it means nothing to you."

She looked out at the glassy surface of the pool, crossing one ankle over the other. Steven was not himself these days. In Wilmington, he had not been cautious. There had been many late nights before Maddy came and after she left, when Bridget, Ryan, and Steven were the only ones in the beach house. They would eat and tell jokes and recount stories, and Bridget was a part of it, but then she would give a one-liner and neither one would hear because they were looking at each other. Understanding that a manager needed to give her client space, she would slip out the door, hearing the men's loud laughter from the windows as she went to her car.

"But they'll say the same things about me if she *does* do the film," Steven said. "I can't stand making it so easy for them."

"There's no reason the content should threaten you. You're a married man. Three years now. *The Weekly Report* is old news. The glossies love you two, the fans love that you're together. She's on bump watch every week, without a baby."

"It's funny you say that." He had a whiskey next to him on the table. He took it into his hand and looked down at it as if trying to read the cubes.

Bridget sat up in the chaise. "Why is that?"

"She just went off the pill. But now she wants to do this film that insults me. She's a mess."

Bridget took out her cigarette case and lit one contemplatively. "Well, there is one way to solve this problem," she said, and took a deep drag.

"What's that?"

"The two of you have to get away. Be together. Take her on a vacation before you go off to do *Flush*." His next film was set to shoot in Providence, a neo-noir about a criminal poker ring. "Try to remember the love you felt for her when you two were first married. Show her you adore her, respect her. And then tell her to do *The Moon and the Stars*."

"I can't," he said.

She held the cigarette off to the side, far from her body, so as not to get smoke in his portion of air. "Yes, you can, Steven. You are a confident man. A confident man wants his wife to do what pleases her."

"I just want her to consider me when she makes decisions."

"She already has. Say you've had a change of heart and give her your blessing. Have a wonderful night together. Show her the depth of your love. You won't regret it."

"I have no idea where she went," he said.

"I'm sure you can find her," Bridget said. "You're her husband, after all."

Kira and Maddy got back from the club at two in the morning. Kira made up the guest room and brought in extra towels, a toothbrush, a washcloth. A gallon of spring water because Maddy had downed too many Seabreezes.

Then Kira sat on the edge of the bed and looked at Maddy. "You're a strong woman," she said. "You're going to be fine."

"Are you spelling 'woman' with a Y?" Maddy asked tipsily.

"You're going to figure this out. You should be with a man who supports you. And if you decide to be alone, it's not so bad. I prefer it, actually. No one telling me, 'Close the window, open the window, let the cat out, leave the cat in, come to bed, don't stay up late, don't drink coffee if I drink tea, don't want sex if I don't want sex.' It's so much easier to be alone."

"I'm not afraid of being alone."

"What is it, then?"

"I'm afraid of making a mistake I can't undo." Maddy stared at Kira and touched her face, ran a thumb over her lips. It was the only time she had ever seen Kira look truly uncomfortable. "Why not?" Maddy asked.

"That's not what you want," Kira said.

"How do you know?"

"Just trust me."

"I'm all alone," she said. "I think I'm scared."

"I know you are," Kira said, "but you won't be scared forever. Keep drinking that water."

After Kira left, Maddy chugged more water and put one foot on the floor so she wouldn't throw up. She listened to the cicadas. There was a low bookshelf in the corner with rows and rows of plays, and a sling chair, and a carved driftwood anchor lamp. Kira had gotten all of this with her own money. It wasn't fancy, and it smelled a little of cat, but it was hers. Maddy hadn't fallen for Steven because of his money, but he had taken care of things for her. And she had let him.

When she'd left Dan for Steven, it had been like removing a speed governor from the mopeds that she and her Potter friends used to ride around. Steven had let her go as fast as she wanted. She had known it all along, accepted it, because she believed that she had talent. Her mission was to act, and if he could expand her audience, then there was no reason to be conflicted about it. That was how she had seen it.

Now it seemed hubristic: the idea that she had a right to be known. Was it the ugly flip side of having had a father who loved her so much, wanted so badly for her to succeed? He had always been interested in the names. The famous teachers and guest lecturers at The New School, the alums who had gone on to greatness. On the street, when they spotted celebs, he had always been starstruck—why, she was not sure. Maybe because he had done theater at Dartmouth and then had to be an English teacher. When she auditioned for famous directors, she would call him to kvell; he craved the stories, the brushes, the proximity.

There was vanity to her hubris, and she was ashamed. It was how she had justified the many gifts Steven had given her: the press, the money, the exposure, the glamour. All of which changed the way that casting directors viewed her when she walked into a room. She had allowed herself

to go from Maddy Freed to Steven Weller's Wife, because Steven Weller's
Wife didn't have to pay dues.

She had let herself be convinced that she was too special to take the
local and instead, she had taken the express. And she had justified it by
telling herself her talent was genuine. Capitalized on the association of
being with Steven, first as a girlfriend and later as a wife. And when he'd
asked her to play Faye, he had been asking her to pay.

But she *had* paid, and she didn't owe him this, she didn't owe him
anything. She was going to bump the Mary Cassatt and take *The Moon
and the Stars*. Even if it meant the end of the marriage. In another week,
it would be their third anniversary. If the marriage ended and all her
money ran out one day, which it surely would, and she couldn't get work
because she was no longer linked to Steven, she would still be all right.
She could always go back to hostessing. She knew how to show someone
a seat.

Maddy spent the next couple of days hanging out with Kira, running,
hiking, and going out to dinners. She met Kira's circle of friends, actors,
directors, musicians, some gay, some not. They were doing comedy showcases or taking acting classes, opening hotel doors or busing tables for rent
money.

She had Zack call Tim Heller to get a postponement on the Mary
Cassatt, and then call Walter to say she would do *The Moon and the Stars*.
Zack loved the script and thought the role was just right for Maddy, who
would get to age a couple of years over the course of the film and show
extraordinary range.

One afternoon she was sitting on Kira's porch when she heard a car
pull up the driveway. She came around the side of the house and saw
Steven's Mustang. He was coming toward her.

"How did you find me?" she asked.

"I have connections."

"Was it Zack? Because I specifically told Kira not to say anything to
h—"

"I had an idea or two of where you might have gone."

"I'm doing Walter's movie," she said. "Zack already told him. If you have a problem with it, then we shouldn't be together. I can't be married to someone who wants to control me."

"You're right," he said.

"What?"

"I'm so sorry. Everything I said was out of line. You should do the projects you believe in."

She looked at him in surprise to see if he meant it. He seemed to. She wanted to believe she knew how to read this man who had been so foreign to her just days ago.

He stepped closer but didn't touch her. "I'm sorry I've been difficult," he said. "Playing Tommy Hall, it's gone to my head. I started to believe I was an action hero. Invincible. I'm not used to being at the top like this, the complete insanity around these movies. Walter is a good director, and *Husbandry* wasn't his fault. I was out of my league."

"I thought the critics were too hard on you. I'm proud of your performance."

"Please forgive me," he said.

"You have to let me be my own person," she said. "I need to be able to have a social life. I'm young. I can stay up later than you. We've been too isolated."

Steven hugged her and stroked her hair. "You can do anything you want to do. You're so talented. I love you so much, and I haven't been appreciating you."

"No."

"That's going to change," he said. "I won't be like this again. It's our anniversary. I want to get out of L.A. and remember what we promised each other. Let's go away. Please say you'll come away."

They flew to Venice. All the palazzo staff members were there, and they seemed happy to see the couple, calling her "Signorina Weller," as they always did, even though it wasn't her name. They went to L'Accademia and looked at *La Tempesta* hand in hand. They went back to the trattorias where he had taken her before she knew she loved him. They went out on the Lido in his motorboat and to the Basilica on Torcello. They dined at Locanda Cipriani, where the gracious host greeted her as if she were Kim Novak.

When they came back to the palazzo, there was champagne in the bedroom and olives and bread and wine and cheese. "I love you so much," he said. "I never want to lose you. You scared me this week."

He got on top of her, and she was grateful that he was being warm to her again; he understood what he had done wrong, and would change. Everything was coming together now, her marriage and her work. She had a partner. Her career would get back on track and Steven loved her and their bodies were close. He moved his mouth on her navel, then lower, and she felt herself opening. "You're so wet," he said.

She closed her eyes and forgot where she was for a moment, and then she was coming. The champagne, the long journey, the jet lag, she wasn't even sure what day it was anymore. He was moving in her, and she was light-headed and drunk, was he pulling out, or it seemed like he was, she couldn't tell. She didn't want to think about anything, she just wanted to be close to her husband who understood her and respected who she was. It was as it had been at the beginning. They were a couple.

Act Four

1

Production on *The Moon and the Stars* began in London in October. On the fourth day, Maddy was shooting a scene where Betty follows her husband out of the apartment and sees him kissing a man in the park. They had already done the kiss, and now they were doing the reaction. It was a difficult, emotional scene, and she wasn't giving Walter what he wanted. She kept feeling dizzy and cold.

"Do less but do more," Walter said, one of those directions that drove actors crazy because it was so meaningless. Maddy did a take where she cried, but he said it was "too showy." She remembered how frustrated he had gotten when she was doing the love scenes with Billy Peck, and she hoped that Walter would not be difficult again. After the seventh take, Walter said, "What do I need to do to get you to listen to me?," and on the word "listen," she vomited onto the grass.

She was convinced it was food poisoning, but then it happened the next day, and the next.

The ob-gyn was in her mid-fifties and resembled Julie Christie. Dr. Liddell. She saw all the London celebs and had been recommended to Maddy by a model who'd had a role in *The Pharmacist's Daughter*. When the doctor came in the exam room looking down at her file, Maddy knew. She hadn't taken any over-the-counter tests for fear she would be noticed in the store. Because of that, she had been able to lie to herself that it was food poisoning, even though she hadn't been running a fever.

"The urine test indicates that you're pregnant," Dr. Liddell said after she took her seat.

Maddy nodded nervously. The finality of it. She wanted to feel joy about becoming a mother, but the pregnancy was so ill timed, she felt only dread. She didn't have anyone to blame but herself. She had noticed that her period hadn't come since she went off the pill, but because she had been on it so long, she had been telling herself it was her body adjusting to the lack of hormones.

She remembered Palazzo Mastrototaro, how she wasn't sure whether Steven had pulled out. She had been drunk on champagne, and jet-lagged, and confused, but none of that was an excuse, she should have made sure he used a condom—every time. She was an actress; to work she needed to be healthy. To work she needed to control her body. How could she have been blasé about something so important to her career?

"Is this a surprise?" Dr. Liddell asked.

"A little," Maddy said. "I went off the pill in August. And we went on vacation and—we weren't careful enough."

"Based on the estimated last menstrual you gave me," said the doctor, "you're about seven weeks along."

"When would you expect me to start showing?"

"With first pregnancies, it can be as long as five or six months. It's different for every woman. I'd like to do an ultrasound today. We should be able to hear the heartbeat by now."

Maddy went to the exam room and waited, and then Dr. Liddell came in. As she put the wand on Maddy's belly, they looked at the screen. There was a little peanut. And she could hear the lub-dub of the heart. "Oh my God," she said. There was a living being inside of her that she had made with Steven, that had come out of their love. If only they had timed their love a little better.

Afterward Maddy asked what she should do about the vomiting, and Dr. Liddell said, "Eat small meals. Crackers. Ginger helps. Eat as soon as you wake up. Keep some food by your bed. If it continues, call me."

As Maddy walked out of the office, she told herself to stay positive. The pregnancy would inform the work; it would make her performance better. She could imagine the excitement on Walter's face when she told him—the vibrancy of an expectant lead. Audiences would see her glow, and costuming would be no problem since it was so early, and the shoot was short.

She called Steven in Rhode Island from the Dorchester. When she told him, he said, "Oh my God. How did this happen?"

"I told you I was off the pill."

"But we were careful, we've used condoms."

"In Venice, the first night, I think. Do you remember?"

"I was so tired," he said. "The jet lag."

"I should have made you use protection," she said. "It was my responsibility." She was quiet and then said, "So are you happy?"

"Of course I am. This is what I've been wanting. I was ready to start as soon as we got married. We're going to have a family. Are *you* happy?"

"I will be when I feel better," she said. "Right now it seems like everything's going wrong." She told him she was worried about the vomiting, had thrown up again as soon as she got back from the doctor.

"It'll resolve," he said. "You'll be fine. You're young. I'm going to figure out how to get a break so I can see you. I want to look at you, look at your belly."

Over the next week, the nausea and vomiting resolved somewhat as she sneaked small meals to the set, nibbled crackers, and bought ginger pills. She was certain that was the worst of it and decided not to tell the costume designer or Walter. It was early, anything could happen.

But about a week after her visit to Dr. Liddell, they were shooting a scene where Betty goes to a poetry slam. It was an important scene, just after her discovery of the affair. They had taken over an old Swinging London café and decorated it to look authentic. There were a hundred extras, all in period clothing. They were shooting day for night, and as soon as Maddy entered the room in full makeup and costume, she threw up all over her minidress. That was when she knew it was the end.

Dr. Liddell weighed her, ran a few tests, and went with her to the ER. She had lost weight since the last visit. In the ER, they put her on an electrolyte drip and moved her to a private room.

Dr. Liddell said Maddy would need to be hospitalized for at least a week, possibly more. She was diagnosed with hyperemesis gravidarum: vomiting so severe it was dangerous to the fetus. She would be put on a drip indefinitely and monitored until she began to gain weight.

As soon as the doctor left the room, Maddy began to weep. On the phone, Steven said he would get there as soon as he could. "I don't want to lose it," she said.

"You're not going to. You're in good hands. I'll be there soon."

She called Zack because she couldn't bear to call Walter herself. He said he would let Walter know. "What about the bonding company?" she asked.

"Let's take it one step at a time, okay? Let's just wait to hear what Lloyd's has to say."

When Steven arrived at the hospital two days later, she embraced him and broke into tears again. Since her pregnancy had been diagnosed, she had barely been sleeping, not taking any lorazepam for fear it might harm the fetus. For the past year or so, she had been taking it three or four nights a week.

With no respite, her mind had been alternating between worries about the baby, the film, and her inability to sleep, all of which were tied together. If she couldn't sleep, she couldn't gain weight, and if she couldn't gain weight, she couldn't get discharged, and if she couldn't get discharged, she couldn't work.

In the hospital that morning, she had complained to Dr. Liddell, who had confirmed that it could cause birth defects, and had sent a doctor to see her, a psychiatrist, a woman, who specialized in reproductive issues. The psychiatrist told her that lorazepam was the safest of all benzodiaz-epines for pregnancy, and that she could take it for a few weeks along with Zoloft, until the Zoloft started to kick in. Then she could go off the anti-anxiety medication.

"What if I can't do the movie?" she asked, burying her face in Steven's shoulder.

"We'll get it worked out. For now you have to focus on getting rest."

"But I want to work. I want to be Betty."

"We have to keep the baby safe," he said. "Maybe Walter can stop the production until you get better. He's very committed to you."

"This has been the strangest couple of days," she said. "I went from not knowing I was pregnant to knowing to worrying about the baby non-stop."

"That's what it means to be a mother," he said. He said it like it was good, but she wasn't sure she agreed.

"I wish we'd been more careful in Venice," she said.

"You can't blame yourself. There's no perfect time for a pregnancy."

"I just wanted to do this film. And now everything's ruined."

"Don't you want to be a mother?"

"I want to be a mother, but I also want to be an actress," she said.

"You're going to get better," he said.

"I've been taking pills at night," she said. She told him she had been relying on them since *Husbandry*, whenever things were bad between them or she had an early call, and then she told him about the psychiatrist and the antidepressant.

"You can't take those when you're pregnant," he said. "They're not good for the baby."

"Are you kidding? Millions of women do and the babies are fine. And I know they'll work. I did well on them after my father . . ."

"I don't want my baby to be born with medicine in his body," Steven said.

My baby. His body. How did he know it was a boy? As far as she knew, it wasn't either gender yet. "Do you want your pregnant wife to be a basket case?" Maddy said. "There's a reason they torture people with sleep deprivation. I'm telling you this because it's your baby, too, but I'm not asking your permission. I have to help myself. And if you care about me, you'll want me to."

"I'm going to do some research on it."

That night, on the lorazepam, she slept. Her relief in the morning outweighed her concerns. She told herself to trust the reproductive psychiatrist about the drugs. She told herself the woman probably treated pregnant patients far more unstable than Maddy.

Steven stayed in London; after a week, she was still in the hospital room, hooked up to an IV. The vomiting had continued, and she was on the drip all day and night.

Production on the film had been halted, and Walter was going back and forth with Lloyd's of London about how to proceed. Steven wanted to stay longer, but she said he should go back. She didn't like him hovering when there was nothing to do but wait. She was like a baby herself, being monitored for weight gain. She had gone from woman to patient.

After Steven left, Zack flew out for a few days to keep her company. They played cards and she would break every hour or so to throw up. She read scripts, though it was impossible to imagine working on any film when she was lying in a hospital bed indefinitely. Zack shared Hollywood gossip. It was good for her mood, but it felt like a Band-Aid. She didn't want to be stuck in a hospital with her agent, lying on her back, talking about deals. She wanted to be on set with her costars, doing the scenes. Doing what she was meant to.

The morning the call came from Walter, Maddy was shaking. "Lloyd's won't let me postpone until after you get better," he said. She put him on speaker so Zack could hear. "I already put in two claims for delays, and the second one was so long, it's cost about two million dollars. I am so sorry, Madeline. You know how desperately I wanted you to do this. I am going to have to replace you."

"I have money of my own," she said. "What if I reimburse Lloyd's the cost of all further delays?"

"If it's about money," Zack said, "we have options. Let's trouble-shoot. Problem-solve."

"I won't be here forever," Maddy added. "I'm already gaining weight."

"You know movie sets are like jigsaw puzzles," Walter said. "I can't lose the other actors. I'm sorry, my darling. We'll work together again, I promise you."

She looked at Zack. "I'm going to get into it with him," he said. Hollywood-speak for fixing something. Like it was simple, an error on a contract or a difference of a few thousand dollars. "Just give me a couple of days."

He flew back to L.A. and called to say he had tried everything, but the insurance company wouldn't yield. He said, "It's out of my hands. I'm so sorry, Maddy."

A few days after that, he called again. "Kira is replacing you," he said. "After it became clear that Walter wanted to recast, we got a call about her. Apparently, he's been a fan of hers ever since he saw *I Used to Know Her*. She didn't even want to go in because you're friends, but then she read the script and . . . she changed her mind. She wanted to call to tell you, but I felt it was my responsibility."

Maddy believed him but was hurt anyway. Kira would be playing Betty in *The Moon and the Stars*. Zack would get his commission. That was what happened, you had a problem and someone else took over. Just like Clint as Dirty Harry and Newman as Butch.

"It's okay if you're angry," Zack said.

She was numb. "I'm not. I would have done exactly the same thing if the roles were reversed."

Throughout Maddy's stay at the hospital, Steven flew back and forth when he could. It made her feel loved that he was taking care of her, but she hated having him see her in the hospital. She felt inadequate for her inability to have a normal pregnancy, and in the back of her mind, she believed it was a result of the surprise. If they had planned it properly, she would be calm, and if she were calm, she would not be ill.

After Kira arrived in London, she called Maddy. "I just wanted to say I'm sorry it worked out this way."

"No, you're not," Maddy said. "You have a job."

"I mean, I know how badly you wanted it."

"When I was in your house and you asked me for the script, were you trying to angle in on it? Tell me the truth. Did you track down a copy and read it before any of this happened?"

"I swear to God, no. I didn't even try. When Zack told me everything that happened, I just felt so sorry for you. But I know you're going to be fine. Morning sickness is a sign of a healthy pregnancy."

Maddy started to say it was much worse than morning sickness, but she didn't have the energy.

"Do you think I could come visit you one day?" Kira asked.

"Probably not a good idea."

"Can't we still be friends?"

"If I see you, I'm only going to feel sadder, so I don't want to see you. I'm sure you understand."

One day Zack called from L.A. and said, "I know it feels like you're under house arrest, but this hospital stay could be an opportunity."

"For what?"

"Well, when you're not puking, you could set up a desk in there and get started on your screenplay."

Before flying to London, she had optioned the rights to the Lane Cromwell bio and bought the life rights for $200,000 from Cromwell's daughter Jean. Only Zack, and Kelly Kennedy, the new entertainment lawyer she had retained shortly after hiring Zack, knew. In Maddy's mind, the money came from her salary on *The Hall Surprise*. She was taking money she had gotten for something bad and using it to pay for something good.

"I'm just trying to keep this fetus healthy," Maddy said on the phone.

"You have a lot of time on your hands. You should take advantage of it."

"I think my mood is too dark."

"That's perfect for the script," he said. "Think about how bleak Lane's life was. Use everything you're feeling, all your frustration right now. You don't need Lloyd's of London in order to write."

After she hung up, she thought about it and tried to take his words to heart. But she was anxious and distractible, and when she tried to type, it didn't flow. To procrastinate and put less pressure on herself, she devoted her time to research. She read the biography of Lane over and over. She read memoirs of the 1930s and *O'Keeffe and Stieglitz: An American Romance*. She read and reread Hemingway to get a feel for war. She read Syd Field's *Screenplay*.

After four more weeks, the vomiting resolved and Dr. Liddell said Maddy could be discharged. She flew home by chartered plane, and Steven stayed with her in Hancock Park a few days before flying off to his set at her insistence.

With the frightening early weeks of the pregnancy behind her and the hyperemesis gone, she tried to enjoy her changing body — her full breasts, her big nipples, her hips and thighs. Because she couldn't act, she focused on the screenplay. In her study, with Steven off in Providence, she began to do index cards, plotting out a structure for the film.

Lane Cromwell had had darkness in her life and had found a way to channel it into art. Maddy was inspired by her but didn't want to hallow her too much, to make her seem perfect or even above the troubled men she was drawn to again and again. The relationship dynamics between Lane Cromwell and Max Sandoval were not so different from modern dynamics; he had been distancing, competitive, and emotionally abusive, and Cromwell always felt he didn't love her quite as much as she loved him.

One day Maddy wrote a few lines, and the next day she wrote a few pages. The writing was painstaking and slow, and every few days she would lose faith in it completely, only to try again and grind out more. It was easy to keep it secret with Steven away, and when he returned near Christmas and noticed that she was often in her study, she told him she was just emailing. She didn't want to show the script to anyone, not even Zack, until it was done, for fear she would lose faith in it.

In January, at the five-month mark, Maddy and Steven went to her ob-gyn, Dr. Sheila Baker, for the big ultrasound. Dr. Baker looked like a Victoria's Secret model and delivered celebrity babies mostly by elective C-section because Hollywood wives saw their vaginas as entrances, not exits. Maddy wanted a natural birth, no epidural, and felt confident that she could have one. It would be the flip side of the difficult early portion of the pregnancy: an uneventful delivery. She was descended from a long line of healthy Boston Brahmins who had birthed big broods; her mother had been one of four.

At the ultrasound, Dr. Baker asked if they wanted to know the gender and Maddy said no, she thought it was better for it to be a surprise; Steven, perhaps sympathetic to her fraught early weeks, yielded.

He decided they needed to build a wing for the baby, complete with live-in baby-nurse quarters. Maddy didn't want one, remembering Irina's prediction that they would get one.

Steven came home with swatches of sheets and crib wood and rugs in colors that could work for either a boy or a girl because he said the whole pink-or-blue thing was stupid.

Though Maddy was eager to maintain her sex life with Steven, he seemed increasingly disturbed by her body's new shape as the pregnancy progressed. More often than not, sex consisted of her fellating him. She was hurt that he didn't seem attracted to her, but he talked constantly about the baby and his excitement, and she decided his desire for family was more important than whatever issues he had with her body.

He began work on a comedy set in a Chicago public school, and most nights he came straight home from set. He no longer talked about Ryan Costello. She asked him once if they'd had a falling-out and he said, "I finally realized he was immature. I was wrong to have thought he was a friend."

One morning in January, shortly after her five-month visit, she met Dan for a walk in Runyon Canyon. "You look fantastic," he said in the parking lot when she got out of the car. "Your tits are big now."

"Yeah, I have actual breasts," she said. "It's weird. I feel like my body's doing what it's meant to, you know?"

"I can't believe you're going to be a mother."

"Me, neither. It's trippy. It's really trippy."

They started on the path, Dan slowing his pace because it was harder now for Maddy to move quickly. She asked if he was dating anyone and he said no one serious. "I'm kind of in this place of wanting to learn to be on my own," he said. "I'm just more into my work."

Silver Spring had been a critical and commercial success, scooping up a slew of critics' nominations and earning a respectable return on its $500,000 budget. On its heels, Dan had scripted another small indie that would be financed entirely by his backers and still allow him final cut. His actors, as they had on *Silver Spring*, would get a percentage of the back end in lieu of a lot of money up front.

He had sent the new script, still untitled, to her at the hospital in England. It was a drama about a young couple in Brooklyn and their friendship with a quirky older male neighbor who becomes entangled in both of their lives. Maddy liked it and gave him a lengthy set of notes, and they went back and forth a few times, Dan asking her for elaboration, Maddy happy to provide it.

"How have you been keeping busy?" he asked as a Rhodesian ridgeback bounded past, the owner trailing behind. "Is it strange not working?"

"Promise you won't tell anyone?"

"Sure."

"I'm writing a script."

"Really? That's fantastic. You've always been a good writer."

"Even though you wanted me to give up my rights?" she asked with a sly smile.

"How many times are you going to make me apologize? I was a Hollywood neophyte. I would never do something like that today. So what's your screenplay about?"

She told him all about Lane Cromwell as they hiked, until they stopped at a lookout, where she told him more. She talked about Lane's affairs, her career, and her mental problems. He listened intently and said it sounded like she had absorbed everything possible about this woman's life.

"Your first screenplay," he said, "I mean the first one you're writing all alone, and it's so ambitious."

"Maybe no one will want to make it. But I feel like I have to finish it. I felt this need to tell her story."

"And you want to play her, I assume?"

"Well, of course. But who knows if I'll be able to make it happen?"

"Of course you will. You're Maddy Freed. You can do anything you want."

"Do you mean Steven Weller's wife can do anything she wants?"

"I mean Maddy Freed. You're a star. Don't you know that?"

"When I had to back out of Walter's movie, I felt like no one would want to work with me again. It was such a mess, being in the hospital and being in England. And then Kira taking over the role."

"Are you still speaking to her?"

"We're . . . cordial." Maddy had wanted to be able to snap back into a friendship with Kira, but felt it would be painful to be near her. "All these things at once, I was losing weight and I couldn't sleep and I was so anxious about the baby. I had to go on antidepressants. I'm on them now." She had gone off the lorazepam while in the hospital and hadn't needed it since.

"You did the right thing."

"Steven was freaked out about it. He said he didn't want the medicine going into the baby. Now we just don't talk about it."

"He's a fucking idiot. It's like on the airplanes when they say you have to put the oxygen mask on yourself before you put one on your child."

"Exactly," she said. He still understood her. "Anyway, I thought I would never work again. And I realized if I wrote something for myself, with a role for me to play, it might be different. When you're an actor, you have to wait for people to hire you. When you're a writer, you can just—write. Please don't tell anyone about this, though."

"No, of course not."

"Zack's the only one who knows. I didn't even tell Steven."

"He doesn't know, and Zack and I do?"

"I don't want him to see it until it's done. I need it to be mine for now. Like how you were with *Silver Spring*."

"Yeah."

They turned and started on the hiking path again. "I envy you," she said.

"Why?"

"Because you're in complete control of your films."

"Yeah, but we did it for a tiny amount of money and a very small cast."

"The scale doesn't matter. You're making your own stuff again, like you were when I met you. And it's going well. If the next one does even a little bit of business, then they'll give you the money to do a third and a fourth, and you can keep working like that until you're old."

"Or until they don't want to finance me anymore."

"That won't happen. People will keep paying for you to make stuff. If you asked me for help again, I would give it to you."

He put his arm around her for a second. "Thank you," he said.

"It's a good investment," she said. "Even if I didn't like you, I'd back you. I put in twenty-five grand and got a hundred and fifty thousand back. You're way better than the stock market."

"That's the nicest thing you've ever said to me."

She panted a little as she climbed, and he asked if she wanted to stop, but she said she was fine. "So . . . are you excited to be a mom?" he asked. "I mean, is it real to you?"

"Now that the baby's kicking, it is. But honestly, I'm just trying to write as much as I can, because once the baby's born, I won't be able to. It's like this ticking clock inside of me. A good one. It's motivating me."

"Can I ask you something?" he said, picking up a stick and holding it out like a cane. "You got pregnant right after you started shooting Walter's movie. And you were so passionate about that role. I know you weren't expecting to get sick, but was the baby planned?"

"Of course it was planned," she said. "Steven has wanted to be a father for a very long time. He's going to be such a good dad. He's not working the first six months. Anyway, yeah, so I thought I would be able to work through the pregnancy, but it didn't happen. There's no perfect time to have a baby."

She glanced at him before striding ahead, and Dan saw that her face had closed. It was the Maddy Freed mask. He'd seen it on the red carpet for *I Used to Know Her* when she gave interviews and he'd seen it again when he watched those clips of her extolling her marriage on daytime, prime time, and late-night. She was a master of her craft, she knew how to appear revealing without being revealing at all. It was a skill she hadn't had until Los Angeles.

What the real circumstances of the baby's conception were, Dan would never know. What she truly felt about building a family with Steven Weller, who had made her so desolate two years ago, that would remain her secret, too. Whatever she felt, she was not going to share. Ahead of him, she moved up the path confidently, and from the back, she didn't seem pregnant at all.

On March 15, the same premiere date as *The Hall Fixation*, Maddy and Steven attended the premiere of *The Hall Surprise*. They had both done a huge round of publicity leading up to it, magazine covers, dozens of junkets. In her interviews, Maddy had gushed about her turn as Faye Fontinell, a feat that took an extraordinary amount of acting. Faye had been the beginning of a string of bad luck: the unplanned pregnancy, the hyperemesis, the withdrawal from *The Moon and the Stars*.

On the press line for the premiere, Steven posed for pictures with his hand on her belly. She wore a red strapless maternity dress with a sweetheart neckline and empire waist and four-inch heels. Reporters asked again and again about the baby's gender and due date, and she had to decline, politely, to answer. You couldn't even say you didn't know the gender, Flora had trained her, because that was too personal and the tabloids would dissect the reasons. Instead, you could say you weren't saying.

On the carpet Maddy was aware of Bridget's presence on the side but avoided her glance. They had not seen each other since Wilmington. On the few occasions when she came by the house to get Steven, Maddy had told him Bridget was not welcome inside.

Inside the theater, she and Steven posed by the posters. There was a little lull while he did some photos on his own, and she stepped off the carpet to watch. By the time Bridget was near, there was no escape. Maddy's hands began to shake. She felt ridiculous for being afraid. Why should she be scared of Bridget now?

"You look gorgeous tonight," Bridget said. "You're radiant."

"Thank you," Maddy said. They stood side by side, watching Steven.

"I know you had mixed feelings about doing Faye," Bridget said, "but I think you should be proud. And I wish you all the best in all of your endeavors."

Before Maddy could respond, Bridget had turned to the door. The CEO and chairman of Apollo, Neil Finneran, a short, bespectacled man with a buzz cut, was coming in with his younger wife.

Inside the theater they took their reserved seats in the middle. As the lights dimmed inside the theater and the Apollo logo came on the screen, Maddy felt a rush of anxiety. The bikini scene was humiliating and the dialogue weak. Even at eight months pregnant, she felt no pride in seeing herself on the enormous screen in peak form. She didn't like remembering that time in her marriage, when she had been so anxious that she'd taken a part she hated, rolled over when her suggested rewrites were voted down, held her tongue when the bikini got skimpier with each costume test. She had to try to forget about Faye Fontinell and focus on Lane Cromwell. Someday Lane would erase Faye.

―――――――

In bed that night, Steven kissed her. It got heated—she was horny, so close to her due date, and so big that he took her from behind, on her side. She realized it was the first time they had had intercourse in over a month.

After he came, he said, "It's going to be soon, now, huh? We'll be a family."

"We're already a family."

"You know what I mean."

As she lay there with her hands on her enormous belly, she said, "I have something to tell you."

"Yes, my love?" he asked, moving his hand around so he could feel the kicks, which were coming all the time now. A reminder that this baby would soon be out.

"I'm writing a screenplay."

"Really? I'm so proud of you. I want to hear all about it."

She told him the broad strokes of Lane's life, and when she'd finished, he said, "Why didn't you tell me about this?"

"I wanted to have something that was only mine. And I didn't know if it would be any good. I'm going to try to set it up, and I want to act in it."

He started to say "That's amazing," but his cell phone rang, and he got up and stepped out of the bedroom into the hallway.

The week after *The Hall Surprise* opened domestically, Neil Finneran took Bridget to lunch at Craft. The film was on track to pass all the benchmarks set by *The Hall Fixation*. At the table, when Neil smiled and said he had something to discuss, she got a feeling that something important was about to happen.

"Bridget," he said. "You know I'll be seventy in December, right?"

She had ordered a white wine and sipped it coolly, wanting to chug. "You don't look a day over fifty, Neil."

He smiled with his lips closed. "I've had a good run, and I'm proud that the Hall franchise has turned Apollo Pictures around," he said. "I have you to thank for it. It was a little rocky there at first, but now it's hard to remember when this wasn't the most successful franchise in our history. I was waiting and waiting to retire at the right moment, and I feel like this is it. I was talking to Bob about how I'm ready to go, and your name was out of his mouth before I said it. You have your finger on the pulse of popular entertainment. With Steven Weller or without, you are going to be making successful movies for a very long time. I want you to take over for me."

It was hard for her to breathe, but she was determined to stay in control. He would be watching her carefully for signs that she was overemotional.

"It's not a hundred percent yet, but I wanted to speak to you before Bob did. Now, should we order some Prosecco?"

She would have to dismantle Ostrow Productions, of course. The hardest part would be saying goodbye to clients. But like a man who knew which friend he would want his wife to marry if he dropped dead, Bridget had ideas about good matches for them. If her clients had any sense, they would take her recommendations. If they didn't, they would look back and appreciate her all the more.

She could imagine the reaction as soon as her appointment was announced. People would say Neil had done this to ensure Steven's loyalty to the studio. They would say she had never been a real producer, merely a highly paid suck-up, and would fail as CEO and chairwoman because of that. Or that she had gotten the job because she was sleeping with Neil. Whenever a woman advanced, there was blowback. But she was prepared. She had been maligned enough that she wasn't threatened by the prospect of cruel lies. Every time a woman took a powerful position, she was said to be fucking someone. It meant nothing. At her age, it was flattering.

She was ecstatic about the possibilities. Her slate would be twenty pictures a year. The palette, the scale! She would have to build on the success of the Tommy Hall movies, find other franchises, make the right hires, bring in more money than Neil Finneran had, merely not to look like a screwup. But she wasn't scared. She was ready.

2

A few weeks after the premiere of *The Hall Surprise*, Maddy finished writing her screenplay. She emailed it to Zack, who loved it but had some notes on the character of Max Sandoval, so she spent the next few weeks revising. She had decided to title it *Pinhole*.

One night in May, she was sleeping next to Steven when she was awakened by Steven's voice. He was on his phone, and though it was only ten P.M., according to the clock, she had already been asleep a few hours. He went downstairs, and when he came back, she said, "Is everything all right?"

"It was Ryan," he said. "He's going through a really hard time."

"I thought you guys didn't speak."

"He got back in touch." He said Ryan had done a crime picture set in 1930s Atlantic City and was upset by his poor reviews. He had gotten involved in a restaurant deal and lost a chunk of money. And his parents had just split up after forty-two years of marriage.

Maddy didn't care what was going on in Ryan Costello's life and wished her husband would never speak to him again. "Anyway," Steven said, "I've never heard him this down before. I'm going to take him out on *Jo* for a couple of days next week."

As soon as he said the name of the boat she felt a wave of nausea and her first thought was that maybe it was labor. "But I'm due in a month."

"That's a long time away. You'll be fine." He fell asleep soon after, but she stared at the ceiling a long time.

————

Over the next couple of nights, Maddy began to have strange dreams. Sometimes they were just old nightmares, like the car-driving dream. But others were sexual. Dan was in many of them, and old boyfriends from theater camp. Her very first make-out on top of a bunk bed. A tattooed jerk from her hallway, freshman year of Dartmouth, who had taken her virginity.

Sometimes after these dreams, when she awakened, she would notice that her panties were wet. Soaked through. She figured the erotic dreams were about the past versus the present. Stress over the change about to come. She and Steven hadn't agreed on a boy's name or a girl's name, and she was anxious about it.

One morning when she woke up and came downstairs for breakfast, woozy from fitful sleep, Steven said this was the day he was taking Ryan on *Jo*. She hadn't quite forgotten, but as the days had passed and he hadn't mentioned it, she had convinced herself that he might not go.

"Look how big I am," she said. "Do you have to leave?"

"You're going to be fine. It's just three days. To Catalina."

"Do it after the baby."

"He's going to Vancouver for a movie, and this is the only window we both have."

"What if something happens? At least take your phone."

"Nothing is going to happen."

"Fine, but will you take your phone anyway?" She gripped both of his shoulders. "Just this one time. Please."

He kissed her gently on the mouth. "Anything for the mother of my child."

He took off in the Mustang. The house was empty and bleak. In the morning, she ran a few errands, arriving home at one for lunch. Around three, she got drowsy. She got in bed to take a nap and dreamed that she was on *Jo* with Steven and the young Alex from the glossy photo. Steven was the Steven of now, but Alex was in his twenties. The men were kissing and she was yelling at them to stop, but they couldn't hear her and went down to the cabin.

She was awakened by a sharp pain in her uterus. Not the mellow kind, like the Braxton-Hicks contractions she had felt before, but a deep, awful one, far worse than her most painful period. The sheets were sticky. She ripped off the comforter and saw a pool of yellowish liquid.

She dialed Steven on his cell, and it rang until it went to voice mail. She left a frenzied message saying she was in labor. She dialed Dr. Baker and said she thought her water had broken. Dr. Baker said to come to the hospital. Maddy called Zack and then Kira, not sure why, but wanting a woman there. Kira was strong and could help her. *The Moon and the Stars* didn't matter now. Maddy left another message for Steven and then dialed Alan, who arrived in twelve minutes in the Highlander. She threw together a bag with toiletries, a few changes of clothes, and slippers before waddling out to the car.

Everything that happened in the two hours after her arrival felt like a wrong turn. The contractions were coming more strongly now, and Dr. Baker put her on an antibiotic drip to prevent infection. Then there was another drip, an IV, she heard someone say. It seemed like tubes were coming out of her everywhere, and when she moved, the drips had to move with her, and the pain, the pain, she wanted to do it naturally, she did the Lamaze breathing she had learned in class with Steven, but the pain was brutal and unfamiliar. She watched Dr. Baker watch a monitor and shake her head. "Late decel." And the doctor was gone, returning with a nurse, who was removing one of the drips. Maddy thought that could be good, fewer drips had to be better.

"Maddy, the baby isn't responding well to the Pitocin, and we don't have a lot of time because your water broke."

"Can't I push? I want to push. I want a normal birth."

"We have to get the baby out because of the risk of infection. We have to do a C-section. You'll be fine. We're going to give you a mini-prep and then we'll go to the OR."

"But I don't want surgery!" she cried, suddenly afraid she might die. This wasn't the way she had envisioned it.

"We have to take care of the baby. You're both going to be fine."

While she was talking, Zack had come in. His first words were "Where's Steven?"

She shook her head violently. "He's on the sailboat with Ryan Costello. You have to find him. Call your mother. His phone is on silent or something. Have them radio him from the yacht club. Bridget will know who to talk to. Or have them call the Coast Guard."

"You don't want me to stay with you?"

"I want you to bring him here."

Zack was gone and a new nurse was in the room, a pretty Mexican girl, shaving Maddy's pubic hair. And then she was on a gurney like in a television hospital show, and they weren't quite running but moving her quickly, and Kira was beside her in the hallway, saying, "I got here as fast as I could." Maddy was numb, not weeping, just thinking about the next moment, getting the baby out of her alive, there was no room to cry, this was happening, they were going to cut it out of her.

"Where's Steven?" Kira asked.

"He's on the boat, Zack's trying to find him. Can you come in the operating room?" Maddy looked up pleadingly at the doctor.

"She can come in," Dr. Baker said.

"What if something goes wrong and I don't make it?" Maddy cried out to Kira. "I don't want to die."

"You're not going to die. You're going to be fine."

And then a nurse was guiding Kira away. They would have to put her in scrubs because it was an operating room and it would be sterile.

An Israeli anesthesiologist injected something into Maddy's back after telling her she had to stay very still. Then she was flat on her back with her arms extended like she was being crucified. A sheet went up in front of her, held between two poles. Kira was on one side of her and the anesthesiologist was on the other. Over the curtain was the baby's team; she wasn't supposed to watch because her guts would come out; they'd watched a video of a C-section in Lamaze . . .

The anesthesiologist was saying something about pressure, and she could hear Dr. Baker talking on the other side, and then there was a loud, startling noise. A baby's cry, healthy and long. Piercing the din.

"I can't see!" Maddy cried. "I want to see my baby!"

"It's a boy," Kira was saying, and Maddy was crying because this wasn't the way it was supposed to be, Kira wasn't supposed to be the one to tell her the gender, they had planned that Steven would tell her, but he wasn't here. "He's perfect," Kira said.

"What's going on? Tell me what's happening."

"They're cleaning him."

A minute later, a nurse was holding the baby, swaddled, against Maddy's cheek, since her arms were still strapped down. She wanted to break out of the straps and touch her son. Her son and all she could do was smell him. He was tiny and scrunched, with dark hair. Blinking, dazed. Not crying anymore. He was in as much shock as she was.

She kissed his cheek, rubbed her cheek against his. Ran her lips over his hair. "I want to hold him," she said, and she began to weep from the frustration of not being able to.

"You'll see him very soon," the nurse said. Maddy kissed him again, but the woman was taking him away. Dr. Baker knew she was on Zoloft, it was in her files, and Maddy had worried about the birth before, the possibility of withdrawal symptoms for the baby. Now he had been early on top of that.

"Kira, go with the baby," she said. "Don't take your eyes off him. I don't want him to get switched."

"Your baby is not going to get switched."

"Just go. Make sure he's okay."

Maddy could hear Dr. Baker talking to the surgical assistant as she stitched her up. Something about plans for Memorial Day weekend. She couldn't move her arms. She had given birth, and the baby was on another floor, probably, where was he? She felt a flood of grief for her mother, who had gone so early, was not here now, when she needed a mother. She missed her father, too, but it was her mother she yearned for, wanted in this room with her.

She remembered her wearing glasses in the morning, she wore glasses when she first woke up and a dark purple robe with two white stripes, and she was squatting beside her in Maddy's bedroom in Potter so their faces were level, and she said, "Is that so?" It was all Maddy remembered, "Is that so?" and the warmth in her mother's eyes.

All these years when people asked about her, she said she didn't remember much, she diminished it, but this was the hole in her life, always had been. To have to learn about tampons from her father. Later, when she lost her virginity to that asshole at Dartmouth, she'd stood in the shower and cried, feeling the burning, regretting that she had done it. She had wanted a mother then, wanted her mother to explain why it had been so awful.

And she wanted her now to tell her it would all be all right, she would get better. Just like her baby needed his mommy, she wanted hers. There was no one here to hold her. She was an orphan and she was alone and her husband had let her give birth without him.

A recovery room. The compression boots made loud, mechanical noises as they rhythmically squeezed her calves. A nurse sat by her, watching TV. They were waiting for a complete blood count, she said; Maddy couldn't be moved until they got it. Kira came in. She said the baby was in the NICU but looked fine. "You should go back and touch him," Maddy said. "Don't leave him all alone in there."

"I feel like I should stay with you," Kira said.

Zack came in, and Maddy shooed Kira away to the NICU. "Congratulations," Zack said.

"Have you seen him? He's so beautiful."

"I came straight to you. They're trying to get Steven on the radio. No one's picking up."

"What about the Coast Guard?"

"My mother tried, but they won't send out boats because they say it's not an emergency."

"Your mother couldn't convince them?"

"She's working on it."

"It doesn't matter anymore. He's born."

Zack looked out the hospital window, feeling numb. His mother had been his first call. Five minutes passed and ten, and he called back and she said the guys at the yacht club were trying to get Steven on the radio. As soon as she told Zack, he knew. The radio was off.

"How can they not reach him?" Maddy asked. "He told me he always has it on."

"I just don't know," Zack said, and felt worse than he had after telling her Kira was going to do Walter's movie.

Maddy was pale and sad, so frail in her gown and the weird boots that kept pumping. She looked off to the side, and then seemed to muster all her strength and said, "I had to have a C-section."

"Look on the bright side. You get to keep your vagina nice and tight." The nurse visibly pretended not to hear this.

"Please don't make me laugh. My stitches will come out." Then she started to cry.

As he put his hand on hers, he felt disgusted with Steven. Steven was a selfish prick and had been as long as Zack had known him. Zack had tried to warn Maddy in Friedenau, but it hadn't worked, and looking at her now, he felt it was his own fault. She had been invited to that dinner party in Mile's End only because he'd called Bridget. Maddy never would have met Steven if it weren't for him.

This was why, when they'd walked in the cemetery, he had tried to convince her to stay away. But at that time they hadn't been friends. He hadn't wanted to come across as a meddler. And he had worried she would relay their conversation to his mother, who had already signed her. He had tried to warn Maddy without warning her.

So many signs over the years. From before he was old enough to know what they meant, until later, when he was.

The funny expression on his mother's face when she would read the gossip items hinting at affairs with men. "I can promise you, Steven is not your father," Bridget had said.

The bad first marriage and the way Steven never talked about his wife, the parade of pretty young things afterward. The women always just right. Hyper-feminine. With their fake boobs and their blowouts and their Kewpie eyes.

Zack had never known for sure, but he had ideas. One night, it must have been senior year of high school, Steven had come over late. Steven and Bridget talked for a long time; he was upset about something. After he had left, Zack went down to the kitchen to get food. His mother was alone at the table and looked sad. "Is he okay?" Zack had asked.

"He's going through a hard time right now. Personal stuff."

And then Zack had blurted it out: "How come he's not married?"

"I'm not married."

"I mean, how come he never stays with one girl?"

"Steven isn't like other men," she had said, and her eyes lingered on his just a beat too long.

"What do you mean?"

"I mean that he doesn't think about marriage the way other men do."

In Berlin, Zack had hoped Maddy would be smart enough to get it, even if she didn't get all of it. Later, after the wedding, he concluded that she was more complicated than he had thought. If not a contract, then an agreement.

And when it became difficult to reconcile his instincts about Maddy with the idea of an arrangement, he worked out other explanations in his head: He had misunderstood all these years and Steven didn't like men, or he liked both, or Maddy had changed him.

Because if he did like men, and Maddy didn't know, it meant she had been duped. By Steven. Or his mother. And if Steven could do such a horrible thing, Zack didn't want to believe that Bridget could. In business she had lied and deceived, but to take another person's life, to use someone as a tool . . . it meant she was a monster.

Maddy found the NICU frightening, wholly abnormal, and too bright. Tiny babies in incubators lined up, all out of the womb too early, purple and skinny, with tubes in them, these bodies so small and weak, hooked up to the big machines. Kira was at the baby's incubator, with a slim, middle-aged pediatric nurse named Lillian. Maddy had already spoken with the neonatologist, who told her there were no signs of withdrawal in the baby, but they were monitoring him. Maddy was relieved to hear that but was agonized by the two tubes going into his tiny hand. "What are those?" she asked Lillian.

"One is antibiotics and one is an IV drip. He had some respiratory distress and we want to make sure he's breathing properly. Do you want to hold your son?"

Lillian lifted the lid of the incubator and took him out. Put him in her lap. She put him to her breast. Lillian demonstrated the football hold. If Maddy held him like a football, to the side, his body wouldn't put pressure on her sutures.

It was hard to coordinate the nursing with the tubes and the monitor strapped to his body, but Lillian and Kira helped her. The baby flailed but took the breast. She had been cut open, catheterized, and shaved, she had morphine and antibiotics in her blood, but her baby was nursing.

"He's perfect," Kira said softly. Maddy stroked his little head.

"Have you picked a name yet?" Zack asked.

"Jake," Maddy said. "Jake Weller Freed." She hadn't been certain until she said it. He was going to have her last name, and her father's. The baby was hers.

She looked down at the baby's little head. The eyes so black. The mouth working hard on her nipple. She wanted to fatten him up so they would let them both go. "He looks like you," Kira said.

"No, he doesn't," she said. "He looks like him."

Maddy was in the NICU, nursing Jake, when she looked up to see Steven standing there. It was a day later. She hadn't even heard him come in.

"You missed it," she said dully. "I told you not to go and you went." Lillian looked up and then down. There was a handful of other parents in the room, but they were focusing on their newborns. It was one of the few times Maddy had been around Steven when no one seemed to notice him.

"I'm so sorry, my love." He leaned down, kissed her head. "They reached us on Catalina and I flew. I got here as fast as I could."

"Why didn't you take your phone, like you said?"

"I left it in the car, at the yacht club."

"And the radio?"

"I thought it was on, but it was off. I feel awful. You had a month before the date. I had no idea he'd come early." He gazed at him on her breast. "He's perfect."

"They want to keep him here longer. I've been pumping my milk so I can nurse him when we get out, so my supply doesn't go down. It's so complicated."

"Hey there, buddy," he cooed softly, running his finger down the baby's cheek.

"I named him after my father," she said. She handed him the baby and Steven took him, sat in another chair, gently avoiding the tubes. "Jake Weller Freed."

He looked a little surprised but then said, "Jake Weller Freed. I like it." He rocked the baby and touched her arm. "Are you in a lot of pain?"

"I'm on Percocet. I don't know how long they'll let me take it. I can't believe you missed the delivery. What's wrong with you? Who are you?" Her voice came out demented and shrill. She didn't care. In every other room of Cedars-Sinai, there were probably bisexual actors in shouting matches with wives recovering from emergency C-section births that the men had missed.

"I shouldn't have gone."

"You care more about Ryan than me." She kept her voice low so the others wouldn't hear, but she was livid. "You're in love with him."

"Nothing you said is true. He's my friend."

This tiny helpless thing was counting on the two of them to help him live. How could they do that when they were so far apart? If Steven loved her, he never would have left. Or maybe he had already left her, years ago, on the boat trip to Cabo, and she hadn't wanted to see it.

"I don't want to be with you right now," she said. "I want to get to know my son."

"Okay," he said. "That's okay. Should I go home or—"

"I don't care anymore. Just go." He gave her an odd look as though about to say something, and then gently handed her the baby and went out.

The morning they left the hospital, Maddy had clothing and heels brought in, and a glam squad for natural-looking hair and makeup. Flora had arranged everything so the media knew when the family would be coming out and no one outlet would have "the first shots."

Dozens of photographers were gathered outside behind the stanchions. It would be an orderly affair. When the time came, Steven and Maddy posed outside with Jake in her arms and Steven's arm around her. Flora was there, overseeing everything. As agreed, the photographers refrained from yelling their names so as not to upset the baby. All Maddy could hear were the digital shutters clicking. They posed for several minutes. Maddy smiled wearily, playing the role of exuberant new mother. It was all cream blush, all fake. No one knew Steven had missed the birth.

But he *had* missed it, and every day since, she had been replaying the delivery, rewinding to the moment when she had the dream and imagining that her water had not broken. She wanted to fix Jake's birth so he hadn't come early and she'd delivered him naturally, in the birthing room they had toured, with the tub and the wood paneling. In this vision of the birth, Steven was there, and he caught the baby and cut the cord, and afterward she could smell the vernix on Jake's face. She was broken and imperfect, her body wouldn't cooperate, a woman's body was supposed to push. It had been the dream that had started it all, the nightmare and then the broken amniotic sac. She shouldn't have napped. If you didn't sleep, you didn't dream.

3

W ho is it?" Zack called out to Natalie from the desk of his new office. They communicated through an open door all day. In September, after two years at the Bentley Howard office in L.A., he had left to launch his own company, Laight Street Entertainment, which he had named after his old block in Tribeca. He had used his trust to capitalize some of it, but the rest came from investors he had met and courted during his time in L.A. Who had been watching him build a better and bigger list, who believed that he could go out on his own at an age when most people would be considered foolish to do so.

When Natalie told him Steven was on the line, he paused before putting on his headset. It had been an insane morning. The script had gone out at five P.M. the day before, and already he had offers from three of the six studios. It was his first submission as independent manager-producer, and he knew the sale price would shape the perception of his company.

Velvet was by a young screenwriter client who had been working on it for a year. It was based on the true story of an Australian jewel thief in the 1980s named Frank McKnight—a tight, edge-of-your seat tale with a coiled, charismatic lead. McKnight was a get for any actor in his mid-thirties. Hyper-intelligent and manic, he had a troubled marriage and a thrill-seeking nature. And he was the greatest fucking jewel thief who ever lived.

The offers that had come in last night and this morning were all in the mid-sixes, which Zack thought boded well. He was hoping for a mil.

He wondered if Steven was putting out a feeler for Zack's management services. Bridget had folded Ostrow Productions and officially taken over as Apollo Pictures CEO and chairwoman just one week ago. Steven was said to be taking meetings with high-profile agents and managers, but there was no way he would hire Zack. A brand-new company, a twenty-nine-year-old manager, even younger than his wife. Steven wasn't the kind of person to take a chance, not in work or in life.

"Put him through," Zack called.

"Zack," Steven said. "First of all, I wanted to thank you again for being so good to Maddy at the hospital."

"Why wouldn't I be?" Zack asked tightly.

"I know, but it was a difficult situation, and you were there for her. She's so grateful to you."

"Someone had to be there."

Steven paused dramatically and then said, "So I read *Velvet*. And I wanted to congratulate you. It's a perfect hybrid. A smart heist movie. Reminds me of the best suspense features of the 'seventies. Like *The Day of the Jackal* and *Three Days of the Condor*. I just—you're a player now. When I met you, you were just a boy."

Zack knew Steven Weller would never call anyone just to say congratulations. He said nothing, only waited. Like a good journalist.

"I was calling because—I'd like to throw my name into the ring," Steven said.

"I'm not sure what you're talking about."

"For Frank. McKnight." Zack tapped his fingers together and pivoted to regard the painting of Kid Berg. Every time he examined it, he saw something new. Sometimes the fighter seemed aggressive, tough, invincible. Other times he looked like a scrappy young kid. "I think I would get a lot of bodies into the theater," Steven was saying. "And you and I would work well together as producer and actor. You remind me of your mother when she was starting out."

Zack stood up and went to the window of his office. A woman in a jog bra was walking a Pomeranian. "Thank you for saying all of that, Steven."

"It's true."

"But I can tell you right now that I would never cast you as Frank McKnight. You're completely wrong for him."

"Really? I feel like I could bring out a lot of the humor, and you know audiences already buy me as an action—"

"I don't mean to upset you, but you're just too old. Frank McKnight is in his thirties. I need an actor with vitality. Someone more warm-blooded."

Zack thought of Berg, who had fought ten rounds against then-unbeaten Cuban Kid Chocolate at the Harlem Polo Grounds in 1930. Berg was persistent and steady and kept it up, and by the end Kid Chocolate couldn't lift his hands.

"We could have a long conversation about whether audiences find my blood warm," Steven said, "but regardless of that, I could bring you attention on a level that . . ."

"That what?"

"That will be hard for you to get from anyone else, given your unknown screenwriter."

"You know, Steven, it's funny you say that. Because I founded this company with the mission of telling good stories and a belief that good stories can also make money. I believe that American audiences are hungry for material that challenges them, makes them think, and provokes them. I've been developing this script for two years, and I have faith that this is a story that needs telling. I will get attention for this movie, wherever we land, and the man who plays McKnight is going to be the one who's most right for him. Because that's part of telling a good story. I have no doubts that this film will find its audience, even without Steven Weller. All right? No hard feelings." And he clicked off before Steven could get in another word.

In the fall, when Jake was a few months old, Maddy and Steven did a family photo spread for *People*. They donated the $1 million fee to World Children's Welfare. The photos showed them cooing over Jake, and they were taken in a studio so no one would have any indication what the nursery looked like. In the interviews, they talked about what a joy it was to be parents, despite the sleeplessness and the crying. They talked about how the experience had changed them. Steven said Maddy was an amazing and selfless mother, but during the sit-down, as she watched his mouth move, it sounded phony and depressing.

She knew she could not stay with Steven, but every time she pictured leaving, she would think about Jake and feel trapped. Only a selfish mother kicked out the father when the child was this young. This tiny baby needed not only Maddy but Steven, too. How could she disrupt her young son's life?

It didn't help her decision-making that Steven had turned out to be a doting dad. During the day, the three of them would go out together. Steven would carry Jake in the BabyBjörn, and they would go hiking or to a playground or the zoo. There would be photographers and people would smile and sometimes she could convince herself that they were happy. But they connected only over Jake.

At home one night, she came in to find Steven making funny noises with his mouth as he read a board book to Jake in the nursery. The baby in his lap, Steven looked like a man who had never been quite so happy. As she stood there in the doorway, she worried not only that Jake preferred Steven, which was painful enough, but also the opposite. Jake was his miniature, his boy. Steven could feel love for him that he could never feel for Maddy, or maybe never had.

That November, in the midst of awards season, *The Moon and the Stars* came out. Maddy watched a screener from bed while nursing Jake. It was excruciating to watch Kira, who put her own stamp on the role of Betty, and Maddy kept imagining the things she would have done differently.

As Jake grew bigger, learned to walk, smile, laugh, and eat, Maddy's mood begin to lift. She decided to go off the Zoloft. At first she was anxious about it, but she went down slowly and found she could sleep at night, and even fall back asleep, after she nursed him. They had let go of the baby nurse and hired a live-in Polish nanny named Lucia.

She started to see a therapist named Dina Friedberg, who had been recommended to her by Dr. Baker. In her visits with Dina, Maddy talked a lot about the night Jake was born. She said she was certain that Steven and Ryan were lovers. She told her about Alex Pattison and the Christian Bernard story and her press blitz.

"Maybe I deserve a husband who cheats on me," Maddy said after confessing about the night she spent with Dan.

"What do you mean?" Dina, who had bony cheeks and hair to her waist, asked from her boxy gray armchair.

"Because I cheated on him."

"But didn't you think he was betraying you before that night with Dan?"

"Yeah. I don't know if that makes it right, though."

In their sessions, Dina would try to pry out of Maddy what fidelity represented to her. And Maddy realized it mattered, it wasn't nothing. She understood that some couples didn't care, but when she had married Steven, she had believed in and expected his faithfulness. Even if she had been stupid to do so. And he knew she felt it was important. To her, fidelity was part and parcel of love. She had felt adrift because she was uncertain of his loyalty, and because of that she had gone to Dan, and it had been wrong, but she couldn't undo it. Now she had to figure out whether to stay married.

Slowly, she began to see the possibility of a future without Steven, though it would be impossible to do anything until Jake was more independent and she was physically back on her feet. She was still nursing him three to four times a day.

Thinking about *Pinhole* and the prospect of someday playing Lane Cromwell, she hired a personal trainer and nutritionist. The pounds fell off. She began to get strong.

Zack had sent out the screenplay, and a New York–based production company, Reckless Entertainment, fell in love with it. The head of the company, Christine Nabors, had been in indie film since the '80s; she flew in to L.A. to discuss her ideas. Maddy, Zack, and Christine had a three-hour lunch meeting at a new Asian restaurant in a condo building in Century City, and Maddy was so taken by Christine's enthusiasm and track record that she decided to go with her without sending it anywhere else. Christine began sending Maddy director reels to watch, and though she took two meetings, she didn't quite click with either director.

One Saturday in December, when Lucia had the day off, Maddy went out for a walk with Jake, who was about seven months old. They returned to find a strange car in the driveway. The light in the guesthouse was on, and suddenly Ryan Costello came out, swept up the baby, and spun him around. "What are you doing here?" Maddy spat.

"Steven didn't tell you? My house in Malibu is being renovated, and he said I could crash here."

"No, he didn't tell me." Jake was crying out with glee. "That's not good for babies," she said, and whisked him away.

Inside the house, she dialed Steven. The call went to voice mail. When he came in a few hours later, she said, "How could you let him stay here without asking me?"

"I'm sorry. I meant to tell you. It's just for a couple weeks. He needs a crash pad and—"

"Ryan can afford to stay in a hotel."

"You've never liked him."

"No, I don't like him. I thought I had already made it clear. I don't want this man in our life."

"It's not up to you who's in my life," he said, then went upstairs into the bedroom and slammed the door.

That night Steven left and didn't come home for dinner, and Ryan's car was gone. Maddy ate early with Jake. She fell asleep for a few hours and was awakened by loud laughter. Out the window, she saw Ryan and Steven in the pool, hanging off the edge. They had whiskey glasses resting on the deck and Steven was saying, "And Brando was so broke, he had to hitchhike!"

Ryan laughed and said, "You're making that up."

"Read it in the memoir," Steven said.

Maddy went back to bed and put a pillow over her head. But she was too restless to stay still.

When she went to the window again, the men had moved away from the edge. They were both in the water, and though they weren't physically close, maybe five feet apart, she caught a glimpse of her husband's face in the moonlight. She drew in her breath. His eyes were dancing. He was besotted. It was the way he looked at Alex in the photo.

Steven had looked at her when he made love to her the first time. It was so obvious now, as it had been obvious in Wilmington. These men were lovers. They had been lovers on *Jo* when Jake was born, and they had been lovers in North Carolina before that. And maybe in between, even when Steven said they were no longer in touch. It could have been going on for two years.

He had installed his lover in their guesthouse and was swimming with him in their pool. As though he no longer cared if she knew. As though they had an "understanding." He wanted her to leave him or he believed she had known all along—or both.

She let the curtain go and went into her walk-in. She moved her hand across the dresses that she had worn to the charity balls and premieres and openings and parties since she moved to L.A. Her fingers stopped at the red strapless Marchesa. She held it up against her body in the mirror. She had been so innocent in Berlin. She had believed she was Cinderella.

To Steven it had all been a grand show. Maddy had never enchanted Steven. Only a man could. A Ryan Costello. An Alex Pattison. A Christian Bernard, who wasn't some grifter but a young man Steven had trusted, who likely had turned on him because Steven had ended the affair. Edward must have known, and Flora, and Bridget, he probably told them the truth while he had lied to her. Why wouldn't he? They were the team, and you had to be honest with your team.

She wanted to be angry with Steven, but she was disgusted with herself for shutting her own eyes. She had loved him so much that she had made herself believe the lies. That had been her fault, not his. In school she had played Elizabeth Proctor in *The Crucible*, and every night, when she had to convince John to sign the confession, she believed that he would, and thus would not hang. Every performance it came as a surprise to her that he had torn up the confession and would die. Her belief was so strong that each night the surprise felt real.

It was the same with Steven: She had acted herself into denial. It was because of her need for him. She wanted to be his more than she wanted him to be faithful. He had been selfish, but there was selfishness, too, in looking the other way. Her desire for him had been so great that she had been willing to accept a kind of lumpy half-love, flawed, temporal, and incomplete.

She stared at her reflection in the mirror, the Marchesa against her neck, remembering her hand in his on the press line in front of the Berlinale Palast. There was no one like Steven, just as Julia had put it.

She heard shouting and went back to the window. Ryan and Steven were having a fight. Moments before, that look of adoration, and now a lovers' spat. She could hear "You're a liar!" from Steven, pained and angry. She heard the words "narcissist" and "dilettante." Ryan ran out of the pool area to the guesthouse with Steven chasing him. They disappeared inside and the door shut and she couldn't hear anything anymore.

Five minutes later, Steven came rushing out and got into the Mustang. There was a squeal as it left, and then she heard the hum of the gate opening.

Jake cried from the nursery on the baby monitor. She went to his room. Lucia was already comforting him when she arrived, but she told her to go back to bed.

Maddy took him out of the crib, sat in the glider, and nursed. "Shhh, shhh," she said as she watched his head bobbing, his mouth taking her so hungrily. His cheeks moving as he suckled. Someone in the house was happy she was there.

Maddy lay in bed a long time, waiting for Steven to come in, but by two in the morning he hadn't returned. She got up and went into the study. "Professor Alex Pattison, Theater Arts, Los Angeles College." She typed the address into her phone.

In the morning, she arose to find that Steven's Mustang was still gone. There was a light on in the guesthouse. In the living room, Lucia was playing blocks with Jake. "I'll be back in a couple of hours," Maddy said, and got in her Prius.

Professor Pattison worked in a low brick building. As she followed the corridor to his office, she felt an instinct to turn around and not come back.

Outside the door, she could hear a man's voice. It was deep and melodious: "And Bérenger is the only one who doesn't think everyone should become a rhinoceros just because they can. He says, 'I will not capitulate,' and we get Ionesco's ideas about the war."

A few minutes later, the door opened and a girl came out. She wore a scoop-necked black shirt and dark jeans with boots, the kind of thing Maddy used to wear to New School classes every day. She did a double take when she saw Maddy. Maddy smiled faintly and waited to knock till the girl was down the hall.

"Come in."

He had a wooden desk and a gray leather chair facing it. Seeing her, he registered surprise and a hint of amusement.

"Professor Pattison," she said. "Could I speak with you? I'm Maddy Freed."

"I know who you are." He gestured to the seat. She closed the door behind her. He wore a dark gray blazer with a gray collared shirt in a slightly lighter hue than the jacket. He eyed her evenly. He would have made a good poker player. She wondered if she was the first. Maybe there had been other visits like this, from other women, over the years. Or maybe Cady and all the rest knew, like Julia most likely had, and Maddy had been the only one delusional or narcissistic enough to convince herself that Steven Weller could ever love a woman.

"I—I wanted to talk to you about Steven," she said.

"Amazing how easy it was to find me, right? Every once in a while an entertainment journalist comes knocking. I've gotten good at turning them away. Probably would have been harder to find me if I'd left L.A., but this happens to a lot of us midwestern boys who have a love of acting. We move out and never go home."

She took a deep breath and held his gaze. "Did I marry a fraud?"

He clasped his hands together on his desk. "How can I answer that question?"

"Is my husband gay?"

"You know," he said, gently rotating a paper-clip holder on his desk, "if you had asked me that two decades ago, I would have said yes. But who knows? I teach these kids, and they talk to me about their personal lives. I guess because I've always been open about my own. And it's so fluid for them. They aren't interested in labels. 'Labels are for cans,' they say. If they do try a name on for size, 'queer' or 'dyke' or 'fag,' they rip it off the next day. We were the opposite. We wore labels as a sign of pride. Because there was so much hate."

"Steven told me about the two of you. He said you were friends. And it got blurry. He said you slept together one night and went back to being friends," Maddy said. Professor Pattison laughed. "It wasn't once, was it?" she asked.

"A lot more than that," he said. "On and off for four years. It went on after his marriage to Julia."

So he had lied to Maddy even after she confronted him with Alex's name. Of course it had been an affair. He had used Alex's book, Alex's quotation, to propose to her, and then lied about how serious it was. If he had told her, after the marriage, that he had been with a man on and off for four years, she would have . . .

"He was so confused," the professor continued. "He fell hard for her and wanted to believe that it meant, that he could . . . She found out. They had a fight and he told her. They split up. We got back together, but he was torn up by the divorce. It made him feel like a failure. Broken. Instead of asking himself why it didn't work, he just wanted to be 'normal' all the more."

"I married a man who loves men," she said. Her face was hot. It was crazy to have tracked down this man on the Internet, like an amateur private detective. But now she was here with him, with a stranger, Steven the glue between them.

"*I* know *I* loved him," Alex said slowly. "Did *he* love *me*? He wasn't sure. We were so young. I can't tell you who he is. Why would I presume to know? I'm not Gay Yoda."

"But you knew him. You knew Steven Woyceck. You have to help me. We have a son, he's still an infant, and I have to—Steven says he's not gay. But there's a man in his life now and . . . I think he's been deceiving me. Do you think I made a mistake?"

"Are you happy in bed with him?"

"Mostly. Yes."

Alex drummed his fingers on the desk and looked out the window. "It seems your problem is the same one we all have. You don't know if you are truly loved. But does anyone? Do I know the secret thoughts and dreams of my partner, whom he sees in his mind when he closes his eyes in bed? Does he know how much it disgusts me to find the cap of the toothpaste off yet again, even though I have told him hundreds of times? To hear the clanging of his fork against his teeth as he eats his fusilli? We are all a little bit despised. Aren't we? Alongside the need to be coupled is an equally compelling need to be left utterly alone."

"Did I make a mistake?"

"Love is filled with mistakes, just varying degrees." He rose to his feet. "I hope you find some answers. Whether that's the same as being happy, I don't know. Is that Gay Yoda enough for you?"

When she returned, Steven's Mustang still wasn't there. She could hear the Rolling Stones blasting from the guesthouse. She opened the door and heard the shower running. She waited on the edge of the bed, imagining that they had made love in it, while she was sleeping, before they got in the pool and had their spat.

The room was a mess; Ryan had books, clothes, and scripts strewn everywhere. She glanced at the titles: up-and-coming action films, all in the Steven Weller/Tommy Hall oeuvre. One day Ryan would be as successful as Steven.

The bathroom door opened. Ryan was naked and rubbing his head with a towel. His penis was long and white, and it looked like he trimmed the hair around his balls.

When he saw her, he jumped and covered himself. "What the fuck?" His torso had the familiar overdeveloped pectorals of many Hollywood stars. Had Steven touched this torso, had Steven kissed Ryan's neck the way he had kissed hers? Did Ryan turn him on in a way she didn't? Had Steven been repulsed by her breasts, her softness, everything about her that made her a woman?

Ryan went to the galley kitchen and started making a pot of coffee. "Does he love you?" she asked.

"I don't know what you're talking about," he said dully.

She hadn't realized until now how exhausted she was. The deceiver wasn't the only one who had to split in two. The deceived did, too.

"Were you guys having sex the night Jake was born?" He stared at the coffeemaker. "Ryan. Steven's not here. It's you and me now. Please. Just tell me."

"Why should I?" he said, pivoting around. "What do I owe you?" With his lip curled out, he reminded her of Steven. The sneer. He had no interest in another person, in imagining what it might be like to be on the other side.

"I know he was with a man when he was younger. And I think there have been others. A lot of them. Please just tell me to my face what's going on between you."

The coffee made bubbling noises, and he poured the brown brew into a modernist mug by Eva Zeisel. Steven had picked all the stoneware for the guesthouse. Steven picked everything.

Ryan held the mug between his hands, blew into the cup, and leaned against the cabinets, sipping. He looked like an ad in an interiors magazine. "Of course we were. It was why he wanted the radio off."

"And that's why he left his phone. So no one could bother him."

"He's crazy when it comes to the phones. Always has to check the bag, the pockets. Like I would take a photo and sell it to a magazine. Like I would do that to myself."

"When did it start? In Wilmington?"

He hesitated and looked down into his mug. "It was weird at first. He thought I was straight. He was cautious. Then one night at the house, we got drunk. It was so easy. My house, his house. Two men. Practical jokers. He felt safe with me because we were doing a movie together and because of my reputation. Sometimes I crashed with him. The paparazzi don't go to Wilmington to stake out homes. Not with all the cutbacks to the tabloid-magazine industry."

She slid down the edge of the bed so she was sitting on the floor, clasping her knees to her chest. "And after Wilmington?" she asked hollowly.

"On and off. There was a period where he was angry, we didn't speak."

"Where did you do it?"

"Always the boat. It was the only place he felt safe. Even after the thing with Christian." Maddy's throat began to close, and she opened her mouth to get more air.

"The thing with Christian."

"You didn't think it was a lie, did you? He made the mistake of getting involved with someone outside of the industry. I told him he was crazy to keep the boat after that, but he said he could trust the guys at the new club. He had them taking even more money than the ones before. He loved that I wanted discretion, too. He would say to me, 'We're the same. That's why this works. We both need privacy. I don't have to explain it to you.' "

He adjusted the towel around his waist. This half-clothed male body in their guesthouse, using their water, their shower, drinking their coffee. He wouldn't put on a shirt for her even as he was assassinating her marriage. "Does he want to be with you?" she asked hollowly.

"He doesn't know what he wants. Sometimes he liked to fantasize that things could be different. He said he wanted to divorce you and be out in the open with me." She didn't believe that he would speak that way about her, that he would denigrate her to Ryan. She wondered if he was making it up. "But then he would get worried about the Tommy movies. He'll never come out, but he likes to play with the idea that he could. He won't change. Only someone really afraid would go to the lengths he does."

"What do you mean, *the lengths he does?*"

"To get married, to throw the scent off."

"Is that how he speaks of our marriage? Throwing the scent off? Is that something he said?"

Ryan turned his back and ran his finger down the edge of the countertop. "I don't think we should talk anymore."

"I can handle it. Keep going."

His back still turned, he said, "Sometimes he said he loved you, but sex with you . . . disgusted him."

He had to be lying. Steven wouldn't say that about her, no matter how confused he was, no matter how angry.

"You're a liar," she said.

"Whatever," Ryan said.

He went to the Roman shades and rolled them up. It had taken Maddy a long time to figure out how to raise Roman shades, but he already knew. She had no interest in window treatments and decor. She had wanted to put her stamp on this house, but in the end, it wasn't about aesthetics. It was about wanting Steven to hear her. She had never cared about couture or designer furniture or modern art. But Steven did, he loved decorating the home, it was part of his identity. She imagined the two men snuggling on the bed in the main cabin and fingering the collars of each other's shirt.

"Why were you two fighting last night?" she asked.

"He asked if there was someone else. I said yes, because I started seeing someone. I never lied to him about other guys before, but last night he just went crazy. I said it was ludicrous to expect me to be faithful when he was married to you. He said, 'What if I left Maddy? Would that change anything?' I said no. And he lost it and drove off."

She stood up. Her legs were weak, like after the C-section, after the spinal wore off. She pushed open the door. "I'm going for a drive," she said. "I'll be back in an hour, and when I come in, I don't want any trace of you."

She got in the Prius and took the streets to the 101 headed northwest, not sure where she was going. Just wanting to drive fast. She had loved Steven. She didn't want to believe it was all a lie. There was a chance that Ryan was making up the story. Maybe he was in love with Steven, and the things he said about Steven wanting a divorce—lies, revenge.

But when he spoke, it felt like the truth. And more upsetting than this affair, even, which seemed an affair of the heart, was that Ryan had probably been only one of many. Maddy and Steven had been separated physically almost half of the four years they had been married. Opportunity abounded. So easy. There could be dozens of lovers. Hundreds. Paid and not. And Ryan had said the Christian Bernard story was true. Her appearances, her testimonials, all a farce. Of course he had paid off Bernard to retract, maybe paid others over the years, others she didn't know about because Steven had told her never to search their names.

She had been shocked and offended when Kira brought up a contract, but they did have a contract. It wasn't written, and there was no salary, but it was a kind of agreement, in that she had let him do what he did.

She had ignored everyone's warnings because in loving and being loved by Steven, she had been part of something huge and important. The charisma, the charm, the stories. He was like Tennessee Williams, shooting three bull's-eyes in a row, all with his blind eye.

She wanted to believe he loved her once. Maybe he had, at the very beginning. The first year. But even after that, he kept making love to her. How was it possible? Always on, never off. In Venice, the time she conceived . . . the way he had kissed her and held her . . . It hadn't felt like he was performing. It felt genuine. He had made love to her and put his mouth all over her, caressed her breasts, buried his nose in her, his tongue, until she came. Even if they hadn't had sex since the baby. Was it so easy to act, to trick her into believing she was desired? There must have been pills, though she had never seen any in his cabinet; maybe he hid them, as she had hid hers. Or maybe he used his mind. Did what gay men had been doing for centuries: closed his eyes and thought of England.

She had married someone with two selves. And like a political wife, she had looked the other way. When the gay men whispered at parties. When he went on the boat, on the trips with Terry, and alone. That time after the *Husbandry* reviews, he had asked her to come, and she had been berating herself for years for saying no, but he'd known she was working. Maybe he'd known she would decline, and had only asked so as to mislead her into trusting him.

She got off the freeway at Mulholland and headed west toward the Santa Monica Mountains. A little past Laurel Canyon, she passed an overlook. She parked the car and got out, staring down at the San Fernando Valley and the trees. She remembered the flash of the cameras in her eyes that night in Berlin, the beautiful blinding light that left spots. The feeling of being on the arm of Steven Weller . . . It wasn't undignified. It was thrilling. As he had risen, she had risen, too. She had seen her marriage transactionally, whether or not she had known it. When Steven took her hand on that press line, she told herself it was an act of generosity, and to some extent it was. But he had been claiming her, announcing that they were together, before she got a chance to decide. And she had let him. She had wanted to be claimed.

She remembered glancing at Bridget and seeing the look she'd shared with Steven. It was some kind of signal. The ever so slight nod of approval. Maddy had read it as a nod about her career, her future stardom. But perhaps it had been something else.

Bridget had managed the marriage. She had been with the two of them all along, she had been at the first party at Mile's End. She'd seen the movie and made sure Steven did.

Every major actress in Hollywood has read for her, but none was right. As though major actresses, far more accomplished and with better résumés, had been unsuitable for Ellie. Or maybe they were right for Ellie but not for Steven. Lael had said she had flown all the way to London and never read her scenes.

They were casting for something more than a movie. The marriage was a script. A script that Walter, Bridget, and Steven had written together. They delivered it flawlessly, they were all off-book.

When Walter had told her she was cast during the dinner at Locanda Cipriani, he'd said it as though it were a foregone conclusion. Bridget and Steven had chosen her for a far more important role than she had thought. Her marriage had been made. Everyone had known it but the bride.

4

When Steven finally came in after three days and three nights, tan, his hair a tousled mess, Maddy was on the living room couch, her knees folded beneath her. Jake was upstairs napping. Lucia was out running errands.

Steven looked like he had been running a marathon. He sat in the armchair across from her, an Ed Ruscha behind his head. An eerie grid of L.A. lights. It had been in the study in the mansion, and now it was in their living room.

"I talked to Ryan," she said, "and I know." He said nothing, merely staring sadly ahead. "You were making love with him when I was having Jake, and you turned the radio off so you could. I needed you, and you sailed away."

"I was afraid of the future."

"You're a phony. You always loved men. You cast me. You and Bridget. You never loved me."

"That's not true."

"Are you just going to keep lying and lying? There's no point anymore."

"I did love you. At first . . . at the beginning, it was Bridget's idea. She was worried about those rumors. Felt I needed to do something. She thought marriage would be a good idea, to the right woman. And then when I got to know you, I believed we could— You were so beautiful and smart. I saw you as an equal. You were my partner. In life and art. I watched you work and I—learned things. You made me a better actor. I fell in love with you after we married. That was the great surprise."

She stared at the grid on the Ruscha. Did he have these pieces because he liked them or because they were the kind of pieces he thought he should have? Did he know what he liked or like what he thought he should? Did he have Ruscha so he could pronounce "Ruscha"?

Steven Weller was interesting, not interested.

Everything in this house was a sham. He was like those *faux marbre* columns she had hated so much in the mansion. He was a gay boy from Kenosha who had transformed himself into Hollywood's sexiest leading man, from Steven Woyceck to Steven Weller. She didn't know Steven Woyceck. Maybe Ryan did.

Maybe Steven Woyceck didn't care for Henry James and pretended to only because Alex had. Alex Pattison had seemed comfortable with himself; whatever taste he had was his own. Maybe Steven Woyceck didn't even like to read. Maybe he had faked his interest in art and literature all his life to make himself seem smarter and more cultured than he was.

"Don't say you loved me," she said. "If you did, you wouldn't have betrayed me."

"But I do love you. I wanted it to be enough. I kept thinking, hoping, that I had changed. It happens. For thirty years you think one thing about yourself, and then you meet someone and you become someone else. But no matter how much I loved you, there was this longing for something different. So I tried to be two people at once. I had my . . . other world, and I had you. I told myself that with men, it was transactional. Physical. Scratching an itch. Sometimes I could believe it. But it became harder. To keep lying and lying. Each time I took out *Jo*, I would say it was the last time, but it never was. You don't know what it's like to have to hide all the time."

"You ruined my life. At our wedding, you vowed you would be true to me and loyal."

"I kept thinking I could get control over it. When I met Ryan, it was confusing. It was different from the other times."

"Ryan said you told him sex with me disgusts you."

"I never said that. I never spoke that way about you, Maddy!"

She didn't know what to believe. She trusted Steven even less than she trusted Ryan Costello. "What about Terry? Was he your lover, too?"

"Never."

"You were with him on that trip to Cabo after your bad reviews."

He shook his head. "That was someone else."

"Who? Actually, don't tell me. What if I had called Terry or Ananda to check on you?"

"They always had instructions."

"So they know."

"They love me. And they understand that this part of me doesn't have to do with what I feel for you."

"They were at our wedding. They were in on this, and she pretended she was so happy for me."

"I told them it's an addiction. It *is* an addiction. I keep trying to fix it, but—"

"That guy, Christian Bernard from the old yacht club. You *did* have an affair with him, and you did coke and poppers and all the stuff the story said you did. Even though you say you hate drugs." His shoulders slumped. "I did those appearances to defend you, and it was true all along. I asked you to tell me the truth, and you looked right into my eyes and lied to me."

He said nothing. She remembered the blue dress she had worn to *Harry*, the roaring elation of the crowd when she'd said he was the best lover she'd had. She had been an actress for her husband, and she had been good at it. Bridget had plucked her for that very reason. "You made a fool of me!"

"I didn't want any of it to be true. No one knows, Maddy. You did such a good job. You changed the tide." He sat next to her on the couch and put his arm around her, but she shrugged it off.

"Who are you?" she said. "Do you know?"

"Sometimes I think I do."

"Do you even like Biedermeier? Did you ever read Nelson Algren, or do you just quote him?"

"Of course I've read Algren."

"Why do you keep a photo of Alex in a box in your drawer?"

He looked as though he was about to protest, to attack her for snooping, but he must have seen something in her face. He couldn't manipulate her anymore. And then he seemed to give up. "I have my things. I had a life before you."

"You think that if you keep a part of yourself in a box, then it's not really who you are, but that's not true. Who took the picture of you on that boat?"

"Bridget. We were all on it together."

"So she knew."

"She thought Alex and I were friends."

"It's not possible. She must have seen the way you . . . She knew. It's why she wanted you to have a wife. So she went and found a director she could manipulate. She knew Walter needed her, wanted his work to reach a larger audience. You used me. You had me sign the postnup because you knew one day you would be done with me, and you wanted to protect your money. I had an expiration date from the very beginning."

"Maddy," Steven said. "When I married you, I *wanted* it to be forever. It was Bridget who suggested the postnup. I didn't care about the money. I was prepared to give you whatever you wanted if it didn't work out, because I wanted it to work out. I love you. And I love Jake. The sex with you . . . It wasn't fake. We could have more children. We can make this work."

"You're just saying that because Ryan broke up with you. You're crawling back to me, but only because he's through with you. If he wanted to keep it going, it would go on and on like this. You would play with Jake in the house, be the all-star father, and then go to the guesthouse at night to be with Ryan. Where am I in that picture? Am I just Jake's mother? Where were you the last couple of days?"

"On the boat."

"With who?"

"No one. I was alone."

"I don't believe you've been alone on that boat once since we met."

"This time I was. I was trying to figure out what matters. It's you. You're all that matters. We can stay together."

"No, we can't."

"Why not?"

"Because I have no respect for you anymore."

Steven nodded at Maddy and went to the bookshelf, running his hands down the first editions. These were the books that Alex had read aloud to him in bed so long ago, and he had wanted to read them to Ryan, but now Ryan was gone, and he would never get the chance.

The night in the pool, when they fought, he could feel him slipping away and wanted to stop it but was angry with Ryan. For not loving him. And he yelled. Ryan had asked to crash but it turned out that he was dating someone, an architect; the guy was working on his house. Of course it was an architect. Ryan was always talking about Julius Shulman and the Stahl House and Richard Neutra, and when he read books in bed, he would put on a pair of reading glasses, though Steven tried them on once and couldn't detect a prescription.

Steven had sneaked on the boat to see him as often as he could after *Office Mate,* but then Ryan broke it off. When he called again and wanted to see Steven just before Jake's birth, he had been excited. Ryan loved him again. That was why he had taken Ryan on *Jo.* They had talked about their future. He said Steven's "choice" was the problem. Steven had said that Ryan was making a choice, too, coy in interviews about his romantic life, escorting pretty young women to premieres. When Ryan said that he was just waiting for the right time to come out, Steven didn't believe it.

Ryan said that if Steven lost the franchise, it wouldn't matter, because he'd already made two Tommy Halls and it was dangerous to get typecast. As for Maddy, he said, "You gave her a perfect life." Steven didn't like discussing Maddy with Ryan. When he was with Ryan, he wanted it to be the two of them. And on the water it was. He could picture Ryan's back as he stood out looking at the blue, so healthy and tan, two dimples on either side of the spine, above his board shorts. Now it was over and he had lost Ryan, and from the look on Maddy's face he was about to lose her, too.

"I loved you," Steven said in the study, turning to her.

"Did you use condoms? Have you made me sick?"

He had been waiting for this. "I'm clean, I'm careful. I never wanted to hurt you. When you got pregnant . . . I thought I could stop all of this. And I will stop. Ryan was the last. I'll be a good husband to you. Not like before. Let's work on this. It will be different. Better." He went to her and embraced her, ran his hands through her hair, began to sob. She looked at him as if he frightened her. He could see the hate in her eyes.

She told him to get his things and go. He headed up the stairs to the bedroom. As he was climbing, he heard her talking and he stopped. "All these years I thought I was the better actor between us," she said. "But I was wrong. You are."

She looks like a crazy woman, Bridget thought as Maddy stood over her desk at Apollo Pictures. Her hair was a mess and her face was blotchy. It was impossible to believe this was Faye Fontinell.

"You knew he could never love me," Maddy was saying. "And you didn't care. You chose me. Like I was some kind of toy. To do with as you pleased."

Bridget was unsure how precarious the situation was. Steven had said only that they'd had a fight and he had left the house.

She had worried that this day would come. Over the years she had imagined what might happen if his boat trips caught up with him. But as the years passed and he was safe, she came to believe that he was changing. Really changing. That was before Christian Bernard, and even then it seemed that Steven had dodged a bullet once again.

She had to be calm and figure out what Maddy wanted. Many women thought their marriages were on the brink, but that didn't mean they were. "I didn't choose you," Bridget said. "You fell in love. The two of you did that on your own."

"You made me think you believed in me, but all you wanted was a wife. And you're a woman. You did this to another woman!"

"I did believe in you. I wouldn't have had you read for Walter if I didn't."

"Walter was going to cast whoever you told him to. He was under your thumb. You were casting me for a life."

"Maddy, that's not true. Dozens of actresses read for it."

"Lael didn't even get to read. You left her alone in a room with Steven. That was her audition. And Taylor Yaccarino—same thing."

"Walter did it differently with every girl. You know he has an atypical process."

"I worked so hard on those scenes. Did you ever even think I was good? When you saw my screener? Or did I just fit the specifications? Did I match some character breakdown in your mind? The Perfect Wife?"

Of course it had been more complicated than that. When it came to Steven, nothing had been explicit. As long as Bridget had known him, as close as they were. To some extent he had always been unknowable, which was what made their relationship work so well. She saw the brand and only occasionally the man. In that way, she was like his audience. It helped her imagine the character they wanted on the screen.

She had wondered, suspected, from the very beginning. But she had looked the other way and seen what she needed to see. In the mid-'80s, after she signed him, when he was still at the repertory company, he would bring around "friends." There were glances, touches, but how could she know? Actors and their games. Young men working for no money to live out their dreams, rooming in close quarters. Later she had wondered about Terry McCarthy, but Terry got married and had children and she put that theory to rest.

There had been one boy, the night she met Steven at the sports bar after *Bus Stop*. He'd stayed later than the rest, and she thought she picked up on something, glances, mostly from him to Steven. Alex, his name was. After Steven started making a little money and bought the boat, the three of them had gone out on it a couple of times. The men gave her the main cabin. They slept in bunk beds in the other cabin. She didn't question it, not then. Though the Alex fellow seemed effeminate, she guessed it was unrequited.

She had been rising as an agent, she knew it would be complicated for Steven if . . . And then he married Julia, and after they divorced, he wouldn't talk about it. From then on it was always beautiful women, maybe too beautiful, but Steven was good-looking and people sought out their own kind. She thought the brief affairs were good for him publicity-wise, but the rumors continued, as though the serial monogamy was proof of something. And then the Internet came along and there was no way to distinguish between legitimate and illegitimate news, and the bloggers, and the young generation with their constant theorizing, it was a mess. With the search fields and other people's searches visible when you typed in your own questions, it fed on itself, became self-perpetuating. People were fascinated by the idea of someone pulling the wool over their eyes. As though every entertainer didn't do the same thing.

The chatter only got louder after Julia's comeback, when the media became curious about the marriage once again, with the blog items and innuendo. Bridget didn't like the new "standards." The actors with wives and big broods succeeded while the single men, who drank more than was "appropriate," and grew paunches, and stayed out an hour or two too late, weren't taken seriously. They were seen as alcoholics, fuckups.

So she'd thought it would be good to quiet the noise. Which was becoming a distraction. They needed a project, and then the Juhasz script landed on her desk and it seemed . . . synergistic.

Bridget came around the desk and tried to take Maddy's hands in hers, but the girl jerked them away. "I always thought you had talent," Bridget said. "I never would have wanted Steven to marry a bad actress. Now, tell me what's going on between the two of you."

"It's over. I know about Ryan."

"You should forgive him," Bridget said quietly.

It was the boat that had done him in. She had hoped that it would stop when he got married, that he wouldn't need it the way he had in the past. But he kept sailing away, and he was sailing when the baby was born, a colossal mistake. A mistake she would have told him not to make if he had consulted her. Leaving the radio off with a wife so far along? No man did that.

"I won't forgive him," Maddy said. "He's gone. This is the end."

"You're crazy to end it. You have everything you could want."

"I don't care about any of that," Maddy said. She went around Bridget's desk and sat in her big swivel chair. "I just wanted to be loved."

"But you are!" Bridget said, spinning to face her. "How can you think you're not loved?"

"He betrayed me, and you knew, and you let him!"

"Marriage is about respect and mutual companionship. You think after five, ten, forty years together that any marriage holds because of the sex?"

"How would you know a thing about marriage?"

"The way you just spoke to me right now, you think you're the first? I know the things they've said about me, that I'm frigid, I'm a dragon lady, I chew men up and spit them out. I'm oversexed or undersexed, I'm over the hill, I'm mannish and no one can love me. I never wanted to be talked about this way. I never wanted to be alone. I wanted to be loved, just like you did.

"I used to think I could find a man who would be attracted to my drive, my ambition, a man evolved enough not to be threatened. I wanted to talk about my day with someone who wanted me to do well. I wanted everything you had. Have. The mutual respect, the shared interests, the family life, the loyalty, the company. The breakfast-table chatter. My home is so silent. Think of what you'll be giving up."

"I don't care. I can't go on living a lie." Maddy headed for the door.

I can't go on living a lie.

It was clear she was angry. She might try to renegotiate the postnup, get better terms, claim she had been defrauded. Bridget didn't know what he had admitted, and hoped he had been cautious. One thing she had taught him over the years was not to be an idiot during a crisis.

It would be difficult enough dealing with the bad PR from a divorce. But a homosexuality-related crisis was another level of headache. She'd thought the studio was going to fire him when the dockworker came forward, and even though Edward had prevailed in the end, it had been harrowing.

If Maddy outed Steven, it would be the end of Steven Weller as Tommy Hall. Apollo would have to let his talent option lapse. *The Hall Endeavor* was starting production in March in Turkey. If Maddy made a statement, they would have to rethink everything, and they could. The movie had several explosive sex scenes between Tommy Hall and a fellow spy to be played by Taylor Yaccarino. No one would believe a gay man as a hard-drinking womanizer.

There was a turpitude clause, but there was also employment discrimination law, and if he got lawyers on it and they tried to prove he'd been terminated because of his status, it could get costly. Gays were a protected class. Public sentiment would be on his side and not the stu-

dio's; he could work the media. This was different from the Christian
Bernard story. He could turn it into an issue of human rights. In the end
she could get rid of him, but at what cost to Apollo? The pay-or-play was
the least of it.

"You'd better not say anything to the press," Bridget said, following
Maddy to the door.

"Don't tell me what to do," Maddy said.

"I've known him a lot longer than you have," Bridget said quietly. "If
you talk, he'll deny it. Demand proof. He'll bring up things from *your*
past. He told me you were on antidepressants. He'll call you mentally
unfit. It'll be embarrassing. He'll wage a PR war, and you know how good
we are at that. It'll affect your custody and visitation. You'd better watch
your step."

"You're afraid of me," Maddy said, a wide, wondrous smile coming
over her face.

"I'm only thinking of you. And Jake. You want a relationship with your
son, don't you?"

Maddy almost laughed. "You've never thought about anyone but yourself. Even Steven was just a meal ticket to you. To this. And you finally got
it. The office, the nameplate. You've made it."

"Of course I care about you, and of course I care about Steven. That's
why I don't want you to ruin his career. And you must feel some love for
him. The American public isn't ready for a gay leading man. Another ten
years, maybe. A gay Steven Weller won't work. A couple of indie wink-
winks, and in ten years it's summer stock in Coral Gables. You can't want
that. The personal life of a Hollywood star has nothing to do with his
talent. But it has everything to do with his earning potential. It will harm
him if you do this, as it harmed the Communists during the 1950s. You'll
see. The names that were named, they couldn't work again. People killed
themselves. Marriages were destroyed."

"My marriage is already destroyed."

"If you love Jake, you'll keep this between you."

"Stop managing me. You've managed enough already."

———

The door closed behind Maddy with a thud. Bridget went to the desk. The swivel chair was still warm from Maddy's body. Bridget picked up the phone and dialed. "She's come unhinged," she said.

"I told you she was hurt."

"I thought she might say something. Issue a statement. But it's all right. I think we'll be okay. I put the fear of God into her."

He had checked in to a boutique hotel on a side street in Beverly Hills, the kind of place doyennes went to recover from face-lifts. It had a private garage and tight security.

Steven sat on the edge of the bed, his arms resting on his knees. After all these years, Bridget still didn't understand Maddy. Maddy wasn't vindictive. She would not punish him. And if she really wanted out of the marriage, surely she understood that it was in her financial best interest to have an ex-husband who kept working.

"You sound more worried about this than I am," he said.

"I'm concerned about the films! The next one's worth potentially five hundred million dollars. We have to be smart about this. You need to make sure she stays quiet. Take control of your wife. You did a beautiful job with that in Venice."

Steven couldn't remember a single red-carpet appearance without feeling Bridget's breath behind him. For almost twenty-five years, she had been there. He could feel her hand resting gently on his lower back. For the shots, you always did low back, never high, so the suit didn't wrinkle, so you didn't look fat. Close but not too close, so people wouldn't get the wrong idea. She had been the one to teach him where to put his hand. All the things he'd never thought about before, like how to hold your chin and your feet, and not to talk while posing because you looked stupid and they couldn't use it. You had to help other people do their jobs while you were doing yours.

Bridget was his partner, his wife, his counsel, his friend, his employee, all rolled into one. Her sunglasses mimicked his over the years, from the wraparounds to the mirrored aviators to the tortoiseshells. She had been his date when he had no other. His defendant and protector, back when the flacks weren't all-powerful. She was there, hovering behind him, and even when she posed for a few obligatories, she was always looking over his shoulder, watching to see who was coming close.

Through it, he had believed that she cared. To employ her, he'd had to believe that she wanted the best for him, not only the most money. He wasn't so deluded as to think she was a charity worker, he knew his films had paid for her house in Brentwood, Zack's college education and trust, her staff, her office, her cars. But even so, he had believed that her faith in him was a kind of love.

Now it seemed like he had tricked himself, as he had tried to trick himself into being the husband Maddy wanted. After all their time together, Bridget had to know who he was. She must have understood the toll it took on him to have to lie, have to run. He was like a bank robber: He could never sit down and rest for a moment, because if he rested, that would be the moment he got caught. She had to have seen it, the exhaustion, the excuses, those hours when she was trying to close a deal and couldn't reach him because he was on Jo.

And yet not once in those years had she asked what it felt like.

Another manager might have encouraged him, maybe not back in the 1990s, but later, when things began to change. Someone else might have dreamed different things for him, not bigger things but different. As important as it was to work, it was important to live. Jake had taught him that. The moment Jake first smiled at him from the crib, Steven realized that life was about so much more, more than he had thought. *Live all you can; it's a mistake not to.*

"I know you want to be smart about this," he said. "You've always been the perfect manager, Bridget." He went to the window.

"I've tried to be."

"You know why?" he asked, placing his palm against a pane that would not open. "Because you always put Steven Weller first."

Steven had stepped out of his car and was coming up the pathway to the house. Normally, Maddy liked Lucia to do the hand-off, but she was sick today in bed and Maddy had been one-on-one with Jake throughout the morning. She would have to hurry if she didn't want to be late; she was headed to Santa Monica to have lunch with the director Deborah Berenson, of *Rondelay* fame, to see if she was right for *Pinhole*.

Maddy had been apprehensive when she first heard the name, remembering that Bridget had said she had a mixed track record. But she'd loved *Rondelay*, and looking back, she thought maybe Bridget had said it to prevent Maddy from wanting to be involved with the project. Maddy was excited to hear Deb's ideas about the script.

When Steven came face-to-face with Maddy, Jake on her hip, he looked uncomfortable. "Lucia's sick today," she said. "Don't look so disappointed to see me."

"I'm not disappointed," he said. "I just thought you didn't—I thought you didn't like to see me. Hi, Jakey!" Jake reached out, and Steven took him in his arms.

Maddy had been living in the house with Jake for a month, but this was the first time she and Steven had been alone, without Lucia there. She couldn't run from him forever. Dina had been telling Maddy to stop blaming herself, had told her she'd done nothing wrong. She'd reminded Maddy that the marriage had not been all bad. They had supported each other, given career advice, laughed, made Jake.

But Jake was the reason she was so angry. Because of Jake, she could never cut her ties from Steven. Not completely. There were no goodbyes when you shared a child.

She had filed and served the petition for divorce earlier that week, using an attorney who had helped half a dozen high-profile Hollywood wives. Steven was using the guy who had negotiated his postnup. Her lawyer had said it would be a matter of days, not weeks, because so much had been hammered out in the postnup.

The tabloids were going crazy for the details of the separation. There were varying reports: She had postpartum depression; Steven was on cocaine; she'd kicked him out because he missed the birth; he was sleeping with Ryan, with Billy Peck, Corinna Mestre, even Kira. Maddy had slept with Billy or Ryan or Munro Heming. Or she was having a torrid affair with Zack, which Zack said he found flattering. Journalists staked out the house and Steven's hotel.

She had packed Jake's bag with a rubber giraffe toy and two wooden trucks he liked, and his lovey, a lamb blanket. It was in the kitchen, and as she turned to get it, she said, "Please, come in."

In the kitchen Jake, now eight months, saw his block set and squirmed in his father's arms to be let down. Jake had Steven's eyes. The eyes that drew you in, made you fall in love in a second. Maddy would watch him squint at something complicated or punch his toys or frown, and it was as though Steven still lived with her.

There were times when she wished Jake had been a girl; if the baby had been a girl, she could have imagined it was hers and not his. There were times when the resemblance was so difficult, she had to turn her head away.

Jake smashed the castle he had built, and the blocks scattered all over the floor. They laughed at the same time at his destructiveness. He was going to be all right. The divorce had happened so early that it would be all he knew: his parents separate, not together.

But one day he would be older, and Maddy would have to tell him why Mommy and Daddy got divorced. She couldn't imagine what Steven might be like in five years, or ten, or fifteen. Maybe he would get a new perspective on it, decide other things mattered more than image, and become a merry sixtysomething gay man, authentic for the first time in his life. Maybe he would trade her in for a new wife, or maybe this was it. Maybe he would wind up with Ryan and they would become an iconic couple.

"I should get going," she told Steven. "I have an appointment."

"Jake! Let's go, buddy."

He scooped up Jake. Maddy grabbed her keys and purse and followed them outside. He strapped Jake into the car seat, and she leaned in and gave the baby a few big kisses on the cheek. Then she closed the door. His car seat faced backward and there was a mirror with colored toys hanging off of it and Jake was reaching forward to touch one.

Steven was starting for the front door when she put her hand on his arm. "What are you going to tell him when he gets older?" she asked.

"What do you mean?"

"When he's old enough to understand, and he asks why we split up, what are you going to say? Are you going to keep lying forever?"

"I don't know what I'm going to tell him," he said. "He's not even one yet." Then he got into the driver's seat and slammed the door.

5

Maddy was surprised when the phone rang in early February and Steven said, "Do you want to come with me to the Oscars? For old times' sake?"

"What?"

"I'm presenting. The editing award." Maddy had not been nominated that year because she hadn't worked. Kira was nominated for *The Moon and the Stars*. Which meant that she would be there, parading around, accepting accolades.

"I don't think I could take it," she said. "With Kira, I think it's just too painful for me."

"I've only been nominated once, and I've gone eight times," he said.

"We're different people," she said. She was on the cordless in the garden with Jake, who was playing with his trucks. "You should probably find someone else."

"I don't want anyone else. I want you."

"Why?"

"I just miss you. I still love you even though we're divorced, you know. Even if you think I don't. And I need a date."

The financial and all other terms of the settlement were confidential. It had taken only ten days. She and Steven had joint custody, she didn't fight him on that, and Steven would get Jake one-third of the time. The settlement contained a clause in which each party agreed not to speak publicly about the other's personal life or the details of their marriage. Because they had been married four and a half years, she would get about $4.5 million. It was strange to think her worth could be quantified. But the lawyers didn't know what she had truly done for him.

Though she could not imagine doing the red carpet with her ex-husband, she knew she was going to have to find a way to coexist with him. She wanted her anger to fade. And he was humbling himself to invite her.

It wasn't good for Jake to have a mother who hated his father. "Why is this so important to you?" she asked.

"I can't tell you now. It's a surprise."

"I've had enough surprises."

"It's a different kind. You won't be disappointed, and you know how good I look in a tux. Please?"

Later that day, Patti came over to consult with her about dresses, and soon Patti was sending over different possibilities. Maddy felt better physically, most of her baby weight gone, the color back in her cheeks.

She selected a strapless champagne-colored Marchesa covered in crystals, with a two-foot silky tulle train. It was like a ballerina bridal dress but form-fitting, and around the neckline were little pieces of fabric that looked like winged birds.

When Steven arrived in a limousine he had rented for the occasion, and she emerged from the house, he stepped from the car and shook his head. "You're beautiful," he said.

"I really hope this isn't a stupid idea," she said.

He came around the side of the car. "We could get married again. People have done it before."

"Steven," she said quietly. "I'm your date tonight, but that's it. I'll never attend another event with you. This is the last one."

"I know."

Alan opened the door and she got in first, gathering her train around her. When they pulled up to the theater, she saw it all. The pen of fans on risers. The line of celebrities walking the L-shaped carpet to the golden entrance with its golden curtains held to the side.

As they emerged, there was a roar and the fans leaped to their feet. The screaming was deafening and reminded her of Berlin. Once again she was a cog in a machine.

She had been wrong to come, wrong to cave to Steven. Now that she no longer had to.

Slowly, they made their way to the video crews, posing again and again for the gathered photographers on one side. Steven took her hand, lacing his fingers through hers. They knew exactly how to stand next to each other, they had done it so many times. She pivoted to her left, her good side. There were shouts: "Can you turn your back, please, Maddy?" and "Maddy, look this way!" and "How about a three-quarter?" Again and again they posed, some together, some apart, so the photographers could get a full shot of the dress.

Finally, they approached one of the entertainment-news crews. Kira, in a dark green V-neck dress, was talking; when she saw Maddy behind her, she turned and embraced her, widening her eyes at Maddy's date, and pulled them both in front of the camera. Kira kissed Steven graciously, and he congratulated her on her nomination. As Kira stepped aside to let the interviewer have his time with the couple, she whispered to Maddy, "You managed to upstage me."

Kira moved to her next interview, and Maddy and Steven answered dumb predictable questions for the dopey young reporter. She said kind things about Kira's performance, and the guy was good enough not to mention that she'd had to back out, even though everyone knew about it.

After they had given half a dozen interviews, they made their way toward the entrance. As they moved up the line, slowly, slowly, the ticket-taking drawn out so the fans could get their last glimpses of everyone famous on the line, Steven put his mouth to her ear. "I've been thinking about what you said," he whispered. "And I don't want to keep hiding. I want Jake to know me. All these years I told myself there was no other choice, but there was. I'm going to tell the world who I am. If I lose Tommy Hall, I don't care."

She was shocked. Did he mean here, tonight? The orchestra was quick to cut off people during acceptance speeches, not to mention any other kind. But he was Steven Weller, and the producers would recognize international news when they saw it.

She looked at him again, her eyes welling with pride. Her ex-husband was about to make history. And the moment would be immortalized on camera, the cameras that had been his friend all these years, the cameras that had brought him everything he had, including Maddy. Including Jake.

They made their way to the reporter waiting to talk to them. Holding her hand, Steven walked just a few steps ahead.

Inside the theater, they sat side by side, watching the endless ceremony, laughing appropriately at the jokes. The beginning was slow. The host, a faded comedian in his sixties, opened with a big song-and-dance number. Steven was to present the best-editing Oscar, to be given out toward the end of the first hour. When a production assistant tapped him on the shoulder during a commercial break to take him backstage, Steven squeezed Maddy's hand. She looked up at him to see if he really meant it, if he was really going to do this thing. But he was already gone.

As Steven made his way up the aisle, he knew that when he walked back down, everything would be different. These were his last moments as the Steven Weller everyone knew, and tonight would be marked as the turning point. It was terrifying, and he still didn't know exactly what he was going to say, he hadn't wanted to memorize it, but when he was done, he would be a different person. A real father to his son. You had to be honest to be a good parent; otherwise you set a terrible example.

Everything was going to be fine. He'd been in the industry long enough that he had earning power, any producer would see that, the studios knew it, and there would be goodwill, especially from GLAAD, an organization that had surpassed the ADL in Hollywood power. He would lose the third Tommy Hall; they would put it in turnaround to "rethink" the casting, he knew that.

But he would bounce back. It might take some time, but he would bounce back. Audiences were sophisticated now, they knew gay people, it was why gay marriage was going to pass, the tide was shifting and audiences could suspend disbelief, they suspended disbelief every time they watched a straight guy play a fag for an award, a beautiful actress don a prosthetic nose.

He was nearing the back of the theater, and he saw Harry Matheson, the late-night host, sitting in the audience next to his wife. It was his red hair that caught Steven's eye. As Steven moved down the aisle, Harry gave him a thumbs-up.

Steven remembered Maddy going on *Harry* and discussing his sexual prowess. She had been "on" that night, herself but not herself, the perfect actress. And then she had come into the greenroom, and it was as though she had been flattened.

One night when he was on the boat with Christian, they'd had a conversation about porn titles. Christian was so young, only twenty-four, that he didn't even know about the days when pornos had stories. Steven remembered one he had watched in the early 1990s, a takeoff of a sitcom called *Jack and Mike*. The porn title was *Jacking Mike*, and on the boat, they had laughed about it. He had felt relaxed in moments like that; those moments were why he went on *Jo* with Christian and the others before and after.

He had been taking a risk with Christian, who was out of his usual circle of agents and agents' assistants and art directors and stylists, who were doing fine on their own and had nothing to gain from outing him. But he was a sweet kid, such an open face. They had flirted every time Steven went to the boat, and he had seen Steven with the other guys, and somehow he had weaseled his way on, though Steven had had an instinct that it was a bad idea. He had let his guard down, but for a month or two, he had gotten away with it, until he got the call from Edward.

When the story broke, he had felt trapped, he had been sure it was the end, but then Maddy had stepped up to help him out. He hadn't even had to ask. That was how much she loved him. Now he would tell the truth, and in telling the truth, he would be outing her as a liar. They would replay her clip ad infinitum, back to back with the speech he was about to give. This was about much more than the stakes for him. It was about more than undoing a fifteen-year-old image and reversing the lengths he had gone to in order to work, in order to keep working, in order to get to the top.

There were stakes for her: She would be perceived as a dupe at best, a conniver at worst. They would mock her *Harry* appearance and the marriage. Maddy had put herself on the line for him, and while he knew she wanted him to be honest for Jake's sake, had she really thought about it, about the repercussions for her own career, her own image? She was talented, more talented than he was, and she would want to keep working.

He loved her, and if you loved someone, you had to put her first, as she had put him first for so many years, not only when she played Faye Fontinell and when she went on Harry's show but before that, when she changed her clothing and makeup and learned how to give sound bites, all so she could be Mrs. Steven Weller. This was about something greater than he, and if he didn't recognize it, if he didn't see the sacrifices she had made, then he was selfish, and he didn't want to be selfish, that was what had gotten him into the mess with Maddy, that was why he had lost her in the first place.

A cameraman scurried up the aisle toward Maddy as the host spoke from the stage. Because of the divorce, the producers wanted to be ready for a reaction, she understood that, even though no one knew what Steven had planned.

"Ladies and gentlemen," the host was saying, "please welcome a man who needs no introduction, because he's so handsome and talented that we all just want to kill him. Steven Weller."

Maddy kept a frozen smile on her face as she clapped along with the others. And then Steven was onstage, resplendent in his tux as always, his body so strong, his skin tan. He looked cool, as though this were nothing, he would ace it, there was no sign of any struggle on his face, he would do this his own way, calm and collected but real. For the first time, real.

"I came here tonight," he said, "to do something special."

A hush came over the audience as they perhaps suspected that the words he was speaking were not from the TelePrompter. "And I . . . I . . ." He seemed to be looking above their heads at something behind them, above them, and beyond the walls of the theater. The silence hung there, no music cue to take it away. There was a lone cough. And then he grinned and said, "I am pleased to share with you the nominees for achievement in editing."

6

The financing for *Pinhole* came together in the spring, a few months after Maddy was divorced. It would be an international coproduction involving four different companies and a handful of independent financiers. Maddy had chosen Deborah Berenson as the director, and after they booked the now-famous Billy Peck to play Max Sandoval, they were able to complete the financing.

They shot *Pinhole* in just forty-four days in June and July, in France, England, and Germany. Deborah hired Victor Ruiz, the director of photography on *I Used to Know Her*. The housing was low-budget and barebones, but Maddy didn't care. Lucia and Jake came along because she didn't want to be apart from him for such a long time. Zack was a producer and was on set every day.

During the shoot, she felt herself rediscovering everything she had loved as an actress, with the added thrill of having written Lane's words. In August, Deborah began cutting the film with the editor, with a plan of submitting it to the Toronto International Film Festival, which Christine thought was a better market than Mile's End.

It was not until after they wrapped and Maddy returned to Hancock Park that she began to think about leaving L.A. She had never liked the new house, even after Steven's art and furniture had been removed. She had always felt like a visitor in Los Angeles, never a resident, and she wanted to move back to Brooklyn. She knew her life in New York would not be anything like what it had been before, but she wanted to raise Jake in the city. She wanted to go to the theater again, to take him to quality children's plays and to the Met. She wanted him to have friends who weren't children of celebrities but normal New York kids.

When she emailed Steven to tell him her plans, he was supportive. He said he would buy an apartment in Manhattan so he could spend time with Jake without having to fly him across the country. His consent came as a relief, because her lawyer had said that a lot of ex-husbands wouldn't have allowed it.

In the fall she closed on a town house on South Elliott Place, just a few blocks from where she had lived with Dan. Jake thrived on the playgrounds and in Fort Greene Park, and Maddy found the parents low-key and friendly but not prying. There were novelists and jazz musicians on her block, actors and academics.

She began to take acting jobs again. The directors in New York were smart, the scripts complex, and the roles for women rich. She did a romantic comedy set in a sex-toy shop, and a thriller about an idiot-savant boy. Never again would she play set dressing, no matter how high the salary.

As a manager, Zack understood that she wanted to work only on projects she valued, and they went over each script carefully, discussing the merits of the roles. It was a type of collaboration she had never experienced with Bridget.

Though Laight Street Entertainment was young and had a small slate, Zack was soaring as a manager-producer. *Velvet,* starring Munro Heming as Frank McKnight, came out in March and did $20 million in its first weekend, a huge figure for a film with no big celebrities and no special effects. Critics loved it, and one of them wrote that the film's success was "reason for confidence in the future of intelligent American cinema."

Around the same time that *Velvet* came out, there was another buzzed-about release: a zombie picture about an ordinary father and husband who tries to save the world, called *The Undead.* The week of the film's release, Ryan, who played the lead, gave an interview to *New York* magazine in which he spoke about zombies as a metaphor for fear. He went on to say, "I guess I'm just really opposed to prejudice and hate being dominant things in our culture. As a gay man, I'm saddened to see that narrow-mindedness and judgment can ruin lives."

This set off a new round of think pieces about casual coming-outs. An *Entertainment Weekly* critic put him, along with Kira, on a list called "The Post-Gay Power Elite."

Maddy read all the chatter, but it took her some time to get around to reading the original interview, which she did one warm spring day on a playground bench while watching Jake, almost two, toddle around. She called Steven from her cell. "Did you read Ryan's thing in *New York*?" she asked.

"Of course I read it. I don't live under a rock." She waited for him to say more, but he didn't.

After he had returned to his seat the night of the Oscars, they hadn't spoken about his moment on the stage. He acted as though nothing was out of the ordinary, as though he had never intended to do anything other than present. And she never asked. They hobnobbed at the *Vanity Fair* party, mingling separately.

Then Steven had gone off to Turkey to shoot *The Hall Endeavor*, and he was said to have started an affair with Taylor Yaccarino. Maddy had chuckled when she read the item, imagining that Taylor knew exactly what she was getting herself into. They were constantly photographed going to dinner and nuzzling in public.

"And what did you think of what Ryan had to say?" she asked Steven on the phone.

"It didn't surprise me very much. He's never married, he's thirty-four, and he grew up in Berkeley."

She laughed and realized it had been a long time since he had made her laugh. "I know you didn't grow up in Berkeley," she said, "but do you think you could ever do something like that?"

"Maddy," he said, "I'm from a different generation."

On a sweltering day in August while she was with Jake on Governors Island, Maddy got an email saying that *Pinhole* had been accepted into Toronto. When she opened it, she screamed, jumped up and down, and called Zack. She felt that her years of slaving over the script, and all her hard work as an actress, had finally paid off. Whether it won anything or not, she would be going to Toronto with a project she had generated from her own mind, out of the story of a complicated woman's life.

Steven offered to take care of Jake in his Gramercy Park apartment so she could be completely focused during the festival. She paid for their

cast and crew to fly over, and rented a huge house near the festival head-
quarters so everyone could stay together.

The first screening of *Pinhole* was at eight on Friday night, a prime
spot. The theater was already packed when Maddy walked in with Deborah and Zack.

Maddy took her reserved seat next to her cast and crew. Lane Cromwell's daughter, Jean, had flown in and would be watching the film for
the first time.

The lights went down.

The opening shot was a point-of-view from a 1920s camera snapping
photos. The shutter closed, and the next frame was Maddy as Lane, posing for a slip ad. The flash popped again and again, and you could see
by Lane's expression that she was uncomfortable and out of her league.
The photographer in the film called out directions off camera and she
vamped, and then there was a freeze-frame and the screen went to black.
Over a gypsy-jazz song, the credits appeared in simple, stark, white-on-
black. Maddy's title card was the last before Deborah's. When she read
the words "written by Maddy Freed," they felt like a prediction.

There was a panel discussion following the screening and she trotted up
to the stage along with the cast and crew. After a few questions about her
writing process and discovery of Lane's story, a heavyset bearded guy with
black-framed glasses raised his hand. "This is the first film you've written
since your divorce from Steven Weller, isn't it, Maddy?"

"Just to clarify, it's the first film I've written," she said. "Ever. I collabo-
rated on some things before, but this is my first solo screenplay."

"I was thinking as I watched it that Lane kept trying to find her happiness in men, but it didn't work. Is that something you relate to personally? Would you say this film is on some level about your anger at your
ex-husband?"

There were whispers in the audience. People seemed to get that the
guy was putting her on the spot, or maybe they wanted her to say something buzz-worthy and scandalous because her divorce had been all over
the news.

"You know," she said, "I would never write a script out of anger. It's hard enough as it is to get independent financing." The audience laughed, and her crew did, too. She could feel the support of Deborah, Victor, and Zack around her. "Filmmaking is first and foremost about storytelling. That's what gets people into a theater. That's why we're all here. To me, this film tells the story of an artist who tried to make work that was meaningful, and at the same time really struggled with her personal happiness. In part because of the sexism of her time.

"But beyond that . . ." The theater was quiet even though there were twelve hundred people in it. "I don't regret my marriage, not in the slightest. I learned so much from Steven. I learned things I never expected to learn." The house lights were bright, and she shaded her eyes. "I guess you could say . . . you could say that Steven Weller made me the actress I am today."

And then someone asked a question about camera lenses, and Maddy exhaled and faced her cinematographer.

Acknowledgments

In inventing the life of Maddy Freed, I found the following books influential and essential: *Is That a Gun in Your Pocket?: Women's Experience of Power in Hollywood*, by Rachel Abramowitz; *Rebecca*, by Daphne du Maurier; *The Yellow Wallpaper and Other Writings*, by Charlotte Perkins Gilman; *Natalie Wood: A Life*, by Gavin Lambert; *In Spite of Myself: A Memoir*, by Christopher Plummer; and *The Female Malady: Women, Madness and English Culture, 1830–1980*, by Elaine Showalter.

A novel about an actress provides an opportunity to watch and rewatch great films. In particular I drew inspiration from *Don't Look Now*, directed by Nicolas Roeg; *Gaslight*, directed by George Cukor; *Inside Daisy Clover*, directed by Robert Mulligan; *Rebecca*, directed by Alfred Hitchcock; and *Repulsion*, directed by Roman Polanski.

For research assistance, thanks to Howard Abramson, Angie Banicki, Gisela Baurmann, John Connolly, Annette Drees, Sara Gozalo, Detective Nils Grevillius, Lillian Hope, Franklin J. Leonard, Terry Levich Ross, Jennifer Levy, Sara Memo, Kelly Bush Novak, Lateef Oseni, Victor Pimstein Ratinoff, Brian Savelson, and Jamie Yerkes. For detail work and production assistance, thanks to Melissa Kahn, Sarah Nalle, and Ed Winstead. For productivity assistance, thanks to Fred Stutzman and Freedom for Productivity, the Brooklyn Writers Space, the Brooklyn Public Library, the Cambridge Public Library, and the Writers Guild of America East Writing Room.

Thanks to Rebecca Gradinger for inspiring this idea over tea at University Restaurant. Thanks to Ernesto Mestre-Reed and Will Blythe for being great critics and great friends. Thanks to Richard Abate for being my consigliere, reluctant driver, and tireless advocate, and to Jonathan Karp for believing in *The Actress* and seeing it to fruition. Special thanks to Millicent Bennett for deep thinking, attentive editing, structural help, and an extremely kind manner.

Most of all, thanks to my husband and my daughter, whose encouragement, patience, and laughter allow me to do what I love.

About the Author

Amy Sohn was born in 1973. She is the author of the novels *Motherland, Prospect Park West, My Old Man,* and *Run Catch Kiss.* She has been a columnist at *New York, New York Press,* the *New York Post,* and *Grazia.* She has written TV pilots for such networks as HBO, FOX, and ABC. She lives in Brooklyn with her family.